TITUS: THE ARISTOCRAT

KATHERYN MADDOX HADDAD

A COMMENTARY IN NARRATIVE FORM

OTHER BOOKS BY THIS AUTHOR

HISTORICAL NOVELS & STORYBOOKS
Series of 8: They Met Jesus
Ongoing Series of 8: Intrepid Men of God
Mysteries of the Empire with Klaudius & Hektor
Christmas: They Rocked the Cradle that Rocked the World
Series of 8: A Child's Life of Christ
Series of 10: A Child's Bible Heroes
Series of 8: A Child's Bible Kids
Series of 10: A Child's Bible Ladies

HISTORICAL RESEARCH BIBLE
for Novel, Screenwriter, Documentary & Thesis Writers

TOPICAL
Applied Christianity: Handbook 500 Good Works
Christianity or Islam? The Contrast
The Holy Spirit: 592 Verses Examined
The Road to Heaven
Inside the Hearts of Bible Women-Reader+Audio+Leader
Revelation: A Love Letter From God
Worship Changes Since 1st Century + Worship 1sr Century Way
Was Jesus God? (Why Evil)
365 Life-Changing Scriptures Day by Date
The Road to Heaven
The Lord's Supper: 52 Readings with Prayers

FUN BOOKS
Bible Puzzles, Bible Song Book, Bible Numbers

TOUCHING GOD SERIES
365 Golden Bible Thoughts: God's Heart to Yours
365 Pearls of Wisdom: God's Soul to Yours
365 Silver-Winged Prayers: Your Spirit to God's

-SURVEY SERIES: EASY BIBLE WORKBOOKS
→Old Testament & New Testament Surveys
→Questions You Have Asked-Part I & II

Genealogy: How to Climb Your Family Tree Without Falling Out
Volume I & 2: Beginner-Intermediate & Colonial-Medieval

Copyright © 2016 Katheryn Maddox Haddad
NORTHERN LIGHTS PUBLISHING HOUSE

CONTENTS

1 ~ I AM TITUS

"My name is Titus Pomponius Brennius, and I am nine years old today."

The boy stands next to a reflecting pool two man-lengths across both ways and surrounding the statue of Augustus Caesar, who had died the year Titus had been born. His hands are at his side. His eyes do not waver from his father, Justus Brennius Antiochus.

"And?" his father prods.

"And the Titus Pomponius of Athens, philoso...philosopher, and writer of many books about our illus...illus..."

"Illustrious," his mother, Kharis, prompts with her ever-present smile that brings out her single dimple.

"...illustrious Cicero, Plato, and other worthy philoso... philosophers and historians." Titus risks reprimand from his father by glancing at his mother for a quick thank you.

"And?" Justus prods again, adjusting his purple-edged toga, which often slips off his lap when sitting.

"And my ancestor, Brennius the Great, leader of the Gauls who dared invade Rome, then settle from there all the way over to our Province of Galatia."

"Well done, Titus." Justus presents his son with a thin smile, stands tall, and brushes back a strand of blond hair from his forehead.

"Sit back down, husband. We have not heard our son

recite his maternal heritage," Kharis pronounces with sternness in her eyes and an abundant smile on her full lips.

"Well, hurry it up. We have things to do today to celebrate this young man's birthday."

Titus, still by the divine Augustus' statue in the middle of the family courtyard, turns to face his mother. His hands remain at his side.

"And Sejanus, Dalmatian official musician of Apollo master of the Muses, with full Roman citizenship bestowed upon him by the illustri...ous Augustus Caesar."

"Perfect," Kharis says, standing at the same time as her husband.

Titus looks at his father. "May I have my birthday present now, sir?"

"Ha, ha. Such impatience," Justus responds, putting an arm around his short and pleasantly-stout wife. "A gentleman and aristocrat displays patience and does not ask for his present."

"Well, how long must I display my aristo...aristocrat patience, sir?"

"To teach you a lesson for being so impatient, you must recite your times tables, the twelve sons and daughters of Apollo, the nine Muses, and the seven planets."

"Justus!" Kharus objects.

"Now, dear, the boy needs to learn."

Parents re-seated, Titus works his way through his penance. For good measure, he ends with a bonus. "Our father god is Jupiter. The Greeks call him Zeus, but they don't know anything. They aren't smart like us Romans. Isn't that right, Father?"

Justus rises and smiles. "That is, indeed, right."

Kharis stands. "Now, we shall begin our celebrations with a song. Where is my lyre?" She looks down at the marble bench on which she had been sitting.

Titus looks at his mother and back at his father.

"Dear, why not save that part of the birthday celebration for our trip to the seacoast," Justus intercedes.

"The seacoast? Really, Father? Is that my present?"

"Cornelius," Justus calls out to his head steward and

gatekeeper.

"Yes, sir. Everything is ready."

Cornelius opens the gilded gate out of the family *palatio.* To one side is Lydia ready with Kharis' stolla of blue. The maid lays it over Kharis' white tunic and secures it with a ruby clasp on one shoulder to match the elegant scarlet trim at the neckline and hem.

Cornelius holds a small toga edged with the same purple as his elder's. "Father, do I have to wear a toga? We're just going to the seacoast."

"You are an aristocrat. You must wear the symbol of your status in public. Once we arrive, you may take it off and play in the sand with just your tunic on."

"When will I be able to wear the plain toga?"

"When you are fourteen. You will wear that one until you are considered a man and must earn the right to wear purple edging."

"When will I be considered a man?" Titus asks.

Justus does not answer.

When they walk toward the stable gate, Titus notices the family litter with the crimson curtains has not been readied for them.

Justus helps his wife up onto her side saddled horse.

Titus looks around. "Well, I guess that means I will be riding behind you, Father."

"No, that is not what it means," Justus replies, his eyes stern and his thin lips even thinner.

Titus steps back against the stable wall. His eyelids fight off unmanly tears. "But it's my birthday, and you promised I could go with you."

"Darling, stop teasing the boy," Kharis chides.

Brutus, the stable master, steps forward, leading a saddled pony.

Titus' eyes grow large at the sight.

"Well, mount your beast," Justus says.

"For me? He's mine?" Titus replies, looking now up into the eyes of his father.

"If you don't hurry, your mother and I are going to leave without you."

Titus rushes to his new pony, rejects the assistance of Brutus, lifts a foot up to the stirrup, swings the other leg around, and sits tall and proud. He jumps back down and rushes to his father, laying his head on the man's chest.

"Oh, Father. Thank you. Thank you. You are the best father in the whole world."

"Don't forget your mother. It was her idea."

Titus hurries to Kharis on her mount, grabs her hand reaching down to him, and kisses it. "Oh, Mother. Thank you. Thank you."

By now, Justus is headed out the stable gate and onto the street. His family follows up Vici Aegeus and turns right at the columned Cardo Maximus.

Titus sees his friend, Stephan, and calls out to him. "Look what I got for my birthday," his single dimple like his mother's flashing.

"Cease speaking, Titus. An aristocrat does not yell at people on the street. Further, I have warned you not to become too friendly with that potter. He is beneath us."

They pass the Temple of Apollo on their right. When they arrive at the artificial waterfall, they turn left onto the equally columned Decumanus Maximus and follow it past the theater and agrarian market with its public forum. They make one last turn out the western gate of Antioch.

Following at a distance are Cornelius with a tent on the rump of his horse, and two light benches tied on each side. Lydia follows him with clothing and cooking supplies on her mount.

On the open highway, they cross the rest of their Gaulish Okondiani tribal territory, now known as the county of Pisidia and part of the greater Province of Galatia. Riding abreast, the three follow the Meander River through the valley with the snow-capped Sultan Mountains on their right.

Kharis can hold it in no longer. Inspired by the fresh air outside the city away from all its cooking and crafting fires and the fires of sacrifices to the gods, she opens her lips and sings to the world.

The strains of her exquisite voice fill the valley, and its melodies rise like the aromas of spring flowers to the mountains, which echo them back.

"Uh, Son," Justus announces as his wife sings, "look in your saddlebag."

Titus, riding on his birthday pony between his parents, obeys. His hand touches something hard. He pulls out a lyre made of bronze, inlaid with mother of pearl.

"Another birthday present," Titus squeals. "Oh, Father, thank you."

"Again, it was your mother's idea."

"Oh, Mother," Titus says, turning in her direction. "Thank you," he calls out above the strains of her refrain.

She winks and keeps on singing.

Titus wraps the reins of his pony around one of the four saddle horns and accompanies his mother on his birthday lyre. His father joins in with his bass voice.

Before they know it, they have arrived at Nyssa in time for an afternoon meal. Both guards at the city gate recognize the Praetor of Antioch and salute him with fists to the heart, followed by raised arms toward the magistrate.

The traveling party stops. Cornelius dismounts and walks forward, leading his horse. "My master's family is in need of refreshment and a place to stay for the night. Please take us to whichever inn you recommend for us."

The soldier turns and leads them into the city. As he marches, people stop along the street and stare, wondering why the Praetor of Antioch no less, is visiting them.

By now, Titus has put away his lyre and is following his father in the procession, his mother behind him, and Lydia behind them. He sits as straight and tall in his saddle as he can to make his father proud.

They arrive at an inn. The city guard knocks on the gate while Cornelius speaks to a stable hand who bows to Justus and takes the reins of his horse. Two more stable hands appear and take the reins of the other two mounts. The proprietor of the inn meets the three at the gate leading into the outer palatial courtyard.

"Most Excellent sir, it is with great pleasure that I welcome you into my establishment. We have a private atrium for our honored guests. Please follow me."

Well filled with cheeses, fresh grapes, bread, yogurt, and nectar of apricots, the family and two servants are led to an exquisite room for the remainder of the night.

The following day, they resume their journey toward the coast of the Aegean Sea. Late afternoon, they reach Tralles. Though the guards at the city gate do not recognize Justus, they understand the significance of the purple border on his toga and salute him.

"Where might my master's family spend the night in your city?" Cornelius asks, once again having dismounted and walked ahead of the family to one of the guards.

The guard leads them to what Titus assumes is the finest inn within the city walls.

As people cheer the magistrate traveling into their city, Kharis leans toward Titus. "Every lip is cheering us. Both upper and lower," she giggles.

Titus glances at his father to see if their untoward behavior has been detected. It has not. He grins in delight at his mother's sense of humor, so different from his father's rigidness.

The next morning, they leave and continue up the highway.

"Did you know we are on one of the silk roads?" Justus says to Titus.

"What's a silk road, Father?"

"Silk roads are scattered throughout the Roman empire, and all lead from one place—China. Do you know the significance of China?"

Titus grins. "Of course, Father. Anyone can figure that out: China is where silk grows."

"Well, in a way, yes. It is where the silkworms grow, and they spin silk threads to make their cocoons," Justus explains.

"And where I get fabric for my finest stolas," Kharis adds.

"Is the stola you're wearing made from silk, Mother?"

"Indeed, it is."

They ride in silence. Then, once again, his mother's angelic voice. The voice of all the Muses blended into one.

Melodic strains that float everywhere bounce playfully off the clouds overhead and swirl around in the glad heart of Titus. He pulls out his new birthday lyre and accompanies her.

That evening, they arrive at Magnesia, former Roman stronghold, and home of many of Antioch's semi-noble equestrian ancestors. Their journey toward the Aegean Sea resumes.

"My father, Justinius, was a Tribune here when Magnesia was a fortress. When he retired, he was granted the land on which our servants grow flax in the valley outside of Antioch," Justus explains.

"He built our house too, didn't he, Father?"

"Yes, he did. I was born there. Too bad he died the year you were born. He did not live long enough to see you."

"And grandmother died when Aunt Chloe was born."

"I was just five then. I did not understand why my mother had to go away from me." Justus is quiet for a long time.

The following day, they arrive at Ephesus on the Aegean coast and go to the finest inn within the city.

"First thing in the morning," Kharis says with a yawn, "I want to visit the great Temple of Artemis. It is the largest temple in the world."

"Do we have to?" Titus asks. "For my birthday?"

"The beach will still be there afterward," Justus chides.

"It will still be there when you are an old man," Kharis mumbles.

"When I am as old as Father?"

"Go to sleep," Justus growls.

Titus closes his eyes. Then it is morning. He hears his father still snoring, jumps up, and tugs on his foot. "Get up, Father. Get up. Today is still my birthday."

Justus sputters.

Kharis smiles, her eyes still closed. When she opens them, Titus is standing beside his parents' bed with his lyre.

"So soon with the music?"

"I haven't played anything yet," Titus responds. "But, I was about to."

Kharis reaches over and kisses her husband on the

cheek, then pinches his nose to interrupt his snoring. He sputters and opens his eyes.

"My dear, you had better not ever do that in public, or I'll send you back to Dalmatia," Justus announces, rubbing his eyes.

"I never lived in Dalmatia. I was born in Rome," Kharis retorts.

"Well, your father was."

"I know lots of words in Dardani, Mother's tribe," Titus announces. "Do you want to hear them?"

"No, not really," Justus says, rising.

"Besides, it isn't the language of just my tribe," Kharis responds. "It is the language of all Dalmatia."

Titus sits on the floor and counts with his fingers.

"What are you counting?" Kharis asks. "All the words you know in my native language?"

"No, all the languages I know. Well, I don't know them, but I am learning. Let me see, Latin, of course, because everyone in our city speaks Latin. Then Greek because the great philosophers wrote in that language. And Gallic spoken by gr gr gr gr grandfather Brennius." He sputters the gr's in quick succession. "And Dalmatian."

"Four, is that all?" Justus says, standing and tickling his son.

"Well, I'm only nine. Hmmm. I may add a fifth language."

"What's that?" Justus asks, picking up the boy and dangling him upside down by his ankles.

"Hebrew," Titus chokes out between giggles. Justus sets him down. "Rabbi Oeneus says he'll teach me Hebrew."

"The language of the Jews?" his father asks with a frown. "They have a strange religion. Only one God and he is invisible, so no one knows what a statue of him would look like. Strange religion. Isn't he the new rabbi in Antioch?"

"I just want to make you proud, Father."

"Well, young man who knows four languages and dares to learn a fifth," Kharis interrupts, "it is time to get dressed, eat something to break our fast, and go see the great Artemis of the Ephesians."

As the sun rises full above the horizon, they leave the inn. Their horses have been saddled and are waiting for them. With the directions fresh in his mind, Justus leads his family half a *mille* to the agora, then turns right. They pass the amphitheater, which he estimates holds at least twenty-five thousand people. Half a *mille* north of that, they pass the stadium and gymnasium academy. They guide their horses through the North Gate and turn right again. Immediately they see on a high hill overlooking the city, the magnificent Temple of Artemis, though it is still another *mille* away.

When they arrive, a man assumed to be the high priest walks with quick steps out to them, followed by three younger priests. He holds up both arms to greet Justus.

"The goddess told me you were coming. How right she was. Welcome, Most Excellent Magistrate. Welcome. These men will help you off your horses and tie them safely to the trees in our adjacent grove. Your servants are welcome to join them."

The temple dignitary waits for the three distinguished strangers to dismount. "My name is Alexander," the high priest announces. "Follow me."

As the trio walks up the forty-eight steps, they stare at the hundred and twenty columns holding up the roof of the holy place.

Once at the top of the steps and on the portico, the high priest stops and turns. It is my understanding that you, sir, are the Flamin of Apollo and your wife, the Flaminica of Apollo in Antioch. Have I heard correctly?"

"Yes, you have," Justus replies without smiling.

"In that case, we will be most happy to allow you inside the Temple of our Mother to gaze upon her greatness."

Alexander turns and leads them between the columns, each of which Justus estimates to be a full man length in thickness.

Once inside, Titus stretches his neck to see the top of the grand marble statue.

"Whoa," Titus mumbles.

"Shhhh," both parents respond in unison.

"On her head is a crown representing the city walls of

Ephesus whom she protects," the high priest explains. "Her many breasts represent her as the Mother of all living things. We are, of course, honored by her presence among us and her protection. You may stay as long as you like," Alexander concludes. "I must leave you now. It is time for the incense offering."

"How can I have two mothers?" Titus whispers.

"She is your spiritual mother, and I am your physical mother," Kharis replies.

They stand in silence, stretching their necks and straining their eyes to see the crowned head nearly touching the arched ceiling high above. In the silence, they try to absorb all that is the essence of the Mother Superior.

"At least, that's what I have been told," Kharis whispers. "Two mothers? How is it possible?"

Justus takes his wife's hand and squeezes it in warning. She remains quiet.

"Father," Titus says, interrupting the silence. "Can we go see the water now before my birthday runs out? I have demon...demonstrated aristocratic patience."

Justus looks down at his little boy. "That you have, Son," he says, turning to leave.

They walk back out between the columns and pause at the portico.

"Look at that," Kharis says.

The city of Ephesus spreads out below them with its colonnaded streets leading through the center of the city and all the way down Arcadian Way to the harbor.

"It's full of ships," Titus says. "Where am I going to swim?"

"I believe that's the Cayster River beside the harbor. Perhaps we can go there," Kharis replies.

At the bottom of the high steps, the three are brought their horses. They work their way back into the city. When they arrive at the theater perched on the side of Mount Pion, they turn west and continue down Arcadian Way and beside the river.

The seagulls are busy flying and perching and squawking. The smell of sea salt fills the air. The breeze flows through their hair. At last, they arrive at a grassy place beside the river and stop.

Cornelius hurries over to his mistress and helps her down from her mount. He returns to maid Lydia and helps her down.

Before anyone realizes, Titus has thrown off his toga and waded into the water in his short tunic. As soon as the water is deep enough, he dives into it, then turns on his back. "Look, Father. Look at me, Mother. I'm swimming."

By the time the parents have taken off their toga and stola, a blanket and two ivory benches have been set in place. They clasp hands and take their seats.

"We did well, didn't we?" Kharis says.

"Indeed, we did," Justus replies. "The gods have been good to us."

Lydia brings them goblets of apricot nectar.

"Which ones?" Kharis asks. "Apollos, Augustus, Jupiter? I sometimes get confused. My people in Dalmatia have one set of gods. The Greeks have another set of gods. The Romans another. And the Jews just one God. Are they all the same gods or different gods in different heavens? Are they all combined into one God? Could the Jews be right?"

"Look, Mother. Look what I found," Titus says, rushing up the beach toward his parents. He hands her a seashell.

"Oh, thank you, Son," she says.

"Did you see me chase the seagulls, Father? I almost caught one. Are you proud of me, Father?"

Lydia takes a smaller goblet of nectar to her young master.

He sits in front of his parents and gulps it down.

"This is the happiest day of my life," he says. "If I live to be a thousand years old, I will never forget it. Never."

2 ~ THE EARTHQUAKE

*I*t is two years later. Titus is walking home from his lessons at the gymnasium academy.

"I'll see you tomorrow," Titus tells his best friend, potter Stephan.

They part where the colonnade Cardo Maximus crosses Veci Aegeus. Titus turns there while Stephan continues on to his house near the South Gate Market.

As Titus works his way closer to home, he rehearses the warrior dance he had learned that day so it will be perfect, and his father will be proud of him.

He arrives at the gilded gates with statues of his armor-clad and sword-wielding Goth ancestor on each side. He salutes Brennius as he walks up to the entrance to his family *palatio*.

"I'm home," he calls out.

Cornelius opens the gate. "Shhh, young master. You know your father does not approve of such open and undignified vocalizations."

Titus hands his clay writing tablet and a scroll to Cornelius and wags his head. He walks through the reception courtyard lined with statues of four muses on each side, a gift from his father to his mother when they married.

By the time he reaches the gate to the larger family courtyard with the muse Calliope on one side and Apollos on the other, Cornelius has passed him and has it opened.

"I'm home, Mother. I'm home, Father."

Lydia greets her young master with a mug of grape juice and piece of flatbread to keep him satisfied until the evening meal.

"Where is everyone?" he asks her.

"Your father is in his *officium* upstairs. Your mother should be home shortly from the Vestal Temple."

The second floor is supported by six pink marble columns on one side of the courtyard representing Apollo's six sons, and an equal number of columns on the other side representing Apollo's daughters.

Just as Titus takes a big bite of his bread, his mother walks in.

"Whew. I had all the Vestal Virgins to teach today, plus three other virgins who are hoping for acceptance into the order. The new ones are so far behind the Vestals in lyre playing, I may have to teach them separately."

She kisses her eleven-year-old son, who is now as tall as her. Other than being tall like his father, the rest of him takes after his mother, including his thick brown hair, big eyes, pointed chin, and single dimple in that chin.

"I see my family has arrived home," Justus says, making his way down the steps leading from the second floor. Sit. Sit. I want to hear all about your day. Titus, what did you learn?"

The family sits on their three usual cushioned benches near the central reflecting pool.

"I taught Mother's poem about her father's rise to fame from barbarian of Dalmatia to the official singer of Apollo and respected Roman citizen."

"Well, that is fine, Son. But you are becoming too much like your mother. You cannot protect Antioch and Rome with an epic poem. Now, what practical thing did you learn today?"

"I learned a new warrior dance. It imitates what warriors do when they crash through the gate of an enemy city."

"Good. Good. Let me see it."

Titus leaps from his bench and immediately squats. His eyes dart both ways, then in front. He takes two steps forward, then runs and leaps in the air, thrusting an imaginary spear as he goes. Leap and thrust, leap, and thrust. He stops and stares at his father.

"That's all?"

"Well, I don't remember the rest. But I will do better tomorrow. I promise, Father. I will make you proud of me. Remember the poem about Augustus becoming a god that I learned last week? Would you like to hear it again, Father?"

Justus rises. "I have work to do. I shall be in my *officium.*"

Titus and his mother watch Justus climb the steps two at a time up to his private domain.

"Son, he is just trying to make sure you grow up to be a man worthy of the title."

"What title? I don't have a title."

"Your father does, and you are an extension of him."

"But he isn't proud of me anymore."

"He is prouder of you than you realize. You should hear him when the judges come here for his advice."

"Then, why doesn't he tell me that?"

"Let me tell you a little story," his mother says. "It happened before you were born, and while I was still living in Rome."

"That's where you and Father met, isn't it?"

"Yes, he was attending the university led by Apollo's priests, and heard my father and me singing."

"Then Father saw your beauty and knew he had to have you."

"That's right, she giggles. "Now, let me tell my story. One year at the solo singing contests held in Apollo's honor, there was a man who scored absolutely no points. Such had never happened before."

Kharis chuckles, showing her single dimple, then returns to her story.

"At the end of the contest, everyone crowded around the man who had made no points. Ha, ha. They were fascinated by him accomplishing such a feat, much to the frustration of the man who won. The poets wanted to write poems about the worst loser in the entire history of the music contests, and the musicians wanted to dedicate songs to him. Ha, ha. He said he had never received so much attention in all his life."

Titus smiles, mostly from watching his mother's enjoyment in her own story.

"So, you see, Son. People can be proud of you for all kinds of reasons."

"Father too?"

Kharis smiles and ruffles her son's hair. "Father too. Now let's think of a song. There is nothing in life that a song cannot help."

Titus smiles and sits in silence next to his mother. *Jewish God, whoever you are and where ever you are, make my mother one of your stars someday. Make her your brightest star.*

"By the way," Kharis interrupts without knowing it, "tomorrow after school, instead of coming straight home, I need you to deliver a lyre to one of my new students so she can practice at home. I will be busy at the synagogue. Rabbi Oenus is teaching me the Hebrew scriptures. I have secretly become one of them."

"You have? Why? Father will be very angry."

"That's why it is a secret. Well, for now, it is. I will teach your father a little at a time until he understands and wants to join us. At any rate, I will put the lyre in a shoulder pouch for you."

"Where does your student live?"

"Just east of Antioch on the Iconium Road. You'll have to take your horse to the gymnasium academy so you can get there and back home before dark."

"Yes, ma'am. I'll be happy to. By the way, how old is the girl?"

"Too old for you. Keep your mind on your education and your future."

The following morning, Brutus has Titus' horse saddled and ready for him.

"Son," Justus says, "after the gymnasium lets out, I need you to meet me at the Temple of Vesta. I am holding court there. A young man was caught marking up Augustus' temple *propylon* and is being tried for treason and blasphemy.

He is just a little older than you. I want you to be there to witness what happens to careless young men."

"But, Father, Mother asked me to deliver a lyre to a student on the Iconium Road after the gymnasium dismisses."

"You can do both. Come to the hearing. It is only a preliminary one with the high priest of Augustus registering the charges. You will have plenty of time to deliver your mother's lyre afterward."

After school that day, Titus heads toward the agora near the West Gate of the city. His father is dressed in his finest purple-edged toga and is sitting on the highest part of the platform as Praetor of Antioch. Below him on the next highest part of the platform are three judges. Titus finds a spot in the crowd sufficient to see and hear what is going on.

"Further, Most Excellent Magistrates and Revered Praetor Justus, this young man was caught in the act. He was painting his name on each step of the *propylon* leading up to the temple of our city's patron, the divine Augustus, now sharing a place with the other gods among the stars."

"Do you have witnesses?" one of the judges asks.

"Yes, Most Excellency. We have four. Sufficient to bring a verdict of guilty and penalty of death."

Titus realizes the young man being tried is an older student at the gymnasium academy who had helped him with one of his warrior dances. Cracius is crying with the hoarse voice of a youth becoming a man.

Before Titus knows it, a continuation of the trial is announced for the next day. He realizes the sun is close to the horizon. *I will never be able to make the delivery now. I guess I can do it tomorrow.*

Praetor Justus Brennius Antiochus steps down off the platform and onto the street. "Son, tie your horse up to my chariot. We shall ride home together."

As they make their way back up the Decumanus Maximus toward home, Titus grows more anxious.

"You can deliver your mother's lyre tomorrow," Justus says, understanding Titus' concerns. "I will speak to your mother, and you will be forgiven. She is a good woman."

"Yes, Father."

They arrive home. Kharis is already there. She is sitting in the courtyard reading.

"Oh, hello, you two. I have been inspired to write another poem. But you cannot hear it yet. I have just begun. Did you get my lyre delivered?"

"Mother, I am sorry. I had two important things to do at the same time. Father assured me..."

"I assured Titus," Justus says, intervening, "he would be out of court in time to deliver your lyre before dark. Yes, yes. I told him to come to court first to hear a special case. The accuser, the high priest of Augustus, went on and on with his orations about the magnificence of our now-deceased Caesar, and before we knew it..."

Kharis stands and kisses the cheeks of both of the most important men in her life. She smiles. "I have no problem with that. I will be free tomorrow morning to deliver the lyre. So, you men can stay as long as you like at your court hearing."

The next morning, Titus kisses his mother on both cheeks. "Thank you, Mother. I just did not know what to do. Thank you for forgiving me."

"There is nothing to forgive you of."

As Titus leaves through the front gate, he hears her humming and knows she will work on her poem a little while before delivering the lyre.

The hours at the gymnasium go by slower this day. Titus looks out the window and realizes the birds are not singing. He sees a rat skitter across the marble floor of the gymnasium academy in broad daylight. The air is still. Everyone in the classroom is quiet. Their lecturer, Fortunatus, too. All quiet. As though waiting for the appearance of something great and wonderful.

Titus' stylus rolls off his lap desk and onto the floor. He looks out the window again. Leaves on the trees are trembling. He hears a dog howl in the distance.

Just as the class is dismissed for a noon-time meal, they hear galloping through the city streets and shouting.

"An earthquake. Out on the highway. An earthquake on the highway!"

The students rush in a body outside to hear more

details, their lecturer Fortunatus leading the way.

They wait for the rider to turn around at the end of the street and return their way.

"Where did it happen?" Fortunatus shouts to the rider as he draws closer. He stands on the road in the path of the onrushing horse. The horse raises up on its haunches to miss trampling the intruder in its path.

The rider reins in his mount, and the lecturer calls up to him again. "Where did it happen? Was anyone hurt?"

"On the Iconium Road!" the rider shouts before resuming his mission of broadcasting tragedy through the city.

Titus runs toward the North Gate near the aqueduct. He hears hoofbeats behind him and moves to the side of the street along with everyone else on foot.

"Get in," he hears.

Titus immediately recognizes his father's voice and dodges other horses to get to the family chariot.

Justus snaps a whip above his horse's head. "Yeeaah!" he shouts. "Yeeaah."

The chariot speeds the rest of the way up columned Cardo Maximus and out through the North Gate. Justus cracks the whip again, though knowing his horse cannot go any faster than it is. When he comes to the Iconium Road, he guides the horse to the right, the chariot rocking and sometimes teetering on one wheel.

They see boulders in the road ahead, and Justus pulls back on the reins. Before the horse can come to a complete stop, Justus jumps out of the chariot. Titus grabs the reins, brings the chariot to a full stop, and he too jumps out.

The men rush to the rubble and immediately move rocks out of the way.

"Stop!" they hear someone shout. "Stop talking, everyone," the stranger says. "We need to listen for voices."

A restless quiet ensues as though there is no such thing as sound anymore. The quiet echoes up the treacherous Mount Karakus, back down, and swirls around in hearts that have stopped their thump, thump, thump.

"Titus," Justus shouts. "Over here! I see a lyre. Move

them. Help me move these rocks out of the way. Maybe we aren't too late."

One by one, the men tug and lift this rock and that out of their treacherous resting places and toss them away. One by one. Closer to their mother and wife. Closer and hoping. Hoping it is her. Hoping it is not.

One rock at a time. Hands working to uncover that which they dread to uncover.

The grand and magnificent Antioch, once favored by Augustus Caesar himself, does not sleep that night.

Funeral processions down every street. Torch lights everywhere. Mourning and wailing, moaning, and screaming. Shouts up into the black sky. "Why?"

Pyres everywhere on the other side of the ancient city walls. No waiting the required five days to make sure the dead is not just in a swoon. Who could live through that? No burials with singers of both the boys' and girls' choruses. The dead are hardly identifiable.

Brutus gallops out of the city to the field hands and tells them where their mistress's pyre will be set up. He returns at the *palatio* where the twenty servants and maids have gathered.

Both father and son now wear the dark toga, symbol of mourning.

Titus looks at his father for the signal. Justus nods. The six men pick up the cot on which their beloved Kharis has been laid, what is left of her mangled body covered with a silk sheet, and attached to the cot itself to avoid it being blown off.

Justus leaves first, walking with slow steps between the statues of the muses he had bought his wife a dozen years earlier. Titus follows.

Kharis and the six servants are next. Behind them, the servants have lined up according to their seniority. All wearing dark tunics.

Titus hears mournful pipes being played by one of them. Another with a flute joins in to make a duet of sorrow as deep as the sea. A third one plays on a lyre changing its former gladness to a sadness that is almost unbearable.

Titus remembers his mother's saying, "There is nothing

that a song cannot help." *You were wrong, Mother. You were wrong.*

Slow and steady steps toward the West Gate in the midnight of their being. Past the Temple of Apollo, then the waterfall. They see ahead of them the Temple of Vesta, protectress of hearth and home. She had not protected their beloved Kharis.

They turn at the waterfall with not enough tears in it to show adequate sorrow for one so sweet and kind. Down the colonnade, past the theater and agora. Out the West Gate to the cemetery. The cemetery not intended for Titus' gentle mother.

All is wrong. This woeful procession should not be. Titus should be at home with both parents, everyone tucked in their own bed and sleeping with happy dreams. Sleeping? Yes, sleeping now. But the sleep of death.

Oh, Mother. Why didn't I deliver your lyre yesterday when you asked me to? Why? I could have left school early and satisfied both you and Father. I killed you. Oh, forgive me. But how can you?

They arrive at the spot on which Justus has instructed a raised pyre be built. The six servants lift what is left of the lovely Kharis up onto the pyre and hand a torch to Justus. Justus steps forward, presses his lips together, pauses, and lights the kindling.

As the flames grow higher, Titus steps back and sits on the ground. He watches what he does not want to watch. He watches as his mother—the one he had betrayed—goes up in smoke.

Oh, God of the Jews. Do not let her soul burn up. Take her soul to where ever your heaven is. Titus looks up into the heavens. The smoke of her pyre rises, and he thinks he sees her soul rise with it.

On and endlessly on. Fire. Smoke. Lost hope. Lost life. Lost everything.

He stands. "No! Not this! Not my mother!"

His cries rush to the cliffs of treacherous Mount Karakus and echo back to him to make sure he feels as guilty as he deserves.

Tears that will not stop. Cannot stop. Tears and wretched groanings that mingle in what should not have been. Reality suffocating in mocking flames that consume his mother as well as his heart.

Titus rushes over to Justus. "Oh, Father, I can't stand this. Father, make it stop. Make this day be only a nightmare. Father, please, Father."

Justus glances at his son and turns away. Titus walks around to face him, but Justus turns again.

Maid Lydia, standing nearby, rushes up to the boy and embraces him. He sobs on her shoulder and wishes she were his mother.

It is morning. Only embers remain under the pyre and charred bones above it.

Justus stands. "Gather them up into an ossuary," he tells Cornelius. "Bury it next to my father and mother."

Justus walks back into the city. Titus follows behind. When they arrive home, Justus goes to his *officium* and closes the door.

Titus is left alone. He sits in the middle of the courtyard on the cold green-and-coral tiles. Cold. Everything now cold. The pyre, his father, his heart. Cold and deserted. And all the fault of Titus Pomponius Brennius, eleven years old.

3 ~ MASKS

*T*hree more years have passed. Once again, it is Titus' birthday.

"Are you ready to become a man today?" Aunt Chloe teases.

Titus looks her in the eye, both being nearly as tall as their father and brother. "I am already a man," Titus replies with his unreliable half-man voice. "This is just a ceremony, so even strangers will know. Do you have it?"

"Your new toga? Yes. It is folded up in that cedar box for your father to take with him."

"It will feel strange wearing a toga with no trim on it, just white."

"True," Chloe responds, "but when you are eighteen, you can choose another trim color. Don't be in a hurry to grow up."

"I told you, I am already grown up, Aunt Chloe."

"Titus, are you ready? The ceremony will begin as soon as we arrive."

"Yes, Father. I am ready. I will make you proud of me."

Justus does not reply. He walks to the outer reception courtyard. It is empty. Titus misses his mother's muses. He tries not to remember the night he had heard the crashing and his father battering them to pieces.

They walk out their gilded front gate where his father's

silver chariot awaits, the same silver chariot into which they had laid what was left of the woman they had both loved and is no more. Titus fights his unmanly tears at the reminder.

"Ha, ha!" he says as they step into the chariot. I wonder what they would say if I wore my new toga backward."

"Titus, I'm warning you."

The chariot turns at the end of Vici Aegeus and turns north at columned Cardo Maximus.

They arrive at the Temple of deified Augustus Caesar. When the assembly sees them, cheering rises on cue.

Father and son walk up the twelve-stepped *propylon* that stops at the portico with two columns on each side, rising to the height of ten man-lengths. At the pinnacle high above is a marble image of Augustus surrounded by banners of his army and the empire on each side. There are two-story wings on either side of the temple itself for the priests.

They turn and face the gathered crowd, mostly of local politicians, priests, and Justus' servants brought in from his fields. Justus steps forward, raising his hands to quiet the celebrating crowd.

He notices that Antioch's quaestor who handles the tax money is there. Also, the aediles who manage the roads, the aqueduct, the market, and other public conveniences and requirements. The censor and governor of Galatia are not there.

"Thank you. Thank you, everyone, for coming to witness a proud moment in the life of my son and me. As everyone here knows, he has excelled in his age group at military dances and the games. He is an excellent mathematician and even better orator."

"Yes, we heard him orating at the South Gate Market not long ago. Ha, ha. What a boy!"

Justus resumes his speech without acknowledging the interruption. "If you have faith in my son as I have, if you believe in him as I have, if you watch him grow into the young man he is today as I have, I declare to you this day of his fourteenth year he will become one of the great leaders of our honored city made famous by Augustus Caesar himself."

Applause. Hooting.

"And now, Titus Pomponius Brennius, step forward," he says to the audience.

As Titus steps up to Justus' right side, two of the magistrates approach him from the left with the cedar box. During the pause, Titus looks out at the audience again and notices Stephan there. Stephan waves, and Titus smiles.

One magistrate helps Titus off with his toga designed like his father's. Justus takes the plain white toga out of the box and turns toward his son just as the first magistrate folds and puts the old child-like toga in the cedar box.

Justus holds it up. "This is a sign you are now your own man," he declares. "There are no markings to indicate the status of your father. From henceforward, you will be expected to earn your own right to distinguished togas."

He steps around behind Titus and puts the end of the cloth over the young man's left shoulder far enough it comes close to touching the floor. He brings his end across his son's back and under his right arm. Titus takes hold of what is left of the length of cloth and drapes it over his left forearm.

Applause from the crowd. Titus looks around for the singers. The boys' chorus always hired to perform at such official ceremonies. No singers. No chorus. No music.

As they ride the chariot on their way home, Justus goes over what will now be expected of his son now, though he never refers to him as son except in public.

"You will be through with your basic writing and poetic analysis courses next year. Then you will be ready to go on to study geometry, astronomy, and rhetoric. I expect you to excel. Is that clear?"

"Yes, Father. It is clear."

Nothing more is said. When father and son arrive home, Justus takes two steps at a time up to his *officium* and closes the door.

Titus sits alone in the courtyard that had, in times past, when his mother was alive, resonated with music and the laughter of happiness. Now silence. Always the silence.

"I am truly sorry your father is acting like this on your special day," his Aunt Chloe says.

"Me too," Titus mumbles at the tiled courtyard floor.

"He's hurting, Titus. He does not know how to handle his loss. We Goths do not express our emotions very well."

"I guess so."

"When I lost my husband last year in Corinth, I felt as though I had fallen into a deep dark hole that was impossible to get out of. Then, when I received word that Kharis had died, I knew I had to come and be a step-mother to you. This time with you has helped both of us."

"But not Father."

"No, not your father."

Titus takes a deep breath, walks around the reflecting pool—still with Augustus' statue in the middle—three times, and raises his forefinger in the air.

"The funniest thing happened at the gymnasium the other day," he announces with a broad grin. "One of the other students decided to say the alphabet backward. When he succeeded, he decided to say it upside down. So—ha, ha—he stood on his head and said the alphabet both backward and upside down. Ha, ha."

Chloe smiles and fights back tears for the boy's broken heart.

"I think I'll go down to the South Gate Market and show off my new toga. I'm my own man now. I don't need anyone now."

Chloe stands. "Indeed, yes. That is what you must do. Now get along, and I—we—will see you when you return."

Titus makes his way to the South Gate Market. He swaggers and swings in a circle to make his new toga flow out in the artificial breeze.

Son, aristocrats do not swing in circles in public, he hears his father say. With that thought, Titus does it again.

"Well, look who's here to show off he's a man now," a baker calls over to him.

"With all the jumping around, he's not going to keep it clean and white for long," a copper jewelry maker says.

"If you're looking for your friend, Stephan, you're going the wrong way," a baker says.

"He has always been trouble. No one likes him. Don't know why you bother with him," a parchment merchant says.

Titus stops in his tracks. "What's wrong with Stephan?"

"What isn't wrong with him?" a weaver says.

Titus walks over to the baker's booth. "What do you mean, I'm going in the wrong direction?"

"I am not going to be the bearer of bad news," comes the response. "But, if I were you, I would check on that friend of yours."

Titus turns around and heads back the way he had come until he arrives at Stephan's mother's small house next to an *insulae*. He knocks on the gate and waits.

In a few moments, a woman opens it. She is crying. "Oh, Titus, what am I going to do?"

"Ma'am, what happened?"

"Come in. I do not want the neighbors spying on us." She steps back so Titus can enter.

Now in the courtyard, he sees all the benches and tables they used to have are gone. Floor cushions are all that is left.

"Sit," Fiora says, dabbing her eyes with a dirty kerchief.

He sits on one of the dirty cushions.

"My Stephan has been arrested." She wipes her nose, then loses control again and weeps anew.

"Arrested for what?" Titus waits for Fiora to collect herself.

"One of the other merchants claims he stole the money that was nearly a full day's sales for him." She breaks down, crying again.

Titus stands and paces, his new white toga dirtied in places. "He wouldn't do that. Not Stephan. Someone else maybe, but not Stephan. How much money was it?"

"Twelve silver coins," she manages to say before burying her face in her kerchief again.

"Who makes that much in a day around here?" he asks.

"The incense seller."

Titus can scarce understand her.

"He's the accuser? He isn't even a Roman citizen. He is a stranger from India."

"He is much older than my Stephan, and they believe him more than they do a mere boy of fourteen."

"He's fourteen. He is a man now. Or almost. Anyway, he

was automatically a Roman citizen, having been born here in Antioch," Titus explains. "They should take his word... Where is he?"

"In the dungeon below the Temple of Augustus."

"That foreigner will wish he had never started this. Wait until I get my hands on him. He will be on a ship back to India before he knows it—if he is allowed to live, that is. He does not know who he is dealing with. I am the son of Justus Brennius Antiochus, Praetor over all Antioch."

With that, he heads for the outer gate.

"What am I going to do? My husband died last year, and it is all Stephan and I can do to keep the pottery business going. What am I..."

Titus does not hear the rest. Within half an hour, he is at the dungeon standing before the guard.

"Sir, my name is Titus Pomponius Brennius, son of Justus Brennius Antiochus. I demand to see one Stephanus Chronus, who has been falsely arrested."

"Demand all you want, young man. No one sees him until the day of his trial."

"When is his trial?"

"Tomorrow."

"I see. That does not leave me much time. Will you get a message to Stephanus from me?"

"If you put it in writing," the guard replies.

Titus is surprised at his answer. He looks around and sees a flat rock on the pavement between the dungeon and the portico of Sanctuary of Men Askanas. He picks it up and takes off his sandal. He pulls off the decorative iron on one of the straps and etches a message on it.

Free tomorrow. Titus

"Here are five copper coins. I will give you five more when you deliver him to the court tomorrow."

"I will not be on duty that early tomorrow, but will pass the word on to the next shift."

"Thank you. I will put in a good word on your behalf to my father."

With that, Titus turns and rushes back in the direction of Stephan's house. Instead of stopping there, he hurries on to Via Salutans, the edge of the market. He rushes to the incense shop before it closes.

"Sir, I would like to see your finest incense."

The merchant looks through shelves below the counter and, when he rises, centers the askance red silk turban on his head. Titus notices he has it clasped together with a pearl.

He hands Titus a small ebony box with a small ball of myrrh inside. When Titus opens the lid, the fragrance floats out to enchant the senses.

"I see," Titus says. "Very nice. How much is it?"

"One silver coin," sir. "I would usually charge ten silver coins, but you look like a man who will come back for more once you get a chance to experience its powers."

Titus holds the small box in the palm of his hand. "And what else do you have for me to experience their powers?"

"Cinnamon," the merchant says, his one broken tooth exhibiting itself when he smiles. He ducks, scoots things around under his counter, and comes up straightening his silk turban.

Titus takes the lid off a small alabaster box and catches the delightful scent of the new spice. He puts that box in the same hand as the myrrh.

"The price?"

"One silver coin."

"And what else do you have down there?"

"I am afraid I have sold out of everything today. It was a good day for me."

"Good for you," Titus responds. He turns and leaves. The merchant calls after him. "Aren't you even going to buy something?"

Titus keeps on walking.

The following morning before daylight, Titus hurries to the dungeon so he can walk with Stephan to the forum at the Temple of Vesta. He is not allowed contact with the prisoner until arrival at the forum, so hurries on ahead.

When Stephan and the guard come into view again, Titus remembers the times when they laughed together, and

Stephan's belly would flop. He remembers times when they mentally sparred with each other—whether it be about philosophy, astronomy, or geometry. Stephan was not popular with the other children for that reason, and Titus knows he would probably have no friends, were it not for him.

When Stephan arrives, he has chains around his ankles.

"Unchain him," Titus demands.

"That is up to the judges, young man," the guard says.

"I have read the law, and that combined with my own experience says prisoners must be unchained—number one, if they have not been proven guilty yet, and number two, if a guard is nearby. He meets both qualifications. Unchain him."

The guard looks around for advice. None is given, so he unchains Stephan's ankles.

"Now, I must consult in private with my client," he tells the guard.

"You are too young to have a client," the guard responds.

"Sir, do you know who I am?"

The guard sighs. "Go ahead. But stay within my view."

Titus takes Stephan's arm and guides him to a corner of the raised platform for the judges, and they sit on the bench for defendants, though Stephan does not know the significance.

"Thank you, friend," Stephan says. "I thought..."

"Listen, this is what is going to happen today. You are going to be given a list of citizens, age forty and above, who are eligible to be a judge."

"Just citizens?"

"That's right. They do not necessarily know the law. They will rely on their own common sense and my father to know the laws. Now, you have the right to choose your judges."

"I do?"

"I know the men that are eligible to serve better than you do, so will you let me choose them for you?"

Stephan looks at his friend. Tears form in his eyes. He says nothing.

"That's okay. I know you are grateful. Now, I am going to draw things out so that it takes all day to select the judges. Court is not allowed to go beyond sunset. My father will be arriving any minute now. Just spend this time praying to whichever god you like most and who likes you most."

"How am I supposed to know that?"

Titus smiles.

Moments later, they hear chariot wheels and the clopping of horse hooves on the smooth cobblestone. Titus and Stephan stand and position themselves facing the high platform on which the judges will eventually sit, and the upper one that his father will ascend to shortly.

Praetor Justus appears and climbs the steps to his coral marble chair. He seats himself and looks out. He squints and motions for the guard to come up to him. They whisper, and the guard returns to his post.

Praetor Justus clears his throat. "Uh, well, I understand we have an accusation of theft by one Stephanus Chronus—twelve pieces of silver. Is that correct?

Titus steps forward. "Most Excellent Praetor Justus. My client's accuser is not here. May I appeal to you for a dismissal. No crime has been proven."

Justus looks down at his son. He furrows his brow and makes his thin lips thinner. He shakes his head and takes a deep breath.

"Am I to understand, Titus, that you have a client?"

"That is correct, Most Excellent Praetor Justus."

"And you are prepared to defend him?"

"Yes, Most Excellent Praetor Justus. You are correct."

Titus covers his smile with one hand. *My oratory classes paid off, after all, didn't they, you old inflated self-righteous lord of the city. What are you going to do about it, now that we are in public?*

Justus clears his throat and looks around. "Oh, I believe the accuser is coming now. We shall recess long enough for him to arrive and make his formal complaint."

"Your Royal Highness, I am so sorry for arriving late. I have so many customers, it is most difficult for me to break away from their presence."

Justus looks over at his deputy.

"Sir, you will address the praetor as Most Excellent. You do not address him as though he were king. That is an offense to the empire."

The Indian bows until his head touches the pavement. He stays.

The deputy watches Justus for several moments and, at last, gets the signal. "You may rise," the deputy says. "Being on time will impress the Most Excellent Praetor much more than groveling."

"Kind Sir Most Excellent, please explain 'groveling'."

Justus interrupts. "State your name."

"Raja, Most Excellent One."

"You have only one name?"

"No, I have three."

"Then state them."

"Raja Vijay Kumar."

"Now then, what are the charges against this boy?"

"That boy is a devil, Excellent Sir."

"Just state the charges."

"He stole from me."

Justus sighs. "And what did he steal from you?"

"Twenty, no, no, twenty-five, no that's not it, thirty pieces of brass, no silver. That's it. Thirty pieces of silver."

Justus runs his long fingers through his receding blond hair. "Sit over there."

He turns to his deputy, and the deputy hands him a scroll. He glances at it and hands it back to the deputy, who then descends the steps to the ground level of the pavement. He gives the list to a clerk who has seated himself at a table between the accuser and accused.

"Maximilius Brochus," he calls out. "Do both parties agree on this man as your judge?"

The Indian puts his hands out, palms up, and shrugs. "If he is a good man, then I approve of his being my excellent one."

Stephan rises, holding his forefinger in the air. "Most Excellent Praetor, I object to this man."

Justus purses his lips and looks heavenward a

moment. "And on what grounds do you object?"

"He is an importer of spices himself and is probably the supplier of the plaintiff. I object to him on the basis of prejudice."

Justus calls down, "Next?"

"Cicero Achaias."

Justus looks at the plaintiff, and once more, he shrugs his shoulders. "Good, good. Good man. I like him. Good man."

"And why is it that you like him?" Justus inquires.

"Most Excellent Praetor," Titus says, standing. "I object to his man being a judge because the plaintiff likes him. That is not allowed in this court."

Justus looks down at his son, then at the clerk.

"Acides Pyrrus."

The Indian raises his forefinger. "I object."

"And why do you object, sir?" Justus asks.

"Because I heard he likes the devil. Uh, that is, he likes that devil Stephan, Excellent Sir."

Justus looks over at his son.

"Uh, no objection, Most Excellent Praetor."

The clerk calls out the next name. "

"Gaius Fortunatus."

"We approve of him," Stephan says, standing in place.

"Well, I do not approve," Raja says.

By this time, Justus has disappeared, and his deputy has taken his place on the high seat.

The hours pass until they have gone through the entire list.

"The two of you have agreed on one judge. The names will be reread from the beginning. You both must agree on three men to be your judges."

Just as the sun reaches the horizon, both parties come to an agreement. The deputy adjourns the court until the next morning.

On Titus' way home, he thinks of the day's events. Becoming a man in the morning and acting the man's part in the afternoon. Though his new white toga is a little grungy in places, he decides it has been a very good day.

He arrives home and walks with a light step through the

guest reception courtyard to the family courtyard. Chloe meets him. Her hands are on her slim hips.

"What in the world did you do today? Your father is livid."

"Huh?" Titus stops and takes a step back. "What do you mean? I thought he would be proud of me."

"Proud of what? What did you do? He came marching in this afternoon, throwing things down, taking the steps two at a time, and slamming his *officium* door.

Titus looks up at the darkening sky above and shakes his head. He presses his lips together. He is still blaming me, isn't he? He will never forgive me."

"Forgive you for what?"

"For killing my mother."

"What? Come sit here. What is going on between you two?"

4 ~ STEPHAN

*T*he following morning before daylight, when Titus opens his bedroom door, he sees a tray of flatbread, yogurt, and fresh grapes. In a basket on the tray is more flatbread, cheese, and fresh apricots—enough for two people. He grabs the bread and the basket and leaves without saying anything to anyone.

Chloe hears him out on the street. Singing? She recalls hearing his mother say many times, "There is nothing that a song cannot help."

"I hope you are right, Kharis," she whispers.

Just as the sun peeks out, Titus walks over to the South Market and the incense booth. Shutters over the counter of the booth are closed and locked. Titus backs away and watches for Raja to arrive.

While he waits, he speaks to some of the merchants nearby who have already opened their booths for the day.

When finally Raja arrives and opens the shutters, Titus notices once again the shelves are empty other than what he apparently has below the counter. Titus turns and heads for the Temple of Vesta, where court will continue shortly.

He arrives and waits for a guard to escort Stephan to the forum. As he does, he notices a few more people from the city arriving and standing in the area of spectators. Soon, Stephan arrives.

"How was your night, friend?"

"I think a little better, now that you are helping me," Stephan replies.

"Well, we have a long way to go, but you will not be punished."

"How about your father? Was he proud of you?"

"I'm afraid it was just the opposite. There is no pleasing him. But I will not allow that to stop us from winning. With all his faults, he is a fair man."

They hear the familiar chariot wheels and clomping of hooves. When Justus arrives, he looks straight ahead and climbs the step to his marble perch at the top. He is following by his deputy. They whisper to each other.

Soon, another chariot is heard. Ammonius Moderatus walks onto the forum pavement and takes a seat on the second level of the forum. He takes the second of the three seats.

Next, Chrispus of Athens arrives and takes the farthest seat on the podium.

Finally, Pollux Antonius arrives and takes the nearest seat.

They are now lined up according to age. All wear the red-purple border on their togas to indicate their position.

Titus rises, and motions for Stephan to follow his example.

"Most Excellent Praetor and Venerated Magistrates. We are ready to commence."

"Well, it looks like this case must be dismissed. There is no accu... Well, here he comes," Justus says from on high.

Indian Raja shuffles over to his bench on the other side of the platform. He sits. He grins. "Excellent One," he begins, "I can explain."

"Don't," Justus replies. "Now, it is my understanding that you are accusing Stephanus Chronus of the theft of either twelve or thirty pieces of silver."

"Thirty, Excellent Sir. Thirty," Raja calls up.

Justus looks down at the clerk sitting between the opposing parties. "So amended," the clerk replies.

"The arbitrator for the defendant may begin," Justus

says, not looking at his son.

Titus rises. "Most Excellent Praetor of the great city of Antioch, and Venerated Magistrates Ammonius Moderatus, Chrispus of Athens and Pollux Antonius." His voice punches at the morning air. "It is with the utmost confidence that my client and I appear before you this day." He swings around and points to Stephan. "I intend to prove beyond any doubt that there was no theft at all, as alleged by Raja." He raises one arm. "None!"

Titus walks to the center of the platform and notices with a quick glance that many of his classmates are among the curious onlookers. One gives him the thumbs up and smiles. Titus winks but otherwise remains somber. He spins and glares at the plaintiff until the plaintiff shows sufficient nervousness.

"Sir!" Raja jumps, much to the satisfaction of Titus, who has only just begun to torment the enemy of his friend. "On what day did this alleged theft take place?"

"I think it took place on Thorsday."

"I see. So, you think it took place on Thorsday, but you are not sure."

"I think I am sure," Raja replies.

Titus paces in front of his victim. "Might it have taken place on Solday? I understand that is the busiest day at the South Market. You would have more money then for someone to steal."

"You may be right. It must have been on Solday."

Titus spins around and looks up at the judges. "So, what you are telling us is that a theft took place on either Thorsday or Solday. Probably on Solday but maybe on Thorsday."

He swings back around and faces the plaintiff again. "Do you know," he pauses, "the days of the week, sir? Do they teach the days of the week in India?"

"Of course, they do," Raja replies.

"So!" Titus pauses. "In India, you have the same days of the week that we do in the Roman Empire."

"Well, not exactly," Raja answers.

"Not exactly? Not exactly?" Titus responds, turning

toward his classmates. They grin broadly, and he nearly loses his train of thought. He turns back to the plaintiff and slams his fist on the clerk's table. It hurts more than he had expected.

"Ouch. That is a hard thing to uh, to understand," he says with a quick recovery that his mother would have been proud of.

"Now then, let us move on to the amount of money that was taken. Was it twelve pieces of silver, or twenty or thirty? Or perhaps ten?"

"Thirty. I am sure of that. Thirty," Raja blurts out.

Titus leans so far over the plaintiff, Raja has to look up to see his face. "You are sure it was not twelve and never was twelve."

"That's right."

Titus steps away, turns his back on his victim, puts his chin in one hand, then turns again to stare at Raja. "Then why did your complaint say twelve?"

"My mind was not good that day. I was mixed up."

"Sir, were you mixed up then, or are you mixed up now?"

Titus does not wait for an answer.

"Now you say the money was stolen at the end of a very prosperous day. When I was at your booth recently, you said your most expensive incense sells for one silver coin, and that most of the incense you carry is worth one silver coin. Is that correct?"

"Yes, that is true."

"Which hour of the day do you usually open your booth?"

"The seventh hour."

"And which hour of the day do you typically close up?"

"Uh, the seventeenth hour."

"So, you are telling me you are typically open ten hours a day."

"Yes, Most Excellent Sir."

"So, you sold incense to an average of three people an hour that day. Is that correct?"

"I guess so." Raja fidgets.

Titus raises both arms heavenward. "Behold!" he shouts to the clouds, "the man is finally telling the truth!"

He looks over at the spectators, then up at the judges, shaking his head and pausing a long moment.

"Venerated Magistrates, I would like to request that four witnesses be called to testify on the morrow."

The judges consult among themselves. The oldest one speaks. "That will be fine. Give your list to the clerk so he can write up subpoenas and serve them this afternoon."

"Thank you, Venerated Magistrates."

Titus looks up at his father, who has his chin in one hand and is leaning on his elbow.

"Uh-hem!" Titus says.

The deputy takes two steps at a time up to the Praetor's coral marble chair and whispers to Justus.

Justus' chin slips off his hand, he jerks and opens his eyes. He stands. "Court is adjourned until tomorrow or the earliest day your witnesses report to the court."

Justus works his way down to the ground level. The spectators part for him. He leaves in his chariot. The judges rise, and they, too, leave. Titus sits back next to Stephan. "Be brave, my friend."

Stephan shakes his head. "Does that man even know how to add and multiply?"

Titus smiles. "I am going over to see your mother, then back to the South Market to do some more watching. So far, everything is going according to plan. Trust me, my friend. We have been best friends for a long time. I will never betray you."

Before Stephan can reply, the guard arrives with the chains to go around his ankles.

"Oh, my Aunt Chloe sent you some food. It is in this basket. She is a good cook."

Titus walks away and makes his visit to Fiora to reassure her. "By the time I am through with this case, you will not only not owe anything, but you will come out maybe even wealthy. I would like to encourage you to come to the hearing tomorrow. You will be proud of your son."

He leaves the modest home, looks toward the market, and changes his mind. His last words to Stephan catch in his throat and will not go away.

He arrives home with the intention of letting Chloe feed him, reading a little from Plato and Cicero, then going to bed.

"What do you think you are doing?"

Instead, his father greets him.

"Oh, Father. I, uh, well, I was hoping you would be proud of me. But, I realized right away that it was not going to happen. At least Mother will be proud of me, where ever she is."

"Do not mention that woman. You are not worthy to speak of her."

"Well, Father, I am going to be back in court tomorrow, and whether or not you admit it, I will make you proud. Good night, Father."

The next day at dawn, Titus hurries to the forum. Spectators have already begun to assemble.

One by one, the witnesses arrive. They are directed by the clerk to sit on the witness bench to one side of the platform.

By this time, there are more spectators than the day before, and the judges have not yet arrived.

"Father and son," he hears people say among themselves. "Father and son. What a spectacle."

"If the judges cannot pronounce a satisfactory verdict, the father will have to. Then what?"

"I wouldn't miss this for anything. I even brought cheese and grapes so I don't have to go home at mid-day."

"Hey, Titus," one of his classmates calls out. "Fortunatus let the gymnasium out today. We're cheering for you."

Titus looks over the crowd, smiles, winks, then walks toward his bench.

The witnesses begin to arrive. One, then two, and three. They report in to the clerk who checks their names off.

The judges file in and step up onto the platform to take their places at the long marble table.

Then the chariot wheels and clomp of horse hooves. Justus arrives and is followed by his deputy to the top-most level of the platform. He looks at his deputy.

"Court will commence," the deputy announces.

Titus watches in the direction of the dungeon. *What has he done to himself? Come on, Stephan. You can get through this.*

Shortly, a guard appears, Stephan shuffling with his chains beside them. The chains are removed, and he scoots to the bench beside Titus.

"Your night wasn't so good, I see," Titus says.

"I think I ate too much. Pain in my intestines all night. What? Why did you bring my mother here?"

Titus looks around and sees Fiora. He rushes over and escorts her to the bench for witnesses.

"Where is the plaintiff?" the deputy asks.

"Most Excellent Praetor," Titus announces, "it looks as though this case must be..."

"Here he is," the deputy says from his perch next to the praetor. "Now, Titus, you may begin to question your witnesses."

Titus stands and saunters to the witness bench. "State your name," he says to the first witness.

"Brochus."

"And your occupation?"

"I am a copper jewelry maker."

"And is your booth within easy viewing distance of the plaintiff's?"

"Yes, it is."

"On average, how many customers does he have a day?"

"On a good day, he has about one every other hour."

"Thank you." Titus looks over at the second witness. "State your name."

"Decimus."

"And your occupation?"

"Baker."

"Now, is your booth within easy viewing distance of the plaintiffs?"

"If you mean, can I see Raja's booth? All the time. My booth is next to his."

"And, on average, how many customers does he have a day?"

"No more than six or eight. He doesn't carry enough incense to sell to any more customers than that."

Titus moves to the next witness. "State your name."

"Eunatus."

"Your occupation?"

"I'm a parchment merchant."

"And, is your booth within easy viewing distance of the plaintiff's?"

"Of course. I am right across from him."

"And, how many…"

"No more than eight or ten, I'd say. Customers, that is. In a day, that is. Never more than ten."

"Fine."

Stephan swings around to the judges, shaking his head. "Venerated Magistrates. I must report that one of the witnesses is missing. May I have your permission to call the witness out at his home today, and every third day according to the Twelve Tablets, the wise ancestors of early Rome posted for everyone's admonition?"

The judges look at each other and smile. "You know about the Twelve Tablets?" Pollux asks."

Titus smiles but does not answer. He steals a glance up at his father, and immediately his smile disappears.

"What about the woman?" Chrispus asks, "Is she your fourth witness?"

"No, Venerated Magistrates. She is the mother of the defendant, the Widow Fiora."

"A widow, you say?" Pollux responds.

Ammonius, being the oldest of the three judges, speaks for them. "You may call the missing witness out every third day in accordance with Tablet Two, but you may not do so more than twice."

Titus looks up again at his father. His father has left. The deputy announces the court adjourned until the witness is found or six days have expired, whichever comes first.

Stephan stands and hurries to his mother. They embrace. His mother leans her head on her son's chest and weeps.

"Don't worry, Mother. Titus is almost as smart as me.

He is going to get me freed. He promised."

The guard arrives and bends over to put the chains back on Stephan's ankles.

"Oh, here. I brought you some bread and yogurt just like you like it. And a few raisins."

"Mother, you can't afford..."

"Yes, I can. I sold one of our cushions today. You must keep your strength up."

The guard prods Stephan with the tip of his sword in the boy's back, and Stephan turns toward the awaiting dungeon.

"Let me take you home," Titus tells the distraught woman. He is careful to take short steps with his long legs so Fiora can keep up without rushing.

"You know, Titus, it has been hard for us with Stephan's father gone now," she confides.

"I know. It must be tearing your heart out. Stephan's too."

"Well, it is very painful."

"Has the music left your life, Fiora? Has the music left?"

"I never thought of it that way, but I guess you are right. The music has left our life."

They arrive at the little house, and Titus walks on. He arrives at a house much nicer than Fiora's, though not as nice as his own. He looks around.'

"Hey, you," he says to someone passing by. "Would you be my witness?"

"Sure. Witness to what?"

"Hector failed to appear in court today as a witness."

"Oh, the three-day solicitation thing you are doing. Sure, I'll stay and witness for you. Hey, Publius, come join us and be a witness for a three-day solicitation. And you, Selucid."

He turns to Titus. "Are three witnesses enough?"

"I believe so." Titus turns and cups his hands around his mouth. "Hector! You in there, Hector. You failed to appear in court today. You must come tomorrow. Hector. Are you in there? Come to your gate if you are. Or wave from your rooftop. Hector? Hector the Rejecter. Come out, come out."

The three witnesses join in with Titus. "Hector the Rejecter. Come out. Come out. Hector the Rejecter. Come out. Come out."

Soon some of the neighbors come out of their houses to see what all the excitement is, and join the others.

"Hector the Rejecter. Come out. Come out. Hector the Rejecter. Come out. Come out."

Titus turns and faces the crowd that has assembled. He holds up both arms. "I think that should do it. Thank you for your assistance."

"What if he doesn't show up in court tomorrow? Will you come back?" Publius asks.

"I am not allowed to come back for three days. If Hector does not show up by then, I will be back."

"Aren't you a little young to be involved in court things, young man?" Selucid asks. "You don't look any older than sixteen or seventeen."

"Hey, you're the son of Antioch's praetor, aren't you?" the first volunteer says. "No wonder. Hey, everyone, we've got to see this. I don't know about you, but I'm going to be in court tomorrow."

The next day comes and goes. A second day. A third. Titus returns. He finds three volunteers to witness his calling out. He calls for Hector. Others who had joined him three days earlier rush out of their houses and begin their chant again. "Hector the Rejecter. Come out. Come out." Soon some are dancing in the street to the cadence.

The following day Titus reports to the judges. They confer and request the clerk fill out a subpoena. Each judge signs it and puts his seal on it. Ammonius, the senior judge, tells the clerk to go to the citadel and bring four soldiers back with him to the court.

The wait lasts half an hour. During that time, Titus approaches the judges. "Venerated Magistrates, it seems the plaintiff never arrived either. He, too, appears to be missing."

Ammonius Moderatus stands and motions for the deputy. His face is red. "If Hector is not located anywhere in his home or at his business," he growls, "search Raja's home. Break down the gates of both places if you have to. We will wait here."

Immediately the deputy leaves on a horse and heads for the citadel to amend the orders.

Stephan's mother is present again. The judges allow Stephan to sit on the witness bench with his mother. He puts his arm around his mother, they whisper to each other, and sometimes he wipes away a tear.

Justus pulls out a parchment scroll and commences to read it in silence. The judges huddle together and whisper. Sometimes one of them stands and paces, or walks up to Justus and speaks with him a moment.

Titus watches his father up on his pedestal. *Look at me, sir. Look at me. I'm your son. I am trying. Why can't you be proud of me?*

The spectators mingle among each other, one of them sometimes calling out, "Hey, Titus. We're cheering for you."

They hear galloping horses. All on the platform return to their seats, and the spectators become silent. Now the clipped marches of soldiers. As they draw closer, it is evident the soldiers have two prisoners. One of them is Raja.

Judge Ammonius motions for the deputy. They whisper, and the deputy climbs up to Praetor Justus. The praetor stands.

"You!" He points at Raja. "You are sentenced to one year in prison for kidnapping a witness. Further, you will reimburse the defendant two times the amount of money you falsely claimed he stole from you. If you cannot come up with the sixty pieces of silver by selling your stock, you will sell your home. Until such time as you pay him in full, you will remain in debtor's dungeon in addition to the one year for kidnapping. You will not mock my court. So, it is ordered. So, it shall be. Take him away."

Silence. Stunned silence. Then the cheering. By the spectators.

"They didn't even lay their verdict on the altar of Vesta to see if she approved," someone says.

"Didn't need to. The judges knew she would."

Some rush to Titus and congratulate him. Others rush to Stephan.

"We were never friends before," a young man about Stephan's age tells the exonerated accused, "because you were too smart for the rest of us. But I guess you're okay after all."

Titus looks around, and among the crowd of people milling around, he briefly sees a woman. The woman looks just like his mother. *Did I just see her ghost?*

5 ~ THE GHOST

*T*itus returns to the gymnasium academy, a hero. It is a hollow heroism. His life at home—the life that matters most—is empty and dark. What used to be will never be again. The love, the laughter, the music gone. All gone. All that is left is anger at what has shattered the very existence of both father and son.

Three more years of living in two different worlds under the same roof. Worlds that have spiraled out of control down into an abyss of guilt. An abyss of no return.

Aunt Chloe returns from the Temple of Vesta, where she teaches girls of all ages how to ready themselves for the female games competition the following year. She has large classes since all girls up through age eighteen are required by law to enter. Some choose to continue in the competition up to age twenty if they are good at it and are still not married.

"What do you think of girls participating in the games?" Chloe asks.

"Some of my friends don't like it, but I think it's fun to watch them—well, the older ones. They put their heart into it. Nothing stops them. I'll bet one of those elephants I heard India has couldn't stop those girls."

"What's your favorite?" Aunt Chloe asks.

"Ha. That's easy. Watching the girls run races bearing arms," Titus says, leaning back against the wall behind his bench. "I especially enjoy watching them run the seven-*mille* race in full armor and fully equipped. I'd sure hate to meet one of them in battle," he says, laughing.

Titus looks over at his aunt. She is walking in circles in the courtyard, tipping her head side to side. "Are you actually singing, Aunt Chloe? You can't keep a tune straight."

"Well," she responds, "anyone who is in love is allowed to sing. Ah. I never thought it would happen again."

"C'mon now. You're too old to be in love."

She puts her hands on her hips. "I am a very young forty-two."

"You're that old? I thought you were fifty or sixty, at least," he retorts.

She picks up a large feather fan and tries to swat him over the head, but he is now taller even than his father, hidden away in his lair on the second floor.

"Okay, so what is his name, and is he aristocratic enough for Father to approve of him?"

"His name is Fulvio, and he is an artist."

"Oh, no wonder you like him. So, will you marry and raise a house full of little artists?" Titus teases.

"He's not that kind of artist. He designs mosaics for homes. He can create any picture you like, even of people. He is very much in demand."

"But, what about…"

"And, if that isn't aristocratic enough for my snooty brother, it isn't going to stop me. I am over forty and can marry whomever I wish. So that's that."

"Why have I never heard of him?"

"He just arrived from Corinth. Says he has pretty much adorned all the luxurious villas there and needs new clientele."

"So, when are you going to do it? Get married?"

"Tomorrow. My new husband will be moving in here. I was raised in this house, and am entitled to bring a husband into it, whether or not my brother likes it. Fulvio has already sent over a fat mutton for us to eat when you celebrate with us tomorrow."

"No other guests to announce your marriage?"

"Not unless Justus breaks down and comes. I don't know what I'm going to do with him."

"No one can get close to him anymore," Titus responds.

"Well, he has responsibilities as the praetor, and I guess that is all he needs," Aunt Chloe adds.

"Or wants."

A week later, upon arrival at the gymnasium academy for his astronomy and oratory lessons, one corner of the lecture hall is abuzz.

"You actually saw him?" he hears among the sons of Antioch's wealthy, the only ones able to continue their education now.

"Saw who?" Titus asks

"Augustus. Augustus Caesar himself,"

"Okay, what's the joke?"

"It's not a joke," Marcus says.

"No, it's true," Lucius says.

"People don't rise from the dead," Titus says.

Sentiments are about equal on both sides of the debate.

"Augustus did," Quintus says.

"It's impossible," Stephan says.

"Hey, Stephan, where did you come from?" Marcus asks, slapping their former schoolmate on the back. "You had to drop out of the gymnasium last year when your sixty pieces of silver ran out."

"I found someone to paint designs on my pottery, and now my vases and bowls are selling so fast, I can hardly keep up."

"Who did you find?" Titus asks.

"Your Aunt Chloe. She not only paints well, but she does not charge very much. I've been saving my money, and now here I am!"

"I know how to settle whether or not it is true," Titus finally says, turning back to the other boys. "Go to Augustus' temple."

"But when?" Lucius asks.

"When is he seen? Day or night? Mid-day? Morning?"

"Night. Sightings have always been at night."

"Fine. So, tonight as many of us can sneak away, meet

at the Sanctuary of Men-Askenos behind the Temple of Augustus."

"Good idea, Titus. We can just hide among the trees at the sanctuary and watch for old Augustus."

"I'll go," Marcus says.

"Count me in," Lucius says.

"I don't have anything else to do at night," Quintus says.

"Well, with Marcus, Lucius, Quintus and I, we have four, and Stephan will make five," Titus says.

"Whoa, wait a minute there. What are you getting me into?" Stephan objects.

"Ghost hunting."

Stephan shakes his fleshy face and hugs himself. "Uh-uh. Not me. Nope. Not going."

"Stephan, ole friend," Titus says, pounding Stephan on the back. "Do you believe in ghosts or not?"

"Not."

"Then you have nothing to worry about. We're meeting tonight at the sanctuary behind the Temple of Augustus."

"Why?"

"Stop by my house on your way there so we can walk together."

"To do what?" Stephan persists.

"I'll explain after school. Here comes our lecturer."

As the day progresses with practicing their oratory and trying to figure out the universe, the five young seniors in their gymnasium academy glance at each other with grins.

After the last lecture of the day, Titus pulls Stephan aside. "All right, this is what is happening. There have been sightings of Augustus Caesar here in Antioch."

Stephan turns and heads toward home. Titus grabs him by the sleeve. "You are not going to walk away from this…this opportunity."

"Opportunity to watch for a man who died the same year you and I were born? I have better things to do."

"Truth. Always search for truth. Isn't that what our lecturer always says?"

"The truth is that he is dead."

"We have to prove it."

"Why?"

"Because."

"Why because?"

"Well, as a service to Antioch and Rome."

"What kind of service?"

"Well, we cannot have two emperors at the same time, can we?"

"Don't waste my time."

"But, he was declared a god. Gods can do anything they want. Truth, my friend. We must discover the truth. Besides, my Aunt Chloe bakes the best baklava you have ever eaten. She made some just yesterday. I'll bring some for you tonight."

"Well.... Baklava, you say?"

"Stop by my house tonight. I'll be waiting outside."

Night comes in Antioch. A night promising to be eerie and exciting to five young men bent on proving Augustus Caesar has indeed returned from the dead. Or not. They are now at the sanctuary.

"We have a full moon tonight," Marcus says. "Perfect."

"Hey, go lean on your own tree," Lucius says.

"Anyone bring food? I'm starved," Quintus says.

An hour goes by.

"Well, it's obvious the rumor is false," Stephan says.

"Wait," Titus says. "I think I see him."

The five all stand and ease their way to the edge of the sanctuary where the pavement behind the temple begins.

The outline of a man emerges from in front of the temple. He is on a horse and wearing thick leather armor, a legionnaire's helmet, and is carrying a spear. The rider looks around.

The young spies drop flat onto the pavement.

The horse takes slow, halting steps working its way south.

The young men stand and walk up a side street to the columned Cardo Maximus. But, by the time they reach the columned street, the horse and rider are lost among the buildings in that part of the city.

"Woah. It really was Augustus Caesar," Marcus says.

"Well, now that we know which direction he goes, we

can change hiding places," Lucius says.

"We can hide behind the Temple of Apollo. The sanctuary extends down that far," Quintus says.

"Okay, tomorrow night, we meet in the sanctuary park behind Apollo's temple. Agreed?"

"No." It is Stephan. "I'm going to sleep all night tomorrow night."

"And miss all this? Stephan, where is your sense of excitement?"

"In my dreams. I'm going home."

Despite his objects, Stephan joins the others with a bribe from Aunt Chloe's kitchen the following night.

Once again, they see the rider emerge from the Temple of Augustus, ride past the Temple of Apollo, and get lost among the buildings in the south part of the city.

The following day, their lecturer, Fortunatus, makes an announcement.

"Tullius has been missing for two days. His family thought he was just over at the Anthius River farther up the mountains fishing. But he still is not home. This morning, I have learned that Lucilius is missing. Pray to your gods for them."

That afternoon when the gymnasium academy is let out, a woman approaches Titus at the outside gate.

"Are you Titus, the one who defended the young man accused of stealing money from the incense dealer?"

She is middle-aged and wearing a tunic with a skimpy toga, required dress within the city walls. Her hair is tangled, and her eyes red and swelled.

"Yes. That was three years ago when I was only fourteen. I didn't do so bad, did I?" He smiles.

The woman does not smile back. Instead, she pulls out a handkerchief and dabs her tears. "Do you remember Eunatus, one of your witnesses? He has been arrested." A new rush of tears.

Titus is not sure what to do. Should he put his arm around her? Should he offer her a fresh handkerchief? Should he try to comfort her but not touch her?

"What is he being accused of?"

"Murder." Her voice is high and shrill, and the word bounces off the walls of buildings on each side of Via Cermalus. "My husband is being accused of murder. Help us, Titus. Help us."

"You mean the murders of Tullius and Lucilius?"

"Please. You are our only hope."

"I'm only seventeen. Well, I'll be eighteen soon, and the case I arbitrated before was just about money, not someone's life. I can't do it. Too much responsibility."

"But your father. He would help you, wouldn't he? Please, Titus. You are our only hope. Please."

Titus walks up the street a little way, turns, walks the other direction, leans against one of the walls lining the street, sits, stands, and watches the woman.

"Well, if you pray for me a lot."

"Which god do you want me to pray to for you?"

"No. I can't do it."

"But you said you would."

"I changed my mind. I have only defended one person in one trial, and it was a long time ago. Can't you get someone more experienced?"

"Lawyers are allowed to charge for their services now. We do not have much money. I thought, considering your age, you would not cost us much."

Titus stares at the women, then at the street and the sky. "Isn't your husband the parchment merchant? I cannot promise anything. I may not be smart enough to get him released. Well, what if I make a trade with you? You provide me with parchments whenever I need them. Let's say for a year."

"Oh, Titus, we will provide you with parchments for the rest of your life."

"By the way, what is your name?"

"My name is Achima."

Titus arrives at the dungeon where Stephan had been he4ld three years earlier. He takes a deep breath and musters up his bravado.

"I am Titus Pomponius Brennius, sir," he tells one of the guards on duty at the iron gate. "I am here to see Eunatus."

"What's his full name?" the guard asks.

"Eunatus Pamphilious the parchment dealer."

Not realizing Titus has just made up part of the man's name and that the man only makes parchments and is not a dealer, the guard lets Titus in.

Titus is led by another guard who takes him down dark, narrow steps with his torch and down a long corridor. The stench envelopes Titus' breath.

At the far end, the guard growls, "Visitor for you." He lights a torch on the wall with his own, then leaves.

"Hello, Eunatus. I am Titus…"

"Yes, I know who you are. You successfully defended that young man falsely accused by the incense dealer."

"Yes. Well, your wife sent me over here. I do not know why. I am not even twenty yet. I'm not sure if…"

"Young man, thank you for coming. We cannot pay you much."

"That's been taken care of. Now, why are they accusing you of murdering Tullius and Lucilius?"

"Because one has a fish booth near me, and the other one has a butcher booth near me."

"Why didn't they accuse someone else in the market?"

"I don't know. Ask your father."

Titus bristles at the suggestion. "Well, I guess the only way to get you freed is to find out who really did murder those two men. I will come back when I have more questions."

When Titus arrives home and is still in the guest courtyard, he can hear his father through the second gate into the family courtyard.

"Where is he? He's late. Go find him."

Titus takes a deep breath and opens the inner gate.

As soon as his father sees he has arrived, he marches forward, jabbing his forefinger at his son.

"You! Are you out of your mind?" he says, still marching. "You are going to resign as the lawyer for that murderer, and you are going to do it now. So, turn right around and go back to the dungeon and tell him. Is that clear?"

By this time, father and son are nearly nose to nose.

Justus' face is red, and his eyes full of rage. He does an about-face, and announces to whoever is within hearing, "Get him out of my sight."

Titus stands by the inner gate and stares as his father once again walks away from him.

"But why, Father?" he calls out. "They cannot afford anyone else."

"A murderer is defending a murder?" he responds on the bottom step of his stairway. "You will do what you are told."

With the reminder of his guilt in his mother's death, Titus sinks to the tile and hugs his raised knees.

"I knew he was mad, but not insanely so," Aunt Chloe says.

"I am sorry, Titus," Fulvio says.

"You didn't do anything, Uncle Fulvio."

"I'm afraid I did. I was setting up a tiled mural in Augustus' temple and heard the priests talking. They apparently learned it from the guards in the dungeon below. I was just making harmless conversion with your father."

Titus looks up and sees Fulvio hovering over him, shaking his head.

"I am truly sorry, Titus."

"You didn't know. Your father was going to find out eventually anyway since he presides over all court cases."

"What can we do for you?" Fulvio asks. "Do you want me to go with you to the dungeon?"

Titus stands and walks past Chloe and Fulvio. He pauses and turns. "No! I am not going to resign."

"Defy your father?"

"As far as he is concerned, I have defied him since my mother died nearly seven years ago. I defied him by living when she is dead. This case is too public. He will not risk people knowing family business. He will say nothing more."

"So, what now?" Chloe asks.

"I have some of the writings of Plato, Cicero, and Seneca, especially about the law. I will study them tonight and start searching tomorrow after school."

"Searching for what," Fulvio asks.

"The real killer."

As he climbs the steps toward his room, he asks himself over and over, *How am I going to do that?*

6 ~ THE UNDEAD

*T*he following day after gymnasium studies, Marcus calls over to Titus on their way out. "Tonight, as usual. Behind the Temple of Apollo."

"I can't go with you. I have more important things to do."

"Oh, we heard. Well, you can't do any investigating in the middle of the night. Go with us."

Titus consents. They take up their usual posts and wait for the ghost of Augustus Caesar to come out of the temple and ride toward the South Market.

The ghost appears, but this time he is leading another horse behind him.

The boys leave their hiding place and follow him, ducking between buildings to make sure they are not seen.

"What is he doing?" Quintus asks. "We've got to get closer."

Titus holds out his arms. "Wait. It is too dangerous to follow him."

"Why?"

"He may be among the undead about which my father used to tell me. He was taught it by his father. It was sworn to as true by my ancestors who lived in Gaul."

"What are the undead?" Marcus asks.

"Corpses of people who died and didn't want to go on to the underworld. They stayed around their home."

"To do what?" Lucius asks.

"Guard their belongings and punish their enemies."

"Well, Augustus had plenty of both," Stephan says. "But, he wasn't buried here."

"They have great powers," Titus explains. "They can rise through the ground or stone or where ever they were buried. They roam only at night checking out what people have done to what they once owned."

"But his temple is in the city," Stephan says. "Why would the ghost or undead or whatever he is of Augustus go toward the market?"

"Food. The undead are always hungry," Titus says.

"Maybe he goes out of the city at night to attack bears in the mountains around us and devour them," Quintus says.

"Or maybe that's what happened to Tullius and Lucilius? Augustus' corpse ate them," Titus says. "But how am I going to prove it?"

"You are not going to prove it because there is no such thing as undead people," Stephan says. "We Hittites believe, once a person is dead, he goes to the underworld, and that's all there is to it."

"But even Plato said people who are enemies of someone who has just died must stay away from their place of burial at least for a year until the dead man lets go and finishes his journey to the underworld," Titus responds.

"Titus, you have been a reasonable person all my life, but now you are insane," Stephan says. "I'll bet your father doesn't believe that anymore. He is too educated to believe it, and you are too. I'm leaving."

With that, Stephan leaves. The other four shrug and decide to go on home too.

The next morning, Chloe catches Titus just as he is leaving for the gymnasium. "May I walk part of the way with you? I have an early-morning class with my new Vestal Virgins."

"Hey, I'll go with you too," Fulvio says. "I'm headed to Augustus' temple and want to get an early start today. They want my design to be completed by the end of the month."

The three walk up Cardo Maximum together.

"Aunt Chloe, do you and Father believe in the undead?"

"Where did you hear about that?" Chloe asks, grinning.

"My father used to tell me about them when I was young."

"He probably told you about them to keep you in bed at night. No, he doesn't believe it. I don't either."

"Well, I am relieved. It just doesn't make sense to me. But, what about the ghost of Augustus Caesar? I have seen him myself. He rides out of his temple every night."

"That part I don't know, Titus. I don't really understand what happens to us after we die," Chloe replies.

"If I were you, Titus, I would concentrate on the living for your answers to the murders," Fulvio says. "Go down to the market after gymnasium and talk to everyone about Tullius and Lucilius. Find out if they had any enemies and things like that. Well, here we are. I will see you two tonight."

Fulvio heads up the *plateia* toward the temple itself. Chloe turns toward the Temple of Vesta on the other side of the street. Titus turns at Via Velabrus for the final way to his gymnasium academy.

He feels a chill. Birds fly overhead. *Is it true that the birds know better than anyone the truth of what humans do day to date?* They fly in circles above his head. *Are they confused? Are they honing in on my answer? Is there an auger I can ask about the murders? Delphi is too far away.*

A raccoon crosses his path. *What is he doing in the city and during the day? Is that an omen of something? What about the clouds overhead? Two are in the shape of a dragon. What does that mean?*

"Better hurry, Titus, or you are going to be late."

Titus turns toward the familiar voice. "Oh, Stephan. I need your advice."

"About what?"

"Truth. What is truth? How can anyone know?"

"Easy there, friend. Your mind is too full. Let's go in and empty our mind a little at our first lecture."

"Ha, ha, Stephan. Better watch it. Just because you are smarter than our lecturer, it doesn't mean you can say it out loud. Do you want to go with me to the South Market after school?”

“Sure, friend. We will both take notes.”

“Oh, I forgot about that. We need to take a couple of clay tablets and a good stylus. What would I do without you watching out for me, Stephan?”

“It’s only fair after you convinced the judges to find me not guilty when I was falsely accused.”

That afternoon, the two leave the gymnasium academy and walk to the market. Their first stop is the poulter’s booth.

“Gaius, I am representing Eunatus and need to ask you a few questions.”

Gaius grabs a chicken from the pen behind his booth and carries it by its head to an empty cage on his counter.

“Couldn’t he get a real lawyer?” Gaius responds.

“He said I was all he could afford. What I need to do is find out who the real killer is. When was the last time you saw the two murdered men?”

“Well, I hadn’t seen Tullius since he left to fish in the river. Do you think he could have drowned instead of being murdered?”

“Stephan, would you write that down? Here’s my tablet.”

“Write it yourself.”

“My writing is not good. I want to be able to read what people told me.”

“Give it to me. But...”

“Remember, you were once in that dungeon,” Titus says

“Excuse me, you two, but I have to get ready for my customers.”

“Oh, sorry, Gaius. What about Lucilius? When was the last time you saw him?”

The afternoon he was murdered. He went home, and I went home. Well, maybe he didn’t make it all the way back. By the way, have you seen Hercules? He’s usually in the booth next to me. He cooks the chickens for me—the ones people don’t want to take home as layers.”

Titus stares at Gaius. He’s missing?”

“Depends on what you consider missing, I guess.”

Titus walks up and down each aisle of the market.

"Have any of you seen Hercules today?"

"Have you seen Hercules?"

"When was the last time you saw Hercules?"

"Another murder?" Stephan says to Titus, not intending for it to be a question."

"Hurry. We've got to go get Eunastus out of the dungeon."

"You've run me to death, Titus. I think I'll just walk you as far as my house, then go home and have something to eat. I'm starved."

"When was the last time you ate?"

"Just before we came here. But it wasn't much."

The young men part and Titus heads toward the Temple of Augustus Caesar declared a god by the Roman Senate.

How can that be? I just don't understand. How can non-gods declare someone a god?

Titus sees something shiny on the street and picks it up. He turns the silver bead over in his palm. *This bead came off a beautiful necklace. If humans can rise to become gods, can gods descend to become humans? If they can go one way, can they go the other way too?*

He walks around the side of the temple until he arrives at the back gate leading to the dungeon. The same guard is there that he had talked to before. He brings his thoughts back to his responsibilities and reminds the guard who he is.

"I am Titus Pomponius Brennius, and I have come to set my client free."

"You don't know much," the guard growls. "You cannot just show up and expect us to take your word for it. Where is your signed authorization?"

"My, uh. I will return with it shortly."

Titus turns around and heads for home, knowing there will be a confrontation worse than the one the previous day. When he reaches home, he does not stop but keeps walking. Three *palatios* down is the home of Pollux Antonius, who still sometimes judges cases when called on by Praetor Brennius. Titus knocks on the aristocrat's gate of silver and copper. A servant opens a small window in one of the gates.

"Yes? Who is it? State your name and intentions."

"My name is Titus Pomponius Brennius. If Pollux Antonius is home, may I speak with him briefly?"

"He is not here."

"Well, look who is standing outside my gate. If it isn't the young man who blustered his way into proving the innocence of his client. We're still talking about it. Ha, ha. So, what can I do for you, young man? Come in. We will talk over some refreshment."

Pollux leads the younger man into his courtyard. His height and blond hair is much the same as most Celtic Goths in Antioch and all of Galatia, though it is receding some now.

The ground of his courtyard is covered with white-and-green marble with marble columns holding up the second floor. All the benches in the courtyard of are mixed colors of marble.

Pollux leads Titus into the solarium. There the ground has been covered with marble tiles to form an elaborate mosaic. Titus makes a mental note to ask Fulvio if he designed it.

"What brings you to my home, Titus? Does your father know you are here?"

"Well, that's what I came about. My father and I have not gotten along well since my mother was...well died when I was eleven."

"I see. We all did notice strain between you two at the trial. So, what can I do for you?"

"There has been a third murder. Hercules, the cook down at the market, has been missing since yesterday afternoon. We asked everywhere, and no one has seen him. This new killing proves my client—uh Eutantus—was not the murderer of the other two because he was locked up when Hercules was murdered. I need a warrant to take to the guard so he will release him from the dungeon."

"Oh, I see. So, you need me to talk to your father for you."

"Not exactly. Would you go see him, tell him about the third murder, and ask him if he would like you to deliver the release order? He will never give it to me, and my client will be forever in the dungeon."

"Well, for a young man seventeen years old—or are you eighteen now—with a client, I think I can do that. Where will you be?"

"Outside our gate, waiting for you."

"You know he will find out about what we did the next day. I can handle him, but what about you?"

"He has never let up being angry at me, so tomorrow will not be any different. Thank you, Pollux."

The following day, Titus takes a large supply of parchment scrolls home, walks up to his father's *officium*, and sets them in a neat pile on his father's writing table. Father and son return to their normal avoiding each other.

Titus continues to go with the other four to spy out the Temple of Augustus Caesar every night. Each time the ghost passes them and works its way to the market, it gets lost in the shadows.

"Where does he disappear to?" Lucius asks.

"Maybe he wills himself to be in Rome after he leaves here. That is where Augustus died."

"Well, I don't believe that undead nonsense," Titus says, "but he might just be his ghost."

Eunatus has been freed from dungeon a week. When Stephan stops by Titus' house on the way to the gymnasium academy, he has bad news.

"Another one has been killed."

"Oh, no," Titus says. "Who?"

"Gaius, the poulter who we questioned."

"Well, at least we know Eunatus didn't do it."

"There is whispering that he did."

When they arrive at the gymnasium, Marcus meets them at the gate. "Well, Augustus' ghost has been at it again. He probably ate all four of the murdered men."

"Stop that," Titus says.

"By the way," Quintus says, "a relative of Eunatus' wife, Achima, suddenly appeared in the city yesterday."

"So?" Stephan retorts.

"He has been estranged from her for ten years," Quintus says. "Why did he suddenly show up? Or has the man been here all along? Did he commit the murders, then get his brother-in-law blamed for it? Some say he lost all his money gambling and now wants to take over their parchment business. It would be convenient with Eunatus in a dungeon and then executed."

"Why Quintus," Titus responds. "I am surprised at you. You have really thought this thing through. You have some valid points. Do you think we can bring them up to Fortunatus, and the entire class debate it?"

"What a grand idea," Lucius responds.

For most of three hours that morning, their lecturer leads them in a debate of the facts. Some of the students are frustrated because he uses the Socratic method of always asking questions, but never giving answers. "Deeper. Dig deeper," he tells them.

By noon, the entire class is convinced Eunatus' brother-in-law is the real killer.

Three days later, another murder is discovered. This time it is Tricho, the perfumer.

"Eunatus' brother-in-law was at the inn all the previous day and part of the night," Quintus says. He had witnesses.

"But, with no body, we cannot prove how Tricho was killed. If it was by poison, he could be at the inn at the time Tricho died," Marcus says.

"He could have sneaked away between the time the inn closed and dawn," Titus says.

The following day there is a sixth murder victim—Tarius, the reseller of copper jewelry.

The brother-in-law of Eunatus is not arrested. Not enough evidence.

A week later, Abaddon returns to Antioch, where he had been born a raised.

"Aren't they having trouble along the Germanic border?" people ask down at the market. "His family is okay. What is he doing here?"

People watch Abaddon as he saunters here and there around the city.

"A deserter. That's what he is. Has to be. No other reason."

"Why did Abaddon come back here? Our city does not

need or want him," men around the city say. "He should just keep going."

"He is the killer. He showed up in the city right in the middle of all the murders," some say.

"It has to be him."

"Why doesn't someone arrest him?"

Nerves of the citizens of Antioch are strained. Tempers flare. People look behind them, especially when walking in the shadows of buildings and statues and columns and trees.

Who will die next?

7 ~ DISCOVERY

"**I**f I could figure out who killed those men," Titus tells Stephan, "My father will finally be proud of me."

The two are at Stephan's little house.

"My father has closed himself off from everyone and is getting worse," Titus continues. "He never did approve of our friendship."

"I know. A potter wasn't aristocratic enough for him. But someday... Well, this is our last year at the gymnasium academy. Then I will start all over again, saving my money."

"Saving money for what?"

"Saving money to go to Rome and study under a famous philosopher there."

Titus stands and picks up the torn floor cushion he has been sitting on. He throws it at Stephan.

Stephan moves onto his knees and stands. He reciprocates with his own pillow.

Titus is no longer laughing.

"Did I hurt you? Sorry," Stephan says.

"No, I just had a thought. Where is something to write on?"

"I have a clay tablet I rubbed down yesterday, so it's fresh. Or I have a small parchment you gave me."

"Write on the parchment. This is important." Titus waits for Stephan to pull it out of a basket of writing supplies in a corner of the small courtyard.

"List these names and occupations. Tullius was a fishmonger, Lucilius a butcher, Hercules a cook, Gaius a poulter, Tricho a perfumer, Tarius a reseller of jewelry."

He waits for Stephan to finish writing.

"Don't you get it, Stephan? Look. They were all merchants down at the market."

"Brilliant, Titus. Brilliant. Why didn't I think of that?"

"Because I am two months older than you," Titus chuckles.

"So, does that mean our killer is a jealous merchant who wants to get rid of his competition?" Stephan asks.

"I don't know," Titus responds. "Let's walk down to the market and make a note of who is left selling."

"You know, the killer could be that brother-in-law of Eunatus after all," Stephan says.

"He would benefit with less competition in the market," Titus says. "After the market, let's go see Eunatus."

The following day, Titus pays a visit to Pollux. He wonders if the same man who designed his family *palatio* also designed that of Pollux.

"So, you think Eunatus' brother-in-law is the murderer. Is that correct?"

"Yes, sir. So, if you would go see my father about it, maybe he'll sign a warrant for his arrest, and we can get rid of him before he kills again."

"First, I thought your client was released. So why are you still investigating?"

"I don't know. I guess because no one else seems to be trying to find out who killed those men. After all, they weren't aristocrats. They were just merchant plebs. It doesn't seem right."

"You are so much like your mother," Pollux says. "Everyone loved her, you know. And she loved everyone."

"There used to be laughter and music in our house. But that was a long time ago."

Pollux breaks a brief silence that follows. "But what proof do you have against Eunatus' brother-in-law, my young friend?"

"Well, I guess none. I just know it. That's all."

"I'm afraid you'll have to come back with solid evidence before I can approach your father."

"I suppose so."

"By the way, there was another murder last night," Pollux announces. "A man named Pontus. He's a street dancer. Not of the war dances, but Dionysius dances."

"What? No, that's wrong."

"Of course, it's wrong. All murder is wrong."

"No, his occupation. Up to now, only merchants in the market have been killed. Pontus' occupation is all wrong."

With that, Titus leaves and goes down to his own house. Chloe hands him a message dropped off less than an hour earlier.

Eunatus has been arrested again.

It is signed by his wife, Achima.

"That can't be. He is innocent," Titus tells his aunt. "It's nearly dark. I cannot go there now," he says, seating himself on his usual bench in the family courtyard.

Chloe brings him and her husband a mug of apricot juice.

"What if it really is the ghost of Augustus Caesar killing them? Fulvio, what are the priests saying over at his temple?"

"The priests are saying it isn't happening. There is no ghost or horse or armor or anything. It's just people's imaginations."

The following morning, Titus stops at the dungeon before going on to the gymnasium academy. The guard lets him in.

"On what basis did they re-arrest you?" Titus asks.

"They found fishing lines, butcher knives, poultry feathers, cinnamon powder, and a small copper broach buried in my yard. I didn't put them there. I'm innocent."

"Do you think your brother-in-law put them there?"

"I don't know. He says he only plans to stay a while; then, he is going to do some traveling."

"I promise you I will get you out," Titus says, trying to

convince himself.

"How?"

Titus does not reply. He works his way back up the putrid corridor and goes outside. He breathes in the fresh air and heads for the gymnasium academy.

"Marcus, are you and the other two fellows still spying on Augustus' ghost?" Titus asks upon entering the lecture hall.

"Yes. But we haven't made much progress. He leaves his temple, goes down into the market, and poof, he disappears. Sometimes he has an extra horse with him, and sometimes he doesn't."

When the academy lets out that afternoon, Titus walks over to Cordo Maximum and follows it past Augustus' temple. He turns west on Decumanus Maximus and arrives at the theater. He sees a troop apparently rehearsing and works his way down to them.

"Uh, excuse me. May I interrupt? It's about Pontus."

When the actors hear the name of their colleague, they become quiet.

"How well did you all know Pontus?" he asks.

"He dances during the intermission between acts," a red-headed man responds.

"He dances on the street to make money to live on between plays."

"Did he have any enemies?"

"Of course. We all do. You toga-wearing aristocrats like to come to our plays, but you scorn us in person."

"You are right. We do. Well, if you hear anything that will prove someone besides Eunatus killed them, would you let me know? You can leave a message with my aunt at the Temple of Vesta."

Titus stops at Stephan's house, and the two of them walk back to the South Market. It is nearly deserted. Fear rules. Those who have kept their booths open eye the two young toga wearers.

"Well, have you caught the real murderer? It wasn't our Eunatus. That's for sure," Hector says. "You aristocrats don't care about us ordinary people. You live off the land that your servants slave over for you. You…”

“Leave the boys alone, Hector.”

“Mind your own business, Decimus.”

Stephan holds out both hands, palms up. “We’re here to try to help,” he says.

“Besides, there has been another murder—Pontus.”

“Pontus? He dances around the market for a few copper coins when he’s not performing at the theater.”

“That’s right,” Titus responds. “The killer is branching out.”

“Maybe it’s two killers.”

“Or three.”

“Maybe it’s Augustus’ ghost.”

“Do you mind if we look around—you know, at the booths of those who have been killed?”

“Go ahead,” Decimus, the baker, says.

Titus and Stephan walk up and down the aisles and look inside each deserted booth, now empty after families have claimed what was left behind.

When they arrive at the end of one of the aisles near the wall, Stephan stops. “Shhh. What was that?”

“What? I didn’t hear anything.”

“Look. Those soldiers just coming in through the gate.”

“I’ll bet they’re after the deserter, Abaddon.”

“Well, once they take him back with them, I’ll bet the murders stop,” Titus says.

The following morning on Titus’ way to the gymnasium academy, he notices soldiers riding out from the Temple of Augustus with a man running behind them, a rope around his neck.

“They will save us having to execute him,” Titus says under his breath. “Now, our city can rest and grieve properly over its dead.”

Just before Lecturer Fortunatus dismisses his last class of the day, he is handed a note. He reads it and shakes his head.

“Everyone sit back down. I have an announcement for you.” His voice is low.

“Has the city been attacked?”

"Has the Temple of Augustus been burned down?"

"There has been another murder. It is Clodius, a street singer."

Fortunatus shakes his head and stares at the floor. "What is happening to the glorious Antioch of Pisidia in Galatia?"

The students rise and walk down the corridor to the outside door in silence.

"I need to go back to the theater and tell the actors if they do not know it already. Then I've got to get the authority to release Eunatus. Do you want to go along, Stephan?"

"No. I want to go back to the market. Maybe I'll hear something that will help."

Titus arrives at the theater. The actors stop rehearsing and glare at him.

"I have bad news for you," he says. "Another one of your own has been murdered..."

"Yes, we know. Antonius."

"No, not Antonius. Clodius. It was your singer; he was murdered."

"You're mistaken. It was Antonius, full-time actor with the rest of us."

Silence. Staring. Watching a spider make his way across a stage that is his whole world.

"Antonius?" Titus asks.

"Clodius?" one of the actors asks.

Titus sits where he is. The other players do also. They stare, and no one says anything for a long while.

"We have a mad man among us," Titus says, standing. "I will find him. There is somewhere else I must go before dark. Pray to your gods."

"Which ones?"

"Your actor gods. Or the weapon gods. Or whatever gods you choose."

Titus works his way back up from there and to Pollux' *palatio.* He knocks on the gate. Pollux answers it himself.

"I suppose you are here about a release order for Eunatus."

"Yes, he couldn't have murdered the last three. He was

locked up."

"I have been told he has an accomplice and is arranging the murders from his dungeon. Your father will not let him out as long as there is any doubt."

Titus runs his hands through his thick reddish-brown hair. "I'm running out of ideas."

"Go back to the market, son. The answer has to be there."

Titus stops at Stephan's house on his way back to the half-deserted South Market.

"Did you learn anything the last time you were there?" Titus asks as they walk south.

"No. Well, yes. Well, I guess."

"What did they say?"

"It wasn't people. It was,   well, a sound. An eerie sound."

"Did you see any light near the sound?"

"No, just the sound."

"Well, we may as well go over there and see if the sound happens again. It's almost dark. Maybe we can watch for Augustus' ghost while we're there. They say it disappears at the wall and never goes through the South Gate."

"Do you really believe it is Augustus' ghost?"

"I don't know what to believe anymore. I am so confused."

They find a large deserted booth and decide to keep watch there. They eat whatever Stephan has brought with them, then fall asleep.

The sound awakens them. The eerie sound that sends chills through them.

"What was that?"

"It sounded like wailing?"

"So, I didn't imagine it."

The wailing stops and is replaced by hoofbeats.

They jump up and head for the north entrance to the market. They do not stop running until they reach Stephan's house.

"You'd better spend the rest of the night here," Stephan urges.

"No, I'll be in worse trouble than I usually am if I don't go home. Cornelius is good. He won't tell my family I came in late."

The next morning Stephan stops by Titus' family *palatio*.

"What do you think the noises were last night?" Stephan asks as they work their way past the waterfall on columned Cardo Maximus.

"My mind is telling me one thing, but my logic is telling me another," Titus says. "All I can think of is what Plato and my ancestors said about people's ghosts lingering around their grave to get vengeance on their enemies."

"But Augustus was not buried here."

"That's right," Titus says. "My logic tells me there are no such things as ghosts. But that is the only answer I can find."

"What are you going to do after we graduate later this year?" Stephan asks.

"I guess go to Pergamum to the university run by Apollos' priests. Their library is world-renowned."

"Maybe I'll open up my father's pottery business," Stephan says. "We are almost out of money again."

"I really admire you, Stephan."

"But someday I will earn enough to go to a university in Rome itself."

"And you will, my friend. You will."

When they arrive at the gymnasium academy, none of the lecturers they see are smiling. Students hurry to their various lecture halls and wait in silence.

At last, Fortunatus rises. He stares at his class of young men still under their twenties.

"Our city has been cursed by the gods. Only a plague could be worse than what is happening to us."

The students wait for the revelation."

He sighs. "Five of them this time. Five. All murdered early last night."

"Uh, sir," Titus says, raising his hand. "What were their occupations? Do you know?"

"Farmhands. Probably one of your father's farmers was among them. I am going to dismiss class today. There is going to be a council of the city fathers today. I want to be there."

"May I have their names, sir?" Titus asks.

The lecturer reads off the names.

"Stephan," Titus says as they leave the academy, "is there any chance your parchment with the list of names is with you.?"

"I have it right here. A list of all victims and their occupations."

Instead of going straight home, they stop at the Sanctuary to Men-Askenos and sit on one of the benches.

"Stephan, you knew the merchants better than me. What were their nationalities? Do you remember?"

Stephan pulls out their list. Well, Tullius, the fishmonger was from Gaul, Lucilius the butcher was from Spain, uh, Hercules the cook was from Africa, Gaius, the poulter was—I think—from Sicily."

He grins at Titus as he begins to see a pattern.

"Tricho, the perfumer, I believe, was from Sardinia."

"And Tarius, the reseller?"

"Germannica. Definitely Germannica."

Titus jumps up.

"Where to?"

"Back to the theater. I need to know where the actors came here from."

They arrive and climb down the risers to the bottom where the stage is.

The actors stop their rehearsal. "Did you find out who killed our friends?"

"Not yet, but I think I'm close," Titus says, "Do you remember where Pontus was from?"

"Ethiopia," one of them says.

Titus waits for Stephan to write the country name down next to the victim's name.

"And Clodius. Where was he from?"

"Arabia," another actor responds. "Definitely, Arabia."

"And Antonius?"

"Egypt. We all loved his Egyptian accent."

Titus' grin is broad. "I think I'm on to something," he announces, already working his way back up the stadium seats rising up to the ground level.

"You can catch up with me," he calls down to Stephan. "I'm going to be at Augustus' temple.

When Stephan arrives at the temple, he sees Titus reading the Latin engraving that covers one entire side.

"I always thought it was boring," Stephan says, catching his breath.

"Oh, The Deeds of the Divine Augustus?"

"All it is about is the people he conquered and the money he gave his people that he stole from the conquered people," Stephan says.

"Well, you have to brag a little to convince the Senate to make you a god," Titus says, grinning but not looking away from the account of Augustus' life. "Look here, Stephan. And here. And here. Read the names of the people he conquered."

"Well, if that isn't the strangest thing," Stephan says.

"All in the same order. Augustus Caesar conquered the Gauls, and the first victim was Tullius, the fisherman. Next, he conquered Spain, and the next victim was Lucilius, the butcher. Third, he lists North Africa. Hercules, the third victim, was a Libyan. Look. Look. Look. All the way down our list. Right in order."

Titus steps to one side to give Stephan a clear view. He grins as he waits. "And I'll bet if you check where the farmhands were from, they'll be from Armenia, Cyrene, Pannonia, Illyricum, and Dacia—all in the same order."

8 ~ TURNING POINT

When Stephen is through reading, he turns around and slides his back down the sacred marble wall of Augustus' temple and sits on the ground. Titus joins him.

"Now what?" Stephan asks.

"I don't know. Did Augustus come back from the dead to take vengeance on some renegades from those countries who didn't succumb to him?"

They sit in silence.

"The only thing we have left is the ghost of Augustus and the eerie sounds over by the south wall of the city," Stephan says.

"I want to go home and read the rest of the day. Something about this list reminds me of Cicero," Titus says.

"Do you want to meet at the same place in the market when it gets dark?" Stephan asks.

"Cicero wrote a lot, but his writing is plain and uncomplicated. I think I will be able to find whatever it is I'm looking for by then. So, yes, I'll meet you there," Titus says.

That evening, just as the sun is falling below the horizon, Stephen walks toward the outer gate of his family *palatio*. He hears the familiar booming voice.

"And where do you think you are going, young man?"

"Uh, Father, I think I will be able to solve the murders tonight. Well, not completely, but close."

"You are going nowhere. Go back to your room."

Titus takes a long, silent look at his father and leaves. In the outer courtyard, he thinks he hears Chloe say something like, "He'll be safe, brother. Don't worry."

He arrives at the same booth as the night before, just as the stars come out. He and Stephan signal to each other.

"I want to walk along this wall before we settle down," Stephan says.

"Me too."

They walk a little way, then stop at a booth opposite the wall and sit. After not hearing anything come out of it, they walk a little farther and sit again. Several hours pass. One punches the other whenever necessary for both to stay awake.

"What was that?" Stephan whispers in a hoarse late-night whisper.

"What?" Titus asks, sitting up on his heels. "I think it's hoofbeats."

The two look both ways down the city wall next to the South Market.

"Hear that?" Stephan says, now standing bent over. "That eerie sound we heard last night."

"Let's follow it."

"What if an undead fellow eats us?" Stephan says with a slight grin.

Ducking their heads and hunching over, the two work their way toward the sound of moaning.

"Light," Titus says. "Hurry, before it goes away."

Titus runs, Stephan follows, gasping.

The moaning grows louder, the light brighter.

Titus stops running. He stares. "Aurelius?" he calls out. "Is that you?"

Aurelius, one of the longest-term priests at the Temple of Augustus, jerks his head around far enough to spot Titus and Stephan.

"What are you doing here?" the old man says, taking off his's helmet and pointing his spear at the boys. "Go on home. This is none of your business."

"What is none of our business?" Titus steps forward and looks down at a hole going under the city wall. "Is this the old escape route I've always heard about?"

"Stay away, I tell you."

Titus walks closer and sees steps down into the hole. He starts down them.

"No! You'll ruin everything. Come back!" the old man growls.

As Titus reaches the bottom of the steps, a man in rags comes into view.

"Food? Did you bring our food?"

"Gaius? Is that you?" Titus says.

Gaius is joined by others—thirteen others.

"Noooo. Noooo!" the priest bellows above ground.

By now, Stephan has joined Titus.

"Where do you sleep?" Titus asks.

Gaius and the others turn and walk back into the darkness.

Titus and Stephan follow.

At the other end of the tunnel is a large boulder. They see blankets on the ground.

"The boulder must have fallen in during an earthquake and blocked the exit," Stephan says.

"Probably the one that..." Titus does not finish his sentence.

"Come with me, everyone," Titus announces. "I am the son of Antioch's praetor, and old Aurelius dares not stop me."

Titus and Stephan climb the steps and stand on each side of the priest and his horse. As the captives reach ground level, they scatter, rushing the best they can in their underfed condition to their homes.

Titus turns to Aurelius. "We're going home now." They leave with Aurelius still pointing his spear, apparently now at ghosts.

When Titus arrives back home, he knocks on his Aunt Chloe's door and tells her what happened.

"Your father will want to hear this," she says. "Go wake him up."

Titus walks to his father's bedroom door and knocks on it.

"What now? Is it morning? Who is disturbing me? Go

away."

Titus opens the door. "Father, they're not dead."

"Who's not dead? You will be punished severely for this."

"No, Father. For once, you are going to listen to me. I am only eighteen years old. That is true. But I am as tall as you and as smart as you, and you are going to be proud of me if I have to knock you over with your own stubborn pride."

"Cornelius!" Justus shouts. "Come get this boy."

Cornelius does not come. Chloe does. Fulvio does.

"If I were you, brother, I would finish waking up and listen to this son of yours. He has accomplished the impossible. If you listen and acknowledge that, you just might be able to get in on some of the accolades that are going to come his way beginning tomorrow."

"I'm awake now." He brushes his thinning blond hair off his forehead and leans on one elbow. "So, what in the world are you talking about?"

"Tell him," Chloe tells Titus.

Moments later, Justus sits up in his bed in stunned silence as Titus finishes explaining what he discovered.

"Further, upon reading Cicero's treatise, *Moral Goodness*, I found the reason Priest Aurelius did this. I think, if you confront Aurelius with this, he will confirm it." Titus hands the scroll to his father.

Justus looks around him.

"I brought your best tunic, brother," Chloe says. "Just washed it this morning. "If you hurry, you can arrive at the temple before daylight and before he can escape justice."

Chloe and Fulvio leave the room. Justus stands and steps over to his son. He puts his big hands on his son's shoulder's, stares a moment, nods his head slightly, and turns toward his clothes.

Titus leaves. Chloe and Fulvio are standing in the corridor.

"Well?"

Titus'' lips break out into a broad grin. "He's proud of me."

"Well, let's hurry. We don't want to miss any of this.

"Lydia!" she calls out. "I need my best tunic and stola."

"Cornelius!" Fulvio calls out. "Get two of the best chariots ready. We're going to a celebration."

Before daybreak, Titus meets his father at the gate. Cornelius opens it for them. Out on the street, Brutus has their finest chariots and horses ready for them.

Justus marches to his chariot. He turns. "Come, Son."

Titus joins him, his heart overflowing and trying to maintain the unmanly tears of joy that keep wanting to show themselves.

Fulvio and Chloe board the chariot behind them.

By the time they reach the Temple of Augustus, the sky is light gray. Justus calls over to the two guards at the front entrance into the temple.

"Hurry to the citadel. I need a *centurie* of men. They will line the twelve steps of the *propylon* up to the temple and the *plateia* approach. They will also line Cardo Maximus up to and surrounding my court at the Temple of Vesta."

"Yes, Most Excellent Praetor."

"When everyone is in place, I want the *cornu* blown at every city gate and in every neighborhood. I want this city fully awake within an hour. It is up to them whether they come to the court, but I want them awake."

"Yes, Most Excellency," the soldier says, pounding his fist over his heart, then raising his arm in salute.

Justus turns to Titus. He looks into the eyes of his son, nods, and almost smiles. "Follow me."

Justus takes the twelve steps into the Temple of Augustus two at a time. When he arrives inside, he sees the priests all assembled. Priest Aurelius stands alone in front of the holy assembly.

Justus takes long steps to the old man.

"You will have a chance to defend yourself when court convenes at daylight. I do not mete out justice for the pleasure of it, but for the fairness of it."

He moves a few steps back from the assembly and motions for Titus to join him at his side.

Though he is speaking to his son, protocol dictates that he do so facing the entire assembly.

"In addition to recovery of the dead from their grave, the final proof of your guilt will now be read."

Titus unrolls the scroll and reads from Cicero.

"Vullgar are the means of livelihood of all hired workmen who we pay for mere manual labor. Vullgar, we must consider those also who buy from wholesale and resell immediately by misrepresentation and lying.   Least respectable of all are those trades which cater to sensual pleasures: Fishmongers, butchers, cooks, poulters. Add to these the perfumers and dancers. Flagrant breaches of good breeding are singing and dancing in the street and acting. We must carefully avoid them."

"But, Most Excellent..."

"You will get your chance to defend yourself in open court," Justus growls at Aurelius, "which will convene the moment the sun is fully up."

Father and son turn their backs on the priests of the divine emperor and hurry down the steps to their chariot.

"Uh, Father, the dungeon is under the temple. May I?"

"Yes, Son, go release the parchment maker. Oh, and thank him for the fine quality he has provided for me. Here is my signet ring. Show it to the guard."

"Yes, sir!" Titus says.

Half an hour later, Titus is at the court outside the Temple of Vesta. Eunatus is by his side. Titus has taken off his clean white toga and put it over Eunatus to hide the filth. He only wishes he had something to hide the stench. He stands next to his client, wearing only a long white tunic with gold trim at the neckline and hem.

Justus is in his marble chair on the highest pinnacle of the court platform. Three judges now file in and take their places at the marble table above the growing crowd of spectators and below the supreme praetor of the city. One of the judges is Pollux. Once seated, Pollux looks over at Titus, catches his eye and smiles. His slight nod is perceived only by Titus.

The priests arrive. They walk in double rows with Aurelius walking between them. They line the steps to the court platform, and Aurelius walks the rest of the way by himself. He is shown the bench of the defendant and seats himself.

"Not so fast, Aurelius." It is Praetor Justus' booming voice. "Stand and hear the charges against you."

Aurelius stands in place. Titus and Eunatus stand at the plaintiff's table.

The court clerk unrolls a small scroll and reads. "The city of Antioch hereby charges Aurelius, priest of the divine Augustus Caesar, with fourteen counts of kidnapping."

"All right, Aurelius. Now is your time," Justus calls down. "Defend yourself."

Everyone on the platform briefly looks down at the spectators. They see the undead in the purest sense. In the minds of everyone, they have risen from the dead. There is Tricho of Sardinia, the perfumer, still in the filthy clothes he'd worn during captivity. Over there is Clodius, the Arabian street singer, and Tarrius, the reseller of jewelry from Germannica. And...

"Defend yourself, Aurelius!" Justus demands. "See if justifying the hideous act you did will exonerate you."

"Most Excellent Justus Brennius Antiochus, I did it for our city," the old priest begins. "Our city has disgraced itself as well as the holy presence of the divine Augustus. The markets must be set up outside the city walls. We cannot tolerate the vulgar inside our city. We are too great, too respected, too Roman to allow such. I could no longer tolerate what was happening and..."

"That's it? That's your defense?"

"Yes, Most Excellent one."

Justus sends his deputy down to the three magistrates. They each read their verdict, beginning with the oldest magistrate. The deputy takes their written judgments down to the street level. There he hands them to the high priestess of Vesta. She takes them to the altar.

After an hour, the high priestess returns with the verdicts in her hand. She walks up onto the platform and holds the decisions high.

"Guilty. Guilty. Guilty."

As she turns to hand them to the deputy, the spectators

break out into cheering.

Once the deputy gives the verdicts to Justus, the crowd grows silent. They know the penalty will be instant death.

"Aurelius, stand." He waits only a moment. "You have been found guilty of fourteen counts of kidnapping. According to our law, your sentence is death. Since you have held such a high and respected office in our city for so long, you deserve a quick death—that of beheading."

A few of the spectators hoot, and Justus glares at them until they stop.

"However, due to your long service to the divine Augustus, I am going to exile you from the Roman Empire. You may choose any island you like. Do not expect a stipend, for you will not receive it. You will depend on your own wits to support yourself. My firm hope is that, in your desperation, you are driven to become one of those workers you so despise. Take him away."

Two guards from the dungeon step forward and escort Aurelius to his cell until such time arrangements can be made over in Smyrna to take him to his island of nightmares.

Justus leaves his chair at the pinnacle of the platform. When he reaches the final steps to the ground, he is joined by Titus. The citadel guards make sure there is a path for the aristocracy to their chariot.

Just before they reach it, Chloe steps over to Titus. "He is proud of you, Titus. I haven't seen him this happy in a long time."

On their ride home, Titus has an overwhelming desire to thank one of the gods. But which one? *Well, Mother, if you are watching, maybe I have you to thank.*

All along the way, commoners of the city stand on either side of the street cheering.

"Hail to Praetor Justus. Hail to Titus. Hail to Praetor Justus. Hail to Titus."

When they arrive home, Brutus takes the reins of Justus' horse, and one of the stable hands takes the reins of Fulvio's. Lydia greets them at the inner gate.

"While you were gone," she pronounces, the other maids and I put together a feast for you and your family. A celebration feast."

"That's fine," Justus says. "I'm sure the others will enjoy it." He walks to the stairway leading to his *officium*. Titus, Chloe, and Fulvio watch him take his usual two steps at a time. He stops at the top, turns, and looks down.

"Uh, Son, I think you will appreciate the university at Pergamum. Your first-year's tuition has been paid. A house with sufficient servants and amenities has been leased for you to maintain your status as son of the praetor. Upon graduation from the gymnasium academy here, you may resume your studies there."

With that, Justus Brinnius Antiochus disappears down the corridor. They hear the door to his *officium* open and close.

Chloe breaks the silence. "I know what we can do. Cornelius! Lydia! Come here!"

The old faithful gatekeeper and head steward of the Brennius household and headmistress come out to the family courtyard.

"We are going to have a feast. Lydia, I want you to take a wagon and all the maids with you, go to the market and buy whatever you need to feed fourteen former captives and their wives and children—and their friends.

"Yes, ma'am," Lydia says with a grin and a curtsy.

"Cornelius," Chloe continues, "if Titus still has his list, send as many servants as you need to the south end of town where the merchants and farmhands live. Invite them to a Freedom Feast at our *palatio*."

"Yes, ma'am," Cornelius says, echoing Lydia.

"While they are gone, send someone to all the markets and buy all the tunics you can find—all sizes. They will be given to every one of the guests as they arrive. And, Cornelius, make sure the tunics are of white linen or wool. Oh, and pick out fourteen togas. We shall dress our fourteen survivors like aristocrats on this their special day."

"Yes, ma'am," Cornelius repeats.

"Now, let me see. I need our butler. We need to make sure we have enough new wine to go around to everyone. And, let me see. Someone tell the butler to find the fattest calf he can and prepare it for roasting immediately."

She looks around. Titus steps over to her. He looks into her eyes, as blue as his own.

"May I?" She holds out her arms, and Titus falls into them weeping. She sways back and forth like his mother used to do when holding her little boy in her arms.

"Do you think it will last?" he whispers.

"I don't know. Your father is a hurting man."

"What if he doesn't approve of what I learn at the university?"

9 ~ AMMONIUS

"Welcome to Pergamum, home of the famous library, outdone only by the library in Alexandria. My name is Ammonius."

The short man with big, laughing eyes extends his hand to tall Titus. Titus grasps the other's hand and forearm, and knows right away they will be friends.

"My name is Titus Pomponius Brennius," he says. "Well, I usually keep the last two names a secret," he adds, matching the grin of his new friend and showing his one dimple. "Just call me Titus."

"And where are you from, Titus with two secret names?"

"Antioch, one of the cities of Augus... There I go again. I just come from Antioch. And you?"

"I was born near Athens in Lamprae."

"Lucky you," Titus says. "The seat of great wisdom and learning."

"True, but I was not even remotely part of what created that esteemed reputation, just born into it."

Ammonius sweeps his hand outward.

"Well, this is the main library, as you can see. And, oh, by the way, as you noticed walking up here, you are in the upper acropolis where the palace, some important temples, and the theater are. You passed the gymnasium academy halfway up in the lower acropolis. Of course, at the foot of our mountain is the Sanctuary of Asclepius, the god of healing."

"I wondered what that was down there," Titus says. "A lot of people being carried in—sick people, I guess. So, you were explaining the library to me."

"Yes, yes," Ammonius continues. "You may have recognized Athena in the middle of this room. We are part of the sanctuary of Athena. Her temple is on the same scale and design as the library. You noticed the benches, flowers, reflecting pools and trees in the vast area between our twin buildings—all to the glory of Athena, of course—goddess of justice, law, and things like that."

"This library is huge," Titus says.

"On the shelves along the walls are two hundred thousand books—though I have never counted them—a few written on stone from our ancient past, some written on Egyptian papyrus, but many on the modern and durable parchment."

"Yes, you're famous for your parchment manufacturing here. Where are our lectures held?"

"Usually in this room."

"When do classes start?"

"Classes start tomorrow. You got here just in time. Do you have a place to stay? I have a room in an *insulae* down in the city. You can spend the night with me."

"That's okay," Titus says. "My father arranged for a place for me before I left home. I actually arrived yesterday and have been settling in."

"Well, then, we shall meet again tomorrow."

Titus hangs back until Ammonius is out of sight. He walks to the end of the library where the banquet hall is, then around behind the building where the stable is. He gives a copper coin to a stable hand and waits. Momentarily, a shiny black Arabian horse with its elegant sculpted head and high arched tail is led out to him.

Titus mounts the horse and leads it down the two *milles* to the lower acropolis. He lets his steed strut all it wants to impress the other horses traveling along the same road.

Rather than continue down the rest of the way to the Temple of Asclepius, he veers to his left to the Selinus River.

At the bottom of the hill, he follows the river along the valley until he arrives at his rented house, a villa.

A stable hand comes out to take his horse, and a gatekeeper opens the gate for him. He goes into his courtyard and up onto his roof. It is a clear day, and he can see the Aegean Sea.

"Well, Mother, I made it to the university. Father made it possible for me. He has changed a lot. Aunt Chloe says it is because he misses you so much. I guess you were his whole world. Mine too. Aunt Chloe also says I look just like my father but act just like you. You were always so happy. Help me find happiness here. Can you hear me, Mother?"

Life at the university is all Titus had hoped for and more. He devours everything taught in his daily classes. He grows impatient each evening for the dawning of a new day when he can learn something else he never dreamed of before.

Ammonius has become a good friend, even though he has to live in a crowded insulae. Titus knows eventually he will have to let Ammonius know where he lives and risk losing his friendship.

At the university, he has three preceptors—Valerius for oratory, Leonides for logic, and Ursus for astronomy.

Yesterday was oratory day. Valerius encouraged Titus to raise his voice, let loose, and see what comes out. Titus obeyed, recalling the days when he was fourteen and defending Stephan. *Maybe I hadn't embarrassed myself as much as I had thought.*

As Titus rides his sleek Arabian up the road to the top of the hill at dawn before the other students arrive, he thinks about the previous week's discussion. Is there a god or not? If so, is there more than one? If not, is there at least a first cause? If there is only a first cause—which some call the god— why does it not have a personality? Why would a first cause make the universe if it didn't have pleasure in anything?

He arrives at the stable just as the sun peaks over the horizon.

Today, they will discuss Plato's, Socrates' and Aristotle's views on the existence of a god or gods. *I think after that class, I'll check to see if the library has any books about the Jewish*

God. They claim there is only one God, but he has personality. My mother liked their God. I was too young to ask her about it.

He enters the library lecture hall and browses among the books until the first student arrives to join him.

"I see you're here early again. Don't you ever sleep?" It is Valerius, master of oratory.

Titus turns and smiles. "Good morning, Preceptor Valerius. Uh, I was expecting Preceptor Leonides."

"He could not come today. He asked me to hold class for him instead. You have been in my oratory class for two months now. I think today would be a good day for you to present us with just what you can do."

"This is unexpected," Titus objects, staring at the short man with wavy hair and bangs combed down slightly onto his forehead.

"Of course, it is. That's part of being an orator. You don't have time to prepare a speech. You may be called upon at any time."

"Are you sure I am ready?"

"Of course. Your father said..."

"My father? When did you meet my father?"

"He has written to me a couple of times about you. He said you defended a young man accused of thievery and won. Then you defended an older man accused of murder and won."

"Well, they were both accidents. I was only fourteen for the first one, and not quite eighteen for the second one."

"See there. You didn't understand what was going on, but you used your wits and came out the winner. That's what I want you to do today. Oh, here comes Ammonius."

Titus looks at a few more books to pass the time until the last two students arrive.

"Attention, everyone. Titus is going to expound for us." Preceptor Valerius sits at the far end of the hall and calls up for Titus to begin.

"Uh, well, fellow Romans..."

"I cannot hear you," Preceptor Valerius calls out from his end of the hall.

"Fellow Romans," Titus says louder.

"I cannot hear you," the preceptor calls out again.

"Fellow Romans," Titus shouts.

"I cannot hear you," the preceptor repeats.

"Fellow Romans!" Titus bellows. He pauses to see if the preceptor complains again. He does not.

"I come to you today to…"

"I cannot see you," Preceptor Valerius calls out.

Titus raises one hand and bellows, "I come to you today to…"

"I cannot see you," comes the dreaded cry at the far end of the hall.

"Titus raises both arms as far as he can stretch them and bellows, "I come to you today to…"

"I still cannot see you, young man. Do something about it."

Titus glares at his preceptor, swings around in an in-place circle, points at the preceptor, glares at him, and bellows, "I come to you today to…"

He pauses, awaiting instructions to do the impossible. Quiet. Approval?

"I come to you today to bring you hope," he bellows.

He jerks his body so he is facing the classmates on his left.

"Yes, I tell you, hope!"

He swings to his right and raises both arms. "Hope is free! Hope sets the imagination on fire. Hope is unstoppable!"

Not sure what to try next to keep his preceptor satisfied, Titus remembers some of his moves from the warrior dances he had learned as a child.

He crouches, his eyes darting back and forth over his classmates. "You cannot keep hope down. You cannot pounce on hope and expect it to cower," he bellows.

He notices his classmates begin to sit up on their marble benches and to follow him more closely.

Time to swing around again. Titus does so, then thrusts both arms upward simultaneously.

"Do not try to destroy hope, for it will rise up. It will rise up again," he lowers his arms and thrusts them up again, "and again," arms lowered and thrust, "and again," he bellows.

His classmates are now smiling. They actually approve.

He remembers the movements to thrust a sword into the belly of an enemy. He faces his audience and thrusts an arm forward.

"We can face the enemy with hope." He thrusts his imaginary sword forward. "We can strive with hope." One more thrust forward for good measure. "We can win with hope!" he bellows.

"So, let us bear up," now thrusting both arms above his head and stretching toward the golden oil lamps near the ceiling. "Let us gather up." Another thrust heavenward. "My fellow Romans, let us cling to hope and rise up!"

With that, the entire class stands and responds, fists in the air.

"Hope!"

"Hope!"

"Hope!"

Titus grins in disbelief at what he has accomplished and toward the back of the lecture hall. But Preceptor Valerius is missing. He stares, his expression becoming blank.

His classmates turn around to see what has gone wrong.

Moments later, the preceptor reappears, carrying a sprig from an olive branch in the sanctuary outside. He weaves it into a circle as he works his way to the front of the hall. He faces Titus and puts the new wreath on his head.

"Congratulations, young man," the preceptor says, reaching up to the much-taller Titus and placing the wreath on his head. "I do not believe I have ever had a student put so much, so much, well animation and vigor into a speech. I must say you will go far in your career as a lawyer. Use your gift, Titus. Use your gift."

With that, Titus turns back toward his classmates, grins, and raises his arms. His classmates raise their arms, and the chant begins anew.

"Hope."

"Hope."

"Hope."

Titus returns to the bench he has been assigned to, still glowing, and the preceptor takes his place at the head of the class.

"Now, for the rest of our time together...Uh, did you need something?" Preceptor Valerius says, looking toward the door.

A messenger works his way to the front and hands him a small wax tablet. He reads it, then stares at his students.

"Someone is going to set fire to the library."

The mood in the second greatest library in the world changes from jubilation to confusion.

"It says a scroll has been placed next to Socrates' last words before his execution by suicide as written by Plato."

"I know right where it is," Ammonius says. As everyone waits, they look at each other but see nothing but a black cloud of bewilderment.

Ammonius returns with the small scroll and hands it to the preceptor.

Valerius unrolls it. "It says a fireball will be catapulted to the library within one week unless the university solves this riddle: 'What good can come from fire?' The correct answer must be delivered to the dock on the Selinus River in a jar lowered into the water by a scarlet rope. The jar will be checked each night. If it contains the correct answer, a banner of Athena will appear in our sanctuary between the library and the temple. If the correct answer is not in the jar within a week, the library will burn."

"Well, hello, everyone. Sorry I am late." It is Leonides, preceptor of logic and debate. He strides in with his long legs and a toga that is falling off his shoulder.

He cannot see the faces of his students but notices Preceptor Valerius' long face. His smile disappears. He stops in his tracks and looks around. He looks back at his colleague.

"What's wrong?"

"They're going to burn the library down," Valerius responds."

"Who?"

"They don't say. Maybe a foreign ship. Or a disgruntled student. Or a devotee of Athena. We do not know."

He hands the scroll to Preceptor Leonides. "I think this is in your field of expertise. I hand this matter over to you while I notify other preceptors, priests, magistrates, and the governor of our province of Asia Minor."

Threatening scroll in hand, Preceptor Leonides takes his place in front of his class. He presses his lips together, then nods.

"Gentlemen, we are going to solve this. Every one of you is going on to be either a philosopher or lawyer. You have a good solid background in the law of both the Greeks and Romans, as well as the great philosophers. You are going to save the library."

Leonides steps to a nearby table and slams his fist down on it. "Do you understand me? You are going to save this library, and perhaps the entire Acropolis of Pergamum if the fire spreads."

Titus raises his hand. "Sir, where do we start?"

"Start with the philosophers. Whoever wrote this threat knows something about the philosophers. His riddle is rhetorical. So, how many of them wrote about fire?"

Ammonius raises his hand. "Plato wrote of Socrates' story about the fire in the cave."

"Then, we shall start there. Ammonius, you go find the scroll and read it aloud to the class. Then we shall discuss how it would answer our enemy's question."

Ammonius reads to the class for half an hour, then steps aside for the preceptor to guide the critical discussion.

"So, here we have people chained in a cave all their life, unable to turn their heads or walk anywhere except straight ahead. They walk randomly around the cave. There is a fire behind them so that everyone in the cave casts shadows. They believe these shadows are other people. This is their reality. But if one of them is freed and goes out into the world, he would see the true reality, not just shadows. If I tried to free the others still in the cave, they would ridicule him and want him dead for disturbing their idea of reality. So, now, what good does the fire create?

"Well," Titus says, "without the fire, they would see nothing. They would be in complete darkness."

"True. Anyone else?"

"The fire provides warmth for them."

"Yes, but the story does not mention that. Do not go beyond the story. Anything else other than the fire provides something for the eyes to look at?"

"The sun above is a fire, isn't it?"

"But the story does not say that. Remain faithful to the story."

The class is quiet.

"Fine. We shall write our conclusions on a small scroll and put that in the bottle. I shall send one of the messengers down to the dock to..."

"Sir, I would like to do that on my way home, if I may," Titus says.

"Good. Let's just hope this is the correct answer."

"Hope!"

"Hope!"

"Hope!"

The preceptor dismisses the class, wondering why they are chanting. He calls over the noise. "Pray to your gods. Pray for their protection. The fate of our library and university depends on us."

Titus does not wait for everyone to leave this time. He goes directly to the stable and mounts his sleek black Arabian. Although galloping is not allowed on the narrow roads leading down from the mountain, he allows his steed to trot, something the steed is, of course, proud to do.

Titus arrives at the dock on the river, dismounts, and looks for a scarlet rope. His steed clop, clop, clops behind him on the wooden planks. He spots the cord, pulls up the jar, and places the hoped-for answer inside.

He steps back and leads his steed to a bench near the road. He watches a while, then remounts.

Instead of heading home, he heads west along the Salinas River. When he arrives at the far west of the city where the Selinus spills into the Cetius River, he urges his Arabian into a gallop. Within half an hour, he and the Cetius River are at the shore of the Aegean Sea.

Although there is no natural harbor there, a ship is anchored just offshore. The ship has a strange figurehead.

Titus stares a moment, dismounts, hurries his steed to

a nearby drinking pool, and with impatience, lets it have its fill. He remounts, presses his lips together, and urges the Arabian into a gallop back to Pergamum.

10 ~ ICE QUEEN

*T*he gate into the Acropolis halfway up the mountain is closed for the night.

"Open up. Open up," Titus calls out. I am Titus Pomponius Brennius, associated with Athena and her university. Let me in. I have urgent news of an enemy on its way."

The guard recognizes the twenty-year-old and lets him in. Titus notices his horse is wheezing and full of white lather. "Please allow me to use one of your horses for the final two *milles* to the palace."

A legionnaire of the respected equestrian rank steps forward with his own horse. "I will take it from here, sir. Thank you for your information. You may go home now."

The legionnaire mounts his horse and gallops up the mountain. Another legionnaire opens the gate back up, and Titus leaves, walking his exhausted steed behind him.

The shadows move in on him, and the only sounds now are of the clop, clop, clop of his Arabian. He wonders about the fire cave and the sun that no one sees. He prays, stops, and raises his eyes toward the stars far above.

"Oh god or gods," he cries aloud, "am I in a cave? I cannot find you. How can I ask you to protect the library and the temples and the city when I do not know who you are? How do I know the names our ancient ancestors gave you are truly your names? How do I know how many you are and where you are? My mother said there is only one of you. How can that be? I do not understand. Does anyone hear me? Anyone?"

He is silent the rest of the way home except for the clop, clop, clop.

Despite a restless night, Titus rises early. He is grateful for Brutus' attentive care of his Arabian and takes a different horse up the mountain.

He arrives at the library at the same time as Ammonius. "Did you hear what happened last night? The library is not going to be burned after all."

"Did they capture the ship? I'm the one who discovered it. So, do you know what happened during the night?"

"No, but we're about to find out."

When they walk into the library, they see all three of their preceptors upfront conferring. The students find their seats and only whisper to each other, "Did you hear what happened?"

"Attention, everyone," Preceptor Ursus calls out, holding his hands up and out. "I was planning to discuss whether the gods actually exist today based on the existence of moving stars and planets, but we have more urgent things facing us. I, therefore, turn my class over to Leonides."

Preceptor Valerius steps forward. "I am in full agreement."

The two step back and give the floor to Preceptor Leonides. Immediately young hands are raised.

"Put your hands down," he begins. "Yes, the ship was captured last night. The crew is being held on their ship, and the captain and his daughter are being held in the palace."

"They say it was like a ghost ship," a student says. "What did the crew look like? Were they hairy?"

"Now, Ammonius, you know better. Get that imagination of yours under check."

"Sir, what about the figurehead on the ship?" another student asks. "Does anyone know what it represents? A god, maybe?"

"It is my understanding that it represents Thor, son of

Odin, their god-king."

"Where are they from?" Titus asks.

"They are from a place Caesar calls Jutland. It is a peninsula jutting out into the Nordic Sea."

"How dare you!"

The preceptor jerks his head toward the door and the woman's voice.

The students swivel around to look behind them.

Standing in the doorway is the most beautiful woman Titus has ever seen. Her long blond hair is almost white. Her green eyes flash. She stands, legs apart, wearing leather sandals up to her knees, a leather tunic down to her knees, and has her delicate hands on her hips.

"How dare you!"

Two soldiers follow her in and grab her arms.

"Our apologies, preceptor," one of them says. "She got away from us."

She elbows them in the middle and pronounces, "Get your hands off me. I did not get away from you or anyone else. The governor set us free. And with his apologies, I might add."

The two guards back away, but stay at the doorway.

The woman marches forward, her green eyes still flashing, and her white-blond hair flowing behind her. She comes within a man-length of the preceptor, glares at him, then turns to face the gawking young men.

"All right. Vhich von ov you decided ve vere monsters sailing in a dragon und bent on destroying dhe Roman Empire?"

The young men stare in momentary speechlessness.

Titus looks around. Ammonius pokes him. "Well, tell her," he whispers with a grin.

"She'll kill me," Titus responds, also with a whisper.

"What a way to die," Ammonius counters.

"You! You back, dhere!"

The strange, frightening, and beautiful woman marches in Titus' direction. She stops by his bench, puts her hands on her hips, and flashes her green eyes at him.

"Stand up, you coward son ov Odin's most verthless offspring."

Titus hears muffled chuckles. His face turns red. He looks around.

"Do you have no ears, you miserable excuse ov a Roman?"

More muffled chuckles. Ammonius elbows his friend.

Titus rises in slow motion. Once he is fully up, he realizes he is only a head taller than the woman.

"Vell, vhat do you have to say vor yourself?

"Uh, par...pardon me," he begins, recalling such interrogations by his father in days gone by. "Uh, I, I don't believe I know what I have done."

"Vhat you have done? Vhat you have done? You have kept my crew up all night, and have brought my vadder, and I bevore your governor, chained like criminals."

"But I..."

Ammonius tugs at Titus' toga. "She doesn't know it was you," he whispers.

"Ah-ha! You dhink I cannot hear? I have ears like any odher man. So, it vas you!"

"Uh, well, all I did was tell the guard..."

"All you did vas tell dhe guards we vere dhe enemy."

Before Titus can reply, the tall woman with the white-blond hair pulls back her hand and slams her fist into Titus' nose.

"Dhat should teach you."

She turns around and marches back to the doorway.

Titus grabs his nose and stumbles after her. "But I don't know who you are."

She spins around. "I am Fjorta, daughter ov Gurrid, captain ov dhe *Sea Dragon*, who is also dhe brodher of dhe king of Jutland. Dhat's who."

She swivels and marches out through the door.

Preceptor Leonides hurries to the door and motions for one of the legionnaires to come back into the library. As he does, all the students look in the direction of Titus, who is nursing his nose with the bloodied edge of his used-to-be-white toga.

Ammonius pounds him on the back. "Lucky you. I would give anything to have been slugged by a beautiful woman who looks like an ice queen."

"Ice is right," Titus mumbles, still leaning over.

"Hey, Titus. Are you going to marry her?"

"Hey, Titus. Will you challenge her father to a contest?"

"Hey, Titus. I know a perfumer who can soften her up for you."

"Hey, Titus, she's getting away."

"Attention, everyone," Preceptor Leonides calls out. "Attention. Return to your seats. Men. Return to your seats."

His class obeys.

"Well, this certainly was a false alarm. Which means we still have much work to do if we are going to stop whoever is determined to set fire to our library. So, gentlemen, get your mind back on what is important. We have six days left to solve the riddle: 'What good can come from fire?'."

He waits.

"Preceptor, sir," one of the students says. "What about Heraclitus? He said the world is like fire, always changing. Further, he said fire is ever-living—it ever was and ever will be. He said the soul is like fire, being ever living. He even said the earth is like fire because it is ever-changing but also ever-living, so the earth may even be a god."

"Anyone have any thoughts on this?"

"Well, he lived six hundred years ago," Ammonius says. "To make the earth god is to make the earth responsible for itself or to have created itself."

"Any other thoughts?"

The preceptor looks over at Titus, who now has his head between his knees, still trying to stop the bleeding of his nose.

"How about putting this in the jar tonight: Fire is ever-changing and also everlasting. So, fire is the essence of the universe."

The class agrees. "Well, let's hope we are right. Our library being destroyed would destroy half the knowledge in the world. Titus, would you like to deliver our answer to the jar since you know where it is?"

Timothy raises his head and tests his nose with a new section of toga. It is no longer bleeding.

"Sir, I believe I can do that," he says with a rather nasal

tone.

After being dismissed, Titus mounts his chestnut horse and walks it to make sure it does not jar the blood in his nose.

When he arrives at the dock, he dismounts, finds the scarlet rope, raises it, stuffs the answer into the jar, and lets it back down into the water.

"Vhy are vou talking to dhe fishes?"

It is a female voice. Titus raises himself up so far, he forgets the jar is still in his hand and attached to the dock. He lets go of it.

"Uh, you weren't supposed to see that."

"Okay, dhen I vill unsee it. Oh, did I bloody your nose?"

Fjorta pulls her white-blond hair back and walks toward Titus. "Aw, let me see."

Titus jerks back. "No, I am not going to let you see my nose. And besides, what were you doing there?

"At dhe sea harbor dhat isn't really a harbor? People sometimes do not trust us."

"Are you a pirate?"

"No, I'm not a pirate, and neidher is my vadder," Fjorta says, swishing her white-blond hair and walking away from Titus.

"Then what are you doing around here so far away from where ever you are from?"

"Why are ve so var vrom Jutland? Ve are going to make dhe rounds of dhe Great Sea bevore ve go on to China."

Titus stares at Fjorta while she steps on top of the bench and swings around on one foot.

"Well, why are you going to China, and why are you so happy? Do you get that much enjoyment out of punching strange men in the nose?"

Titus sits on the bench, almost on Fiorta's foot, and she leans her elbows on his back.

"I'm happy because my vadder has been trying vor years to meet vith your governor about trading vith your people."

She jumps down off the bench, turns to face Titus, and throws her hands up in the air. "Und, ve vinally did. Granted, ve vere in chains, but dhat changed vhen he vound out ve vould be uv benefit to him."

"Fjorta! Get on dhe horse. Your vadder is ready to leave."

She takes one last glimpse at Titus, runs to the horse, leaps, settles behind the horseman and waves.

"Will I ever see you again?" Titus calls.

But all he sees now is her white-blond hair floating behind her as the strange Norseman takes her away from him.

He sits on the ground and leans on the bench. *I think I just fell in love with an ice queen.*

The next morning, he is back at the library where the other young men crowd around him.

"You lucky fellow, you."

"So, do you think you will marry her?"

"Where did she disappear to?"

"If you must know," Titus says with a grin, "she is on her way to China."

"You saw her again?" Ammonius asks. "He saw her again," he says, raising his fist and shouting. "He saw her again!"

"Class. Class. Be seated, everyone. There was no banner in the sanctuary of Athena. That means we have not come up with the correct answer to the riddle about the goodness of fire."

The young men disburse to their seats.

"Now, we must find the answer today. We are running out of time," Preceptor Leonides says.

Silence. Leonides paces.

"Sir, what about the stoic philosophy? Stoics believe the entire earth was fire at one time and would become fire again, thus beginning the cycle of eternal life all over again."

"Well, gentlemen," Leonides says. "What do the rest of you think?"

"I thought fire destroyed."

"Not completely. It always leaves ashes."

"Then, ashes float up into the air and fall down on all things, thus merging with them."

"The fire starts all over again being earth."

The discussion goes on for three hours. In the end, Preceptor Leonides sums up the discussion.

"Therefore, from fire came the earth. And although it will return to fire someday, it will provide a new beginning for a new earth. Is that what we have decided?"

"Yes, sir," Ammonius says. "I have written it down on this small scroll I brought with me today."

"Fine. Would you like to be the one to deliver our answer to the jar?"

"Yes, sir. That is, if Titus does not mind."

I may as well get it over with. Ammonius knows I live near that dock. "That is fine with me," Titus responds.

"I saw you on a chestnut horse yesterday," Ammonius tells his friend on their way to the stable. "I thought you had to walk everywhere."

"Well, it's a little more than that," Titus responds. "Actually, a lot more."

Two stable hands bring out the young men's horses. Ammonius' is a black Frisian horse. It stands taller than the sleek black horse also being brought out.

"Ha, ha! I thought you were poor and lived in an *insulae* in town."

"I assumed you were poor and had to walk everywhere."

They mount their steeds and ride side by side down the mountain as their respective animals compete to see which one can high step and prance the best. They arrive at the dock, and Titus tells him where the scarlet rope is. He waits while Ammonius kneels down, puts today's answer to the riddle in the jar, and lowers it back into the water.

"Is it empty each time you put an answer in it?"

"Yes, each time. Whoever our enemy is, he takes the answer out during the night."

"Well, let's hope we are correct this time. I thought it was a splendid answer. Perhaps tomorrow, when we return to the university, there will be a banner in the sanctuary. Uh, which way are you going, Titus?"

"I am going that way. Uh, I guess I live along the river."

"I will confess I only stayed in the *insulae* long enough for my things to arrive, and I could move into better quarters. So, now you have to show me that little house you say you live in."

The two young men grin at each other and remount. Titus takes his friend along the river about a *mille* and stops.

"Ammonius, I don't want to lose your friendship. Please do not hold it against me."

"What against you?"

"Well, I guess I live in a villa."

"Ha! This I have to see. Let me in."

Brutus comes out of the stable and takes their horses. Titus knocks on his gate, and Cornelius answers it.

"Two servants? You've got two servants?"

"Well, maybe a few more than that," Titus confesses. "But you promised to remain my friend, despite our differences. The physical means nothing. What is in the mind and soul is what means something."

"Agreed. Now, let me into your little villa," Ammonius says, following Titus into the courtyard, with its green-and-white tile, reflecting pool in the middle, and matching columns of green and white marble holding up the second floor.

Titus stares at Ammonius, who is standing by the pool turning in place to take in the beauty. He is still smiling. "Do you ever go up on your roof?" he asks Titus.

"Of course. Well, I have a view of the Aegean from there."

"That's not all you have a view of, my friend." Titus takes the steps two at a time, as his father always had. His shorter friend follows, taking one step at a time.

They walk across the roof facing west. "Indeed, you do have a view of the Aegean from here. There is something else you have a view of."

He walks closer to Titus, takes hold of one shoulder, and points over the other shoulder. "See that village over there where the three trees are? That's my villa!"

Titus turns toward his friend. The two men form wide grins and embrace, pounding each other on the back.

"Then that must be why we are so much alike. We have rich parents. Or at least I have a rich father," Titus says. "And you?"

"As I said, I was born near Athens. I had two older siblings—a brother and sister. My parents had married just within the limit of thirty before they were taxed for not marrying and not having children. So, my parents are old and gray haired. But, if you ever meet them, do not tell them I said that."

A maid comes up on the roof with drinks and some cheese, flatbread, yogurt, and grapes.

"Sit, my friend. Let us indulge in our riches together," Titus says.

"Indeed, yes."

The following morning, Titus and Ammonius meet at the bottom of the mountain and ride upon their respective black steeds to the library together.

"Oh, no," Ammonius says when they see there is no banner in the sanctuary between Athena's temple and the library.

"And this is day five," Titus adds. "We're doomed."

11 ~ THE RETURN

*S*oon they are inside and in their assigned seats. Preceptor Leonides walks out. He is not happy.

"This is day five. Time is running out. We must find the correct answer to the riddle about the goodness of fire. It must be done today. Now, let us begin."

Once again, their preceptor paces while the students think. At last, one raises his hand.

"Preceptor, sir. Empedocles who lived just before Socrates, said there are four elements in the world: Earth, Air, Water, and Fire. He said Zeus—our Jupiter—is in all fire. Fire is the shiniest and brightest thing in the universe. Therefore, fire represents the greatest of all powers in the universe. Fire is king."

Questions follow. Challenges. Thinking. Dissecting. In mid-afternoon, the preceptor makes his announcement. "Then we shall submit this as the answer to the riddle on the goodness of fire. Someone write it out. Which one of you wants to deliver it to the river?"

Titus and Ammonius raise their hands in unison. They look at each other, grin, and keep their hands raised.

"Fine, you shall both take our answer to the river. The answer will ride with you, Ammonius, and be placed in the jar by Titus."

Once again, the message is put in the jar, but on the

morning of the sixth day, there is no banner flying over the sanctuary.

All levity of previous days is gone. In one more day, their library could be up in smoke.

Leonides has brought Valerius and Ursus back. The three preceptors pace in a circle in front of the assembling students.

All talking among the young men stops at the door. They enter and find their assigned seats in quiet.

"Sirs," Titus says. "Yesterday, I found a copy of the Hebrew writings of Moses, their lawgiver, and took it home with me. I read all night, hoping the religion of my mother would shed light on our growing dilemma."

"Your mother is a Jew?" Preceptor Ursus responds. "Strange religion. They only have one God."

"My mother did become a Jew. She has gone to the Jewish heaven now."

"That is something I would love to hear more of someday—that is, if our library survives to exist another day," Preceptor Valerius says.

"Continue," Preceptor Leonides says. "Continue."

"Well, the Hebrews believe fire represents two things—purification and the presence of their one God. They receive purification whenever they sacrifice an animal, especially on their Day of Atonement. On the other hand—or perhaps related to it somehow—God appeared to Moses in a bush that was afire but did not burn up. God put his words in that bush. Then later, God appeared at the top of Mount Sinai in Arabia, where he spent many days dictating what the Hebrews call their Law of Moses. In fact, his finger of fire etched the first and most famous Ten Commandments right into two stone tablets."

Silence.

"That's it?" Leonides asks. "In that case, let us debate it. Who has a rebuttal? Anyone? Questions? Affirmations? Challenges?"

The next four hours are spent in discussion.

"This one has to be the correct answer to the riddle. If it is not, tomorrow our library and university will be no more,"

Preceptor Ursus announces. "The soul of our books will be reunited with the soul of the universe."

The entire class goes with Titus down to the dock. They watch him put their final answer to the riddle in the jar hung by the scarlet rope.

"We have decided to spend the night here," one of the classmates says. "We are going to catch the culprit when he rises out of the water to claim his answer. We will grab him, arrest him, and have him crucified."

The side of Titus that takes after his father is in agreement. The side of him that takes after his mother is hesitant. He and Ammonius stay until dark, then sneak off to their respective villas.

The following morning at dawn, they both check at the dock. Their classmates are still asleep.

"Well, did you grab him? Are we safe now?"

"Huh?"

The young men waken and look around to reorient themselves.

One lunges at the scarlet rope and pulls up the jar. The jar is gone. Students without horses of their own ride up the mountain to the Acropolis behind their friends who do have them.

Hearts beat fast. Silent prayers are repeated over and over to their respective gods. Muscles strain, stomachs churn, they look up in the sky for the promised fireball that will doom their library forever.

They rush past the now-open gates and up past the gymnasium academy, the baths, the Temple of Hera, and the Temple of Demeter at the lower acropolis.

Their horses lunge and gulp air as they gallop on up the road leading to the top of the mountain. Riders still watch the sky for the fireball praying to every god they can think of.

Beat the enemy there. Grab all the books possible and take them outside before they go up in smoke with the library. Save what they can. Hurry. Beat the fireball. Save something. Try to recompense for their failure at properly answering the riddle of goodness in fire.

On they go, daring to hope with the hope Titus had

taught them just a week earlier. Was Titus right? Does hope keep everything alive? Will hope put out the fierceness and destruction of the fireball? Or was Titus wrong?

They gallop past the upper market and the great altar. They reach the temple of Athena and slide off their horses. They look up. Instead of the fireball, they see the banner flying high between the temple and the library.

"Hurrah!"

"We did it!"

"We solved the riddle!"

"Hey, who is that man running away?"

"That's him. Go after him, men!"

The class of future philosophers and lawyers speed across the sanctuary to catch the enemy.

Titus, the tallest, reaches him first and tackles him. When the others catch up, they sit on him, hold his arms and legs down, and spit on him.

"Hey, let me up," the enemy begs.

"Why, so you can go back to your ship and send your fireball down on us?"

"Was the banner you just put up to throw us off, so we weren't ready after all?"

"Who are you, anyway."

"If you let me up, I'll tell you," says the boyish voice with grass in his mouth and up his nose.

Titus moves aside. All the others do except those with his arms pinned down. They pull him up.

"Now talk. Who are you? And why are you so young?"

"My name is Numinous. I am from Athens. I have been trying to be accepted into the Academy of Plato, but so far, they have not let me in. They finally gave me this riddle and said if I could solve it, they would let me in."

"You could always apply for admittance another year."

"No, it isn't that simple. My father is ashamed of me and said he would disinherit me if I was not accepted this time."

Titus looks at the younger man and thinks of his own father. "Well, did you get your answers?" he asks Numinous.

The young man smiles. I got six answers. I have been adding them to my reply to the preceptors at the academy and will have them ready to submit by the time I get back to Athens."

Silence.

"How did you get here all the way from Athens? And how are you going to get back?"

"I crossed the Aegean on a strange ship called the *Sea Monster*. The people on it talked funny. Then there was this girl who was always bawling the crew out. The crewmen didn't mind because she was..."

"Was so beautiful," Titus finishes for him.

"Yes. How did you know?"

"Is the *Sea Monster* back?" Titus asks.

"It went to China, but I don't think it will be back for another year or two.

"Ha!" Ammonius says. "When I graduate from here, I plan to go to your famous Academy of Plato and become famous myself."

Titus laughs and pounds his friend on the back. "I believe you will, my friend. I believe you will."

Another year passes. Titus writes to his father monthly. His father never replies. One day he receives a letter from his old friend, Stephan.

Congratulate me, Titus. I am getting married. Her name is Arelia, and she is beautiful and funny and musical and reminds me of your mother. You will love her. When are you coming home?

Another two years pass. Tiberius Caesar dies. Caligula Caesar takes his place as emperor of the Roman Empire. Titus has learned about all the oratorical techniques and debate methods that exist along with a new understanding and appreciation of the firmament with its star gods looking down on humanity.

"I guess this is it," Ammonius tells Titus on their last night together, watching the sun go down behind the Aegean. "We go our separate ways."

"We will write each other," Titus says. "And no matter how big and important you become, Ammonius, you will remember our years together at the beginning."

The next morning when Ammonius leaves his villa for the last time, Titus is waiting for him on the road.

As their horses walk at a slower pace than is their wont to do, Titus begins to sing.

"Where did you learn that song?" Ammonius asks.

"From my mother. She always said there isn't a problem in the world that a song can't cure."

"Hmmm."

When they arrive at Smyrna, where the ships are docked, they dismount, embrace, and pound each other on the back for the last time. Titus turns toward home but decides to go south along the coast until he reaches the place where the Salinas River spills into the Aegean. There he will follow it upstream until he reaches home. The home he will only have for one more day.

As he comes into view of where the river meets the sea, he hears bells. He looks toward his right.

"The *Sea Dragon!*" he shouts. The seagulls fly off their perches and squawk. More bells. He looks out over the sea and not too far offshore is the Nordic ship that had brought him his ice queen three years earlier.

He slides off his mount and, with the tide lapping at his feet and his hands cupped around his mouth, he shouts at the ship.

"Hellooo. Hellooo out there. Send me a boat and permission to board."

"Vhy vould you vant to do dhat?"

Titus turns and sees his beautiful ice queen with the white-blond hair spilling over her shoulders in graceful strands. Her smile is broad and warm and welcoming.

"I see your nose has healed."

Titus rushes over to his Fjorta and lifts her feet off the ground. He swings her around and around until they both fall onto the shore.

"Vhat are you doing to my daughter, young man? I vill have you hung by your dhumbs."

Titus jumps up and faces the voice he is confident belongs Captain Gurrid, father of the one he loves and brother of the king of Jutland.

"Uh, sir..."

"Vadder, I vill not be returning home vith you. I am staying here to marry—vhat did you say your name vas? Oh, yes, I am going to be marrying Titus."

Silence. Fjorta walks up to her father and puts her arms around his neck. "I love you vadder, but now it is time vor me to leave. I promise to have many grandchildren vor you."

The captain looks down at his daughter. "You are vivteen und a voman now." He looks over at Titus.

"I promise to give her a good home," Titus says, answering his future father-in-law's unasked question. "I will build her the finest *palatio* in Antioch. My father is the, uh, the governor of our city. Everyone will honor her. I promise, sir."

"Then I pronounce you married," the captain growls. He says no more. He embraces his daughter, turns, re-enters the rowboat he had come to shore in, and orders his oarsmen to make all haste back to his ship. He does not turn back for one last glimpse of his daughter.

Titus and Fjorta watch him until he is back on his ship. They hear the bells and know he has ordered the ship to weigh anchor and head back out to sea.

Titus takes her into his arms. "I will keep my promise. You will be the most honored lady in the city of Antioch."

"And I vill be married to dhe most handsome man vith a single dimple in all dhe vorld."

As Titus and his bride ride on the broad Roman road back to his home, he thinks of his mother. *If I hadn't killed her, she would be waiting for us at home and would love her new daughter-in-law.*

They arrive in Antioch. As he enters the city with Fjorta riding behind him with her white-blond hair flowing in the breeze, people stop and stare.

"Who is that?"

"It must be Titus all grown up and a man now."

"Not him. Who is that strange woman?"

Titus and Fjorta both wave at the people as they pass.

Now home, they face Justus Brinnius Antiochus,

praetor of Antioch.

"You did what?"

"We married, sir. Isn't she beautiful?"

"Beauty has nothing to do with it. You will unmarry her immediately."

"Father, I cannot do that. I love her, and she loves me."

"Without my permission. You dare to bring disgrace on our family and our illustrious ancestors?"

"But, father."

"Look at her. She's wearing leather, and her tunic only comes to her knees. She is shaming me."

Fjorta starts to say something, but Titus motions for her not to.

"Who did I hear in our courtyard?" Aunt Chloe walks out from her weaving room. "Oh, Titus, you have brought this beautiful young lady to us. How delightful."

She immediately embraces Fjorta. "Come with me. We shall finish making a lady of you."

Fjorta looks at Titus. "She is my, she is our Aunt Chloe," he explains. "You will love her. I will be here when you come back."

Titus turns toward his father, but the man has now returned to the infamous steps that take him to his *officium* on the second floor. No more does he take the steps two at a time. Titus shakes his head slightly. *I wish I could tell him as he grows old that I still love him.*

Titus sits on his regular bench in the courtyard, and a new maid he does not recognize brings him some apricot juice for a brief refreshment before the evening meal.

Just as he finishes his drink, he hears his aunt.

"Ta, da. Behold your bride."

Titus turns and sees Fjorta floating toward him like a goddess, wearing a gold stola over a long white tunic trimmed in gold at both the neckline and hem. She wears gold earrings, a silver chain with a ruby on the end, and three gold bracelets. There is also an anklet of gold worn next to her delicate linen-woven sandals.

"Oh, my love. You are beauti..."

"Dhey itch," Fjorta announces.

"Oh, my ice queen," Titus laughs. "I do not want you to be anything but yourself. Aunt Chloe, I appreciate what you have done. But, she is not comfortable wearing our type of clothing."

He turns to his new wife. "Sweetheart, what if Aunt Chloe has a long white leather tunic made for you?"

"Would that be enough compromise?" Chloe asks Fjorta.

"Und a cloak?"

"Yes, for the cool nights, a cloak. What would you like your cloak to be made of?"

"More vhite leadder, I dhink," she replies.

"So, it shall be." He turns back to Chloe. "Do you think you can do this for us?"

"Oh, this is so exciting. Of course. We shall begin in the morning. Fjorta and I will go to the market and visit with a tailor. Oh, and a tanner. He may know how to turn leather white."

"Iv he doesn't, I know how."

"You wore white leather in Jutland?"

"Ov course. I am dhe niece of dhe king."

Titus smiles and glances at Chloe. "I should have known."

During the following days, Chloe works in close collaboration with the local tanner and tailor who make daily trips to the *palatio* of Justus Brennius Antiochus, Praetor of the free city of Antioch.

On one of those days, as Titus is going through some of the writings on the law he has brought with him from the university, he hears a familiar voice from the other side of the gate. He rushes to it and opens it before Cornelius has a chance to.

"Stephan! My dear friend Stephen, how have you been?"

The two men, now twenty-five years old, go into a bear hug and pound each other on the back.

"Oh, and this is my wife, Arelia," Stephan says.

A freckled red-headed girl with frizzy red hair Titus estimates to be ten years younger than Stephan, steps out from behind her husband.

"Aren't you lovely," Titus says. "Both of you come sit. We have a lot of catching up to do. My wife is busy creating a wardrobe that compromises her Nordic clothes with our Roman styles. I think you will find them fascinating."

A week later, Chloe makes an announcement. "The Vestal Virgins are going to be singing at a special sacrifice for our city in a few days. I taught them all myself. It would be a perfect time for you to present your Fjorta to the city officially. The crowds will love her."

The day comes. Justus climbs on board his silver chariot and rides to the Temple of Vesta alone. There, he climbs the steps to the pinnacle of the platform where he normally holds court in order to preside over the ceremonies.

Titus and Fjorta ride in another chariot, not as elegant as the father's, but spectacular in its own right. Behind them are Chloe and husband Fulvio.

Once again, people stand on both sides of the columned Cardo Maximus as the chariots of their aristocrats roll in slow motion to the center of the city so everyone can absorb the beauty of Titus' ice queen with the white-blond hair and green eyes.

They reach the Temple of Vesta and climb the steps to the platform where three specially-chosen magistrates are seated at the table. One of the magistrates is Pollux. Pollux smiles and winks at Titus.

Titus, his bride, his aunt, and his brother-in-law stand on the platform facing the crowd on the street level below them. They smile and wave for the excited spectators.

The spectators do not smile or wave back. They do not cheer. They do not chant or sing or clap their hands in approval. The faces down on the street are blank.

Something must be done. Titus steps forward.

"Fellow Romans," he begins. Still blank faces.

"I come to you today to bring you hope," he bellows.

He jerks his body around so he is facing the audience on his left.

"Yes, I tell you, hope!"

He swings to his right and raises both arms. "Hope is

free! Hope sets the imagination on fire. Hope is unstoppable!"

He crouches, his eyes darting back and forth over the crowd below. "You cannot keep hope down. You cannot pounce on hope and expect it to cower," he bellows.

He notices a few of the spectators beginning to smile a little and follow him more closely.

Time to swing around again. Titus does so, then thrusts both arms upward simultaneously.

"Do not try to destroy hope, for it will rise up. It will rise up again," he lowers his arms and thrusts them up again, "and again," arms lowered and thrust, "and again," he bellows.

Most in the crowd are now smiling.

He faces his audience and thrusts his sword arm forward.

"We can face the enemy with hope." He thrusts his imaginary sword forward. "We can strive with hope." One more thrust forward for good measure. "We can win with hope!" he bellows.

"So, let us bear up," now stretching both arms above his head and reaching for the golden sun above. "Let us gather up." Another stretch heavenward. "My fellow Romans, let us cling to hope and rise up!"

With that, the entire crowd raises its arms in response and shouts in echoed approval.

"Hope!"

"Hope!"

"Hope!"

Titus motions for his bride to step to his side. He holds her hand and drinks in the love he feels for his city and her citizens, who now love the one he loves.

Will his father approve? Finally, approve? Will his father now love him again?

12 ~ GODDESSES

"This is one of the happiest days of my life, sweetheart," Titus tells Fjorta, sitting on a bench next to her bed.

"Vell, my *kareste,* here is your daughter."

Not admitting how unsure he is to take such a delicate and breakable creature into his arms, he overcomes his fear and takes the little one.

He looks down at her silky skin and touches her nose. She twitches it. He pulls slightly on her chin, and she puckers her lips. He leans down and kisses her on her forehead, and she opens her eyes and blinks.

"Green. Her eyes are green like yours, my love."

"Und her hair is dark like yours."

"A little bit of both of us. Our daughter."

"Vhat shall we name her?"

"Would you mind if we named her after my mother, Kharis?"

"Dhat is a beautiful name. Ov course."

The baby sniffs a couple of times, opens her eyes, and lets out a wail.

"Oh, where did that come from?" Titus says, startled.

"She is hungry. Ov course. Give her to me."

Titus hands his daughter over to her mother and stands. He turns in place in a full circle, raises his hands above his head and shouts. "I am a father, world. I am a father!"

He sits back down and watches mother and daughter bond. "I must remember to start wearing a sword by the time she reaches her tenth birthday. No young male will be allowed even to touch her. She will be too holy for them."

Fjorta laughs. "Even vhen she wails vor her dinner, she is holy?"

"Well, maybe not then. Well, sometimes."

"May I come in?" Aunt Chloe asks, peeking into their room. She does not wait for an answer but opens the door the rest of the way. "Would you like to present your daughter to Vesta? She is the goddess of hearth and home and protects our city. She will also protect your little girl."

"When could it be done?" Titus asks.

"Tomorrow, if you like."

Titus looks over at his wife. "What do you think?"

"I dhink it vould be vonderful," she tells Chloe. "Dhen ve can present her to my goddess, the vife of Odin--Vrigg." She turns to her husband. "Vould dhat be acceptable?"

"Well, what does your Frigg look like?"

"She keeps her long yellow hair in pigtails, und she vears armor und holds a sword all dhe time. I brought a small statue vith me. I alvays carry it vherever I go, so she vill protect me."

"Fine. We can do it now, or after the ceremony with Vesta."

"Oh, let us do it now. Here, hold your daughter vhile I go get Vrigg out uv my basket."

Fjorta climbs out of her bed and stands. "Vhew!" She puts a hand up to her forehead. "I'm a little dizzy."

"Maybe we should do it tomorrow," Chloe says.

"No, I'm okay. Ve shall do it now." She walks over to the basket and takes out her statue of Frigg.

"Let us put her out on your reflecting pool next to vour Augustus."

"I don't think my father would approve."

"Oh, vooey on your vadder. He'll never know."

The three walk out to the courtyard, Fjorta sets her

statue of Frigg on the ledge of the reflecting pool, kneels, then turns to Titus, still holding their daughter.

"Join me," she says.

Titus bows before Frigg. Fjorta raises her arms. "Åh, Vrigg. Vi dedikerer vores datter til dig. Beskyt hende, og hun vil leve vor dig."

She looks at Titus and smiles. "Okay. We're done. She's dedicated. I can go back to bed now."

"That's it?"

Chloe takes the baby so Titus can help his wife stand. She follows them back to their bedroom.

"Just what did you get our daughter into when you said those words," Titus says, glaring with a half-grin and single dimple.

"I said, 'Oh, Frigg. We dedicate our baby daughter to you. Protect her und she vill live vor you."

"Would three days from now be satisfactory for dedicating Kharis to Vesta?" Chloe asks.

"Will you be up to traveling by then, sweetheart?" Titus asks.

"Ov course, my *kareste,*" she replies, sliding down into bed and closing her eyes.

Three days later, Titus, his wife, and his daughter go to the city center with Chloe and Fulvio behind them in their own chariot.

When they arrive, the Vesta Virgins are lined up outside by the altar. To one side are a dozen girls wearing white togas and simple wreaths on their heads.

As they sing their sweet song of dedication, Titus hears chariot wheels. He turns and sees his father come in to view. Their eyes meet for a moment until Justus turns toward the steps to the raised platform. He climbs them only as far as the magistrate level and sits on one of the benches.

"They will be sacrificing two turtle doves for Vesta's blessing," Chloe whispers as the bell-like voices of the singing girls die away.

At the end of the sacrifice, the family is escorted to a small table where they are served pieces of the turtle dove along with bread, dates, and apricot nectar. They hear chariot wheels leaving, but do not turn around.

Another week passes. Titus hears people at their outer gate. He watches Cornelius open it. In walks everyone who has ever served as a magistrate under Justus, as well as the city questor and the all the high priests in the city.

"Welcome to my home," Justus says, walking down the steps from his hideout. "Thank you for helping us celebrate the arrival of my grandaughter."

Titus stares at his father. His father looks over at him, nods slightly, and returns to his guests.

Titus rushes up to their bedroom, followed by Chloe. "He made me promise not to tell you," she explains.

"Fjorta," Titus says, stepping to the mother who sits singing to her daughter, "people from all over the city are here to celebrate our little Kharis. Hurry. Put something special on so you greet our guests."

"You take the baby. We girls will be out in a little while," Aunt Chloe says, handing Kharis to him. "Now, shoo."

Titus returns to the courtyard and makes the rounds of the officials looking at the baby, saying something silly to get her to laugh, and complimenting her on her name. "Your mother would have been pleased," many say.

In what seems to be half an hour, Titus hears the familiar voice. "Okay, I am ready. Vould vou like to share our daughter vith me?"

Conversation becomes muted as people behold Titus' ice queen wearing a long tunic of pure white leather and matching cape of white fur.

"What, in the name of the divine Augustus, is she wearing?" the wife of one of the dignitaries says.

Justus climbs four steps leading to his *officium* and stops. "Ladies and gentlemen, may I present to you my daughter-in-law, niece and therefore somewhat heir to the throne of the king of Jutland."

All who had been watching him now look over at Fjorta. As they do, Justus walks over to the woman who had made the earlier curt remark and says, "You may bow to her."

The lady looks at her husband, he shrugs, she walks forward, and curtsies to Fjorta.

The guests are escorted into a seldom-used banquet hall along one side of the courtyard. The maids are ready and bring out dish after dish of fresh fruits, and mutton. The feast lasts the rest of the day.

As the last guest leaves and Justus is on his way up to his *officium*, Titus calls up to him.

"Thank you, Father. You have no idea what this means to me. And, Father, I do love you."

Justus pauses, nods his head slightly, and resumes his climb—slower these days—up the stairs.

Five weeks later, Titus approaches his wife sitting near the pool. He sits on his bench, watching her suckle their child.

"My mother became Jewish," he tells Fjorta. "I have been reading her Jewish *Torah*. They dedicate their babies to their God. In my mother's honor, I would like to do that. Being dedicated to one God and two goddesses surely won't hurt. What do you think?"

"Ov course," Fjorta replies. "Vhen shall ve do it?"

"Tomorrow is their Sabbath. Let's go over to their synagogue tomorrow and ask about it."

The next morning, Titus takes his wife and daughter in his chariot to the city center along Cardo Maximum. He turns left at Via Velabrus. At the end of the street near the city wall is a large synagogue.

They climb out of the chariot, and Titus hands the reins to a shabby man standing nearby. As the young family walks toward the front double doors, the Jews on their way in stop and stare.

"What's he doing here?"

"Spying on us, probably."

"Going to shut us down."

Titus approaches a man standing by the double doors. "Could you tell me where Rabbi Oeneus is?"

"I am he. May I help you?" The rabbi is not smiling.

"I am Titus, son of Kharis."

"Oh, I remember her. She converted to Judaism about...uh..."

"Fourteen years ago."

"Tragic, tragic what happened to her," the rabbi says.

"I was wondering, since she came to believe in only one God and he is Jehovah, if I could dedicate our daughter to her God."

The rabbi stares at Titus a moment, looks down at the marble flooring, out toward the street, and up to the sky.

"Of course, we don't have to if it is against your rules," Titus adds.

"We would be most happy to dedicate your daughter to Jehovah, but you would have to become a Jew first."

"Okay, I can do that. What are the requirements."

"Mostly, you have to be circumcised."

"Huh?"

"You must be circumcised. Then vow to keep all the Laws of Moses and come to the synagogue every Sabbath."

"Well, could I do the last two without the first?"

"Absolutely not."

The rabbi looks around and sees they have drawn the attention of others newly arrived.

"Come in. Come in. I will think about this situation and speak with you afterward."

Titus and Fjorta enter the synagogue and notice the men and women sit on separate sides. They divide up and accommodate the custom.

They observe reading of the *Torah* and the prophets, prayers, and hymns by a king they call David.

Afterward, Oeneus rushes to the back door and motions for Titus to follow him.

Out on the columned veranda of the synagogue, the rabbi whispers, "for a donation to our orphan fund, I can come to your house and read the words of the *Torah* blessing your daughter. But that is all I can do until you are circumcised."

By now, Fjorta has joined them. Titus wishes the rabbi good day and takes his wife to the chariot.

Titus is never circumcised. But for a donation of thirty silver coins to the synagogue's orphan fund, Rabbi Oeneus goes to his house and reads a blessing from the *Torah* for the granddaughter of their proselyted former member, Kharis.

Every Thorsday afternoon—which Fjorta duly explains

was named after her Thor—Titus goes to the pottery booth in the South Market and visits with his childhood friend, Stephan.

Near the end of the year, when Titus arrives at the booth, he sees Stephan packing his pottery in baskets.

"What are you doing, ole friend?" he asks.

"Getting ready to move."

"Oh, to the West Gate Market? It is very prestigious at that forum. You will probably be able to demand higher prices there."

"No, to Rome."

Titus stares at Stephan. Stephan stops packing, and his eyes lock with Titus'. "I have been wanting to tell you, but did not know how."

Titus looks at the ground, over at a booth down the lane, up at the sky, and back at Stephan. "Well, I did leave you for four years to go to the university in Pergamum. I guess this is payback."

Stephan smiles. "Whatever you say, old friend. In reality, I have been saving my money these past six years since we graduated from the gymnasium academy. I now have enough to pay a famous philosopher to tutor me."

"Who?"

"Well, since Rome got rid of its spoiled brat Gaius Caligula, Claudius is now Caesar, and everyone is looking forward to a good era under his rule.

"But who will you be studying under?"

"Gaius Musonius Rufus. He is close to our age but way smarter than us."

"Someone out there is smarter than you?" Titus responds.

"Yes. And he is all I can afford and still pay for an *insulae* for us to live in. This man is going to be famous someday. I am sure of it."

"Stephan, we shall see each other again someday. The Fates have always brought us together."

"Yes, they have indeed."

Two more years pass. Little Kharis is now three years old.

Titus delights in sitting on his bench in the courtyard and watching her romp around the reflecting pool.

If only my mother could be here to enjoy her. Oh, Mother, can you ever forgive me? I didn't mean to kill you. I didn't mean to. I didn't know.

"Papa, guess what?" a squeaky voice says.

Titus smiles at his bubbly daughter. "What, my precious one?"

"I'm old enough to go to school."

"Ha. You're old enough?"

"Mudder says I am. I get to go to the Temple of Vesta and will have twelve Vesta Virgins watching me. Papa, what's a virgin?"

Titus set her on his knee. The Vesta Virgins serve a great goddess who watches over little children. And I believe there will be more than you at the temple. All little ones go there for three years before entering a real school."

Kharis jumps down and puts her hands on her hips. "It is a real school. Mudder said so. Would you like to hear my song, Papa?"

Titus slaps his knee. "I definitely would."

Sometimes when she sings in her high-pitched lyrical voice, Justus comes down the stairs partway and listens to her. Titus notices but keeps the uneasy pact that is between them. At the end of her performance, Titus will look up at his father, his father will nod slightly, then return to his *officium.*

After that, each morning, Titus mounts his black Arabian, Cornelius hands his daughter up to him, and he takes her to the city center where she is watched for six hours by the Vestal Virgins and their assistants. And each afternoon, he is there waiting for her when it is time to go home.

Every evening, the family gathers around the table on their respective couches for an evening meal—Titus and his wife and Chloe and her husband. Kharis is provided a miniature couch but does not stay it on very long at a time.

"Chuhc, chuhc," Kharis coughs.

Fjorta holds out her arms to her daughter. "Come to Mudder, sweetie," she says.

Kharis shuffles to her mother, and Fjorta feels the child's forehead. "You are a little hot," she says. "Come up here on mudder's couch."

Kharis climbs onto the couch and lays her head against Fjorta's leaning arm.

"Chuhc, chuhc," she coughs again.

"Here. Dake a drink ov dhis nectar," Fjorta says, holding goblet up to her daughter's lips.

Kharis takes a sip. "Chuhc, chuhc, chuhc."

Fjorta sits up and lays her daughter's head onto her shoulder. She stands and walks around the courtyard humming.

Kharis continues to cough. "Chuhc, chuhc, chuhc."

Titus stands. "Cornelius," he says to the household steward who is never far away. "Do you know where our doctor is?"

"Probably in his room. I will fetch him for you."

"Quickly."

Shortly, the family doctor appears. He takes Kharis in his arms. "Hold out your tongue to me. That's it. That is very good." He pokes her in the tummy and she giggles. And she coughs again.

"Chuhc, chuhc, chuhc."

He hands the girl back to her mother. Titus takes him aside.

"You look worried, doctor. What's wrong? It's just a simple cold, isn't it?"

"Has our city had any children from other cities move here and enroll at the temple?"

"Yes. One family from Colossae. Why?"

"I think they have brought with them something terrible."

"What?"

"Plague."

13 ~ PLAGUE

"You've got to keep your child away from that temple. If you do not, she will—how can I say this? She will die."

Titus stares at the doctor. "No, you're wrong."

"I wish I were."

"How do you know?"

"Colossae has had its gates closed for a month and is not letting anyone in or out. They use ropes to let their dead down the outside of their walls in a basket filled with kindling, then throw torches down to offer them as sacrifices to the gods."

"Which gods?"

"Their priests and augurs do not know. They do not have the luxury of sending an augur or flamin to Delphi to find out what Apollo knows."

Titus stares at the old doctor who has been with the family since he was a teenager.

"No, you're mistaken."

"Chuhc, chuhc, chuhc."

He turns and rushes over to his wife. He takes their daughter out of her arms, cradles her, and holds her against his chest. Tears rush to his eyes. He stands and place and slowly turns in a circle. He raises his eyes heavenward.

"Which one of you is doing this to us?" he shouts. "Stay

away. Stay away from my family. Do not hurt us. Do not hurt...."

Fjorta takes the child back, and Titus stares at his wife, his face now pale, his eyes overflowing with premature grief.

"No. No. The gods can't do that to us." He turns to the doctor. "You're wrong. You're always wrong. You have always been wrong. You will be wrong this time too."

Lydia walks over to the couple. "Mistress, would you like me to put the child in her bed just for a little while?"

"Yes, a little vhile," Fjorta replies, still uncertain what is going on, and dreading to know.

"I will put together the strongest elixir I know for cough and fever," the doctor tells them. "Together, we will defy the gods, sir."

"Yes, defy the gods," Titus replies. "That's what we shall do. Hope. Hope! Never keep down hope. Hope rises and will turn into victory."

"I will need the use of your chariot, sir," the doctor tells Titus, "to get to my herb garden."

"Yes, yes," Titus replies. "Out the South Gate. "Yes, go as fast as you can."

Within an hour, the doctor is back and handing a warm tea to Fjorta in the child's bedroom. "This is Eucalyptus. I purchase my starter plants from a merchant from China. They are good quality. I mixed in some mint also. It should stop her cough."

Fjorta lifts the child's head, half-asleep except for her growing cough, and burning with fever.

"Here, dake dhis, my little one."

She holds the warm tea up to Kharis' little lips.

"Dake dhis. You von't cough so much. Dhat's right. A liddle more now. Just a liddle more."

"I will be back shortly," the doctor says. "I will make some borage tea for her. It will help take some of the poisonous heat out of her body."

Titus stands as the doctor leaves the sick room. "I am sorry I lost my temper with you, doctor. It's just that..." Titus' tears will not allow him to continue.

The doctor lays a hand on the younger man's shoulder.

"I understand. We will get control of this. But, be sure to pray to the gods also."

"Which ones? There are so many. I just don't know which ones."

The parents sit up through the night with their little Kharis. Dawn comes. Her cough is deeper.

"If I could use my svord to chop avay dhe sickness, I vould," Fjorta says. "I do not know how to vight somedhing dhat is invisible."

"Apollo is supposed to be a healer," Titus announces. "We will take her over to the Temple of Apollo. Surely he will heal our baby girl."

"Brutus!" he calls out. "Someone get Brutus. Tell him to get my chariot ready. Quickly."

Titus picks up his daughter along with the blankets that have been around her. Fjorta reaches over and tucks them between her daughter and Titus' big hands so they do not fall off.

He paces. "Where is my chariot? Where is my chariot?"

Cornelius opens the gates to the outside. Titus hands Kharis to his wife, and they board the chariot. He secures the back guard gate and tells Fjorta to sit on the floor. She settles down, and he snaps the reins over his horse. "Yahhh. Yahhh."

The horse breaks out into a gallop. All along the Vici Aegeus to the columned Cardo Maximus, people jump out of the way.

"Yahhh. Yahhh."

They arrive at the temple, and Titus helps his wife stand. He unlocks the guard gate and walks as fast as he and Fjorta can with their long legs up the front walkway to the grand temple. He charges in.

"Help us! Help us, someone."

The high priest rushes toward them. "You cannot be in here. It is only allowed for the priests."

"I must. For my daughter. She must receive Apollo's healing. Just let me lay her at his feet. Please. I must do this."

"I vill ask Odin to bring good luck to you und not curse you," Fjorta says.

Seeing the distress on the faces of the parents, and

knowing he is dealing with the praetor and former Flamen of Apollo, he relents.

Another day. Another long, long night.

Titus paces. Fjorta kneels, raising her hands high, then touching the marble floor with her head. Little Kharis' cough deepens and she begins to struggle for breath.

"Åh stor Odin, helbrede vores datter. Åh stor Odin, helbrede vores datter. Oh, great Odin, heal our daughter."

Dawn.

"This is not working. Odin has no powers. Apollo has no powers."

"Vhat shall ve do?" Fjorta asks.

"We shall go to Pergamum to the Temple of Asclepius. He is the greatest god of healing. He knows things even Apollo, his father, does not. He has powers even Apollo does not. Hurry."

"Titus picks up his daughter, now pale, with breathing that is loud and insufficient.

"Dhat is a long vay," Fjorta objects, following her husband and daughter out of the temple.

"It is a little over one hundred *milles*. There are many posts along the way. I will buy a new horse every forty *milles*. If we start now, maybe we can be there by dawn tomorrow."

"Travel all day und all night?"

"All day and all night."

"We vill need vood," she says.

"No time."

They reach the chariot, and Fjorta settles on the floor with their daughter struggling to live.

Titus snaps the whip above his steed's head, and it takes off in a gallop. Titus directs it west to the theater, around it, past the agora, and through the Western Gate.

Out on the highway, he snaps the whip again, and his horse stretches its legs longer. "Yahhh. Yahhh."

When the sun is low in the sky, Titus stops at a traveler's station along the way. He pulls out a bag of silver coins he had grabbed up just before leaving home.

"How much for your fastest horse?" he asks the government innkeeper.

"If you're going to treat it like you have this one," he says, eyeing Titus' black Arabian, we have no horses for you. You could kill the next one."

"Please, sir. My daughter. She is... She is..." Dare he say it? Dare he say the word? "She will be gone forever if we do not get her to the Temple of Asclepius in Pergamum. I will give you thirty pieces of silver for your best horse."

"I just can't."

"Forty pieces. Fifty. Name your price. I will pay whatever it takes to save my daughter."

"Oh, all right," the government innkeeper. "Give me fifty pieces of silver. But I'm warning you. You had better not kill it."

"Thank you, sir."

Moments later, when the fresh horse is harnessed to the chariot, Titus snaps his whip in the air, and the horse breaks into a gallop.

"Yahhh. Yahhh."

On they go through the valleys between the mountains. Along the rivers. Keep going. Keep going.

Darkness overtakes them.

I hope this horse is familiar with the terrain. We are traveling blind.

Titus eases up with the whip and the reins and trusts the horse to know its way. He thinks he hears his daughter's wheezing grow stronger.

Dawn. Time to stop and arrange for a new horse. As soon as Titus spots the next government stopping point, he directs his horse and chariot to its front gate. He rushes in.

His hair is down in his face. Dark shadows make his bloodshot eyes look like those of an undead man. His toga is on the floor of the chariot to help keep his wife and baby warm. With only a tunic on now, his arms are scratched from overhanging trees along the road.

"I need a new horse," he growls. "How much?"

"Our horses are not for rent, sir."

"Not to rent. I want to buy one."

"They are not for sale either. By the looks of the horse you brought in here, you are the last person I would want to sell my horse to, even if it were for sale."

"Sir, my baby daughter is in the bottom of the chariot with my wife. We are trying to save my daughter's life. She is so weak and helpless. Please, sir."

Titus' eyes fill with tears. The government innkeeper walks out and looks in the chariot. Fjorta raises her head, looks at the innkeeper through swelled eyes.

"Fifty pieces of silver I will give you for your best horse."

The innkeeper stares at Titus.

"Sixty pieces of silver," Titus says. "One hundred. Man! Stop thinking about it and give me your best horse. I've got to get my daughter to the temple before... before...."

"All right. For one hundred pieces of silver, I will sell you my best horse."

Titus counts out the money, and a servant brings out the coveted horse. The exhausted horse is unhitched, takes three steps, and crumples to the ground.

Titus says nothing. The innkeeper says nothing. The servant hitches the fresh horse to the chariot. He directs it to turn northwest and snaps his whip over the horse's head.

"Yahhh. Yahhh."

The horse stretches its legs and works its way closer to the Aegean Sea.

Titus begins to sob. "Oh, gods, whoever you are, help my little girl. I cannot lose her."

By mid-afternoon, the scenery begins to look familiar. Titus lets his mind drift to the day he met his sweetheart and the following day when he decided he loved her. He thinks back on her sea captain father, and her wedding dress and the day little Kharis was born.

At last, he sees the magnificent Acropolis on top of the mountain. The Acropolis with its gargantuan temple to Zeus-Jupiter, the other temple to Athena with its magnificent library, the palaces above them.

Instead of heading straight up the mountain, he veers his struggling horse to the left. He reins in the exhausted horse, runs with his long legs, and pounds on the front gate.

"Let us in. Let us in. My daughter. She is... She is..."

He hears scraping as the bar is moved out of the way

and rattling of hinges. One of the priests opens the gate for him.

By this time, Fjorta has arrived at the gate with Kharis in her arms.

A priestess comes and takes the child.

"What is wrong?" they both ask in unison.

Unsure whether they will take a child with the plague, Titus replies, "Her breathing. At first, she coughed, but now she just cannot breathe."

The two officials rush the child to a nearby room and call out for others to come with water, medicinal teas, and prayers.

"Where is Asclepius?" Titus asks.

"Of course. I shall take you to him," the priest says. They rush through the large courtyard doubling as a sanctuary and arrive at the magnificent statue of the greatest healing god known to humankind.

Marble Asclepius sits high on his throne, holding his staff with a great snake curled around it. His toga has fallen to his waist as though the business of healing takes far more precedence than proper codes of dress.

Titus throws himself onto the floor and kneels before the great one.

"Oh, healer. I lift up my little one to you. We have not yet dedicated her to you, but as soon as you heal her, we will. We will dedicate the rest of her life to you."

He stretches out his arms and torso and reclines completely on the marble floor of the great healer.

"Hear me, oh, Asclepius. Hear me. Hear me. Hear…"

He feels a hand on him. Fjorta lays her head on his back. They remain there prostrate before Asclepius, the mighty healer god, for a long time.

Long shadows form. Titus raises his head. Fjorta sits up. He turns. He looks into her eyes, drowning in tears that flow like an unending wellspring.

At last, he speaks. It is in a whisper.

"She is gone, isn't she?"

Fjorta slides her arms around his neck and buries her face in his chest. Together, they fall once again to the floor, arm in arm, trying to comfort that which cannot be comforted.

They remain there before the useless god the rest of the night.

When daylight begins to break through, Titus whispers. "We need to clean her up and take her home."

"Yes, ve need to do dhat," Fjorta groans.

They help each other stand and lean on each other as they walk back to the room where they had laid her.

The priestesses have washed her and placed a white tunic on her. Her fuzzy red hair is combed, and her hands are crossed on her little chest.

The parents cry anew. This time soft weeping. Their tears fall onto the face of their Kharis.

"Your horse is rested, but I do not think he can make the trip back. His lungs are still exhausted."

"That is fine," Titus whispers. "Here. Take my bag. Take the rest of the silver in it. Give me one of your horses, and we will be gone."

"We have already done that. You need not pay us. You have suffered enough."

"No! I have got to pay you. I must pay you."

Startled at Titus' sudden outburst, the priest takes the money and leads them out to the chariot. It is bent and scratched.

"We replaced one of the wheels."

"Thank you," Titus groans.

Mother and father enter the chariot. Fjorta chooses to sit on one of the side seats, holding their lifeless daughter in her lap.

Titus clicks his tongue, and the horse ambles forward. Forward toward the east where once his family laughed and was happy.

It takes five days. Each night they pull into a government-owned inn along the highway. Titus tells them who his father is, and they allow him to stay on credit.

At last, they see Antioch before them. They are grateful for the cool nights and days. But when they draw closer to the city, they know they must make one more stop.

Titus leads the tired horse to the cemetery where he and

his father had buried little Kharis' grandmother when he had been eleven years old.

He sees an old shovel sticking up from a fresh grave. In a daze, Titus digs. In a daze, Fjorta watches and waits.

It is time. Together, mother and father take their fuzzy red-headed daughter with green eyes and a squeaky voice to her final resting place. They kneel and place their little Kharis next to her grandmother.

He covers her up with the dirt while Fjorta looks around for stones that have worked their way up during the last rain. Together, they place the stones over the little mound.

"I do not know who to pray to, Fjorta. I do not know."

They return to their chariot and guide it slowly into the city of Antioch.

People stop along the way when they see the couple with hair down in their face, black circles under sunken eyes. Scratches on their arms and dirt on their torn clothes. No one cheers. Everyone knows.

They arrive back at the family *palatio*, sit at the gate without knocking, and wait for someone to discover them. Brutus does and knocks on the gate for them. When Cornelius unlocks the gate, he calls for Lydia.

Mother and father stand, lean on the servants and shuffle into the family courtyard.

Chloe sees them and screams, "Justus. Justus. Come quickly."

Justus runs down the stairs and rushes toward his son and daughter-in-law. The four kneel, and cling to one another, not speaking, not even moaning—in an existence that is not an existence. They remain together in their silence for a long time.

When the shadows of the evening overtake them, Cornelius and Lydia approach them.

"Come. You need to go to your rooms. You may not sleep, but you need your beds. Come."

The four rise and wander to where their servants have instructed. In the midst of their emptiness, they wonder. Titus, most of all, wonders. Now thirty years old, he questions all the more. *Where were all the gods?*

14 ~ THE APOSTLE PAUL

*T*hree years have passed. Each year on little Kharis' birthday, Titus tells whoever is near him, "She would have been four this year;" "She would have been five this year;" "She would have been six this year."

During the first of those empty years, Titus decides to return to what he had intended to do after graduating from the university at Pergamum. He tells his friends he will become a lawyer, an arbitrator, for anyone who needs him.

It fills the time and helps heals the wounds. He defends thieves in the marketplace, thieves of temple property, thieves of water during drought, children whose fathers have hit them too much, wives whose husbands have beat on them, slaves whose masters have whipped them into submission.

There is another earthquake. The edge of it hit Antioch, just enough to crack the statue to Augustus Caesar in the reflecting pool of the family courtyard. Justus has it hauled away.

"I wonder where our little Kharis went after she left us?"

"I don't know," Fjorta says. "I try not to dhink about it."

"Why?"

"Because dhere are two places ve who live around the Nordh Sea believe souls go afder dhey die: Valhalla or Fólkvangr. Bodh are vor warriors—men or vomen—who die gallant deaths, mostly in wars."

She is silent.

"Dhere is no place vor little girls. Dhere is no place vor people who are just good, and dhat's all. Vhat happens to us?"

"Well, our Roman beliefs are about as complicated as yours are simple," Titus replies. "We are taught the god Hermes comes to get our souls when we die. He leaves our soul at the River Styx that divides the land of the living from the land of the dead.

"If we have gold on us—hopefully placed under our tongue before we are buried—a ferry takes us across the river. There we are judged by three gods—a son of Jupiter, a wise king of Crete, and another son of Jupiter, who was an earlier king of Crete.

"And the kings became gods," Fjorta says," trying to understand.

"Something like that. Anyway, we are sent to one of three places upon being judged. The best place is happy, blissful fields of flowers reserved for heroes and those who turned into gods. The next one, a deep dark dungeon reserved for bad people. The third place is kind of misty and is for ordinary people whose good deeds equaled their bad deeds."

"I remember vhen I vas in China, Fjorta says, "they told us dhat dead people just go to another physical world and continue dheir lives dhere."

"I read that the people of India believe a person's soul is put into another body, and he has to start over again living on earth—as a human or animal or even a rock," Titus says. "He has to keep living life all over again until he is perfect. Then he can be absorbed into the universe and become kind of a god with no personality."

"What are you two talking about?" Chloe asks, bringing them some fresh grapes she had just picked up at the market that morning.

"Do you have any idea where little Kharis went after she died, Aunt Chloe?" Titus asks.

"I have no answer to that. One religion says one thing, another religion says another. Well, the Jews believe your mother went to heaven, a place where the throne of the one God is, and she gets to talk to him anytime she wants because he loves her. When you're finished with those grapes, I have raisin cakes for you."

"Wait," Titus says. "A God that loves people? I have never heard of such. The gods are always so busy with their own problems, they don't have much time for us. We have to do a lot of sacrificing to get their attention."

"I'm just telling you what Fulvio said to me."

"When did he begin associating with Jews? The Jews refuse to associate with us."

"He created a floor for them in their synagogue. They do not believe in drawing or carving images of people or animals, so they had to create a mosaic with words on it."

"Magic words?" Fjorta asks.

"Words of a great king who was supposed to become the ancestor of the king of the world."

"What a mighty king," Titus says. "What were the words?"

PSALM 42:1

"I shall have to look it up in my mother's *Torah*. Well, if it isn't there, she also bought songs and warnings of the prophets."

A knock on their gate. Cornelius shuffles over to it, never complaining of the pain in his knee, and answers it.

"Sir, is Titus the lawyer home?"

Titus steps forward. "Yes, I am an arbitrator. Are you in need of one?"

"Oh, sir. I need your help. They are going to arrest me for theft. But I had to. Oh, sir, help me."

Titus leads the young man to an *officium* he has set up in a large former storeroom on the first floor. Fulvio has created a mosaic on the floor that looks like a meadow, and on one wall that looks like the sky.

A writing table is in the middle with two marble benches before it. Behind his writing-table are baskets—one with blank scrolls in it, another with the scrolls of law books by Cicero and Plato, another with miscellaneous writings of Socrates, Aristotle, and others. A final basket holds scrolls with the laws of the Jews, which they call the *Torah*.

Titus steps behind his writing-table and seats himself, the stranger following his example.

"Now, what is your name?"

"My name is Nestor."

"Nestor, what?"

"That's all. Just Nestor."

"And you say you were accused of stealing. Who did you allegedly steal from?"

"Ophelos Orestes."

"The banker?"

"Yes."

"Well, did you steal from him?"

"Yes."

"Then, if you admit you stole from him, why are you here? I cannot do anything for you."

"Oh, sir. The highwaymen. They made me. I was up in the mountains of Phrygia, where the highwaymen are so bad. I had to cross them to the seacoast, and on my way home is when they kidnapped me."

"That's terrible. How did you break loose?"

"They threatened to beat me to death if I did not get their stolen money back."

"Money Ophelos Orestes stole from them?"

"Yes, sir."

"Did he steal from them?"

"I don't know. All I know is the highwaymen had me tied up to a stake and were debating whether to burn me alive or beat me to death."

"Has a trial date been set?"

"Not yet. We have not decided on judges yet."

"Of course. Both of you are required by law to agree on whoever judges you."

"Every time I agree on a judge, he disagrees. Then he selects someone, and I have no idea who he is."

"Well, I believe I can remedy that."

"Now, do you have any witnesses to your ideal in the mountains south of here?"

"When they let me loose, I escaped to the highway. I

hadn't eaten in a long time—they never fed me—so I was weak, and my clothes were torn and dirty. Some people came by and helped me get back to Antioch."

"How kind of them."

"They were on their way here anyway. They live over on Via Venerius."

"In the Jewish part of town?"

"Yes, they were Jews. They said they weren't supposed to associate with Gentiles—whatever a Gentile is—but God wanted them to be kind to everyone in distress."

"Their names?"

"Uh, Cephas. Cephas Hillel. And he had a wife. Sarah was her name. Cephas and Sarah."

"I believe that is all I need from you, Nestor."

"Uh, I have some excellent pottery I can give you in payment."

Titus' curiosity is piqued. "Who made it?"

"Stephan, also of Antioch."

"How many pieces do you have?"

"Twelve."

"Fine, I will take them all and consider myself paid."

Titus stands. "Do not worry about judge selection. I will take care of that for you. I know them all, and I believe I can handle that ole banker."

"Thank you, sir."

Soon after Nestor leaves, Titus puts on his toga and leaves also. It is a good day for walking. He heads toward the city center and the small stone building of Ophelos Orestes, the banker.

"Well, what brings you into the financial center of Antioch?" Ophelos asks, rising from his writing desk.

"A small matter of helping a friend of mine select judges you both agree on."

"Oh, him. I'm just giving him a hard time because he stole from me."

"How much?"

"I didn't actually count it, but believe it was around thirty pieces of silver."

"Okay. Here is a list of men who usually volunteer to be

judges. Pick three."

Ophelos looks over the list Titus has made on a small scroll."

"That one, that one, and that one."

"Now, Ophelos, you know you cannot choose your relatives."

"That boy won't know the difference."

"I do. Now I choose this one, this one, and this one."

"I don't know…"

"Then, it is settled. I will submit the names to my father's deputy, and he will give us a court date."

"Are you defending that boy? This is going to be fun."

The day arrives. The usual number of spectators stand around on the street, ready to enjoy the spectacle of a rich man suing a poor man for theft.

Titus and Nestor arrive first and take their place on the defendants' bench. The three judges arrive next. Ophelos arrives next. Finally, Justus Brennius Antiochus arrives and takes his seat at the pinnacle of the outdoor courtroom.

Titus quickly takes everyone through the proceedings. Nestor confesses he took the money. Titus calls Cephas, who testifies he and his wife rescued Nestor from known highwaymen on that road through Phrygia. His wife, Sarah, testifies the same.

"Now then, judges and praetor of our fine city of Antioch," Titus declares, "you must declare this young man not guilty. Why? Because of Cicero's law written in his *Moral Goodness* wherein he stated that a vow made to anyone, including an enemy, must be kept. If it is not, the person who betrays the vow is to be punished by his own citizens.

Banker Ophelos glares at Titus. Titus smiles at the judges. They take out small scrolls, write on them, and hand them to the deputy. The deputy shows them to the praetor, and the praetor sends them back to the judges to be sealed.

One of the Vesta Virgins walks up the steps to the platform, takes the three decisions, and lays them on the ledge of their altar to Vesta. Prayers are offered up along with a slaughtered calf. That done, the city auger looks at the ashes and determines the final decision of Vesta. He walks up to the platform and whispers to the deputy. The deputy climbs the steps to the pinnacle and whispers to the praetor. Justus Brennius Antiochus stands and bellows out, "Not guilty."

Ophelos glares at Titus. "I will get you for this."

Titus walks down to the street level and hears his name called. It is Cephas Hillel.

"Sir. Sir. Your mother was Kharis, wasn't she?"

Titus turns. "Yes, she was. She became a Jew not long before she, before she, well left us."

"We had an interesting man speak in our synagogue last week. His name is Paul, and he is a very educated man from Tarsus, home of a great library."

"Yes, I have heard the reputation of the city," Titus replies.

"He told us about a man who claims to be the predicted one we Jews have looked for over the centuries—the one who is supposed to be king of the world, not just of the Jews."

"How interesting."

"I think you would like to hear him. Our Rabbi Oeneus invited him to come back and speak this Sabbath again.

"I don't know," Titus replies. "I have believed in all the gods, and none of them seem to care. Why would I want to learn about another one?"

"Because our God is one, and he predicted he would send his Son to rule the world someday. Paul claims this Jesus the Christ proved he was the Son of God by letting people put him to death, then coming back to life three days later."

Thoughts of Titus' mother and daughter rush to his mind. "No, that is not possible."

"This man, Paul, said he saw the man before he died, saw him die, then saw him after he came back to life. You must come hear him."

"I will think about it."

Titus does not go directly home. He goes over to the Sanctuary of Men-Askenos, where he and his friends had hidden to follow the ghost of Augustus Caesar so long ago. He sits on one of the marble benches scattered around the grass and flowers.

As the sun touches the horizon, he decides to hurry back home before the women in his household begin to worry.

That night after eating, Titus goes up on the roof. Fjorta, Chloe, and Fulvio follow him.

"You have something on your mind, Aunt Chloe says. "We all know it. So, you may as well come out with it."

Do I dare try to believe in another god? They have all failed me. They have failed us all. I don't know if gods even exist anymore."

He stands and walks to the other side of the roof. He looks down on the dark streets below and turns toward his loved ones.

"Most philosophers believe there are gods. They base it on the fact that the heavens are always moving in a predictable direction, always returning where they started, but there is something that makes them move. That something is the first cause which most philosophers call some kind of god, a creator god.

The other three have learned not to interrupt Titus when he is contemplative like this. His mind goes far too deep for them.

"Plato claimed that this world we live in is not reality; that reality comes in the next world after we die. Our world will be destroyed someday, and the next world cannot be destroyed because it is eternal."

Titus sits back on his bench.

"Aristotle claimed that first cause is mind. This mind is so pure, it cannot think on anything but itself. Therefore, his god created the world, then left us on our own because we became evil. If he thought about us, he—being mind—would then become evil and go out of existence."

He takes a drink of new wine served by Lydia.

"Then there is the afterlife. Socrates agreed with Plato that the only reality is after we die here and that only a fool wants to stay here when actual life begins on the other side."

He stands and faces the other three. "How can anyone know? They are all theories and unprovable. So why would I want to go hear that Paul talk about yet another god?"

"You vill go, Titus, because your *moderr* believed in

dheir God. You vant to learn more about dheir God who loves us like children."

Titus sits back next to his wife and puts his arm around her. "And that is one of the things I love about you—besides your white-blond hair, which is as beautiful as the day I met you. I love you because you listen to me talk, talk, talk, and in one sentence, help me understand what I just said."

The next day is the Jewish Sabbath. When Titus walks to the gate, he hears footsteps behind him.

"You didn't dhink you vere going to go hear him vithout us, did you?"

The day is warm and clear and fresh. The four walk toward the synagogue.

Upon their arrival, they see the inside is full. All the windows have been opened so latecomers can stand around outside and hear this stranger with news about a king of the world, Son of God.

Titus and the others hear voices inside the building and become quiet. Someone reads from the *Torah*—the Laws of Moses. Someone else reads from their prophets—something about the deliverer of the world having his hands pierced. Finally, the guest speaker is heard.

"Brothers," he bellows. "You no longer have to keep the Laws of Moses. There were six hundred of them, and they were impossible for us to keep. All they accomplished was to show us how imperfect we are."

You mean I have been learning all those laws for nothing? Titus thinks to himself.

"Jesus, the Son of God, was perfect for us—something impossible for us to be. Not only that, but he lived every prediction made about him through our prophets hundreds of years ago. Even his being pierced was fulfilled. He was pierced on a cross; he did not die the usual Jewish way of being stoned. He was pierced."

They put the Son of God through a crucifixion? Barbarians.

But he did not stay dead. God brought him back to life— yet another thing impossible for us to do. He promised that, if we believe Jesus really was the Son of God, he will bring us back to life when we die, and we will live with him forever in his heaven where the sun never goes down, and there are no more tears. Come, everyone. Become Christians and live forever in the eternal love of God."

"We don't believe all that, Paul," someone inside the synagogue calls out. "Prove it. You can't do it, can you?"

"I see you have a hand missing, sir," Paul bellows, still aware of the listeners outside. "Come up here."

The skeptic rises and walks to the front. "What are you going to do? Make it grow back?" he says, chuckling to the audience.

"By the power of Jesus the Christ, your hand has just grown back," Paul declares.

"Huh?"

The man looks down at his stub. It is gone. Growing out from it is his hand. The man stares at it. He runs down the aisle and out into the street. "He made my hand grow back, everyone. Look. My hand is back!"

"I know that man," Titus says to his family. "His hand has been missing as long as I can remember."

Shouting is heard inside the synagogue. It is Rabbi Oeneus.

"I must interrupt. I must warn everyone. Brothers, be careful. We trusted this man, Paul, to speak to you, but he has introduced a strange sect that is against the Law of Moses. This is blasphemy, Brothers. Blasphemy!"

"Can we sit any longer and listen to this?" someone in the audience shouts.

"Our elders are against this new sect. We must obey our elders," another shouts.

"Stop them!"

"They're trying to destroy us!"

Titus and the others hear Paul's voice again. "Do not reject Jesus. He loves you!"

A Son of God that loves people?

The crowd standing outside hears feet shuffling and stomping, people apparently running into the pews or falling on them or throwing them. They look at each other.

Another voice close to the door is heard over the

shouting, a deep bass one. "You have proven yourself unworthy," the voice declares. "We turn now to the non-Jews. It is they who shall be rewarded in heaven."

"Yes!" Titus shouts.

Two strange men rush out of the synagogue. By the way, everyone is chasing them, Titus assumes they are Paul and a companion. He rushes over to them.

"I am Titus. Follow me."

15 ~ A NEW REALITY

Paul and Barnabas follow Titus and his family down the street and through the city. Behind them is a crowd of Gentiles. They arrive at Titus' stately home. "My father stays isolated. He won't mind you all being here."

People file in, all welcomed by Titus, Fjorta, Aunt Chloe, Uncle Fulvio.

For the first time, Titus realizes what Paul looks like—nothing unusual except that he seems to be very muscular. His companion is tall like Titus but bulkier.

"My name is Titus," he says, reintroducing himself.

"My name is Paulus, though everyone calls me Paul. This is my companion, Big Barnabas."

"I am honored to meet you, Titus," Barnabas says in his deep bass voice.

"Come sit on these benches," Titus says. "Tell us more about—what do your call yourselves? Christians."

Paul spends the next two hours answering their questions.

"What about Aristotle saying God is just a first cause mind and can only think about itself," Titus asks.

"Aristotle's God is selfish and self-absorbed. Besides, why would Aristotle's great mind create a universe if all he can think about is himself?"

"What about Plato's god, which he also called the first

cause that guides the movement of the stars, which are all angels?" Quintus, a boyhood friend of Titus, asks.

"Plato's god has no love. His god is logic, and that is all."

Aunt Chloe interrupts with a tray of goblets filled with apricot nectar.

"What about Homer and all his gods?" she asks while passing around the goblets. "They don't have time for us because they have so many problems of their own."

"Homer's gods are just overgrown humans. Just because they are bigger than us, it doesn't make them gods."

"What about Augustus and all the other heroes of war?" Uncle Fulvio asks.

"Just because someone says they are gods, it does not make it so."

"The Roman Senate must approve all new gods. Have the Christian God and his Son been approved by the Senate?" Urias asks.

"Oh, you're the one the only true God gave his hand back to," Paul says, recognizing the man with a broad grin.

"God needs no approval by a little child who he made."

"How do we know the Christian God loves us?" Fjorta asks.

"You saw the miracle. God does not perform miracles of destruction like storms and earthquakes. He loves us like a father loves his children. He is a gentle God."

"And you notice we're speaking Latin," Barnabas says, seeing Paul is beginning to grow tired and taking over the conversation. "Nobody in the empire speaks Latin except government officials and the military. But God gave us the gift of tongues, meaning we can talk in any language on earth, even though we did not take the time to learn it."

"Say somedhing in my language," Fjorta challenges.

"Gud velsigne og bevare dig," Barnabas replies.

"My vadder took his ship to China once," she says. "Let's see iv you can say somedhing in their language."

"Shàngdì bǎoyòu nǐ, bǎochí nǐ," Barnabas replies.

"What about my language?" Cornelius asks, hoping his master does not mind his stopping work to hear these men with their amazing story.

"Dio vi benedica e ti protegga."

"What did he say?" Chloe asks.

"He said God bless und keep you in my language," Fjorta announces.

"He said the same thing in my mother tongue," Cornelius replies.

Everyone in the group looks at each other and grins.

Nestor stands and paces a moment. They wait for him. He turns back around. "What will happen to us when the Senate finds out we are refusing to worship Augustus Caesar and are worshipping an unknown, unapproved God instead? It is dangerous not to worship whoever the Senate tells us to worship."

"God will protect you. But sometimes he will let you be killed.   Death is just the door to the greatest existence possible—the very throne room of God himself."

"No.   No," Achima objects. "My Eunatus was falsely accused of theft once. How could I go through that again? Or worse?"

Her husband reaches over and takes her hand. "We will be strong as long as we can," he tells her.

"True, people will make up things about you," Paul says, having recovered a little strength. "If they attack you, it will only be because they are afraid of you. People don't attack children. They attack giants."

"Well, how are we supposed to act?" Cephas Hillel, who Titus had defended to the banker, asks.

"Jesus said for us to be as wise as snakes and harmless as doves. You will try to be like Jesus, who went around helping the poor and sick and teaching people how to get along."

"What about worship? Do we sacrifice anything? If so, where is his altar? And who will be our priest?" It's Decimus, the baker.

"As Christians, every one of you will be priests. You will offer your bodies to God every day for his use."

"No blood sacrifices?" Brutus, the stable hand, asks.

"The blood sacrifice has already been made."

"The sacrifice? Just one sacrifice? That's it?" Hector, the

weaver, asks.

"God loved humans so much that he gave his only begotten Son to die in our place. When we sin, we belong to Satan. But Jesus set us free by paying the ransom for us. His blood bought our freedom from Satan."

"So, we do not worship?" Marcus, Titus' boyhood friend, asks.

"Of course, you do. You meet every Solday—the day Jesus came back to life—to remember his death, burial, and resurrection. You sip a little red wine representing his blood and take a bite of unleavened bread representing his body killed on the cross down in Jerusalem. And of course, you pray and sing hymns, but you can do those things any day of the week."

"Once a week?" Lucius, another of Titus' boyhood friends, asks. "Not once a month or annually?"

"Once a week for the remembrance ceremony. Every day for praying and studying the scriptures. Does anyone here have a copy of the scriptures?"

"I do," Titus says.

"They will be your guide. And I will write to you sometimes, and perhaps come back and visit you," Paul says.

Their host stands and walks over to the large reflecting pool in the middle of the courtyard.

"I don't know about the rest of you," he says, "but I believe and want to live the way you say Jesus lived, and want to be baptized. I want to be a Christian. You performed an incredible miracle to prove your words were from the only real God, not a god from some philosopher's imagination."

Fjorta stands and walks over to her husband. "I believe Jesus vas dead und now is alive vorever."

"And you spoke in all those tongues you never learned," Titus adds, taking his wife's hand. "What power. Superhuman power. I believe Jesus came back to life and will bring me back to life in heaven when I die." He looks at Fjorta. "I do believe that."

"Me too. I vant to be baptized," Crasius, who had been falsely accused of defacing Augustus' temple years earlier, says.

"Don't leave me out," Lydia, the ever-faithful maid, says.

"Can we all be baptized?" Hera, Nestor's wife, asks.

"Wait. You are going too fast. First of all, how many of you believe Jesus was the Son of God come to earth to save us with his blood sacrifice?"

Everyone in the group—some of whom were sitting on benches and others on cushions on the floor—stands.

"It looks like we all do," Titus answers for them.

"You believe. Good. Do you repent of all your sins and promise to live as good a life like Jesus' as possible?"

"We do," everyone replies.

Paul's eyes sparkle. "In that case, you may be baptized. In so doing, you are dying to your old sinful nature, just as Jesus died for your sins. You will be buried, just as Jesus was buried. You will rise up out of your watery grave the saved, just as Jesus rose up out of his grave, the savior. Your soul is reborn and will never die again."

People line up.

"Uh, Paul has not been feeling well," Barnabas intercedes. "I will baptize you."

They spend the rest of the night praising God. Titus keeps them going. "Teach us another Psalm."

At last, Barnabas stands. "As much as we rejoice with you, Paul needs to rest now."

"Where are you staying?" Titus asks. "You can stay here for what is left of the night."

"We already have our night paid for at the hostel. We will be fine," Barnabas says.

They leave. One by one, all the guests leave.

"Tomorrow is Solday. Come back tomorrow," Titus urges. "We shall worship as Christians tomorrow."

Just as the last guest leaves, they hear a familiar voice.

"What's going on down here?" Justin calls out from the top of the stairs. Go to bed. All of you."

Titus has trouble sleeping, though he does doze a little and dreams he is standing before the throne of the real God who is smiling at him.

He has another dream too. He and his father are next to his mother's funeral pyre, but suddenly his mother is standing in his place, and he is on the funeral pyre. His father begins to laugh, but his mother calls out for her son.

"Titus. Titus. Titus. Time to get up. Ve have an exciting day ahead ov us." It is Fjorta.

Still morning, Titus is sitting at his writing-table reading through the Jewish prophecies his mother had purchased. *Hmmm. Paul said the life of Jesus was written hundreds of years before his birth. I have got to find it.*

There is a knock at his gate. He walks out to the courtyard to see if someone had come to talk about Jesus. It is Paul and Barnabas.

"We must be on our way," Paul says, looking better than he had the night before.

"Did vou have a good night's sleep?" Fjorta asks, coming out to the courtyard. "At least, vhat vas left ov it?"

"Well, someone threw a rock through our window. Then, when we went outside to go to the market, stones were thrown at us from both sides of the street. We complained to a magistrate, but he threatened to throw us in jail for causing unrest between the Jews and non-Jews in the city."

"Which magistrate?" Titus says. "He had no right to say that. No one goes to jail without a proper court hearing," Titus responds.

"Well, come in. My aunt is preparing a mid-day refreshment."

"No. We must be on our way. It is Solday, but we will stop and worship on our way. We do not want our presence to bring any trouble for you," Barnabas says.

"Jesus said 'Where two or three are gathered in my name, I will be among them," Paul adds.

"Where are you going next?"

"Iconium. Then Lystra. Then Derbe."

"Gud velsigne og bevare dig," Fjorta says.

"Und "Gud velsigne og bevare dig, to you too," Paul replies.

"I hope no one throws rocks at them on their way out of the city," Chloe says.

"If I hear about it, they will see my fists," Fulvio says.

Chloe pokes him in the rib with her elbow. "Uh uh," she

says, "can't do that. You have to be as harmless as a dove from now on."

The four seat themselves in their usual spots in the courtyard.

"Oh, we vorgot to invite everyone to come back to vorship togedher today," Fjorta says.

"Then, the seven of us will worship together."

"Seven?" Fulvio asks.

"Ve vill not leave out Cornelius, Lydia und Brutus," Fjorta answers for her husband. "Lydia, vould you vix some vlat bread and red vine vor our ceremony?"

"Yes, ma'am."

Chloe stares at the sky above the courtyard.

"What's wrong, Aunt Chloe?" Titus asks.

"The ceremony. For the very first time in our lives, we will be worshipping the one true God. We have found him."

They hear a knock at their gate.

"Uh, is Titus here?"

"Nestor! I'm here," Titus says, walking toward the gate. "Come in. Come in."

Nestor and Hera walk in. "Uh, well, could we do the ceremony with you today? It will be our first time, and we are not sure we will do it right."

"It will be the first time for all of us," Fjorta replies.

"Cornelius, would you ask one of the younger men to bring in another bench for our company?"

Before he can go back to his own bench, there is another knock on his gate.

Cornelius shuffles over to open it.

It is Decimus and Hector.

Titus walks toward them. "Would you like to join us for our very first celebration?"

"You read our minds," Titus old boyhood friends reply.

Titus looks over at the young man bringing in another bench.

There is another knock at the gate.

Titus calls out to his servant. "Bring them all out."

Lydia brings out more flatbread and red wine and sets it on the ledge of the reflecting pool.

Titus stands before his friends. "I guess just about all of us are…"

Another knock on the gate. Urias walks in. He is not smiling.

"What's wrong, Urias?"

"Our friends at the synagogue threw rocks over our gate all morning. I guess they learned we became Christians."

Titus leads them to the last bench in the courtyard, then stands to face everyone.

"Two days ago, we were just friends. Today we are brothers and sisters. We are the family of God. Paul said the family of God is sometimes called the church."

He looks over at Urias and Sofia. "I think we are going to have much joy and much sorrow. We need to pray for Paul and Barnabas after what they went through before leaving our city. And Urias and Sofia. But I am not sure how we are supposed to pray. This is all so new."

Urias stands. "I know how. I am still a Jew. I have let go of the Laws of Moses and will follow the Laws of Jesus now, but he is the same God. Will you allow me to lead us in a prayer?"

Before Urias has a chance to begin, there is another knock at the gate. Cornelius, seated by the gate, gets up and answers it.

"Is Titus here? We need a lawyer," a young man says, holding close what seems to be a baby. "We're desperate."

"Come in, come in, friends. Come join us. We are just beginning our worship."

"Without permission? Which god? We need your help. No god can help us," a young woman who apparently is his wife, says.

"You would be surprised what this God can do," Titus replies. Come and just watch. Afterward, we will talk about your problem. I promise you as a Christian."

"What's a Christian? Oh, Titus, we need you," the woman says.

A loud banging interrupts.

"We know you're in there," comes the booming voice. "You cannot run from us forever."

"What did you do?" Titus asks.

"It's not us," the young man says, unmanly tears coming to his eyes. "It's them."

The young lady looks up at Titus, tears streaming down her face. "They're trying to kill our baby."

16 ~ CHALLENGES

"Come sit," Titus says. "We must worship first."

"No!" the woman shouts, her hair falling onto her face as she shakes it back and forth. "No, no, no."

"Open up," they hear out on the street again."

Sarah, seated near the front of the group, stands and walks toward the gate.

"Come back here," someone else says. "You're not going to desert us already."

"You're not going to abandon Jesus already."

"Besides, it's too dangerous out there."

When she reaches the inner gate, old Cornelius smiles at her. She smiles back, then turns and sits, leaning her back against the gate.

Silence.

Soon Cephas stands, walks to the inner gate, turns, and sits next to his wife.

Marcus stands. So does Quintus. They walk over to the gate, turn, and sit next to the others.

One by one, the others walk over to the gate, turn, and sit.

The couple with the baby, Titus, and Urias are the only ones left standing.

Titus remembers what his mother used to say so long ago. *There is nothing that a song cannot help.* He recalls one of the simpler songs Barnabas had taught them the day before.

The Lo'rd's my she'pherd, I'll not wa'nt.

Urias already knows the song and joins Titus.

He ma'kes me lie do'wn in pas'tures gre'en.

His wife, Sophia, sitting in front of the gate, joins in.

...eat in the pre'sence of my en'em'ies.

One by one, the others add their voices.

Fjorta stands, walks up to the couple, touches the younger woman's arm, and with gentleness leads her over to sit with the others. Her husband with the baby follows.

...li've in the hou'se of the Lo'rd for'ev'er."

Silence. In the courtyard, out on the street. Marching is heard. Footsteps marching away.

"This is how we pray," Urias says. He kneels on both knees. The others in the new congregation do the same. Their worship has begun.

Two hours later, Titus dismisses the group.

"Do we meet again next Solday?" someone asks.

"Yes," Titus replies."Again next Solday. Or tonight if you want to. Or every day. I think it is up to us as long as we keep Solday holy."

The courtyard is empty now except for the couple still clinging to their baby. Now in the arms of its mother, it stirs. Stretches its arms, and lets out a baby's wail.

The young lady stands and walks with it around the courtyard, tears still flowing freely.

"My baby," she coos. "My sweet baby."

"Come sit over here," Titus tells the young man. "I do not even know your name."

"I am Comonius. My wife is Hathor. Our baby is Helios."

"Did you say someone wants to kill your baby? That can never be. A baby is a gift from God." He fights the impulse to think of his baby daughter.

"Why? Why would anyone want to kill an innocent child?"

"She is deformed," Hathor says, walking over to join the men. She sits, lays the baby in her lap, and takes the blanket away.

"As you can see," Comonius says, "one arm is normal, the other arm ends at her elbow, and there is no hand. The same thing with the leg."

"But he is a handsome baby. Don't you think so, Titus?"

Being exposed to a slight chill from not having his blanket to snuggle into, little Helios opens his eyes and looks around.

"Ha, ha. He is, indeed, a handsome boy."

"Do you see how busy his eyes are, checking everything around him?" Helios adds.

"He is very smart. Don't you think?" Comonius asks.

"I must agree with you on both points. Well, has anyone taken you to court over your baby's problem?"

"No."

"Then, we shall. I will draw up a subpoena to the culprits tomorrow. Today is my day of rest and worship. From henceforth, Solday will always be a special day for me now that I am a Christian."

"What is a Christian?"

"Someone who follows the Christ, the Messiah, the Savior of the world from Satan."

"What or who is Satan?"

"He is pure evil."

Titus explains what he knows to the couple until they hear someone at the outside gate.

Cornelius shuffles out and opens it.

"We want to worship again. We cannot get enough of it. Will you join us to worship some more today?" It is Nestor and his wife.

"Come in. And do you mind if this fine young couple with their beautiful baby joins us?"

Worship resumes with a reading of the old prophets, a few hymns, and prayers. As they worship, other new Christians arrive and join them. By late afternoon, the courtyard is filled again.

"What's all the commotion down here?"

"These are our new friends, Father," Titus calls up to Justus. "They are just leaving to go home."

Justus walks back up the stairs and disappears again.

"That was your father?" Comonius asks.

"Yes. He is very busy in his *officium* all the time, what with having the responsibilities of the entire city on his shoulders."

"He must be very patient with all of us here and getting a little loud with our singing sometimes."

"I guess you could say that." Titus presses his lips together, rubs his fingers together, and looks down at the floor.

"Well, come back tomorrow at noon, and I will give you a list of judges you may select from. And God bless you."

"Which god?"

"I think we can discuss that further tomorrow also."

The last guest leaves. Titus sits on the tiled ground, leaning against one of the marble columns, his knees drawn up and hugging them. Then it is dark.

"Oh, my dear *kareste*, vhat are you doing out here in dhe dark?" She sits next to him and puts her head on his shoulder.

"Why did he have to do that, Fjorta? Why did he have to come down and embarrass me like that? He stays hidden up there in his *officium* as though he is too important to associate with his son."

"Aunt Chloe says he misses his vife."

"And he blames me for murdering her. I didn't know. I didn't know the earthquake was going to come. Can't he ever forgive me? I was eleven years old then. I am thirty-five years old now and will be thirty-six soon. How long is he going to punish me?"

"Vell, at least you are still living vith him."

"We are in the same house, but we are not living

together."

The next day, Titus goes to the Temple of Apollo.

"Is the augur here? I need his guidance."

"Did I hear someone needing me?"

Titus looks around and sees a man about the same age as his father. His hair is long. He has a bird on his shoulder.

"Adelphos, I need your help again. I am looking for the identity of...the identity of..."

"Who, my son? Whose identity do you seek? The birds, as always, will help you find your suspect or witness or whoever he is this time. We can always depend on the birds."

Titus backs up. *What am I doing here? I am a Christian. Those birds he consults do not tell the wisdom of the gods. There is only one God. What am I doing here?*

"Oh, nothing. I do not think I will be needing your services anymore."

Titus rushes out of the temple and sits on the edge of the artificial waterfall nearby. "God, who lets me call you Father, forgive me. I am still learning. It's just that, I need to learn the identity of the men threatening baby Helios' life."

"You know we will find that deformed monster eventually, and it will be destroyed."

Titus looks up and sees his friend since childhood.

"You, Hypos? You're the one trying to kill that innocent baby?"

"Oh, not innocent, my friend. No monster is innocent. That babe brings a curse upon our city."

"Hypos, how can you say that?"

"Plato himself said so."

Titus looks over at a young man approaching the two. The stranger puts his hand on the shoulder of Hypos.

"And who are you?" Titus demands, standing.

"My name is Deimos, recent graduate of the prestigious Academy of Plato in Athens. I am going city to city to make sure they are pure."

"What do you mean by pure?"

"For one thing, getting rid of monsters. We are watching the *insulae* the parents of that monster are in and will make it a gift to your river Anthius."

Titus brings his shoulders back, tightens his muscles, and sets his feet wider apart.

"Number one, who put you in charge of the Roman Empire? Number two, who made you God?"

The young man grins. "I intend to become a god someday. The Senate will appreciate what I am going. I will be right up there with Plato. Plato himself will thank me when I get to the underworld. You shall see. Isn't that right, Hypos?"

"He is staying with you while he destroys everything decent in our city?"

"Well, he is my nephew. But I agree with him. He has been showing me passages in Plato where the state must be the guardian and in control of all children."

Titus glares one last time at Deimos, turns his back on him, and heads toward the *palatio* of Lykonius, Censor of Antioch. There he obtains subpoenas for Deimos as the defendant and Hypos as a co-conspirator, and a second subpoena to Deimos to appear at the public forum at the West Gate the following day. They will go over judges lists together until they come to an agreement on three of them. He hires a guard to deliver them all, then makes one last request of the censor before leaving. Permission is granted.

Titus hurries to the insulae where his clients live. "Come with me," he says when Comonius answers the door of their third-floor apartment. "Grab clothing and whatever you will need until the trial is over, and come with me."

"What has happened?" Comonius asks.

"Nothing yet. But you are being watched. Your baby will not live long enough to be saved at the trial. Hurry."

Within the hour, Titus has the young couple and their baby at his home. "The servants' quarters are on the other side of the kitchen area. You may stay there during the trial. The trial will begin tomorrow."

The following morning at dawn, two armed guards arrive. Titus sends instructions for them to wait inside the guest courtyard. His father comes down the stairs dressed in his purple-bordered toga. Father and son nod at each other, and Justus leaves in his silver chariot.

Titus brings the couple and their baby to the guest

courtyard, where the guards take their place in front and behind.

By the time they arrive at the platform in front of the Temple of Vesta, a crowd of spectators has begun to assemble. As word spreads about the cause of the lawsuit, more citizens of Antioch arrive.

Titus and the couple sit on the plaintiff's bench. The three judges come up the steps and sit behind their long table facing the plaintiffs and defendants. The defendant and witness arrive next and sit on the bench of the accused. Finally, Justus arrives and ascends the steps to his pinnacle above and behind the judges and is followed by his deputy.

Where has Father been? To his grandaughter's grave?

Titus stands. "Most Excellent Praetor Justus Brinnius Antiochus and esteemed judges. God made all of mankind. God does not make mistakes. God is perfect in all things. Therefore, everything he makes is perfect."

He swings around and points to Deimos. "This young man, barely out of university, dares come into our esteemed city and declare who is pure and who is not."

He walks over to his clients and, in a soft voice, continues. "This couple and their precious...the precious...uh, baby only want to be left alone to be a family and, uh, raise that child to adulthood."

Titus takes control of his emotions and walks toward the judges.

"Sirs, I urge you to find both of them guilty of attempted murder."

Titus sits. Deimos rises. He looks up at the praetor and bows.

"Most Excellent praetor and magistrates," Deimos announces. He raises his right hand. "I come to you on behalf of the venerable Plato, giver of laws, giver of hope, giver of all that is good in the world."

He raises his left hand. "Nothing can and ever will discredit that noble man who, today, is a god, so far advanced he was above all others."

"Get to it," Justus calls down.

"It was he who upheld the divine Twelve Tablets. Tablet

IV said, and I quote, 'A dreadfully deformed child shall be quickly killed.' "

Deimos swings around and points at the object of his scorn. "Uncover the monster. Uncover him and hold him up for all to see and repulse."

Titus tells the couple they must comply. Mother Hathor lays the baby on her lap and uncovers it, tears like dewdrops falling.

"Hold it up, I tell you," Deimos declares. "Hold up the monster. He can never live a normal life. He will become a beggar, which, according to Plato's Book 11 of his *Laws*, must be exiled."

Comonius gently picks up his child with only one arm and one leg and holds it up for everyone to see.

Gasps.

The child looks around and smiles.

Sighs.

Titus tells the father to give the baby back to his mother. She takes the little one and holds it against her breast.

"Most Excellent Magistrates," Titus declares, "I call your attention to the venerable Cicero who condemned such atrocities. Also, Philo, respected in Alexandria, condemned it."

Without pausing, Titus holds his hand out toward the spectators. "I now call a witness who I just discovered among our spectators."

The judges all agree.

"I call Urias Philon."

The spectators step aside to let Urias up onto the platform.

Titus motions for him to stand in front of the witness bench.

"Sir, does someone without a hand or foot end up as a beggar and disgrace to his city?"

"As everyone here knows, I was without a hand for many years. I was never a beggar. I married and have been a successful dyer of cloth, as everyone knows. A man of God and ambassador for Jesus the Christ came here and made my hand grow back by God's power, which also everyone here knows."

"Thank you, Urias, for your testimony.

"One more thing," Urias adds. "I want to adopt the father of this baby and bring them into my home as my own." He smiles at the young couple.

Deimos stands again. "This baby is cursed and will bring curses down on this entire city," Deimos declares. "I demand death to this monster!"

The three judges have heard enough. They write on the three small scrolls provided to them and seal them. Their decisions are handed to the deputy who, in turn, gives them to a Vestal Virgin to place on Vesta's altar nearby. Two doves are offered. The Vestal Virgin returns the decisions to the deputy who takes them up to Praetor Justus Brennius Antiochus. He reads them and stands.

"The baby lives."

Suddenly they hear screaming. "My baby!"

17 ~ CONFUSION

"Stop him!" Titus shouts.

By now, Deimos has pushed his way through the shocked crowd and is running toward the Sanctuary of Men-Askanos and the river. When he sees a high cliff ahead of him, he veers south toward the artificial waterfall on columned Cardo Maximus.

Justus hurries down the steps from his pinnacle and down the final steps to the street. People move aside, and he rushes for his chariot. He jumps in, grabs the reins and his whip.

"Yahh! Yahh!" he shouts as he cracks the whip over the head of his horse. "Yahh! Yahh!"

People on the street scramble to get out of the way. When he arrives at the artificial waterfall between the Temple of Augustus and Temple of Apollo, he jumps out, whip still in his hand. Just as Deimos reaches the waterfall, Justus' whip wraps itself around the escapee.

Justus reels him in and grabs the baby. Just as he does, guards on duty at the court run up, spears ready to plunge into the would-be baby killer. Behind them is Titus, and behind him are the child's parents Comonius and Hathor.

Justus hands the baby back to his mother. Without even a pause, he climbs back into his chariot and returns to the platform.

The three judges are still there. Also, the young man's uncle, Hypos. Justus climbs past them to his perch on high. He remains standing.

The guards bring the captured Deimos up the platform, spears still trained on him.

Justus looks over to Hypos. "Exiled for life," he growls. He points and glares at Deimos, his dark eyes even darker. "Death by drowning."

He says something to his deputy, climbs back down to his chariot, and leaves.

The deputy approaches the judges. The oldest one nods his head and writes something on a small scroll. He seals it and motions for Titus to come take it.

When Titus opens it, he looks over the crowd to find his clients. They are in a huddle near Urias. He kneels on one knee on the platform and touches the shoulder of a spectator. "Would you notify Urias to come here, please?"

Moments later, Urias is on the platform with Titus.

"Here is your documentation. You have officially adopted Comonius and all who belong to him."

The two men smile.

Behind Urias, Titus can see Deimos being led to the river with a small crowd of people behind them.

Titus sits on his bench awhile, watching the three judges descend the steps and the spectators to disperse.

Alone, Titus thinks of his baby girl. *I must remember to ask Paul where she went when she died. I hope beyond hope she is in the arms of God.*

After a while, he goes down the steps to the street and walks through the columned Dacumanus Maximus, past the theater and market, and out the West Gate. He walks out into the country a little way, then down a path with colored rocks on each side. Ahead he sees the chariot.

He walks over to the graves of his paternal grandparents, his mother, and his daughter. He stands next to his father. They are silent. Their tears silent. The words silent. *If my father would just let me touch him. Like he used to do before...*They stand there a long time.

Weeks come and go. The family resumes its routine.

Justus is back in his *officium.*

Solday again. Titus tells Cornelius just to open the outer and inner gates wide and let anyone in who wants in.

Urias arrives with his wife, Sofia, and new son, daughter-in-law, and grandson. Behind him are what Titus estimates to be twenty or thirty Jews.

"What happened, Urias?" Titus asks, pounding his Jewish brother's back. "Steal half the synagogue?"

"You do not know the half of it," Urias replies. "Rabbi Oeneus has been sending the elders out to every city in Galatia, warning them not to let Paul or Barnabas preach for them."

"Oh, no. Paul said he was going to Iconium, Lystra, and Derby. That much I know for sure."

"I think Paul can handle himself. Anyway, yesterday, when I tried to attend synagogue, the rabbi wouldn't let me in. So, I walked around and looked in one of the windows. Only half the congregation was there."

"So, I suppose the missing members are behind you."

"We would surely like to be let in so we can learn more about the Christ," someone behind Urias says.

The two men grin and step out of the way.

The service begins. There are not enough benches for everyone, so many sit on cushions on the floor.

The gates are closed, and their worship of the only true God begins. They sing their hymns, and Fulvio stands to lead the Lord's Supper ceremony.

Just as he does, there is a knock on the outside gate.

"Who could that be?"

"The Rabbi and his elders?"

"Guards from the citadel?"

Cornelius shuffles over to the gates and opens them. When he does, a crowd of people pushes their way past him. The congregation stands, ready to defend themselves, or—as Paul had explained to them—die for the Christ who had died for them.

Instead, the crowd is smiling.

"Are you the Christians? Ever since Urias showed his new hand to everyone at the trial a few weeks ago, we have been curious and decided finally to do something about it. We want to know how that Christ you talk about can have that kind of power."

Fjorta and Chloe walk toward the newcomers.

"Welcome. I'm afraid we are nearly out of room, but that can be remedied." Chloe turns and says something to Cornelius. Cornelius shuffles to the other end of the courtyard and speaks to one of the servants.

"Since everyone is already standing," Fjorta says, "please allow dhe servants to take avay dhe benches. We vill all just sit on the tile. Dhen dhere should be room vor everyone."

Soon, the Christians are settled back down, and the gates closed again. Fulvio takes his place at the front of the congregation.

"We are about to eat unleavened bread as Jesus instructed. He told us to take a bite of it every Solday to remember his body that was tortured for us."

Men with baskets hand around enough flatbread, everyone can have a bite. It is a quiet time. A time of reflection, contemplation, remembering events on a hill outside of Jerusalem some fifteen years earlier that they have only heard about. And a time of once again asking forgiveness for impure deeds and thoughts committed, and good deeds left undone.

Fulvio stands again. "We are now going to take a sip of the red wine representing Jesus' sacred blood that escaped his body one drop at a time for hours on end until he was drained of life. 'Remember me,' Jesus had said. 'Remember my body. Remember my blood. Never forget.' Amen, Lord God, the only God, we shall never forget."

Quiet again. Quiet and thinking and absorbing. How could God put his Words in a body to send to earth? God walked the earth? Like he did with Adam and Eve in the Garden at the beginning? Silent prayers again. Prayers asking for strength to do better.

By the end of the service, the congregation has nearly doubled. And Justus had not come down to complain about the noise.

Two weeks later, Urias comes to see Titus. "We have a

grand congregation of believers in the only true God, don't we?"

"Indeed, we do."

Urias' smile fades. "But, well, I guess we have one problem. It shouldn't be hard to solve, though."

"What is it? Titus asks. "Of course, we will solve it."

"We Jews believe, since Jesus was prophesied throughout the Jewish scriptures and since Jesus was a Jew, all Christians should become both Jews and Christians. What I mean is, become Jews just enough to be circumcised. That's all. Easy to remedy."

Titus stares at Urias. "What are you saying? We have all been baptized. Isn't that enough?"

"Well, it wouldn't hurt. That way, everyone will be happy."

Titus stands and paces. "As much as I love the Jewish prophecies, I do not see how being circumcised according to the Jewish laws would make us any more Christian than we are now."

"It would make the Jewish Christians happy. Isn't that worth something?"

Titus stands. "That is something I suppose we all must pray over and search the prophecies about."

The following day, there is another knock on the gate. Titus steps out of his *officium,* where he is studying the ancient laws for his next case. When Cornelius opens the gate, two men walk in, and Titus stops in his tracks.

"Titus, he needs someplace to sit. Quickly."

Paul, once so full of energy, leans on Barnabas as they shuffle farther into the courtyard. Paul has a band around his head that goes across one eye.

"Stop that, Barnabas. I just walked too far today. I'm perfectly fine, and you know that. So, quit making people think I'm not."

Titus grabs a gilded couch from the banquet hall and brings it out for Paul. "No. I sit on a bench like everyone else. Take that soft fluffy thing away."

"What happened?" Titus asks Barnabas.

"Lystra is what happened. Apparently, some of your

Jewish elders arrived there about the same time we did and stirred up the people against us. Since Paul was doing the preaching, well, they stoned him."

"What?"

"It was nothing. God healed me. Barnabas says God brought me back to life. Either way, here I am. God did not heal one of my eyes, though. He said his grace was sufficient, and I needed to be satisfied with what I got. So, I am."

Fjorta joins the men, bringing goblets of nectar to them, then sitting to hear the conversation.

"Sweet *kareste*," she says to her husband. "Tell them what Urias and the other Jews want every man who was not born a Jew to do."

"Don't tell me," Paul says. "I can guess. They want you to be circumcised."

"How did you know?"

"The Jews just won't let go. It was a commandment God gave to Abraham, Isaac, and Jacob, then centuries later, started it up again in the Law of Moses. We Christians do not keep the Law of Moses. That was God's last will and testament for the Jews. When Jesus died, Jesus left behind a new last will and testament, leaving the old will no longer in effect."

"Do you think you can talk to them, Paul?"

"Well, we came by here on our way back to the other Antioch down in Syria. We can stay for a few days.

Two days later is Solday. Paul speaks about the two testaments of God and that they are not to be mixed together. "When a will and testament is replaced, the old one is no longer good. We now obey the Christ. No longer Moses. It was time for Moses to step aside."

The congregation breaks up at noon and relaxes with each other before resuming mid-afternoon.

When they reassemble, Titus makes an announcement.

"Paul says there are enough of us we should be able to select elders to lead us—not just one elder, but several."

Slate tablets with styluses are passed around for everyone to scratch in the name of someone they respect and would be willing to follow. Names are announced and discussed.

"Remember, he must have just one wife, have believing children, is respected in the city and knows enough to teach others," Paul says.

Voting follows. They select three. The next day, Paul and Barnabas leave, telling them they may have to divide up and meet in different homes if they keep growing.

A week later, a woman knocks on Titus' gate. Cornelius lets her in. She is crying. He leads her to Titus' *officium* just off the courtyard.

Titus hears the weeping and meets the woman at his doorway. He guides her to a gilded chair with cushioned seat. He hands her a handkerchief, a supply of which he keeps in a basket on his writing desk, walks back around to his own seat, and waits.

"It's my husband," she says with a frightened voice. "He beats me. I am afraid of him."

"You should leave him. Do you have parents living nearby you could move back in with?"

"No. Yes. No. I mean, it is too late."

"Too late?"

"Too late to move away."

"But, if your life is in danger..."

"Not anymore."

"I am confused."

"Just before I came to see you, I killed him."

She breaks down in sobs. Titus is unsure what to do. He stands and walks back around, stands by her chair, and she leans her head on his arm, clinging to it.

He looks around and sees Fjorta walking past. He prays she will look his way, and she does. She rushes over, and Titus steps aside. Fjorta kneels by the woman's chair and puts her arm around her. The woman leans her head over, and it touches Fjorta arm.

"Shhh. Shhh, my wee one. Shhh. Dhings could not be so bad."

Titus clears his throat, Fjorta looks over at him, and he shakes his head.

"Shhh," she resumes. "I'm sorry. I'm so sorry. Shhh, my wee one."

"What is your name?" Titus asks. "I need to know your name."

"Semele," she answers, taking deep breaths to control her emotions.

"Good, Semele. A very nice name. Now I need to know your husband's name."

"Kreon."

Titus etches both names into a wax tablet. "Can you tell me what happened?"

Semele breaks out into loud sobs. She stands.

"No, don't leave," Titus urges.

Wailing at what she has done, Semele holds out her hands. In it is a bloody knife.

Titus takes one of the handkerchiefs in his basket and holds it up for her to drop the knife in.

"Does anyone else know?"

"Just you," she says, re-seating herself, lowering her head to her knees, and shaking.

"Oh, my poor wee one," Fjorta says. "Vhat did he do to you?"

"He beat me. Every day he hit me," she says, once again trying to control her sobs.

"Do you have proof? Did anyone ever see him hit you?" Titus asks.

"No."

"Did he have a temper that he showed around other people?"

"Never. He…he controlled it around other people. They all thought he was nice."

"Did you ask anyone to intercede?" Titus prods.

"Yes, but no one believed…believed me."

"Was he living off the labor of servants or slaves on an estate, or did he have a trade?"

"He was rich. I do not know why he was rich. He would never tell me."

"So, he did not have employees."

"I think he did, but I never knew who they were or where they were—other than the ones at our villa."

Titus stands and calls Cornelius into his office. He

whispers something, and Cornelius leaves.

"We need to go where the body, where your husband's remains are. You must lead us."

Fjorta helps her stand. When the woman does, her stola slips off her shoulder. Fjorta stares at the woman's back. It is full of scars.

Fjorta squints her eyes, furrows her brow, and clinches her fists. "Did he do dhis to you?" she demands. "If he vere still alive, I vould do dhe same dhing you did."

Titus sees the scars too. "You will not be charged."

He leads them out to the street and steps on board his chariot. The women are seated on the built-in benches on each side behind him. Old Brutus secures the gate.

"Which way?" Titus asks.

"Out the North Gate by the aqueduct," she says almost in a whisper. "We lived in the mountains."

Titus guides his chariot up the Cordo Maximum and through the North Gate. They follow the road that parallels the aqueduct up into the mountains. At the end of the aqueduct, he stops.

Semele points to a narrow pass. He works his way through it and sees a villa in the small vale on the other side. He stops.

"You are going to have to lead us to him."

She takes short, uncertain steps. Titus and Fjorta are on each side, supporting her.

When they arrive in the room where the body is, another man is already there: Censor Lykonius. He looks up.

"Are you the wife?"

"Yes, sir."

"You are under arrest for murder."

18 ~ FAILURE

Fjorta stands between Semele and Censor Lykonius.

"Never!" she declares, her eyes cold as ice.

"Sweetheart, we cannot interfere," Titus urges. We will go to court, and she will eventually be freed."

"Eventually vreed? Imprisoned on top of everydhing else?"

"Sir," Titus says to the censor. "Would it be acceptable for her to ride to the dungeon in our chariot? My wife can keep her calm."

"As you wish," Censor Lykonius replies. "Follow me."

Semele has stopped crying. She now stares into nothingness. Wherever anyone guides her, she follows without seeing, and steps without knowing. The ride back into Antioch seems to be in a different world.

"I vill bring back blankets und vood vor you to eat, wee one," Fjorta says. "Und I vill tell you about Jesus. He is part ov the only true God und vants to help you live in heaven widh him someday."

The following day, Titus meets with the prosecutor, Censor Lykonius. They look through the list of men volunteering to be judges and select three they both agree on.

Titus arrives at the platform in front of the Temple of Vesta. Shortly, two dungeon guards lead Semele out of her dungeon behind the Temple of Augustus, across the road. She walks slowly, the chains around her ankles clanging and scraping as she goes. Her eyes are swollen.

When they reach the bottom of the steps, Titus looks at the guards. "Really?"

One of them reaches down and unlocks the chains. Titus steps down and helps his client up to the platform. They sit together on the defendant's bench and watch as the three judges arrive and sit behind their long table facing the other benches.

They wait. Eventually, they hear the clop, clop, clop, and know Praetor Justus Brennius Antiochus has arrived.

He climbs to the top of the platform and seats himself. His deputy makes the announcement.

"You may begin."

Censor Lykonius rises. "Most Excellent Magistrates," he bellows, his thin gray hair blowing in the breeze. "I present to you a murderer." His brows furrow, his eyes grow dark. "A cold-blooded murderer who deserves no less than what she did to her benevolent husband."

"Your Excellencies," Titus says, rising. "No one has proven the dead man was benevolent."

Justus glares down at his son, and Titus sits back down.

"Most Excellent Magistrates," the censor repeats, bowing this time, "the unfortunate victim—Kreon—was a benefactor of the arts, having donated ten thousand pieces of silver for refinements of our grand theater. He donated ten oxen that were sacrificed at the Temple of our divine Augustus Caesar on the anniversary of his death last year, and another ten oxen sacrificed at the Temple of Apollo at the games the year before. Further..."

"I think we get the idea, Censor Lykonius," senior judge Crispus of Athens says.

"On the other hand," the censor continues, his eyes growing dark, we have this worthless woman." He swings around, points at Semele, and holds his position as long as his arm holds out.

"Has anyone ever heard of her? Of course not. She stays up in those mountains where she does not have to contribute to society. Never has she been seen at the Temple of Vesta—or any other temple for that matter. Never has she been seen at the market carefully choosing food for her family as normal women do. Never has she been seen at the cemetery, mourning our city's ancestors. Never has she apprenticed a young girl to learn how to dress properly or to write a poem or to sing a song. Never has she hosted a reception or feast for her husband's friends. Never has she been known to do anything except selfishly hide herself up in those mountains."

Lykonius lowers his head and paces. The spectators and judges wait until Justus clears his throat in a long series of clearings.

"The victim was doomed from the day of their betrothal to have a wife who went from being vivacious—at least, that is what they tell me—to being weak, cowardly, and cowering. He would even have to order her to his bed. Never a loving word from her. Only groaning and complaining. How do I know this? The victim, her husband, was my friend and told me so himself. I am not here only to honor his memory, but to prosecute and condemn his killer. That is all."

The prosecutor sits on his bench. Titus rises.

"And do you know why this harmless little woman got to be the ways she is? Her husband's threats."

He pauses and looks west toward the theater.

"But before we get into that, no one ever knew where Kreon's money came from. He owned no tillable soil that we are aware of. He had no trade. He did not belong to a family of means. He never held public office. Rumors have it that he was actually..."

"May I interrupt, Excellent Magistrates," Lykonius objects. "We cannot mar these proceeding with rumors."

"His treatment of his wife was deplorable," Titus continues. "He never allowed her to go to the market or anywhere else in our city or the immediate surroundings of our city such as our cemetery. He never allowed her to participate in any of the ceremonies held at the Temple of Vesta. He never allowed her to have a normal conversation with anyone outside of him, and that included his servants. He never allowed her to give them instructions, or give him her opinion of anything, or to laugh, or to even sing. He never allowed her to go around any of his friends."

"Prove it," Censor Lykonius demands, standing. "You cannot prove it. These are just silly excuses for a heinous crime."

"It is true, we have no witnesses, honored Magistrates. As soon as he was dead, Semele found his strongbox of money, called the servants together, and divided the money so they could escape that horrid place in the mountains and return to their families. And, since she was never allowed out in public, no one else saw him be harsh or heard him speak with rudeness."

Censor Lykonius leans back, folds his arms, and gloats.

"However, honored Magistrates, we do have one witness. It is the strongest of all witnesses. It is the woman herself."

"She is too stupid to defend herself," the censor objects. He turns around to the spectators to bring them in on his jokes. Many respond accordingly. "Ha, ha, ha."

Titus whispers to Semele and helps her stand. She shuffles over to stand in front of the judges and turns her back on them.

"Honored magistrates, the defendant did not want to do this. It is very humiliating to her—both to expose her body as she is about to do, but also to admit the man she loved did not love her back."

Titus gently takes her stola off, leaving only a short, sleeveless tunic. The neckline is cut low in the back. The spectators move around so they can see what he is revealing and gasp at the welts and scars.

He leads her over to the witness bench where she sits. He puts his hand behind her crooked calf and foot. More gasping.

He helps her stand again. He holds out her arm, also crooked. Some in the crowd groan.

He turns her around with her back to the judges again and parts her long dark hair so they can see the jagged scar. Moaning in the crowd.

He helps her face the judges. "And this."

He raises her chin, and red scarring is seen across her neck.

Some of the spectators have turned their back. Others gawk. Semele weeps as Titus returns her to her bench.

He stands before the judges in silence. At last, he breaks the silence with a soft question. "What more can I say?"

He stares at the three judges, up at his father, and back to the three judges. "You must, by all that is decent and fair, let this woman live."

Titus sits back down and puts an arm around the weeping woman a moment, then takes it down. His head is bowed.

Each judge takes out a small scroll writes on it, seals it, and gives it to the deputy who hands it down to one of the Vesta Virgins. She sets them on the edge of the altar, and a cow is offered as a sacrifice.

After an hour of chanting, the Vesta Virgin picks up the verdicts, hands them to the deputy, who then takes them up to Justus, the praetor.

He does not open them. He watches the three judges below him. They are watching the censor. The censor sometimes winks.

Justus stands without breaking the seals or opening the verdicts. He stares down at Semele and his son. He stares down at the spectators and Vesta Virgins and the cow still being roasted on the sacrificial fire. He stares at the smiling judges, down at Fjorta and Chloe among the spectators. He stares toward the West Gate where the cemetery is.

Without a word, he descends his steps to the lower platform, more steps down onto the street, climbs aboard his chariot, cracks his whip, and urges his horse in a gallop toward home.

Censor Lykonius stands, motions for the deputy to bring him the three verdicts still unopened, takes them in his big hand, and raises his arms toward the spectators.

"By the authority vested in me by Claudius Caesar, I declare my rights as a defender of the city and regulator of decency, I shall now pronounce sentence."

"You haven't opened up the verdicts yet!" someone in

the crowd shouts.

"Open up the verdicts!" Another shouts.

"Yeah, open up the verdicts!"

"I was just getting to that," the censor replies. He sets two unopened scrolls on the judges' table and breaks the seal of the first.

"Guilty."

Semele gasps.

He sets it down and breaks the seal of the second one.

"Guilty."

Titus puts his arm around the shoulder of his client.

Lykonius sets it down and breaks the seal of the last one.

"Guilty."

The spectators thrust fits in the air. They roar their disapproval.

"Never."

"Never."

"Never."

Censor Lykonius climbs to the pinnacle of the platform and faces the citadel on the hill behind and to the north of the Temple of Augustus. He waves both arms back and forth, then returns down the steps.

He sets his legs farther apart and waits.

"Never."

"Never."

"Never."

At first, the crowd does not hear the galloping of the equestrian legionnaires. But when the horses plow into the masses, and the legionnaires themselves raise their spears in ready to find their mark, the spectators back up.

Quiet.

A quiet that echoes through the city and out into the mountains where the hidden house, once the dungeon of Semele, catches the sound and weeps.

"Censor Lykonius punches the air with both fists.

"Death!"

"No!"

"No!"

"No!"

"Sentence to be carried out immediately in the dungeon."

More legionnaires from the citadel have arrived by now and form a fence between the spectators and the platform.

Fjorta convinces one of them to let "a relative of the advocate" to ascend the platform. She rushes to Semele and embraces her. They rock back and forth.

Titus looks out over the south part of the city and sees his father's chariot still speeding down the street toward his affluent neighborhood and home.

Looking at his client and wife, then at the crowd being disbursed by soldiers, the three judges, and the crowing censor, Titus' muscles tighten. He looks up at the clouds bumping into each other overhead.

"Why? Why?"

The two guards who had escorted Semele to her trial, now return and place the chains once again around her ankles. They move to the top of the steps leading to the street and pause.

Five legionnaires stand in front of them, shields touching. They step down, and three legionnaires on each side march into place, holding shields out to their side. Once the guards and condemned are off the platform, five more legionnaires move into place, twisting so that their shields touch each other behind them.

Titus watches from the platform. His wife stands there only a moment. She jumps down the steps and follows them, shaking her fist and screeching. "No! Do not soil your hands widh dhe blood of dhis pure voman."

One of the legionnaires threatens her with his sword. Titus jumps down, joins her, puts his arm around her, and turns her away.

They walk in silence all the way home. When Cornelius opens the gate for them, he whispers, "I am sorry."

Once in their family courtyard, Fjorta walks to the reflecting pool, puts her head down on her knees, and rocks back and forth.

Titus paces. He stops. He raises his face. He shouts.

"Why?"

He walks in a circle in place, still looking up into the heavens. *Did I believe in the wrong god? Are you, Jesus, as make-believe as all the other gods? Where are you? You did not listen to me. You let that poor abused woman die for the sins of her husband. Why? Are you there? Are you real? Have I been fooled again? Or do not care?*

He falls to the pavement on his hands and knees. He slides his hands forward until completely prostrate. His tears wash the floor, and their dirt mingles with his tears, making him as dirty as the Consul, all the judges, the legionnaires, the people of Antioch who let it happen.

Titus opens his eyes. It is dark. He hears footsteps, though muted. He hears whisper sometimes. The servants tip-toe around him, respecting his agony. Respecting his unanswered questions. Respecting his failure.

Oh, God, where are you?

The stars come out. Stars that look down in shame upon the son of doom.

I am a failure. Nothing but a failure. My father is right. He has been right all along. Why didn't I see it? Why couldn't I admit it? Father, I am not worthy of your love.

He lifts his head. It is morning.

Titus sits up. He moves to his hands and knees. He rises but is stooping. He makes his way to the *officium* where only two days earlier, he had told his client she had nothing to worry about. The client he pushed to her death.

I am now the killer of three. Mother, please forgive me. I didn't know. Sweet Kharis, my baby, please forgive me. I didn't get help in time. Dear stranger Semele who lived an undeserved nightmare, and now this. I was not qualified. Forgive me.

Titus calls for Cornelius. "Get me a board."

"How big, sir."

"I don't care. Just get me a board."

After some time, Cornelius returns with a board about as long as two arms.

Titus grabs it out of the hands of his faithful old servant. He glares at nothing with sunken eyes behind a field of red-brown hair, surrounded by the dirt of his filthiness.

He lays the board on his writing-table and gets out a jar of blackener. He dips his finger in the blackener and writes. When he is through, he calls Cornelius back.

"Nail this to the front gate."

After a while, Titus hears banging on the front gate. Cornelius returns to his master. "But why, sir? Why would you resign as an arbitrator and lawyer?"

The rest of the day goes by in a mist. A dark mist of soul wandering. Like the mist over the River Styx in the underworld. Like the Asphodel Meadows full of the wandering souls of ordinary men. Like the blackness of Tartarus where all the failures wander in their filthy nothingness.

Night comes, the night that has been his blackness since the beginning of his existence.

Oh, that the gods had killed me at my birth. No! That's wrong. Those gods don't exist. So, why didn't the God kill me at my birth? Oh, Jesus. I am not worthy of you. Do not love me. I am not worthy of even a misty drop of it. I am only a killer. Killer of mothers, of daughters, of the world's innocent.

Dawn again. Titus realizes he has fallen asleep at his writing desk.

"My dear *kareste*, please come out ov here and dake some refreshment. Eat a little, shave, bathe, put on clean clothes. I am worried about you."

He leans his head on her, and she brushes the hair out of his eyes. Come, my *kareste*. You did not know. Dhe judges and censor must have conspired to take over dhat cruel man's estate. Dhey knew somedhing no one else did. Dhat's for sure. Now, come, my *kareste*."

Titus lifts his eyes to his wife. "Would you hand a scroll to me out of that basket over there? Then leave me alone a little while longer. I will come out after I have written this. I promise." He tries to smile.

Fjorta hands the scroll to her husband and leaves.

From Titus of Antioch, Pisidia, in Galatia, to Paul of Tarsus now of Antioch in Syria. How can I greet you as a brother? Paul, I am sinking. Soon not even the only real God will be able to lift me up. Pray for a man who has wasted thirty-five years on earth and is drowning in a cesspool of shame. Perhaps your God (and mine if he can still tolerate me) will listen to you.

Titus rolls the scroll up, seals it, writes Paul's name and location on the outside, and takes it out to Cornelius. "Can you get this to Syria?"

Fjuorta hears him and comes to Cornelius' rescue. "I know someone, my *kareste,* who is going to Ephesus lader today. He vill get it on board a ship bound for Syria. I am sure he vill."

She walks to Titus' *officium,* takes a key off her sash, and unlocks a gold-covered box. She takes out some silver coins and put them in a leather pouch. With that, she puts on her stola.

"Vhen I get back vrom town, I expect you to have some clean clothes on und—ooeey—dhat smell gone."

Titus' wife hurries out the gate. He stands in place, watching her leave. "If I am here, that is. If I am here."

19 ~ THE TEMPLE

*T*itus leans against the railing of the ship and watches Ephesus grow smaller and more insignificant, befitting his worthless life.

He holds the letter from Paul and reads it once again, though he no longer opens it to remember what it says. It had taken nearly a year for his message to be delivered to the other Antioch, and for Paul's reply to arrive.

From Paul of Tarsus in Antioch of Syria. To Titus Pomponius Brennius of Antioch of Pisidia, Galatia, your brother in Christ. I have been where you are. All great soldiers of our God have. We are in a war. A war of good against evil. Sometimes Satan wins. But he only thinks he does. He may win a skirmish, but God will win the war. Come join us. We are going to Jerusalem. Come with us and see where Jesus, our Lord, walked and taught and died to overcome death and hell for us. Come, my brother. We will leave as soon as you arrive and not before. Then we will talk. You are not the only one with murder on your hands. Come, my brother.

A day passes. Titus has rented a tent that is put up on the main deck for him to sleep in and for his general privacy. He is grateful for it. When his mood becomes too gloomy, he escapes into it. Inside, he broods for hours.

Just like my father. I am becoming just like my father.

Two days later, the ship docks at Cnidus. He takes the

ramp down to the docks and wanders around the market, always keeping the ship in his sights. That night he sleeps on board in his tent.

He wakens the next morning to bells and shouts to weigh anchor.

He wanders around the ship. *The Christians at home were very patient with me when I descended to this abyss. But I think I took advantage of their patience. I know I did. And Fjorda's. She always defended me to them and told them things I said with more enthusiasm than I had actually said them. Why can I not pull out of this depression?*

The ship docks at Patara and Mira, taking two days at each of those ports.

Titus, as usual, walks around by himself. Sometimes a passenger out sightseeing on the dock tries to strike up a conversation with him. He manages to slip away from them.

He recalls telling his father about his journey. He had knocked on the upstairs *officium* and walked in without being invited. His father had looked up from his writing desk and grunted. Titus had told him he was going to Jerusalem, and he had grunted again. That was it. *Rebuffed by my father, just like I am now rebuffing everyone. I am becoming my father.*

The merchant ship takes a full week to stop at all the ports along the coast of Cilicia. Another week Titus wanders in his nothingness, trying to figure everything out.

Who am I? Why? Who is God? Why? Can that God actually love a worm like me? A murderer of mother, daughter, and innocent client?

At the end of the second week, the ship arrives at Seleucia, seaport serving Antioch, a buffer between the classical city and pirates of the seas.

Titus finds a small caravan going the fifteen *milles* up into the city and joins them. As they draw close, he can see high on a hill what he concludes is the palace. They work their way around the Orontes River, cross it, and enter the city through the North Gate.

He walks straight along the colonnaded street to the market.

"I am looking for a Christian by the name of Paul," he

asks a shopkeeper. "He is from Tarsus up in Cilicia, but I think has lived here a long time."

No response.

"He has a companion by the name of Barnabas—a big man. Perhaps you remember him."

No response.

"Do you know of any Christians in the city?"

The shopkeeper, without looking up, points to his right. Titus turns and walks up a street he hopes will lead him to the Christians. He walks three blocks, then sees a Jewish synagogue on his right. He walks up to it and knocks on the double doors. A big man answers it. They stare at each other.

"Barnabas, is that you?"

"Titus, is that you? Ha! You have found us. Come in. Oh, don't worry. This is not a synagogue anymore. There got to be more Christians than Jews, so we bought out the Jews. Come in. Come in. I think Paul is around here somewhere."

Barnabas looks over the heads of the other men in the large room. "Paul! Are you still here?" he calls out.

"Yes," a familiar voice says, coming out of an adjoining room, "and it looks like you have found our Titus."

"Actually, he found us."

Paul walks over to Titus, taller than him, and forcing a smile.

"Well, now that you have arrived, we can leave. At dawn in the morning, we will walk down to the port and catch a ship headed south. Maybe even on the ship you arrived in. Those merchant ships always take at least a couple days to unload and load back up."

"I know," Titus says, trying to be civil.

"Then we will talk, you and I," Paul says, his eyes serious. "You will be surprised," he whispers.

He smiles again. "Then I trust you can begin rebuilding yourself and your faith. Oh, it is so good to see you again, my brother."

Barnabas walks up. "You are going to go home with us tonight. We need to go to bed early so we can get up before dawn and arrive at the docks before the ships begin pulling out.

Once at Barnabas' house, the three men eat, pray God's blessings on their upcoming mission to Jerusalem, then try to sleep, though sleep is always hard to come by the night before a journey.

By the following mid-morning, they are on their way south along the coast of the Great Sea. Along with the three, they are also accompanied by Lucius and Manaen, leaders in the congregation at Antioch.

Everyone finds a spot to sit and pulls out whatever he brought to do on the way—read someone's writing, do his own writing, mend a tunic, or just sit back and decide what animal the clouds above have formed into.

Paul stands and motions to Titus. "It is time. Come."

Titus stands, and the two men walk away from the others. They lean against the railing and watch the waves, though they do not actually watch them.

"So, you murdered someone. Is that what you said?"

"No, not someone. Three. I have murdered three times."

"And what weapons did you use?"

Titus looks down at Paul. "What do you mean?"

"Exactly that. What weapons did you use?"

Titus gazes back out at the rolling waves. "You are too literal, Paul. I did not need weapons."

Paul is silent.

"The first time it was my mother," Titus continues. "I was eleven years old and selfish. My mother asked me to deliver something to a student out in the country. My father wanted me to observe a trial. I thought I couldn't do both. I thought. I didn't think. I could have delivered the lyre before I went to school that day. But I didn't. Instead, I decided my father was more fierce than my mother, so I would please him and do what he wanted."

Paul remains silent.

"I thought I could just deliver the lyre the next day, but my mother said she had some free time and would deliver it."

Titus stops. He walks up the deck a little way. Paul watches his back tremble as he puts his face in his hands. Paul waits.

After a while, Titus returns. He takes a deep breath.

"There was a horrible earthquake and…"

Paul puts his big hand on Titus' shoulder. Tell me about the next time.

Titus presses his lips together, looks up in the sky, and begins to shake again. He stares at Paul. "My daughter. I killed my baby daughter. I didn't have my doctor check her in time. I should have done it earlier. I should have known a three-year-old would not be strong enough to…"

"Titus," Paul says, facing him and putting his hands on his shoulder. "Tell me about the third time. Tell me."

"She was a little woman. Her husband was big and strong and hateful. He treated her worse than an animal. She had scars all over where he had…"

"So, she killed her husband out of fear."

"Yes, and I could not defend her properly. They found her guilty, and two days after killing her husband, she was dead too. I should have done a better job. But I didn't. I killed…"

Once again, Titus walks off.

Paul waits a while, then steps over to Titus. "When you are ready, I will tell you of the people I murdered, and the weapons I used."

Titus stares at Paul. "You used weapons? Real weapons?"

"Sit," Paul says. He leans his head against the hull and takes a deep breath.

"I was born a Jew and determine to die a Jew. I hated Jesus. He was drawing people away from following the priests. I hated Christians. They were ruining my religion. Everything was falling apart. I wasn't going to let that happen."

He looks Titus in the eyes. "I went house to house hauling people into the dungeon. I tortured them. I used spikes, blades, darts, spears, knives—anything I could think of to make them suffer for what they were doing to the sacred Jewish religion."

Titus stares back. "You did?"

"I was mean and cruel and didn't care. I no longer had a heart. I was like Satan walking on earth."

Both men are quiet.

"Men and women both. I didn't care. I wanted them all dead. When I couldn't get my fill of hatred in Jerusalem, I decided to go to other cities hauling people into the dungeon, torture, and their eventual death. Then I went to Damascus."

"Out of Palestine and all the way up to Syria?"

"Just outside the city, it happened."

"What happened?"

"Can you imagine hearing the very voice of God? I didn't imagine it. I actually heard it. He spoke to me out of heaven in a light so bright I could not tell what was up or down. I fell in the road. The voice of God said to keep going into Damascus, and there someone would explain to me what I had to do. Not could do, but had to do."

"Did the light follow you into the city? Did you crawl there?"

"No, the light went away, but I was left blind. I had an entourage of temple police with me, and they led me into the city. I went to the house of the man I had intended to stay with in the first place and was blind three days."

"Obviously, God let you live."

"No, he killed the old Paul. The old selfish, egotistical, maniac, blood-thirsty Paul. At the end of three days, a man named Ananias came to the house where I was, healed me of my blindness and told me to rise up, be baptized, and wash away all those sins."

"Those were his very words?"

"Those were his very words. I was thirty-one years old then—a little younger than you—and now I am forty-eight. I have spent the past seventeen years trying to make it up to my Savior Jesus Christ, the Word of God who walked on earth."

Silence.

"I never knew," Titus whispers. "I thought I was bad."

Paul laughs and jabs Titus in the shoulder. "So, just because you're better than me…"

"I did not say that," Titus says, smiling in return.

Silence.

"We have a great God. None of those make-believe gods of the Romans or Greeks or Gauls or Egyptians or anyone else would have forgiven what I did—that is, had they been real."

Tears come to Paul's eyes.

"So, you see, young man, you are not alone. You have been forgiven for your small failings and me for my great failings. And now we are equals—forgiven sinners."

"What are you two over here talking about?" Barnabas asks, standing over them. He takes a second look. "Oh. I see Paul has told you his story."

Titus shakes his head. "I just had no idea."

"Well come on, big guy," Barnabas says, tugging on Titus' hand. "We have opened up our baskets of food and are about to indulge. Join us, brothers. Join us."

At the end of a week, the ship docks at Azotas. The five men disembark and walk the rest of the way into Jerusalem.

"See those two towers up ahead?" Paul points out to Titus. "That's always the first thing you see when approaching the legendary holy city from the west."

They enter the city, and Titus takes in all that he sees. Most startling are all the men he sees with beards. The longer the beards are, the more proudly the men seem to walk.

They walk straight ahead and pass two small palaces. "These are the homes of Ananas, the senior High Priest, and Caiaphas, the junior High Priest."

"What's that ramp up there?"

"It leads up to Mount Moriah and the temple at the pinnacle," Barnabas says. "You are a non-Jew..."

"What you Jews call a Gentile. Right?"

"Yes, a Gentile. You will be allowed to walk around all you want in the grand courtyard, but you will not be allowed into the courtyard of the treasury, which some people call the courtyard of the women. Nor farther into the sacred altar. Beyond that, no one is allowed inside the temple except priests and Levites."

"I understand."

"I am going to stay with my sister while I'm here, Titus," Paul says. "Would you like to go with Barnabas or with me?"

"I'm going to the house of my aunt and my cousin, John Mark. You are welcome to go with me if you like."

"Well, I guess I'll go with Barnabas, Paul. You will have

a lot of family catching up to do with your sister.”

The next day is the Sabbath. Barnabas takes Titus with him to the synagogue he attended while a student at the temple in his youth.

The rest of the day, since no work is allowed, John Mark thinks of something enjoyable to do with his company.

“Okay, everyone,” he says, sitting in the solarium of his mother, Mary. “Titus tells me he has been studying the *Torah* and the *Prophets*. Let’s have some competition. Barnabas, you challenge Titus and me to the correct answer.

“This is John Mark’s favorite pastime,” Barnabas tells Titus, “So you’ll have to go along with it, so he doesn’t kick you out onto the street tonight. Okay,” he says, “which prophet foretold that a prophet a lot like Moses would come to earth someday? Titus, you get the first chance.”

Titus grins, then shakes his head. “I don’t guess I know that one.”

“It was Moses who said one would come after him just like him but greater than him.”

“Oh! Ha! Well, give me another chance.”

“All right,” Barnabas says, “which prophet told what city Jesus would be born in hundreds of years later.”

John Mark looks over at Titus. “Well, whoever misses a guess gets to answer the next question first.”

“Micah did. Micah did,” Titus answers, a broad grin on his face.

That night, Titus sleeps soundly for the first time in two years.

“Get up, sleepy Gentile,” John Mark says, coming into the supply room Mary has turned into a guest bedroom. “It is Solday morning.”

“Oh, where does the church meet here? Are you scattered all over the city like we are in Antioch?” Titus asks.

“We are lucky. There are six thousand of us...”

“Six thousand?” Titus puts both hands on top of his head and swings around in place. “Six?”

“Yes. Six thousand, and we meet along the portico of the general courtyard outside the actual temple area. Solomon’s Portico is half a *mille* long, so there is plenty of room for everyone."

Titus walks with Barnabas' Aunt Mary, John Mark, and Barnabas up the long ramp to the top of Mount Moriah. They enter the courtyard that is behind the temple facing east. As they walk toward the portico where the Christians are assembling, Titus stops.

"Angels. You said there are angels in heaven. Is that what angels sound like?" he asks.

"Probably so," Aunt Mary says. "Let's go join the angels."

After our worship," Barnabas explains, "we will be taking care of the business they came to Jerusalem for."

"I didn't know you came for business. I thought it was just to see your families again," Titus says.

"It's about circumcision. You in Galatia are not the only ones with that problem. Jewish spies are making the rounds of every city that has Christians in it, and going in to stir things up. 'You have to be a Jew before you can be a Christian,' they declare. They're not trying to help us. They are trying to divide us and destroy us."

Titus is enthralled with the worship service he is able to participate in. *I can't wait to get back to Antioch and tell them what this has been like. They'll never believe it.*

When the time of worship is over, Peter announces that some business needs to be taken care of, but anyone who cannot stay may leave now.

Most leave, but about two hundred stay.

Peter stands. "We are privileged to have Paul and Barnabas with us today. They have come here from Antioch in Syria with a couple of their other leaders and with one of their Gentile converts—Titus of Antioch in Pisidia of Galatia. We have asked Paul and Barnabas to report on their work in the province of Galatia."

The two missionaries take turns reporting the establishment of congregations among both Jews and Gentiles in cities of Galatia, Pisidia, Lycea, and Cyprus.

Amos rises. "Did you circumcise them before or after their baptism?"

"We circumcised no one," Barnabas replies.

Back and forth, the discussion goes. Old arguments

Titus has often heard. New arguments he has not yet heard.

He hears his own name called out.

"Titus? Never," Paul replies, almost irate. "He is of Gaulish ancestry on both sides of his family. They have never had any connections with Jews. There is no reason for him to be circumcised. I will not allow it."

The debate about Titus subsides. The debate about circumcision ends.

James, the half-brother of Jesus, rises.

"Brothers, Simon Peter has reminded us how God has blessed the Gentiles. Therefore, in my opinion, we should write the Gentile Christians a circulating letter telling them to abide by three things: Don't eat anything with blood still in it, don't eat anything offered to false gods, don't commit sexual sins."

The next morning, the five walk back toward Azotas and pay the fare for a ship heading back north. When they reach the port serving Antioch of Syria, Titus stays on board.

"I am ready to go home, Paul."

"Are you okay now?"

"Yes. I am invigorated and ready to get back to work serving my family, my city, my congregation, and my Lord Jesus the Christ, Son of the only God."

"Your faith has recovered. Good, Titus. Good."

"No more earthquakes, no more plagues, no more disruptions. Everything back to normal again. Isn't that right, Paul?"

Paul does not reply. He turns and steps off the ship.

20 ~ ASTONISHMENTS

"Did you hear the news?" passengers aboard the ship ask each other.

Titus decides, now that he is alone again, he will refuse to return to his old gloomy self.

"No, I don't guess I have. I've been out of touch recently," he tells a friendly passenger.

"Claudius has deported all Jews from Rome."

"What? Why?"

"Don't know. He just says they're always arguing and rampaging against each other and causing constant disorder in his city."

"I wonder if he knows the difference in Christians and Jews."

"What's a Christian?"

"Oh, you don't know? Let me tell you all about it. We have a week or two together. I think I can get it all explained by the time we get home—or wherever you are going."

As others overhear Titus, they ask to listen in. Within a few days, most of the passengers are sitting around Titus and his rented tent learning about a God who is the only real God.

"How do we know? There are a thousand gods in the world? Who is telling the truth and who is making things up to make them look important?"

"Miracles. Their leaders can perform miracles. They can

go anywhere in the world and speak the language of the local people instantly. They don't have to take lessons. They just automatically know all those languages."

"So, our prophetesses can all speak unknown tongues."

"There's a difference. These are not unknown. They are not gibberish and blathering like the Pythias of Apollo and other gods do. They are actual known languages."

"So?"

"They can perform other miracles too. I saw one of them make a man's hand grow back instantly."

"Can't be done."

"Of course. Not by humans. Their God, who claims to be the only real God in existence, proved he is telling the truth.

Questions and answers. Day after day.

At last, they hear the captain call out Titus' destination. "Everyone debarking at Ephesus, gather up your luggage, and turn in your tent if you rented one."

Once on shore, Titus looks through his money pouch. *Just enough left*, he tells himself. He walks over to a stable and buys a delicate Egyptian horse. "Perfect for my delicate ice queen."

He gives away all his luggage and heads for home. He stops on the way twice, stays in government hostels along the Roman road, waters and feeds his mount and goes on his way. On the third day, he rides into Antioch.

People look twice when they see him.

"Is that you, Titus?"

He waves back. "Yes. And isn't it a beautiful day?"

The word spreads fast. But not as fast as Titus. He puts his Egyptian into a prance and hurries toward home.

"Let me in Cornelius. I'm home. I'm home, everyone!"

The gate opens. Fjorta comes running toward him, her arms outstretched.

Titus slides off his horse and rushes toward her. He picks her up in his arms and swings her around.

"Look. Your dimple is back," she squeals.

"What's wrong?" he asks. "You don't feel right. Are you okay?"

Fjorta backs away from her husband.

She has lost her smile, her laughter.

"Yes, I'm all right?" she whispers. "Ve both are."

"Aunt Chloe too? I'm glad for her."

"Not Aunt Chloe, silly. Us. Us."

She takes Titus' hand and places it on her swelling.

"Baby? We're going to have a baby?" Titus yelps.

"Yes, my sweet *kareste*. Ve are going to have a baby."

"When? It must be soon. You are, well, big."

"Yes, soon. I knew as soon as you left."

"So, you are giving me a homecoming gift. Well, I have one for you."

"A present vor me? All dhe way vrom Palestine?"

"Farther than that. All the way from Egypt."

He hands her the reins of the delicate Egyptian horse. "She is yours."

"Oh, I can't vait," she squeals.

"You do not have to wait."

Before she can object, Titus has lifted her up to sit sideways on her gift. He takes hold of the halter and walks the horse up the street a little way and back. He steps around and helps her down.

They embrace for a long time.

"You're back," Fjorta whispers. "I have you back. All ov you."

"Yes, all of me. I learned so much from Paul. He even took me to Jerusalem, the capital city of the Jews. And I saw the temple, and..."

"What are you two doing in the middle of the street?" It is an old voice. A sweet voice. The faltering voice of Lydia, their maid now for nearly three decades.

"Brutus!" the sweet voice of Lydia calls out in a shriek. "Come get our master's horse."

"No, Lydia. It is my horse. My *kareste* brought back a horse ov my very own."

"Come get our mistress's horse," Lydia corrects.

Brutus hobbles out to the street, grins, and welcomes his master home.

Titus and Fjorta walk, holding hands back into Titus' childhood home.

He looks around. "Nothing seems changed."

"You veren't gone dhat long, my *kareste.*"

"What about the church? Are we still hosting it, or at least part of it?"

"Yes. But ve have been suffering vithout much leadership, vhat vith Fulvio gone."

"Fulvio's gone? Where?"

"To Corinth. Vhen Claudia made all dhe Jews leave Rome, many of dhem vent to Corinth. Some vent to Athens, but Corinth vas better because it is a vairly new city."

"You're right. It was rebuilt about twenty-five years before my father was born. As cities go, Corinth is just an infant."

"An invant all ready to grow up and be vancy. Und to be helped vith all dhe Jews vrom Rome. New houses, especially.

"Perfect for Fulvio and his picturesque tile business," Titus responds. "It won't take him long to be rich. So, I suppose Aunt Chloe went with him."

"Yes, dhey are both gone. Hey, vhere is your baggage?" she asks, one hand on her lower back and the under her swelling front, walking toward her new and cushioned chair.

"I gave it away in Ephesus. So now, it's just you and my father. How is he, anyway?"

"He is beginning to show his age. Remember how he used to come halv vay down dhe stairs und bawl everyone out vor all our noise vidh dhat big, gruff voice ov his?"

Titus smiles. "Do I ever."

Lydia walks out to the courtyard with a large goblet of new wine for Titus and the smaller one of peach nectar for Fjorta.

"Vell, he is sixty-von years old now und can't yell as loud anymore. He had a birdhday vhile you vere gone."

"How did you kitow?"

"I didn't get here yust yesterday," she says, wagging her head. "Vell, I am a little tired. I dhink I shall dake a little nap."

Titus helps her stand and gain her balance and walks her to the guest bedroom, which she takes possession of during the day.

She lies down, and he goes to his *officium.* He pauses at

the door, remembering. He looks at a basket on his writing-table and remembers the last person he had shared a handkerchief with from it.

I am not going to look back. If Paul can handle it, I can too. Satan, stay away from me. You are not going to pull me down anymore.

He walks around and sits on a chair behind his writing-table. He looks over to his left and sees the basket with some of the Jewish prophecies belonging to his mother that he had left behind. He pulls one out and begins reading.

"Is our vamily doctor here?" It is Fjorta's voice.

Shocked, Titus looks up and drops the scroll onto his writing-table. He rushes out to his wife and helps her to her chair in the family courtyard.

"Cornelius! Lydia! Someone! Call the doctor."

"I believe he is with your father upstairs," Lydia responds.

"Why? What's wrong with my father?"

"Oh, I think he is just wanting a little attention," she says, smiling.

"I'll go get him," Cornelius says.

"Oh, no, you won't. You can hardly shuffle around down here. You are not going to climb stairs."

Cornelius obeys, and Lydia disappears upstairs.

"The doctor says he will be down as soon as he is through with your father."

"What's going on?"

"I think they are having a friendly game of dice," Lydia says with a twinkle in her eye.

"Tell him to hurry," Titus urges. "I am not going to wait too long this time..."

"My *kareste,* ve are not going to dhink about dhose earlier times."

Titus takes a deep breath. "You are right, Fjorta. You are right."

A little past midnight, Fjorta gives birth with the assistance of the doctor and a midwife.

Lydia goes into the guest room with water, towels, and swaddling bands. Half an hour later, she walks out with the baby in her arms, wrapped snugly in the bands. She hands the baby to its father.

"You have a baby boy, Master," she says.

Titus takes his child in his arms, tries not to weep, and does anyway.

"Your wife will be clean and fresh in just a few more moments," she adds.

Titus sits with his son on a bench around the reflecting pool. He looks up, and for a moment sees a nine-year-old boy standing beside it, reciting what he has learned in school to the delight of his very young father and mother.

The flash of memory excuses itself, and he returns to his own little boy. "I will be proud of you all your life. No matter what you do or don't do, no matter what you say or don't say, no matter what you become, I will never stop being proud of you. And loving you."

"Did you say somedhing, my *kareste*? Don't expect vour son to answer you. Not vor anodher veek or two, anyvay."

Titus looks up. "What are you doing out of bed?" he asks.

"Visiting my two *karestes*. Dhat's vhat."

The baby wrinkles its nose, opens its mouth, and lets out a tiny noise that is akin to the warbling of a bird.

"I think he wants his mother. Why don't you go back to your room and sit up in bed? He may be wanting his dinner."

"Vell, his middle-ov-dhe-night dinner anyvay."

Mother and son get settled, and Titus seats himself where the doctor had been.

"Have you thought of a name, my little ice queen now with a little ice sickle to take care of?"

"Vell, yes, I have been dhinking. But I don't dhink you vill like it."

"Tell me the name and I will let you know."

"Vellll," she scrunches up her lips and wiggles her nose. "I vas dhinking ov maybe naming him after my vadder."

Titus is silent.

She watches him.

"Or, maybe not."

"Guthmar," Titus muses. "Hmmm."

"My vadder has dhree names. Vould you like to know dhem all?"

"By all means, let's consider them all. And I will choose one of them to be our son's name." *What am I getting into?*

His dhree names are Guthmar Asmunder Sirius.

"Sirius? Really?"

"In our language, Sirius means a dog."

"In our language, Sirius is a bright star."

Titus smiles.

"You like it?" Fjorta smiles back. "You like Sirius?"

"I do, my love. I do."

"So our son vill be named avter my vadder. Uh, oh. Vill your vadder be jealous?"

"Well, Justus means being 'just and fair'. I would think 'light' and 'justus' would nearly have the same meaning."

"So, ve vill tell your vadder ve named our son avter him in my native language."

"That might work. Anyway, our son's name will be Sirius Titus Brinnius. I like it. I will go tell Father now."

"Titus does. His father looks up from his writing table, sets down the scroll he is reading, walks past Titus, down the stairs, and into the guest bedroom. Fjorta holds the baby up for Justus to see. He grunts and returns to his *officium.*

"Your vadder is pleased. He likes his new grandson."

"How do you know he is pleased?"

"He grunted und almost smiled."

"Oh, what a woman I married," Titus says, grinning.

Over the next few months, Fjorta spends most of her time with baby Sirius.

Titus takes a few legal cases—wills, border disputes, water rights and such like— but refuses to go to the Vesta court or to be paid.

One afternoon, there is a knock on the gate. Cornelius shuffles to it. "Where is that Titus?" the gruff voice bellows.

Titus stands and hurries to the courtyard.

"Paul. It's brother Paul," Titus exclaims, striding with his long legs toward his friend.

"And who do you have with you? Where is Barnabas?"

"Oh, well, he and John Mark went to Cyprus. But this

is Silas, a friend I have had since early school days in Tarsus. And this is Timothy from Derbe. He has just joined us and will be traveling with us. Well, aren't you going to invite us to sit down?" Paul says, walking toward a bench. He sits.

Silas offers his hand to Paul. "He has been like that his whole life," he says, winking at Titus. "He'll never change."

"Well, have a seat around our pool," Titus responds.

"So, I guess that leaves me," Timothy says, holding out his hand.

"Well, it looks like we see eye to eye," Titus says. I assume you are Gaulish like my father and me.

"All except my mother's side," Timothy says. "She is the one I inherited the red hair from.

"Who do ve have here, my *kareste*?

Titus hurries to his wife.

"Paul, look what my wife presented me with when I got back home."

Paul jumps up and steps over to the baby. "And what do we call him?"

"Sirius Titus Brennius."

"An excellent name," Paul says while easing little Sirius out of Titus' arms and into his own. He walks over to his partner and lifetime friend.

"Look," he says. "This is Uncle Silas. His name almost sounds like yours. You must be twins."

Paul walks next over to Timothy. "And this is Uncle Timothy. He looks a lot like your papa. They must be twins."

He sits on the side of the round reflecting pool, turns the baby over on his stomach, and holds him out over the water.

"Ughhh," Fjorta says, throwing her hands to her cheeks and heading for Paul. "Give me my baby!" she screeches.

"Look, this is you reflected in the water," Paul says. "You must be twins."

Before Fjorta can get to him, Paul steps over to Titus. On his way, he holds the baby out in front of him so he can see Paul's face. "And I am Uncle Paul. I am too ugly to have a twin, much to the relief of the saner world."

He turns the baby around and holds him up to see his

father just as Fjorta arrives at his side. He turns the baby around, now holding him out to face his mother.

Fjorta snatches her baby and walks away from Paul while he laughs. She turns around facing Paul but looks down at little Sirius. "Dhat man who just had you is bad, bad, bad."

Paul and his companions laugh. Titus only half laughs.

"Sirius und I are going vor a valk," she announces as Cornelius opens both inner and outer gates for her. The men settle on gilded chairs situated around the pool.

"Well, the Jews keep wanting to control the church," Paul says. "They are a hard-headed bunch. I ought to know. I am one of them—well only by nationality now."

"They keep wanting to turn you Gentiles into Jews first so they can claim you, then allow you to be Christians," Silas says.

"The Jews never give us rest," Titus says. "However, some of them have decided you gave valid proofs that day, and Jesus really was the Son of God. So they have joined themselves to us at great jeopardy to their own safety."

"And they don't bring up circumcision to you?" Timothy asks.

"Not much. We Gentiles—as you call us—far outnumber them. You must remember, this city has a strong Gaulish aristocracy," Titus explains.

"I'll bet your local synagogue keeps trying to get them back," Paul says.

"They try harder even than the worshippers of the Roman gods," Titus says. "So, are you just passing through, or can you stay a while?"

"If we can be of any help, we thought we'd stay a couple weeks," Silas replies. "All you have to do is let us loose in the city, and we will do what we do."

The next morning, Timothy announces he wants to go over to the Temple of Apollo. "There are always men my age standing around, wanting to talk about the Olympics and how proud Apollo is of them."

"I think I'll go over to the market, mention Jesus a little loud to a few merchants, and see if anyone wants to hear more," Silas says, putting on a toga he does not wear much but is entitled to as a Roman citizen of Tarsus.

"Where is your library?" Paul asks, draping his own toga around his athletic but scarred body.

"Over in the gymnasium academy at the far northeast side of the city beyond the citadel," Titus explains.

"I will cover the library," Paul says. "Maybe I can find someone interested in learning about a god they never heard of. Then I will explain he is the only real God and that his Word walked on earth for a while."

"They won't all like it," Titus warns. "Be careful."

21 ~ UNSPEAKABLE

"*T*itus, I am going to valk over to dhe Demple of Vesta to pick up Sirius. He does enjoy playing vith dhe odher children. I just vish the city vould let us keep our children home until they are school age."

"We will just have to keep teaching him that Vesta is not a real goddess," he says, walking out of his *officium.*

"Vhat can you teach a dhree-year-old?"

"I don't know. We can just keep teaching him until he is old enough to understand," he says, kissing his still beautiful ice queen with the white-blond hair. "Will you be coming right back home?" he asks.

Fjorta reaches up and tugs on a hair at his temple. "Vhat is dhis? A gray hair?"

"No, it is not a gray hair. Men at age forty do not have gray hair."

"Perhaps I vill buy some charcoal on my vay home vor you to hide it under." She grins, reaches up, kisses her husband, turns, and Cornelius opens the gate for her.

Titus returns to his *officium.* "Now let me see, I was categorizing all King Solomon's proverbs so I can find them easier when needed. Too bad he didn't think of things to say in categories."

"What did you say, Master Titus?" Lydia says, walking toward the female servants' quarters in the back.

Titus looks over at her. "Oh, nothing. You look very nice today."

"Oh, my. I have not looked nice in nearly fifty years, Master Titus. But thank you, anyway."

"Master Titus. Your wife has not returned yet," Cornelius says. "Do you think we should worry?"

Titus looks out through his open door at the courtyard. "Is it that late? I thought I have just been reading this a few moments."

He walks out to the street. He looks in the direction his wife and son should be arriving from. He sees many people returning home, but not his family.

"Brutus," he calls out, "saddle my horse."

Moments later, Titus is urging his horse through the streets of Antioch as fast as he dares with all the foot traffic. He cuts behind the Temple of Augustus and slows his horse so he can watch the trees and park benches along the Sanctuary of Men-Askenos.

He speeds up again as he rides past the citadel and the gymnasium academy. At the north city wall, he slows again, turns left, and enters the Nymphaeum. He dismounts and walks his horse between the columns, statues of the muses, and around the waterfalls and lily ponds. Still, no family.

He works his way west toward the North Gate, where the aqueduct from the mountains spills into the park. He pauses at the gate and decides to turn back and go through the park a different way. As he does, he thinks he hears a lamb bleating for its mother. Once more, he goes through the North Gate.

A strange place for a lost lamb. He looks back toward the aqueduct again. The sound is still there. He looks around and does not see anyone. His horse neighs and walks forward. Titus loosens his grip on the reins and follows the horse. It stops where the hill slopes down into the valley at the base of the aqueduct.

He hears the sound of the lost lamb again, looks around again. He dismounts and works his way down the slope. He hears a scream. He all but stumbles down the remainder of the hill.

"Over here, Titus. Over here!"

He lunges in the direction of his wife's voice and sees his son wandering in circles crying like a little lost lamb. He grabs up his son. "Where is your *moderr*, Sirius?

The boy clings to his father around the neck, still crying, and points behind him.

Titus hangs tight onto the boy and scrambles the rest of the way to the concrete base of the first aqueduct arch.

"Dhank God. Dhank God."

He sees a piece of blue cloth and knows it is his Fjorta. He looks behind a bush and sees her on the ground, the blue leather tunic is torn and pulled half off her. There is blood on one arm, her face, and part of her tangled hair.

Titus shifts his son over onto his back to cling to him there and kneels by his wife.

"What did they do to you?" He embraces her and rocks her back and forth. "Oh, my darling. What did they do to you?"

"You should have seen vhat I did to him," she says.

Titus eases his hold on her and jerks his head back. "What did you say?"

"You should have seen vhat I did to him."

Fjorta sits up. "Vhile ve vere in dhe nymphaeum, I heard a scream. I could tell it came vrom dhe odher side of dhe city vall. I heard dhe scream again, grabbed up Sirius, und ran dhrough dhe gate und down the gulley."

Sirius has now loosened his grip on his father's neck, slid down his back, and stepped around to lay his head on his mother's legs.

"Ouch, sveetheart. Dhat hurts *moderr*."

"What did they—he do to you?"

"I vas getting to dhat. I followed dhe sound of dhe scream und saw a young man vorcing a girl down onto dhe ground. So, vhat could I do? I could not yust let it happen. I ran down into dhe gully, jumped on dhe young man und rolled him off dhe girl. Dhen I punched him in dhe face. He tried to reach my neck, but I am too tall. I yust leaned back und kept punching."

"Yup. *Moderr* punched and punched and punched," Sirius responds, shadow boxing.

"I made him promise to leave dhe girl alone, und he did. So, I let him up und he ran avay."

"And the girl?"

She disappeared too.

"And left you like…" He pauses. "Why can't you get up?"

"Vell, before dhe young man ran avay, he picked up a tree branch laying dhere und batted it into my legs. I guess so I could not vollow him."

Titus moves her skirt out of the way and feels around both legs.

"Ooo," Fjorta says, "dhat one hurts. It must be broken."

"Are you hurt anywhere else? I do not want to move you if you are."

"Vell, my knuckles are preddy sore," she says.

Titus shakes his head. "Oh, my Nordic ice queen. Let's get you out of here."

Sirius climbs onto his father's back again, clinging to his neck. Titus lifts his wife onto her one good leg, then sweeps her up in his strong arms.

Titus works his way back up the slope. When he reaches the top, he whistles for his horse, now grazing. The big Arabian trots over, and Titus lifts his wife onto it, side-saddle.

"Sirius and I will walk," he says.

When they reach the North Gate, one of the guards steps over. "What happened?"

"There seems to have been a serious altercation at the bottom of the gully. Did you hear anything?"

"Nothing other than crows."

"Did you see a young man with a bloody nose run through here?"

"No. Everything has been quiet. Most people have gone home for the day."

Titus walks his black horseback into the city and proceeds straight on the columned Cardo Maximus. The few people left on the street before the sun goes down stare at the familiar threesome. He proceeds at a slow gait past the Temple of Vesta on his right, then the Temple of Augustus Caesar on his left, the artificial waterfall, and the Temple of Apollo. More people stop beside the street and watch them go by.

"What's wrong with Fjorta?" ask. Others stare a moment, shrug, and flip their hand as though shooing away a menace. On the other side of Apollo, Titus turns at the Vici Aegeus and arrives home.

"Brutus! Cornelius! Lydia!" he calls out.

Cornelius comes out first. Then Brutus who takes hold of the Arabian's bridle. Finally, Lydia.

"Oh, my poor baby," she says, reaching up to pat her mistress on the hand. She reaches for Sirius.

"Run get the doctor," Titus instructs Cornelius. "Is he here?"

"Probably upstairs playing a board game with your father. I will call him."

Titus eases his wife off the big steed and carries her to the family courtyard. He situates her on a couch brought out from the banquet hall.

Just then, the doctor arrives, armed with swaddling bands, a couple sticks of different lengths, and a jar of herbs. He hands the herbs to Lydia to make anesthetic tea, then kneels before his mistress's couch to wrap her injured leg.

The next morning, Titus leaves early and rides over to the *palatio* of the new censor of Antioch, Ammonius Moderatus.

Upon seeing Titus, the censor stops in his tracks. "I am surprised to see you here, considering the trouble your wife is in."

"My wife?" Titus challenges? "She rescued a girl about to be ravaged."

"That is not what I have been told. The father of the girl has already been here demanding a subpoena for her arrest."

Titus backs up. "What? No. You're wrong."

"The girl claims she was strolling along the hill opposite the aqueduct when your wife suddenly appeared, attacked her, and shoved her down into the gully."

"That is not true," Titus insists. "The girl is wrong!"

"That is what I have been told. Apophis is an honorable man. He would not lie. "If I were you, I would hurry home. A legionnaire from the citadel is probably there now."

Titus turns and rushes back out onto the street. He

mounts his horse and gallops the two blocks to home.

Two legionnaires stand guard at his gate.

"What is the meaning of this? Do you realize where you are? This is the home of Justus Brennius Antiochus, Praetor of Antioch."

"We know that, sir, but must obey the law." Just then, another legionnaire arrives with a small cart.

"Put her in here," he growls.

Titus turns to rush into his house when he is met by a legionnaire carrying his wife out.

"Put her down!"

The legionnaire says nothing and deposits her in the cart.

"*Moderr, Moderr.*" Sirius toddles after his mother. Titus grabs him up in his arms and hands him over to Lydia.

"I am here, Fjorta. I will not leave you," He shouts. "You will be freed tomorrow. I promise."

"Halt!"

The voice is powerful.

"Halt! You will not take that woman out of my house."

Justus stands at the railing of his roof next to a transplanted tree and ivy. "Take one more step, and your life will be at the mercy of Nero Caesar himself."

The legionnaires stop and stare up.

"You will leave her here. I will personally escort her to court tomorrow morning."

Titus sweeps his wife up in his arms and rushes her back into their home. Brutus grabs his Arabian's halter to lead it away, and Cornelius follows behind Titus to close the gates and secure them.

"Vhy vould dhe girl lie vhen I probably saved her life? Or at least her honor," Fjorta asks.

"I intend to find out."

Titus spends the rest of the day questioning people at the nymphaeum, asking if they had been there the day before and if they had heard or seen anything unusual.

One of the legionnaires comes out of his guardhouse at the North Gate and marches over to the nymphaeum nearby. The people spot him and wander back toward the city.

Titus backtracks to the Sanctuary of Men-Askenos. He walks his horse between the pine trees and park benches, approaching anyone he sees.

"Were you here yesterday? Did you see anything unusual?"

Once more, he sees legionnaires marching toward him.

"Move along, sir. We do not want the citizenry of Antioch disturbed."

With that, visitors to the park turn toward the city.

It is mid-afternoon. Titus mounts his horse and heads toward his neighborhood. When he reaches it, he rides past his *palatio* to that of his father's old friend.

"Come in, come in, Titus," Pollux says. "I know why you are here."

"What is going to happen tomorrow at court?" Titus asks.

"Tomorrow at court, the truth will be revealed. That is what is going to happen. Now go on home. Your wife and son need you."

The following morning before dawn, Titus rides his black stallion toward the Temple of Vesta. When he arrives, spectators are just beginning to assemble. He takes the steps up to the platform, looks around, takes the steps up to his father's perch at the top, sits in his chair a moment, stands, looks at the city toward the nymphaeum, then walks back down to sit on the defendant's bench. He bows his head, then raises it to the rose-colored sky of the morning.

"Give me wisdom. Give us all wisdom."

Sometime later, Apophis arrives. His daughter is not with him. He looks around, climbs the steps to the platform, and sits on the plaintiff's bench.

Titus looks around for his wife. She is not yet in sight. But soon, the three judges arrive.

Finally, he hears his father's chariot and the clop, clop, clop of his horse's hooves. He prays again. *Give me wisdom. Give us all wisdom. Give us all mercy.*

The horse stops, and he hears his father's familiar footsteps. He walks up to the platform carrying his daughter-in-law. Tall and straight, his father takes broad steps over to the defendant's bench, sets her down, then seats himself next to her.

Fjorta is wearing her white leather tunic and white cloak edges with white fir. Titus kisses his wife's cheek and whispers, "Where did he get that strength? He is over sixty."

Titus looks at his father. Justus stares back, then nods. Titus nods back. No words are exchanged.

Everyone waits. The spectators below wait. Titus and his wife's enemy, Ammonius, wait. The three judges wait. Justus waits.

They hear chariot wheels again and clop, clop, clop of horse hooves. The chariot stops.

Titus closes his eyes tight.

He hears footsteps toward the platform. When he opens his eyes, he sees Pollux.

Pollux climbs to the pinnacle and sits in the praetor's seat. The deputy joins him and makes the announcement. "You may begin."

Apophus stands. "Most Excellent Magistrates. I am honored to stand before such men of wisdom as you. If my daughter had been able to be here today, she would have come. But, friends and Romans, she was accosted in such an inhuman way, she still has not gotten over the trauma. She, only thirteen years of age, is afraid to leave our house."

He looks toward the spectators for approval.

"As her father, I intend to prove that this vicious woman—he swings around and points at Fjorta—this, this barbarian, daughter of barbarians, has done all she could since arriving in this city to upset every tradition of goodness we have here."

He looks down at the spectators, then up at the acting praetor. "She has finally done it." He raises his voice. "I demand that she be punished for treason and put to death."

The spectators gasp. Titus clings to his bench, and his knuckles turn white. Justus does not react. Fjorta bows her head.

Titus begins to stand, but his father's hand reaches over to his chest.

Justus stands. The spectators grow completely silent.

The judges stop fidgeting. He is wearing his purple-bordered toga, strands of his now white hair lifting briefly in the morning breeze. He looks down at the spectators then up at his substitute.

"Romans, proud citizens of Antioch," he growls. "Today, you shall see justice. Today, you shall see the honor of all Antioch defended and upheld."

"Uh, Praetor Pollux," Apophis says, standing. "My witnesses have just arrived."

Everyone on the platform and among the spectators turns to see three legionnaires marching from the citadel. When they arrive on the platform, they salute the victim's father.

"Reporting as requested."

"Stay standing," Apophis responds. "Now, all three of you were on duty the of the vicious assault of my daughter."

The legionnaires respond with "Yes, sir," each in turn beginning with the oldest.

"And did you see my daughter that day?"

"Yes, sir," come their replies.

"Was she with anyone?"

"No, sir."

"She was just strolling along the top of the hill overlooking the aqueduct."

"Yes, sir."

"Did you see anyone else after that?"

"Yes, sir," each in turn.

"If she—uh the person—is here today, will you please point her—or him—out?"

The three legionnaires raise their arms in synchronization and point to Fjorta.

The crowd nods its approval.

22 ~ THE MEETING

"Young men."

The voice is loud, but not as booming as Justus' voice.

Everyone looks up at the praetor's perch above all others.

"Take those faceplates off your helmets. The very idea of appearing in court with your identities hidden."

The young men comply. Fjorta squints to see them better.

"Do you recognize anyone?" Titus whispers.

"Shhh," Justus mutters.

"You. Yes, you with the scratches on your face. Take your helmet off." It is Chrispus of Athens, the oldest judge.

The legionnaire looks over at Ammonius, hesitates, then takes off his helmet.

"Dhat's him," Fjorta calls out. "Dhat's him."

"Young lady," Chrispus of Athens warns, "get control of yourself."

"I believe we have one more witness," Pollux announces from on high. "Oh, here she comes."

When the girl approaches the steps up to the platform, she screams.

Apophis' face turns red with rage. ""What is my daughter doing here? I demand an explanation."

Fjorta stands and rushes down the steps.

"Stop her!" Ammonius shouts.

Immediately Fjorta puts her arm around the girl and helps her up the steps. The girl cringes and hangs back.

"Do not look at her," Acting Praetor Pollux calls down to the witnesses.

The legionnaires return to facing Ammonius. Fjorta slips the girl behind them and takes her over to the witness bench. They sit, Fjorta still holding her close.

"I demand this be stopped, and my daughter returned to the protection of her home," Ammonius shouts, his face still red. He looks up at the acting praetor. "Do something. This is illegal."

"I did something, sir. I personally subpoenaed your daughter to appear in court today." He looks down at the frightened girl. "You may remain where you are. We just need you to point out your assailant to the court."

The girl raises her head from Fjorta's shoulder, sobs, and points to the youngest legionnaire, the one with scratches on his face. "Him," she whispers.

"Now we wait again," Acting Praetor Pollux commands.

Silence on the platform. All except the three judges mumbling to each other, and the spectators stretching their necks to see what is going on, anxious to know the outcome of this strange trial.

"Hutt, hutt, hutt." It comes from the direction of the citadel

Everyone turns and watches as the commander is escorted toward the forum by two lesser legionnaires.

The commander steps up to the platform and faces the judges, his legs apart and flexing his chest and arm muscles. The veins on his neck throb.

"Commander, I am placing you under arrest." Acting Praetor Pollux pronounces.

Gasping. The crowd stirs and mutters to each other. The participants on the platform squirm.

"You have bribed a man who used to be respected in our city in order to save the honor of your consortium. You, sir, have brought yourself down lower than any of the men serving under you."

Ammonius stands. "He initiated it. He forced the money on me. I did not want to take it!"

Justus smiles. He looks over at his son and nods. Titus nods back.

"This trial has revealed the souls and true nature of people in our city who everyone has heretofore respected. I am ashamed," Acting Praetor Pollux announces. "Before I turn the proceedings back to our judges, I must declare new charges against all those who have perjured themselves on this dark day in the city of Antioch."

"Charges of perjury against the three legionnaires.

"Charges of bribery against Commander Festus.

"Charges of accepting a bribe against Ammonius.

"Charles of slander against Ammonius.

"Charges of bone-breaking against Legionnaire Vlassic.

"Charges of assault and attempted ravaging against Legionnaire Vlassic.

Pollox leans forward to see the judges below better. "Did you get all that? Good. Now, write your verdicts."

The three judges are given five small scrolls each.

At the end of an hour, the verdicts have been placed on the side of the altar to Vesta, and an ox offered as a sacrifice, all amidst chanting by the Vestal Virgins.

Everyone waits. At last, the high priestess pronounces them approved by the goddess, and they are handed up to Acting Praetor Pollux.

"All have been found guilty. Everyone stand."

"You three legionnaires will forfeit pay for one year and never be allowed to participate in any of Rome's Olympic games as long as you live. Two of you are dismissed. Vlassis, you stay."

"Ammonius, you condemned yourself when you admitted you took the bribe to lie about Fjorta and Vlassic. Thank you." Pollux grins. Justus grins.

"You will stand on this platform every morning for one month, confess your sins, and publicly apologize for defaming Fjorta Brennius. Next, you will deposit three times the amount of the bribe with the city treasurer to be given to your daughter, and your daughter alone, at the age of twenty-five or until she marries, whichever comes first. If you do not deposit the money in one week, you will be confined to debtor's dungeon until you do. Dismissed."

"Commander Festus, you will put on deposit five times the amount of money you bribed Ammonius with. Table VIII of the ancient Laws Tables states that you, not only a false witness but the instigator or creating other false witnesses, must be taken to the top of the cliff behind the Sanctuary of Men-Askenos and hurled down from it into the river below.

However, we are not barbarians. You will resign your position, be beaten with one hundred stripes, and exiled from the Roman Empire the rest of your life. Guards, take him into custody."

"Last, we have Legionnaire Vlassic. I understand you are only seventeen years old. Interesting. That is the age of our new Caesar this year—Nero. I hope your malicious behavior is not any portend of what he will become."

Stirring among the spectators.

"Because you broke the bone or bones of Fjorta Brennius, your bones will be broken in the same places. She has the right to do the honors herself, or may pass the deed on to another."

"Now for the most heinous of crimes—violating a little girl. I tend to agree with Plato in his Book 8 of *Laws*. The little girl is thirteen years old. You are seventeen years old. Combined, that is twenty years. I am sentencing you to twenty years hard labor. The procurator of Thrace is a friend of mine. I'm sure he can use you in his silver mines."

Pollux looks over at the legionnaires standing by at the bottom of the steps. "Guards, get him out of my sight."

The spectators turn to each other and commence discussions of the verdicts.

"We are not through here, everyone," Acting Praetor Pollux announces. We have one left. Fjorta Brennius, will you step forward."

He waits. Fjorta stands straight and tall, her white-blond hair flowing easily behind her.

"You risked your life to save another. That does not go unnoticed. I do not believe you are interested in money.

Instead, I am granting that for the next two years, whenever we have games in honor of Apollo, you will lead the procession through our streets."

Pollux whispers something to the deputy. The deputy calls out, "Dismissed."

Two years pass. Everyone returns to normal. Titus studies the old prophecies and writes opinions of them, though he doubts he will ever show them to anyone.

Fjorta continues to dote on their son and begins giving lessons in spear throwing to any woman in the city who wants to learn. The husbands tolerate her; Titus thinks his ice queen is more amazing all the time.

Justus has returned to his *officium* on the second floor. The doctor has died, and Justus has not found a replacement for checking on his ailing bones and challenging him to a board game. He recedes into himself even more.

One afternoon, there is a knock on the gate. Old Cornelius answers it.

"Is Titus here? He is not expecting me, but I am Paul of Tarsus."

Titus recognizes the voice as he walks around the reflecting pool to stretch his legs. He rushes to the gate and opens it for Cornelius.

"Paul! Yes, yes. Come in. Come in. It has been a long time. I think the first time you had another man with you, an older man. Yes, Barnabas. Where is Barnabas?"

"Well, he had somewhere else to go. He is not with me now."

"The next time you came through another man was with you. What was his name?"

"Silas. But this is Timothy. He is a fine young man from Lystra. He was with me on my second visit to your fine city."

"Oh, yes, I remember you, Timothy," Titus says.

"Come sit. Have some grapes. My servant just brought them in from the market."

"How has the church here been doing over the past eight years?" Paul asks. "I trust it is still strong and perhaps growing."

"Indeed, it is. As you know, the native Jews ultimately

rejected Jesus. It's as though Jesus was from another star." Titus pauses, grins, and shakes his head. "If they only knew. Anyway, we Gentiles—as you call us—welcomed your message. Some of the Jews who rejected you have come over and become Christians, but not many of them."

"How many Christians are there now?"

"There are one hundred and twenty of us."

"Marvelous," Paul says.

"Most are formerly worshippers of Augustus Caesar, Apollo or Men-Askenos. This is a large city, and we are far from being a majority. But we are doing okay."

"What about the Jews over at the synagogue? Are they leaving you alone?"

"Now and then they harass us, especially Hector, the Necktor. Watch out for him. He looks a little like Timothy."

Paul smiles as he watches Titus. "You remind me so much of Barnabas. Now, why should we watch out for Hector the whatever?"

"He struts in front of Christians whenever he sees one of us like a rooster stretching its neck ready to crow."

"Well, we would like to meet with the congregation here," Paul says. "The first day of the week is in three days."

"We are divided into three congregations meeting in three different homes," Titus says, growing serious again. "Everyone stays until dusk, so you should be able to get to all three of them on the one day."

"In the meantime, there is someone we want you to meet," Paul says. "Do you know Pollux?"

"Pollux, the copper exporter? Of course."

"He wants to know more about Jesus," Paul explains. "He broke his leg in the earthquake on the way here, so perhaps we can go to his home tomorrow."

Titus grows silent, looks at the sky above the courtyard, and regains control. He smiles. "We felt a few shakes of the earth here, but nothing serious."

"It was bad out on the road," Paul says.

"I have an extra room. Please stay with me as long as you like. Get settled in, then perhaps later we can discuss the earthquake."

The next day, the three Christians go see Pollux. Paul leads the taller Timothy and Titus.

A servant shows them to his quarters.

"Welcome, friends. Please forgive me if I do not stand and greet you. Do be seated. And tell me more about Jesus. Did Timothy say he is actually king of the world?"

"Indeed, he is," Paul says.

"How is that possible?" Pollux asks. "A man cannot just up and claim to be superior to Caesar and take his place."

"It happened anyway. Now Jesus is king of the world."

"You keep saying that. But how? Caesar is both man and god."

"Caesar will die, just like all other Caesars before him died."

"Of course. But while he is alive, he is a god."

"Not true. God does not die. God cannot die."

"You say God as though there is only one. There are many gods."

"God is not a statue. God is everywhere at once."

"That is impossible. No one can be everywhere at once."

"A person cannot, but God is Spirit, Holy Spirit. He made the world and causes all living things to move and breathe. God is Life."

"Is that why God cannot die?"

"Yes."

"But Timothy told me that this king, this Jesus, is God, and he died."

"Only the body he temporarily put his voice into died. God's Word never died. Three days after that temporary body died, it came back to life. Jesus went through all that to prove he can bring us back to life after we die."

Pollux calls over to his servant standing nearby.

"Would you get these gentlemen something to drink. I need to think."

"You look rather tired," Titus tells his father's friend. "I want to show these men the addition to the gymnasium academy's library. We will return after you have had a sleep."

Before Titus is through speaking, Pollux's eyes are closed, and his breathing heavy.

Titus takes Paul and Timothy back into the city. They walk over to the Temple of Augustus Caesar and watch the worshippers go in and out.

"Jesus is the king of your heart," Paul tells some of them. "Come to Titus' house on the next first day of the week and find out about it."

Timothy goes to the other side of the steps and tells people the same thing.

Titus goes to a marble bench facing the grand temple and grins widely. "Hey, Paul," he calls out. "If you make any of them mad, send them to me. I'll show them my sixth finger."

After a while, Paul returns to Titus, then Timothy does too.

"Do you think he is awake now?" Paul asks.

"I wonder what he dreamed about," Timothy says.

"Looks like we never made it to the library. This was better," Titus says with a grin.

"How old are you now, Titus?" Paul asks.

"Forty-two. I've been a Christian nine years. Sirius is five, and—remember you told me about Jesus' beatitudes? Well, he has memorized them all."

The three men backtrack and end up again at Pollux's *palatio.* Their footsteps echo on the marble floor.

"Okay, how can this Jesus be king of the world if Caesar is still on his throne?" Pollux calls out from his quarters.

The three Christians grin and walk back into where Pollux is now half seated and half reclined on a large couch with a high back on it.

"Because he is king of hearts. Caesar can still be your king. But Jesus wants to be king of your words, your thoughts, your actions."

"Tell me again how this Jesus is related to the Creator of the world, the one God."

"Jesus is God's Words. God can and has put his words in scrolls. He does not become a scroll, but his words are there," Paul says. "God put his words in the body of Jesus. He did not become that body, but his words were there."

"You know Jesus actually lived?" Pollux asks.

"I saw him both before he died and after he came back

to life.”

“How do I know what you are saying is the truth? You could have made it all up.”

Paul kneels before Pollux and puts his hand on the broken leg.

“Get up now, Pollux. Your leg is whole.”

“What?”

“Get up. Both legs are healed. You can stand and walk around like you always did. Come. Take my hand.”

“Well, I have to admit the pain is suddenly gone.”

Fascinated, Pollux takes Paul’s hand. Paul’s firm grip pulls on Pollux. At first, he uses his free arm to push himself up but realizes he does not need to.

Paul steps back, jerking Pollux up, and takes away his hand.

Pollux looks down at his legs. He unwraps the bandages. He looks up at Paul.

“How did you do that?”

“I did not do it. The power of Jesus Christ, the Word of God, did it. Now, do you believe?”

“Yes! Yes!” he says, looking around his room and watching everyone grin, including his servant.

“Then you may be baptized. It is a way of imitating Jesus’ death, burial, and resurrection so that your dead soul can be buried then brought back to life.”

Paul looks at Titus. “He is going to be in your congregation. Why don’t you baptize him?”

Titus presses his lips together and stares at Paul. “I have baptized others. What are you getting me into?”

Paul only smiles.

The next day, Pollux sends for his friends to come hear Paul speak about the Creator of the world. They come. Many become Christians.

“So, which congregation will you and your friends be a part of, Pollux, sir?” Paul asks.

“How many are there?”

“Three,” Titus replies. “But with the addition of you and your friends, we may have to start a fourth congregation. Our homes are not large enough to hold one hundred fifty or two hundred people."

"Ha! That is easily solved. Come with me."

Pollux leads them to his banquet hall. "Look. Enough for three hundred people to feast together. Why not three hundred feast on—what did you call it, Paul—the bread of heaven? I seldom have feasts anymore. I'm getting too old. I will move all the feasting couches out and replace them with rows and rows of benches. With cushions on the benches too."

Pollux looks at Titus and waits.

"Bring everyone to my home," he urges. "It is too large for me. Now it will be perfect for the church. As the church grows, I will even add on to this room."

Two days later is Solday. Titus has sent word to the owners of the other two congregational meeting houses, and they, in turn, have sent word to their attendees.

Paul speaks. Timothy teaches them two new hymns. Titus leads them in prayers. Pollux reads scriptures to everyone.

Paul explains that the Christians in Jerusalem are suffering lost jobs from persecution, fathers and mothers have been martyred, and they—the original church—need help. They take up a special collection.

"It's the least we can do for them," Titus says.

The next day, Paul announces they will be leaving for Ephesus. "You will have to come see us there."

23 ~ CRIES FOR HELP

*T*itus walks from his *officium* over to the reflecting pool where Fjorta is listening to Sirius tell her what five times five is.

"I was just a little older than Sirius when I think I lived through the happiest week of my life," Titus says, watching his son recite in almost the exact same spot he had stood thirty-six years earlier. It was my ninth birthday. After I was through reciting everything I could think of that I had learned in school, my father rewarded me with a pony. Then we rode to the Aegean coast, picnicked and played on the beach. My mother sang all the time, and sometimes my father and I would join in and sing with her."

He pauses and smiles at the clouds.

"You have wondered where I got my single dimple. I got it from my mother."

"You never told me chose dhings," Fjorta says. "I had no idea."

Well, that was before…before, you know."

"Your mother."

"Yes. After we lost her, it was never the same. All the happiness went out of this house, and all the light went out of my father."

Sirius steps over to his father. He tips his head and puts his hands on his hips. "Papa, that is so silly. People don't have light in them.”

Titus reaches over and puts Sirius on his lap. “Well, there are different kinds of light. There is the light of love, and the light of knowledge, and the light of... You know what I think I’ll do?”

“What, Papa?”

Titus sets his boy down. “I am going to go into the city and declare the truth at the forum.”

“The druth about vhich dhing?” Fjorta asks, squinting and tipping her head.

“Don’t worry, dear. I am only going to challenge Hesiod and Socrates.”

“You mean, how dhe vorld vas created and how humans vere created? You had bedder vatch out. You do not vant to bring down dhe wrath of all dhe priests in dhe city.”

“It’s early. I think I’ll do it now while a lot of people are at the market by the forum.”

“No, Titus. Do not do dhis dhing.”

Titus walks to the forum by the West Gate—the main gate into the city. As he does, he calls out to people on the street.

“Would you like to know how the earth and humans were created? Follow me.”

“We already know,” most call back.

“Hesiod and Socrates were just guessing. I know the facts.”

“Hey, everyone. Perhaps Titus has received an oracle from the gods. “I’m going.”

“Me too.”

“Don’t waste your time.”

“I want to hear what he has to say.”

“This is going to be fun.”

“You can’t prove anything.”

“What does it matter? I’m going to work.”

By the time Titus has walked the *mille* to the West Gate Forum, there is a trail of people behind him.

“What’s going on?”

“Titus says he’s smarter than Socrates.”

“I’ve got to see this.”

Titus steps up to the platform and holds out his arms.

"Shhh, everyone," he hears.

"You don't want to miss this."

"Fellow Romans and Antiochans. I bring you greetings."

"Get on with it, Titus."

"We have been told all our lives that great philosophers like Socrates, Plato, Aristotle know how we got here. We have been told we must believe our ancient ancestors who witnessed the creation of the gods. I am not sure how that is possible, but that is what they always tell us."

"Eight centuries ago, Homer introduced us to the gods. A little while later, Hesiod told us how they came into existence. Hesiod said poof, the first god came into being. Do you remember who he said that was?"

"The god Chaos," someone shouts.

"Right. Then suddenly, poof, which god came next?"

"The god Earth," someone else shouts.

"Right again. Then suddenly, poof, which god came next?"

"The god Tartarus, the scary one."

"And the last god that suddenly, poof, came into existence?"

"The god Eros, the fun one."

"So, they hadn't always been. They only became eternal after they were, well, born. Further, how can the thing which we see and feel be gods? That rock over there? Is it a god? When darkness comes, is that a god?"

"What are you getting at, Titus?"

"Socrates—how many of you have read Socrates?"

Two of the spectators raise their hands.

"That's what I thought. Well, Socrates is confusing. He said there was a Creator, but does not describe the Creator. He created other gods, but we don't know which ones. But he and Plato and the others urge us to just believe because our ancient ancestors were sons of those gods."

"Huh?"

"What's he talking about?"

"So, my friends, if our ancestors were sons of the gods, that means we are gods too."

"Titus, you're confusing us."

"It's not me. It's those men our school teachers told us to believe. Now I'm going to tell you how Socrates and the others claim humans were formed. Get ready for a real laugh, my fellow Romans."

"Are you sure you should be saying all this? Won't you be arrested?"

"Be careful, Titus."

"The Creator created two balls in the shape of the universe, then handed over the design of the rest of our body to lesser gods. One ball was our head where they put our lesser soul, and the other was our chest, where they placed our heart, the greater soul. They put our heart next to our lungs because, when we get agitated, our heart heats up. With the wet lungs nearby, they can cool the heart off. But our two round balls would "tumble about among the high and deep places of the earth." So, they gave our body flexible arms and legs so we could get around. And they put our various internal organs far from our mind because they do not need much instruction."

"That's not what happened," someone says.

"Aha!" Titus responds, pointing at the spectator. "Of course, not. It makes no sense that the gods would be so ignorant and make humans two balls without arms and legs."

"Look out, Titus. I think the high priest of Apollo is headed this way."

First, let me tell you who that Creator was that Socrates and the others could not name. He was Jehovah. He made the heavens and earth in five days. When it was just right, he made humans. Why? Because Jehovah loves us."

"A god who loves?" something calls up to Titus.

"Hey, Titus, the high priest has some legionnaires behind him. If you leave now, you can duck out through the West Gate until they cool now. It's been fun, but..."

"Well, if you want to learn more, go to the house of Pollux the first day of next week. You will learn the most amazing..."

"Now, Titus!"

A big man in the audience reaches up, grabs Titus'

hand, and jerks him down to the street level.

"Run, Titus!"

Several in the crowd surround Titus and rush *en masse* with him out the West Gate.

They stay on the road out of the city just briefly, then scramble down into a gully full of bushes. They stoop and watch the high priest and legionnaires look for the escapees, then see them go back into the city.

"That was close, Titus. Just what were you trying to do? You know only the Senate can announce a new god?"

"Well, I, for one, want to learn more about this Jehovah, the one and only God," Stethos says. "He certainly is less confusing than all those thousands of gods we have been taught to believe in."

"Stethos, you are welcome to join us. But come early. Our number is growing all the time," Titus says.

"How many are there who believe in only one God?"

"Over one hundred and fifty of us."

"I had no idea."

Stethos looks at the other five men who had whisked Titus out of danger. "Why don't we circle around and go back into the city at the South Gate?"

The others agree, and late in the afternoon as the sun begins its descent to the horizon, Titus arrives home.

"I vas avraid you had been arrested," Fjorta says when he walks in. "We had a visitor vhile you vere gone."

"Who?" Titus asks, taking off his toga and sitting in his favorite gilded chair by the pool.

"A messenger vrom Greece on his vay to Lystra."

"Greece? Who do we know... Oh, that's right. Aunt Chloe and Uncle Fulvio are there. So, what did they have to say?"

"I did not read it, my *kareste.* It vas addressed to you," she says, handing the scroll to him.

Titus leans back in his chair, breaks the seal and reads. "Oh, no."

"Oh, no? Vhat has happened in Greece?"

"My uncle died. Aunt Chloe says some bankers claim the bank owns her house and are trying to take it from her.

She wants me to come help defend her."

Titus stands and paces around the courtyard. Fjorta watches. Sirius runs to his father's side and stretches his legs to pace beside the man he loves to imitate.

"You know vhat you must do."

"Yes. She came to live with us after my mother died. She was a substitute mother to me. Even when she married, she stayed here and continued to look out for my father and me."

"I know you swore you vould never practice law again. But you owe it to her.

Titus stares at her a moment. "You are right. I owe a lot to her."

"So, vhen vill you leave?"

"I think the second day of next week. It will give me time to pull out my old law books, and maybe go into the city to see if I can buy her something special."

"Is Papa going away?" Sirius asks his mother.

"Can I go with you?" he asks his father.

Titus picks up his son and taps the end of his nose. "Not this time."

"When I'm bigger?"

"Yes. When you are bigger. Now I need you to stay here with your mother and take care of her while I'm gone."

"I'm big," Sirius says, displaying the muscles in both arms at once.

"You certainly are. And I am proud of you."

The day of worship arrives, and Titus takes his family to Pollux' spacious *palatio* with the banquet hall large enough for the congregation.

"We are pleased to have with us today," Pollux announces, "a brother from Derbe. You may remember Paul and Timothy, who have visited with us. Gaius is Timothy's cousin. Gaius, would you like to say a few words?"

"Paul has opened a school in Ephesus that is becoming very famous. In fact, it is now part of the Academy of Tyrannus. I am going there to enroll in Paul's school. If any of you would like to enroll also, we can keep each other company on the road, and perhaps rent a room together upon our arrival."

Three hours later, when worship has recessed briefly while everyone eats, Titus finds Gaius.

"Did you say you are on your way to Ephesus? I am too. I am leaving tomorrow morning. God has surely provided mutual companionship while we travel."

A week later, Titus and Gaius are in Ephesus. As they enter the city through the southeastern Magnesian Gate, Titus wonders where the beach is he had played on with his parents to celebrate his ninth birthday. *The happiest week of my life. I need to do that for Sirius when he turns nine.*

They work their way past the east gymnasium academy, and some government buildings, then see the baths.

"I think I'll stop here," Gaius says. After you purchase your ship passage, come back and join me. We should, at least, be presentable when we see our apostle again."

"You are right, my friend. I will meet you back here as soon as I can."

Titus continues up Via Curetes to the market, turns, passes the theater, then turns again to go on the columned Arcadian Way down to the docks.

"Is your ship going to Corinth?"

"By any chance, might you ship be headed for Corinth?"

"What about your ship? Do you expect to go to Corinth soon?"

At last, he finds the ship he needs. It will be leaving the following morning, much to Titus' satisfaction. He pays his fare, is given a token as proof, and hears a familiar voice.

"You took so long, my skin was beginning to shrink in the water," Gaius says. "So, what's next? I've never been here before."

"I was here once before, but I was only nine," Titus responds. " I guess we need to ask where the School of Tyrannus is," he adds.

"Well, well, well. Look who is here?"

The men turn and see someone walking toward them.

"It's Timothy," Titus says, grinning. "Were you sailing somewhere?" he asks.

They embrace, pounding each other on the back.

"No, I just like to come down here sometimes and watch

the ships," Timothy replies. "So, what are you doing here?"

"This is my traveling companion, Gaius."

"I want to enroll in Paul's school if he will have me," Gaius responds.

"I am going to see my aunt in Corinth," Titus explains. "I found a ship leaving tomorrow morning."

"Perfect," Timothy responds. "Come with me. I know Paul will be most happy to see you. We are staying in the home of another Gaius. I'm sure he will have room for you to spend the night."

From the docks, they turn south until they reach the *palatio* of Gaius.

"Gaius is entertaining two brothers from Corinth. I will introduce you," Timothy says when they arrive at his gate.

A gatekeeper lets the men in.

"Look who I found down at the docks," Timothy announces. "Our very own Titus, fresh from Antioch not far from my hometown. Also, Gaius, my cousin from Derbe."

Copper Gaius rises. "I do not believe I have had the pleasure of meeting Titus or Gaius." He reaches out his hand. "There seems to be three of us named Gaius here now," he laughs. "They call me Copper Gaius, they call Aristarchus' friend Silver Gaius. What is your occupation?"

The young man smiles. "I am a potter," he says.

"Then you shall be Clay Gaius," he responds with a grin. "Now, have a seat."

"What brings you here?" Timothy asks. "Paul is surely going to be glad to see you two."

"I am coming to enroll in Paul's school," Clay Gaius says. "Also, our congregation heard about the plight of the Christians down in Jerusalem and decided to send them some money. Since Paul goes to Jerusalem sometimes, they told me to give him the money so it will eventually get to the right people."

"And I am on my way to Corinth to visit my Aunt Chloe. I received a letter from her a week ago," Titus says. "She and my father are brother and sister. She wants me to help her with something to do with her estate. She says a banker there is not treating her with fairness."

"Then Paul will be doubly excited to see you," Timothy says.

"Because my aunt is having problems?"

"No. Because he received an urgent letter from your Aunt Chloe just a couple days ago and has written a reply. He has been looking for someone he can trust to take a letter from him to the church in Corinth."

"You said the letter he received was from my aunt," Titus responds.

"It was. But she wrote about some problems with the church there. So, he wrote the whole church."

Two hours later, Paul arrives. His lips are pressed together, his forehead is furrowed, and his dark eyes darker.

"Those silversmiths are spreading rumors about Christians again," he says, looking at the floor. There is no response. He looks up, stares a moment, and smiles.

"Oh, Titus. And Gaius. Where did you come from? It is so good to see you after all this time. What is going on with you? When did you get here?"

Paul embraces them both, pounding them heartily on the back, but shifting around far enough that they do not reciprocate on his badly scarred and sensitive back.

"Have a seat, everyone," Paul says.

As they talk, Timothy watches Paul's forced smile.

"Gentlemen," Timothy says to Titus and Clay Gaius, "Paul's school is growing so much, he has had to rent the largest room in the School of Tyrannus. Even then, it is crowded."

"But?" Titus asks.

Timothy takes a deep breath. "But, as you know, Christianity is attacked everywhere we go. It is no different here. The stronger we get, the stronger the opposition gets."

"Timothy is right," Paul says. "Demetrius, the head of the silver guild, is telling everyone the Christians are meeting in secret at my school plotting ways to overthrow the city government and take over."

"They are afraid of you."

"I know that, Copper Gaius. But it angers me how people resort to lies. He even says the goddess Artemis is greater than Jesus, and that Jesus never existed anyway."

"I have seen riots before," Titus says. "So have you. You need to have a plan in case things get out of control here."

"Titus, of course, you are right," Paul says. "When we passed the silver guild hall, there were more men milling around outside than normal."

"Looks like they are up to something."

"What are your plans, Titus?" Paul asks. "I need to make sure my letter to the church in Corinth gets there."

"I am leaving tomorrow morning. I already have my fare purchased."

"God knew we needed you and sent you our way," Paul responds.

The next morning early Paul, Timothy, and Copper Gaius walk with Titus on the Arcadian Way to the docks and wait for him to board.

The anchor is pulled up, warning bells are rung, the sails are hoisted, the tackle stashed, and the ship begins to slip out of the harbor.

As it does, angry waves churn, and Titus hears thunderings back onshore.

"Great is Artemis of the Ephesians."

"Great is Artemis of the Ephesians."

"Great is Artemis of the Ephesians."

"Oh, Jesus. Protect your church. Especially your apostle. Protect Paul."

24 ~ CHLOE

The voyage across the Aegean Sea over to Greece is disturbing. The wind is relentless against the ship, and the anchor is lowered for stability. The red tanbark sails are taken aback with winds shifting and filling them from the wrong direction.

"All passengers, below deck," the sailors growl as they make their way around the ship, hanging on to ropes.

Titus had hoped to study his laws again. Instead, he now sits below in the blackness, leaning against a post and steadying himself against the rolling of the ship. No light. Only darkness.

He wonders how his apostle to doing. He wonders how his aunt is doing. Everything dark. He is glad his wife and son had not come with him and that God will keep them safe until his return.

Hours later—he cannot tell if it is day or night—the wind dies enough he can hear the pounding of feet above as the sailors work to save their ship and keep it from ramming into any of the tiny islands between Anatolia and Greece.

Then the hatch overhead is opened. Titus' eyes are shocked by the sun but delighted. He and the other passengers climb the ladder and go above board. The air is fresh, the sea is calm, and the crew is busy securing whatever had broken loose during the storm.

Titus finds a place to sit along a rail which he trusts is out of the way of the crew. He opens a leather pouch in which he had stored bread, cheese, and dried apricots for the trip. He eats a little, takes a few swigs from his waterskin, and prays that Paul is as relieved of danger as he is.

On his other shoulder is another large leather pouch. He opens it and finds it as protective of his law books as his food had been protected. He pulls out one of the scrolls.

He reads Cicero again, the one he respects the most. He reads Plato, though he is a little old fashioned and too idealistic. Cicero is much more practical.

Sometimes, Titus walks around the deck, watching all the islands drift by and wonders how many villages, if any, are on each.

Then he sees ahead a long island, much larger than the others.

"Sir, could you tell me the name of that large island up there?"

"That's not an island," the first mate replies. That is Greece. Up at the top of the peninsula is Athens."

"Oh, that's wrong. I am supposed to be going to Corinth," Titus replies. "Did I board the wrong ship."

The first mate laughs. "Athens will be on our right. Corinth will be on our left. See that island on the left? That's not really an island either. That's another peninsula. Where the two of them meet is where Corinth is. We have just entered the Saronic Gulf and should be near Corinth within an hour."

"That's good. I have an aunt who lives there. It shouldn't be too hard to find her," Titus responds.

"Well, Corinth is on the other side of that meeting point. It is actually on the Corinthian Gulf side."

"Huh?"

"We will put in port at Isthmia. You will have to walk or hire a horse to take you the last eight or nine *milles* to Corinth," the first mate explains.

"Can't the ship go the rest of the way to Corinth?"

"Everyone wishes it could. The Aegean Sea between Anatolia and Greece, and the Ionian Sea between Greece and Italy almost meet on either side of Corinth. The seas are only four *milles* apart and so close. We will be headed to Rome after we leave here and will have to go all the way around the south end of Greece and back up again. Or, the captain may arrange for slaves to take our ship up onto the planks of the portage road through there and pull us to the Ionian Sea on the other side."

"Four *milles* should not be so hard to dig through," Titus says.

"Two emperors have tried it and met with violent deaths—Julius Caesar and Caligula. They say Nero is considering it, but so far is afraid of the curse. I must leave you now."

An hour later, Titus is on land at the city of Isthmia. He looks up a steep hill on his left, sees a temple of Poseidon, and grunts to himself at people's gullibility.

He walks the eight *milles* between the port of Isthmia on the Aegean side, arrives at Corinth on the Ionian side of the isthmus. He proceeds through the gate next to a reflecting pool and into the South Market. He continues until he senses he is at the center of the city. Five streets meet there.

"Sir," he asks someone with a beard who he assumes is a Jew, "could you tell me which way I would go to a neighborhood of rather nice homes?"

"Hurry, Father," a girl who seems to be marriage age but apparently is not yet claimed, tugs at her father. "We are going to be late."

The stranger calls over his shoulder, "Via Lechaion is to your north, Via Philus to your west, a temple to Poseidon and others up on that hill to the south. You should go west."

"Thank you, sir," Titus replies, not sure the stranger hears him. "I guess I will go west," he mutters to himself.

The stranger with the beard stops and restrains his daughter.

"Hurry, Father," she repeats.

The man pulls his daughter's hand away from him and walks back toward Titus.

Did I do something to offend him? Titus wonders.

The stranger walks closer and stares at Titus. "Uh, what is your name?" he asks.

"I am Titus Pomponius..."

"Brennius!" the stranger finishes for him with a broad grin.

"Huh?"

"Titus. It's me. Stephanas!"

Titus has but a moment to stare back before the man with the beard is embracing him. They pull apart.

"Oh, my beard," the man says, stroking it. "But it's really me, old friend. Do you still live in Antioch? How is your aunt? Your father? Did you ever get married? By the way, this is my youngest daughter, Lupa."

Stephan turns toward his daughter. "Lupa, say hello to the best friend I ever had. Remember I told you when I was a boy I was accused of stealing someone's money? My mother and I were poor after my father died, so Titus defended me. And he won. And we were only fifteen years old."

Lupa stares.

Titus stares at the man and grins. "It really is you, Stephan. Your voice hasn't changed at all. Where did all that fat go? You're skinny now."

"That was baby fat. I outgrew it as soon as we started having children. I have four now. And you?"

"Uh, I married a couple years after you. We have one son."

"Good. Is your family with you?

"No, they're back in Antioch. But my Aunt Chloe is here. I came to see her."

"I know exactly where your Aunt Chloe lives. Let me take you to her house. We have a lot of years to catch up on. Just go without me," he says to his daughter, putting his arm over Titus' shoulder and leading him west.

"I thought you went to Rome," Titus says as they walk.

"I did. And I studied under Gaius Musonius Rufus just like I said I would. But, perhaps you heard that Claudius Caesar made all the Jews leave Rome."

"But, you aren't..."

"I converted to being a Jew, old friend, so I had to go when they left."

"Well, how did you find my aunt? She is not a Jew."

"Because we both belong to a group of people who follow Jesus the Christ in Corinth."

Titus stops in the middle of the street and stares at his boyhood friend. "You do?"

"Yes. Two years after I arrived here, a man named Paul came to the city and began the church. I was his first convert."

"He did? You were? And my aunt is a Christian now?"

"Huh?"

"Stephan, I am a Christian too. That same Paul came to Antioch twelve years ago, and I was his first convert there."

Stephan backs up and leans against the wall of a building lining the street and slides down until he is seated. He looks up at Titus. "God moves in mysterious ways," he says.

"Indeed, he does," Titus says, sitting down next to his old friend. "Indeed, he does."

They sit a while, not speaking. As they had done in years past. Just absorbing their old friendship.

At last, Stephan stands and jerks at Titus' arm.

"Well, let me show you where Chloe lives. She will be surprised to see you."

"I doubt that," Titus says, resisting his tug. "She wrote me that she is having trouble keeping her house since Fulvio died."

Stephan shakes his head. "Yes, sad situation. Well, if anyone can straighten it out, it will be you."

"She also wrote a letter to Paul in Ephesus. Paul wrote back a long letter. I have it in my pouch. Apparently, the church here in Corinth is having its problems."

Stephen reseats himself. "Indeed, it is."

"Well, you may as well have the letter." Titus hands the scroll to his friend, and Stephan slips it in a wool pouch he wears at his waist.

They sit in silence a little longer. Titus elbows Stephan in the ribs. "I thought you were going to show me where my aunt lives."

The two men stand, put their arms across each other's shoulders, and continue west.

"Well, this is it," Stephan says, stopping in front of a

double gate."

"I should have known. Fulvio decorated the entire gate with tiles depicting, depicting what?"

"It's a map showing Corinth up here at the top right and Olympia down here at the bottom left."

"We're close to Olympia?"

"Under a hundred *milles* away."

"I always dreamed of going to the Olympic Games."

"Well, tryouts are done just outside Corinth at Isthmia. Your ship probably docked at the shores of Isthmia."

"I guess it did. Well, we need to knock and quit talking," Titus says, grinning. "But where? I'd hate to knock down one of those tiles."

"Try over here on the mantle. Ole Fulvio put up a steel door knocker."

"I'll bet that's my Titus Pomponius Brennius knocking at my gate," a familiar voice says as the gate opens.

"How did you know, Aunt?" Titus says as he steps up and embraces the woman who so well filled in for his mother after she was gone. He swings her around, and she screams in delight.

"Well, come in," she says, untangling herself from her nephew. "I see you brought Stephanas with you. Come in, both of you."

Titus jerks his head around to his friend. "Stephanas? Since when did you become Stephanas?"

"Since Rome. And the people here call me that too."

"Well, you'll always be Stephan to me, so get used to it," he replies with a grin and elbow in his friend's ribs.

They enter her courtyard, and Titus stares. "I should have known."

The floor is in a geometric pattern with the smiling face of Chloe in the middle. The columns holding up the second floor are tiled, each one depicting a different kind of tree.

Titus turns in place, absorbing Fulvio's talents, and stumbles into someone. He looks down and sees an elderly lady.

"I am so sorry, Miss," he says.

The lady looks straight ahead. "That's okay. I should

have watched where I was going better."

Aunt Chloe chuckles. "Oh, Phylidda, you make me laugh." She sees Titus staring at both women with a blank stare. "Well, Phylidda is blind. She can be so funny sometimes. We are doing each other a favor. After Fulvio, well, died, she moved in with me. She is widowed like me, and so is her son. She needed a place to stay while he is up at the mines, and I needed company. Come sit over here in the solarium, Titus and Stephanus."

They settle in on marble benches around a small reflecting pool.

"Thank you for coming, Titus. I am not sure who is trying to get my house from me. The bank will not tell me. But they claim my husband borrowed money from them continually to keep his business going. It doesn't make sense. He had more work than he could handle. He hired eight men to help him."

"Aunt Chloe, it has been a long time since I have been in court. Ten years, to be exact."

"Why?" she asks, shaking her head.

"I lost a case. A case I should have won. The young lady was executed the next day." He shakes his head, grits his teeth, and stares at the tiled floor. "I have caused the deaths of too many people, Aunt Chloe."

"Now listen to me, young man," she says, moving to sit next to her nephew. "It was not your fault that your mother died, and it was not your fault that your daughter died."

Titus puts his face in his hands. "If I had just done things differently," he says.

"Stop that this instant," Chloe declares. "I am twenty years older than you, and I am smarter than you. Well, about some things. I still need your help with those bankers trying to take my home from me. So you just concentrate on that. Okay?"

She takes the face of her nephew in her hands, leans over, and kisses him on the forehead.

"Well, I have to be going," Stephan says.

Stephan leaves. Titus and the two women eat a final meal for the day.

"Come up on the roof with me, Titus. You will enjoy the breeze and the view."

He follows her up. They look all around them. "See that light over there?" she asks. "That is a lighthouse between Isthmea and the Aegean coast. It watches over the ships, although the local people say it is the eyes of Poseidon. And look over to the west. See those little dots of light? Those are ships docked at the harbor on the Ionian Sea side, waiting to be pulled overland to the Aegean Sea side. I think sometimes I can see Rome from here, though I know I can't."

"Isn't Athens nearby?" Titus asks.

"Yes, straight north of here. It's on a hill, but too far away for us to see—forty *milles* or so. Don't you love the breeze here? A little from the east and a little from the west."

"Well, I know it is still daylight, but I guess I am a little tired."

"Of course you are, Titus. I will show you to your room," Aunt Chloe responds. "I will bring you a copy of the deed and Fulvio's will."

"Tomorrow, I will go into the city and start investigating," he promises.

Once in his bed, his thoughts drift back to the family he has left behind in Antioch. "Jesus, keep them safe. Father too. Don't let anything happen to them. Sometimes I become so fearful of losing them."

He closes his eyes, then opens them again. It is night. He hears a scream.

He quickly tries to orient himself as to where he is, then rushes out into the hallway. He sees Chloe running toward him and follows her down the stairs. Immediately they see smoke.

"The house is on fire!" Chloe shouts.

Titus follows her down the steps to find the origin of the fire and try to put it out. He grabs an ornate urn from between two columns in the courtyard, runs to the solarium, and fills it with water from the reflecting pool. He runs out to the courtyard.

"Aunt Chloe. Where are you?"

"She runs out from the kitchen end of the courtyard. "In

here, Titus!"

He runs in her direction, sees the flames on the goat-hair canopy overhead, and throws the water at it. It falls mostly on the floor. He rushes back to the solarium and fills his urn again. Back to the kitchen area. Chloe runs out, choking.

"It's no use. The wood beams overhead and along the walls have caught fire. Where is Phylidda? Phylidda!" she shouts as she runs toward her friend's room on the first floor. "Where are you, Phylidda? Phylidda!"

Her screams grow louder and more frantic. Titus follows, then passes her when he sees smoke coming out of one of the side rooms. He rushes in, choking.

Despite the smoke and his aunt screaming, he can hear someone choking down by the floor. He feels his way in that direction, and nearly trips on the blind woman. He leans down and picks her up in his strong arms.

"Aunt...Aunt Chloe," he chokes. "Where are you?"

"Over here. Come toward my voice. Over here!"

Titus stumbles out of the smoke-filled side room into the night air of the courtyard. Wooden beams anchored to each other on the second floor overhead are now aflame.

"This way," Chloe shouts.

Titus follows her to the front gate. She fumbles with the bronze latch. "It's too hot," she says.

Titus realizes the blind woman in his arms has passed out and may be dead. He looks around.

The flames leap out at them from overhead.

"To your right, Aunt Chloe. That tapestry on the wall. See if you can yank it off."

A beam falls from the second floor onto the face of Chloe formed from intricate tiles in the middle of the courtyard.

She tugs, and the small tapestry comes loose. She turns back to the gate.

Another flaming beam crashes down.

Her hands protected by the tapestry, Chloe flings the gate open, and Titus rushes out onto the street. Moments later, even the front gates are aflame.

The two step back and watch all that Chloe has left of

Fulvio turn to ashes as though it had never been.

She leans her head against Titus' shoulder, forgetting he is still holding Phylidda.

A neighbor comes running out to the street. "Come in here," Nikanor shouts.

"No, I cannot," Chloe replies.

Titus accepts the invitation and goes through the gates of the neighbor across the wide street.

"Put her over here," Enyo says. "Go back to your aunt. We will take care of Phylidda."

He runs back out onto the street and puts his arms around his aunt, the one who had comforted him in his own loss so many years earlier when he was only eleven years old.

He rocks her back and forth, back and forth as they watch the hungry flames attack in the darkness of her night.

"Titus," she whispers, looking up into his eyes. "The will and deed to the house were in there. Now my only proof is gone. I have lost everything."

25 ~ UNTOUCHABLES

"What am I going to do?" she whispers to Titus.

"We will figure something out," he replies.

"There is nothing left I can do," Chloe says. "Not only did my house burn down, but all my proof did."

"Aunt Chloe, is this what you are talking about?"

Titus pulls out some small scrolls from his leather shoulder pouch.

Chloe stares at the scrolls. She reaches up and hugs Titus' neck. "But how?"

"I heard you bring them to me when you thought I was asleep. After you left, I put them in the pouch with my law books. I grabbed my pouch when I got up in case a thief had broken into your house."

He smiles, tucks the documents back into his shoulder pouch, pats his aunt on her cheek, and kisses her on the top of her head.

"I remember when I used to do that to you when you were a boy," she whispers.

"Yes, you did. You comforted me and encouraged me and helped me through some hard times. It is now my turn."

"Well, I'm not sure what there is left to do."

"Aunt Chloe, I am going to find whoever did this to you and take them to court."

"But, I thought you gave up the law."

"Maybe so. But now I'm taking it up again. Anything for my Aunt Chloe."

"Well, Son, you will need someone to show you around the city. But you'll have to tell me where you need to go."

"I think I know."

Titus turns and sees Stephan standing near the gateway, still open so Chloe can keep watch on what once was.

"Why don't you three come home with me. We have an extra bedroom the women can sleep in. Titus, you can sleep on the roof in a tent or under a canopy, so the dew and rain don't get you."

Titus looks at his aunt. "What do you want to do?"

"You cannot carry Phylidda all the way to Stephanus' house," she half-whispers.

"I brought a cart," Stephan says. "Titus can take the reins, and you women can ride in the back. Come. My wife, Arelia, is anxious to see Titus again. She is not sure she remembers you. Well, we've all changed. Oh, here comes Nikanor with Phylidda."

Chloe walks over to the cart leaning on Titus. Nikanor lays Phylidda in the cart next to Chloe, then puts his arm on Titus' shoulder. "We are sorry about all the things happening to your aunt," the neighbor says. By the time they arrive at Stephan's modest home near the South Market, the sun has appeared.

"Stephan, I cannot rest while it's daylight," Titus says when they get settled in.

"You want to check out the public records, then start interviewing people. I have a tunic here that my son Nicon—who is taller than me—wears. It should fit you. We need to go over to the baths before we do anything. You smell like smoke," Stephan says, "and a few other things," he adds with a wink.

Bathed and properly dressed, Titus walks over to a linen-cloth seller and purchases enough to make a toga to indicate his aristocratic heritage.

"This will help me intimidate people into talking to me," he tells Stephan. "Now, take me to the public records building."

"Right behind you is the Julian Basilica. The records are in there."

Before entering, Titus finds a bench and studies his uncle's deed and will. "I'm ready," he says.

An hour later, upon finding what he was looking for, Titus pays the clerk double to have the records copied and ready for him by late afternoon.

"Now, where?" Stephan asks.

"How many banks does Corinth have?"

"One."

"Take me to it."

They walk farther north until they come to the Temple of Augustus. "The bank backs up to the temple walls.

"Everyone knows this bank connected to the priests of Augustus," Stephan says. "There is one banker here—Nomiki. Everyone knows there are more, but they keep their identities secret."

Titus gives Stephan a list of questions to ask. Did your bank loan money to Fulvio? How much was it? When did the loan come due? How much interest was charged? Who are the other officials in your bank?

"Ask them yourself. You've become lazy in your old age."

"I have my reasons. I will be right over there. Whenever the banker answers, look at me just in case I signal you."

"Signal to do what? You are as strange as you ever were, Titus Pomponius Brennius."

Titus grins. I'll explain later."

Complying with Titus' instructions, Stephan approaches the first and only-known banker while Titus stands at a distance where he can watch the man, and where Stephan can see Titus.

Every time the banker replies, Stephan glances at Titus, who either shakes his head no—meaning he has to ask the question again—or yes. With a yes, Stephan goes on to the next question.

After Stephan runs through all the questions with the banker, Titus joins him, and they walk outside to a bench along the via.

"Okay, I always knew you were strange, but this is the

strangest thing you have ever pulled," Stephan tells his old friend. "Why would you trust me to ask the questions and write down the answers?"

"I was reading their bodies," Titus replies. "If they're lying, their faces or hands or feet do certain things."

"Like what?"

"They may cover their mouth, or talk too much, or watch the door, or tap their fingers."

"Most smart people know that. So, why didn't you question them yourself?"

"Their words would have distracted me."

"Titus stands. "I would like to go back to see what is left of my aunt's villa and do not remember where it is."

"You are going to send a bunch of bankers to jail, but don't remember how to get to a house you went to just yesterday."

"That's about it, friend," Titus says, grinning.

Titus pokes around in the smoky and charred remains of Chloe's villa. "Okay, the government records I ordered should be copied for me by now.

They make their way back to the Julian Basilica for a copy of the records on file, then on to Stephan's home.

The two old friends arrive at Stephan's modest home. Red-headed Arelia is still red-headed, though her once thick, frizzy hair is now thin and frizzy. Her freckles remain.

"You are just in time," she says. "Juno and Lupa have fixed their most delicious dishes in your honor, and Nicon and Tycho are overjoyed their empty and angry stomachs will finally be filled and happy again."

Stephan introduces his children to Titus.

"Nicon, the last time I saw you, you were five years old. And you, Tycho, were three," Titus says.

The boys, now twenty-three and twenty-one, press their lips together in fake smiles, which Titus immediately catches.

"Your oldest daughter was just a baby. And, Lupa, you weren't even a twinkle in your father's eye yet."

The girls giggle.

That evening, the men put their heads together and figure out which answers were the truth, then Titus prepares his strategy.

"I need you to take me to the city's censor tomorrow morning."

At daybreak, Titus is in Stephan's small courtyard pacing.

"So, you still pace, I see?" Stephan tells his old friend. "We cannot go see Censor Sethos until the sun is at least halfway up the sky."

Arelia and their daughters prepare flatbread and yogurt for everyone to break their fast. Nicon and Tycho head up the street to the pottery shop.

"Okay, let's go," Titus says.

"It's too early."

"Then we'll sit outside his gate until he gets embarrassed and lets us in," Titus retorts.

By noon, Titus has subpoenas for all bankers, reluctantly signed by Censor Sethos. Titus pays double for his cooperation and for them to be served.

"How did you know who they were?" Stephan whispers.

"They have to record their officers with the city government. That's one of the things I picked up yesterday."

The following day, Banker Nomiki arrives at the Julian Basilica to look over the roster of judges. He assures everyone the other bankers—who he had initially denied existed—had given him full authority.

Titus and Stephan wrangle back and forth with Banker Nomiki most of the day. They come to an agreement on judges just when a clerk is preparing to lock the doors. The next day the judges are notified, and the trial set to begin the day after that.

As arranged, two days later, Titus dons the finest toga of the finest, whitest linen he can find in the city. He trims his hair, shaves a close shave, and cleans his fingernails. As a final touch, he purchases a pure gold chain with a large ruby dangling from it and a matching ruby ring. *I hope I don't run out of money before I win this case for Aunt Chloe,* he thinks to himself.

He rents a chariot for the occasion, and Aunt Chloe rides in it with him. He brings blind Phylidda along just because she wants to hear the proceedings. He has purchased conservative clothing for them both.

When he arrives at the forum near the Julian Basilica, a crowd of spectators has already begun to form.

He walks up the steps to the platform, Aunt Chloe behind him. Blind Phylidda stays on the street level with Stephen and his family. He instructs his aunt where to sit, then begins to pace.

One at a time, the bankers arrive and take their seats on benches on the defendants' side. Next, the three judges arrive and take their seats behind a long table facing the accused and accuser. Finally, the Praetor of Corinth arrives and climbs to his gilded chair above the judges. He announces, "You may begin."

The crowd mumbles, grins, frowns and generally settles in for the spectacle about to unfold.

"First of all, Most Excellent magistrates and Praetor Basileus, may I introduce myself?" Titus says, standing as tall as he possibly can. "I am Titus Pomponius Brennius, named after the great Titus Pomponius of Athens just north of here, and close friend of the Most Excellent Cicero."

Titus paces with his chin resting on two fingers as though in great thought. He stops and stares once more at the judges, then Praetor Basilius.

"More importantly, I am a direct descendant of the great Gaul General Brennius who succeeded in conquering Rome, then decided to settle there. Families of his warriors settled all the way from Rome to what is today Galatia. My grandfather Brennius was granted land and settled in Antioch, made sacred at that time by Augustus Caesar himself."

Once again, Titus pauses, then holds out both arms. "Greetings, I bring to you, Oh Excellent Basileus from my father, Justus Brennius Antiochus, Praetor of Antioch." He pauses for effect, lowers his arms, and raises them again. "He sends you his kindest greetings and invites you to his *palatio* any time you are in Antioch."

Praetor Brennius smiles and clears his throat. "Of course. Of course. And I extend the same to your illustrious father."

Titus bows to the praetor, looks at the judges, at his Aunt Chloe, and at the five bankers. His eyes darken, and he jabs his fist at the bankers.

"Most Excellent judges and praetor, these men—if you can call him men—have deceived and deprived my, uh, this woman, this widow, of her hearth and home out of jealousy. Pure malicious jealousy, and I intend to prove it."

Banker Savvas stands and pounds his fist into his open hand. "Liar. He is a liar!"

"Do you have something to say in your defense?" the oldest judge asks.

"I would not lower myself to explain anything to this foreigner." With that, Banker Savvas sits back on his bench and folds his arms protectively across his chest.

"Most Excellent magistrates," Titus continues, "may I have permission to question these bankers? In so doing, I will prove they are malicious frauds and cheats, not only of my, of this widow but of half the people in your magnificent and famed city of Corinth."

"You may proceed," the oldest judge says, his elbow on the marble table in front of the judges and waving from his wrist.

"Now Banker Ikaros, Titus begins, "tell the magistrates here whether you ever loaned money to Fulvio, the tile artist."

"Yes, we did."

"And did you set a date for him to pay you back?"

"Yes, we did."

"And did he pay you back?"

"No, he did not."

"Liar!" Titus declares, jabbing his fist at the banker and swinging around to face the magistrates. "He is lying."

He turns back to Banker Ikaros.

"Would you like to try again?"

"No, I was telling the truth."

"You do realize the penalty for perjury three times is death. Now, would you like to reconsider?"

Banker Ikaros' eyes dart around. He looks at Titus. "No."

Titus picks up a small scroll from the table in front of

the plaintiff's bench.

"Are you sure?"

"Well, maybe he did."

"Thank you. Now we move on to Banker Khryses. Sir, how much did Fulvio borrow from the bank?"

"Three thousand *sestertii*."

"Are you sure?" Titus asks, staring at the banker's eyes.

"Yes. Definitely three thousand *sestertii*."

"Are you willing to bet your life on your answer?"

"Of course, I am. No. I mean, there is no contest. I am telling the truth."

"If I ask your partners, will they give the same answer?"

"Naturally."

"Moving on to Banker Minos. Have you recently purchased a new villa?"

"Well, yes, I have, but the money I paid for it with was honest money."

"How do I know that? How do our honored magistrates know that?"

"Because I am an honest man," Banker Minos replies, looking Titus straight in the eye.

"Can you prove it?" Titus dares.

"Yes, I can prove it. I sold my shares in a silver mine to get the money."

"Who did you sell the shares to?" Titus demands.

"Well, a ship captain. He is down in Egypt at the moment, I believe."

Titus peers at the Banker Minors. He draws closer and closer to his face. When they are almost nose to nose, Titus stops and turns.

He looks at the magistrates, smiles, and swings his fist around to point at Banker Nomiki.

"Sir, how late was Fulvio in repaying the bank?"

"Very late."

"How late?"

"Well, I keep excellent records. I keep everything up to date at all times. I remember the very day he finally came in with his money. It was raining that day. But he had his money pouch with him. It was made of cow leather and dyed blue. I remember that because it matched his tunic that day. And…”

“Banker, Nomiki,” Titus interrupts, “who are you trying to convince?”

The spectators chuckle, the magistrates grin.

“Well, no one. Everyone.”

“So, tell us how late he was in repaying the bank. That is, if you know the date as well as you know the color of his money pouch.”

Titus turns and grins at the magistrates, then turns back to the defendants.

“Well, It may have been a month. Or two months.”

“Liar! Or, is it that you are telling the truth and Banker Ikaros is lying? He said Fulvio never paid the bank back. So, which one of you is the liar?”

“Banker Nomika glances at Ikaros. Ikaros does not reciprocate.

Titus paces then looks out over the spectators.

“Fair citizens of the great city of Corinth. Have you believed anything these men have said?”

“Nooo,” comes the rumbled reply.”

“Imprison them all,” someone in the crowd shouts.

“Exile them all.”

“Kill them all.”

Titus looks back at the magistrates and shrugs. He takes a paper off the table in front of his aunt and walks back over to Banker Khryses.

“Sir, would you like to repeat what you told me earlier?”

“About what?” the banker replies.

“About what? About what? He does not even remember his own answer?” Titus says, turning back to tell the magistrates. He raises a small scroll over his head.

“Tell us again how much Fulvio borrowed from the bank.”

“Two thousand *sestertii*,” he replies.

“But, earlier you said it was three thousand. Which figure is the truth?”

“I had trouble remembering.”

“I hold in my hand the proof of what he borrowed. Would you like to change your answer?”

"Well, maybe it was four thousand *sestertii*. I have the evidence that's how much it was."

"That's him. That's him."

Titus turns toward the spectators. It is a woman's voice. He sees a hand raised. Someone helps her walk forward.

"Phylidda, would you like to come up and testify? Are you a witness? Just what did Banker Khryses do?"

Titus walks down to the ground level and helps the blind woman make her way up to the platform. He seats her on the witness bench.

"What did Banker Khryses do?" he repeats, kneeling in front of the old woman.

"He burned Chloe's house down."

Titus stands, his eyes grow wide, he sucks in a deep breath. He kneels again. "How do you know that, Phylidda?"

"His voice. I wasn't sure until I moved closer. But now I know it was him."

"When did you hear his voice?"

"He was talking to someone on the other side of the back wall. I had just gone to the kitchen area for a drink of water before retiring for the night. I heard his voice. He said, "Let's do it now and destroy all the evidence.""

Titus pats Phylidda on the knee, and Chloe moves over to sit with her.

He turns to the bankers and sees them gathered around Banker Khryses. "What did you do?"

Titus faces the judges and the praetor. "I have in my hand the evidence Banker Khryses had intended to destroy in the fire that destroyed this woman's home. It is a copy of a letter Fulvio sent to him. He made two copies. One was on the backside of a large marble tile, which I found when I returned to search what was left of his house, and one was recorded in your hall of records."

He turns to Banker Khryses and opens the scroll.

Dear Banker Khryses. I know what you did with my money—all ten thousand sestertii. If you do not refund my money, I will expose you to the other bankers. You have one week.

Titus walks over to the plaintiff's table, picks up another scroll, and turns back to the magistrates. I have here the date of his death as recorded in the hall of records. He died of unknown cause the day after writing and recording this threat. I suggest to you that the unknown cause was poison and that, if you question the apothecary in your fair city, he will confirm my suspicions. I now leave this in your hands."

Titus steps over and sits with his aunt and the blind woman. Murmuring among the spectators. The magistrates pull out their small scrolls, mutter to each other, then write their verdicts, seal them and hand them to the deputy. The deputy takes them up to Praetor Basileus. He reads them and stands.

"One hundred lashes! After that, you will be burned at the stake."

"No!" Chloe screams. "You can't do that."

26 ~ THE LETTER

*C*hloe wipes her eyes as she steps over to the judges. "Please, do not torture him like that."

"Why not?" Praetor Basileus says. "You brought him to court. If you didn't mean it, why did you bother all of us with it?"

Chloe brings her hands up and folds her fingers together, as though in prayer. "Please."

"Why?"

"I am a Christian and do not want him to suffer."

"He made you suffer."

"True, but our Lord says we were not to repay evil with evil."

"And who is your Lord? Does he live here in Corinth? Or perhaps in Rome?"

"He lives in heaven."

"That is interesting. A new god. And what is this god's name?"

"Jesus of Nazareth."

"Did he go to war for Roman? Did he conquer kingdoms?"

"Uh, Most Excellent Basileus," Titus says, interceding. "It is my understanding that Tiberius Caesar received an appeal from Pontus Pilate, governor of the Province of Judea, to make Jesus a god. Tiberius, in turn, submitted the request to the Senate in accordance with law."

"And?" Praetor Basileus says.

"I think the appeal has been lost and never acted upon."

Praetor Basileus looks back at Chloe. You sued. I sentenced. That is the end of that." He looks over at the guilty banker. "Take him away."

"Wait," Chloe says. She walks over to Khryses and holds out her down-turned hands.

"How can you forgive me after what I did to your husband and now to you?" he asks.

She stares at the man with tears still misting her eyes. He takes her hands in his, and she nods. Through his confusion, he nods back.

The legionnaires lead the condemned man away. His former partners follow just long enough to leave the podium, then walk away from him.

The praetor leaves next. Then the three judges. Last Titus, Chloe, and her blind friend, Phylidda.

"You certainly did wax eloquent up there, Titus," Stephan says, pounding his old friend on his back. "You are going to have people lining up for your services. You're going to be so popular and in demand, you are going to have to move your family here and stay."

Titus does not reply.

"Come on back to our house," Stephan says. "We must celebrate."

His sons, Nicon and Tycho, walk on one side of their father. Titus, Chloe, and Phylidda on the other side on the broad street.

Titus takes his aunt's hand, and sometimes they look into each other's eyes without speaking. They both know.

When they arrive at Stephan's house, he calls for his wife to bring everyone some new wine.

"I'm not going to do it again," Titus says.

Stephan takes a gulp of his drink, then sets his mug down. He tips his head one way, then the other, and smiles. "And what is it that you're not going to do again, my brilliant friend?"

"I will never represent anyone else in court. Never

again."

Stephan wrinkles his brow, dips his head, and looks up. "You what?"

"I swore I would never do it again when my client was sentenced to death. Now I have repeated history, only this time it is the death of my opponent. I know justice must exist, but there has to be another way."

"There is another way," Chloe says.

Stephan stands, walks to the other side of his small courtyard, and stares at Titus and his aunt. He looks up at the pure white clouds overhead. He steps over to his gate, opens it, and leaves.

Arelia joins them in the courtyard. "Our son, Nicon, told me what happened. My Stephan used to be shy as a boy. I guess you remember that, Titus. Now he sometimes overdoes it the other way with his enthusiasm."

"What do you think you will do now, Aunt Chloe?" Titus asks. "You have nothing left. How are you going to live? Do you think you'll return to Antioch?"

"And watch my brother continue to destroy himself? He hasn't changed, has he?"

"No, he hasn't changed. But the congregation there is a good one."

"Maybe I need to stay and help our congregation here. I have a pretty good hand where it comes to writing. Perhaps I can advertise that I will do scribe work for people. I suppose you will be returning to Antioch and your family now that— you know—you did the best you could for me."

"Aunt Chloe, tomorrow, why don't you and I go over to what remains of your house. Wear dark clothes so the soot doesn't show, and see what we can salvage. I think most of the tiles are still good. Perhaps, if we could borrow a cart, we could put the tiles in it and sell them at the market."

The hinges on the gate rattle. Stephen walks through and reseats himself where he had been before. He leans over, puts his elbows on his knees, and lets his clasped hands droop. He looks down at the floor.

"I know," Titus says. "I was caught up in the moment too. Not only did Cicero and Seneca say justice must never be meted out for the joy of it, but Jesus also said we must love our enemies."

"It's my fault," Chloe says. "I should have never written you that letter to come help me."

"Well, your house hadn't burned down yet. I think that led us all to start thinking with our emotions instead of our heart and mind. Jesus said we were to love our enemies, and we did not do it."

"We disobeyed our Lord, and look what it led to. How are we going to live with ourselves now?" Stephan says.

Chloe looks over at her nephew. Titus is confident he detects the sliver of a moment when there is a gleam in her eyes.

"We shall turn the matter over to God now," she says

They sit in silence a while.

There is a knock on their gate. Stephan's son, Nicon, answers it.

"Is Titus here?" Sosthenes asks.

At hearing the familiar voice, Titus stands. "How was your trip back from Ephesus?"

"I heard about the riot there and left from Smyrna. It was all right," he says, pulling at his sharp nose. His beard is long and white, while his hair is black with many white streaks in it.

"We need to talk," gray-haired Erastus says, standing beside his friend. The bulky man with a broad nose and large mouth steps into the small courtyard

"Thank you for delivering my letter to Paul," Chloe says to both Sosthenes and Erastus.

"That's what we came to talk about," Sosthenes says. "Stephanas gave us Paul's reply after he ran into Titus his first day here. We have read it. It is a powerful letter. It may run some people off. But it is from an apostle. If they are run off, it will be because of their pride, not their humility."

"Two days from now is the first day of the week. We need everyone to stay after our worship and hear Paul's letter. It will take all afternoon to do so," Erastus says.

"So, who should do the reading?" Sosthenes asks.

"I suggest Titus do it. Sometimes people get mad at the

messenger, even though he didn't write the message. Titus doesn't live here and can escape back to Antioch. Isn't that right?" Stephan says, trying to lighten up the dark mood that is returning to his home.

"We have to be going now. We shall pray much tonight that our congregation does not end up worse than it already is," Sosthenes says.

"Paul is a wise man and is led by the Spirit of Christ. Let us trust in that," Erastus says.

They leave, and Stephan's two daughters call everyone to partake in their evening meal. They enjoy cheese, grapes, flatbread, raisin sauce, and olives.

"Your daughters are amazing cooks," Titus says. "By the way, do your church members meet in homes around the city?"

"No," Stephan says. "At first we met in the home of Gaius. He exports copper and has a relatively large villa. But we grew so fast, before we knew it, we had outgrown his house. So we negotiated with the Jews because there were about as many Christians as Jews by then. We agreed to share the synagogue building with them using it on the last day of the week and us using it on the first day of the week. After all, we Christians had helped pay for it while we were still Jews."

"So, you still have that arrangement?" Titus asks, popping the last grape into his mouth.

"Oh, no," red-headed Arelia says. "We eventually bought the Jews out. Their numbers got so small, they couldn't keep up with their half of the upkeep. Was Sosthenes mad!"

"Sosthenes? Why would he be mad?"

"Because after Crispus, ruler of the synagogue, became a Christian, Sosthenes took his place. He tried everything to destroy us, even to having Crispus arrested for theft, which never happened."

"Ha, ha," Stephan intercedes. "We had a time with that man, but eventually converted him."

"So the synagogue became the meeting place of the Christians," Titus says in conclusion.

"No. That's when we only had two hundred and fifty

members."

"Only?"

"Yes," son Tycho jumps in. We now have six hundred Christians here in Corinth. We had to double the size of the building,"

Titus drops the last of his bread in his plate. "No! You couldn't possibly have that many."

"And there are all kinds of us," daughter Juno says.

"Yeah," daughter Lupa continues. "We have city officials who promised not to be crooked anymore, and sailors and athletes who promised not to run after women any more. We have lazy philosophers and former pagan priests and repentant temple prostitutes..."

"And potters like us," son Nicon says.

"Is that why you are having so many problems? You have so many differences?" Titus slaps his knee. "Well, that certainly explains it."

"Yup, I guess so," Tycho says.

"And you expect me to get up in front of that wild bunch of Christians and read to them and not expect someone to throw date pits at me?"

"Something like that," Stephan says. "As I said, you're not from around here, and you can always escape back to Antioch."

Titus looks over at Chloe, who has just brought in more bread for everyone.

"Whatever happened to the execution? I thought they were going to, you know?"

"I heard he escaped," Chloe replies.

"He was too well guarded. That's impossible."

"Maybe the guards looked away at something else just long enough for him to..."

Titus stares at his aunt. Chloe says no more.

Two days later, the family and guests leave Stephan's home and walk past the North Market and the North columned walkway. On their right is Corinth's theater for plays and some athletics, and an odeon for musical performances and plays. Across from the odeon is a large building with an old side and new side.

They enter, and Titus realizes he is the center of attention. "I think I'll sit in the back," he whispers to Stephan.

"Can I go back there with him?" Tycho asks.

"No."

The worship time is entered into with gusto. They sing a hymn, and someone goes up front, waves at everyone to stop singing, and announces, "Stop. Stop. I have a prophecy." They resume singing, and someone jumps up in their seat and announces another prophecy that must be said on the spot.

Finally, the hymn is completed. Erastus stands before the group and makes announcements about who is sick and needs visiting, who is traveling and needs prayers, who has lost his job and needs financial help.

He is interrupted. Someone stands and speaks something in Persian. Someone else stands and speaks something in Egyptian. Someone else stands and speaks something in Germanic.

Erastus finishes his announcements with members raising their hand that they will go see whoever he mentioned.

Stephan stands and explains it is time for the Lord's Supper. He retells the story of Jesus' terrible death.

Everyone pulls out their own bread and wine. Some have a few bites, while others have enough for an entire meal with some left over. Those with just one or two bites of the bread and one or two sips of the wine wait around while those with a whole feast of it finishes their meal.

That done, Gaius, the copper exporter and second convert of Paul's after Stephan, stands and leads a prayer. He is interrupted by someone praying in Gaulish. He continues his prayer but is interrupted by someone praying in Chinese. He hurries up and finishes his prayer.

Sosthenes stands and opens a scroll displayed on a cedar table with ivory inlays. He begins reading the prophecy of Isaiah but is interrupted.

"Wait, I just got my own prophecy. Listen to this, everyone."

Sosthenes resumes reading. He is interrupted.

"I have an interpretation of what he just read. Now the meaning of that passage in our everyday life is..."

The reading is resumed and completed.

They sing another hymn, which seems a little fast to Titus. *Perhaps they are rushing through it before someone interrupts them,* he thinks.

Three hours later, the worship of the Christians is over. It is now early afternoon, too long—some believe—to go between meals. Nearly everyone has brought something to eat, and each person eats what he or she has brought—if anything. Some take their foot outside and sit on benches scattered around.

"Come outside and eat with us," Stephan urges Titus.

"No, thank you. What you gave me to eat for the Lord's Supper was plenty. I am not hungry."

Two hours later, everyone has filed in and taken their seats. The sailors from down at the docks sit together. The athletes practicing for the Olympic tryouts sit in another. The merchants in another area, the craftsmen in another, the farmers in another, and the city's elite in another.

I wonder if they're further subdivided by former Jews and former pagans.

Titus walks to the front with Paul's letter and begins to read. He reads about cliques, wisdom that is foolish, and foolishness that is wise. So far, so good. No one has left.

He rests while the congregation sings a song. He reads a little ahead silently and tells himself, *Uh-oh. Things are going to start getting sticky now.*

Paul bawls them out for bragging they accept anyone in the church, regardless of their sexual activities. Despite that, they turn right around and take each other to court for sometimes petty. Then the letter goes back to their immorality.

"Do not be fooled. People committing sexual sins and thieves and people who get drunk and people who gossip and people who swindle others—none of them will go to heaven. You are the body of Christ, and his Holy Spirit is in your body. How dare you do those things with the body he has made holy!"

Titus sits back down. The congregation sings another hymn, but not with the zest it had earlier.

"Now, regarding the things you wrote **about**." Titus

reads about being married to unbelievers and advises them not to marry if they can handle being single because of growing persecution against the church.

Another rest for Titus' voice and to let everyone absorb what he has read thus far. Another hymn. He thinks about the odeon across the street where songs to the gods are sung, and full orchestras to those same gods perform.

"Now about eating food the pagan priests offer to idols and eat as part of their worship: If you don't believe those gods exist and buy leftover sacrificial food in the market, you are not sinning. But don't tell new Christians who used to believe in those gods where you got your food; they're still weak in their faith. I try to fit in with the customs of whoever I am around so I can save them. If they are weak, I become weak. I am running a race to heaven, I am boxing Satan, I keep myself spiritually fit and ready. If it is your custom to pray with your head covered, do it. If not, don't do it. Women, submit to men as examples for the way they have to submit to Christ."

Titus sits again. Another hymn is sung. Someone stands to speak in a Celtic language. The others make them sit down. Another stands to teach everyone a new song that is in his heart. They get him to sit down. Someone else thinks it is time to stop and eat again. He is outvoted. Paul's letter is going to make for a long afternoon.

Back standing, Titus continues. "In the first place, your worship services are doing more harm than good. You have cliques, some of you turn the Lord's Supper into a feast and let the others go hungry, some of you even get drunk on the wine. If you expect me to praise you, you are wrong."

What kind of congregation is this? I hope Antioch never gets this bad.

"When you eat the Lord's Supper, examine yourself quietly. Judge yourself weekly, so God's final judgment on you will not be severe. You are not only abusing the Lord's Supper, but you are abusing the spiritual gifts I bestowed some of you with when I was there. Someone has the gift of speaking languages he never learned and thinks he is most important. Someone else has the gift of healing and thinks he is most important. Another has the gift of prophesying God's words and thinks he is important. What is wrong with you?"

Titus hears some shuffling and looks up from his reading. Three men and two women have marched out of the assembly and slammed the door behind them.

"Just like the parts of your body that are hidden are most important, those of you with quiet gifts, no one notices are most important. If a stranger visits your worship, and everyone is speaking a different language, he will think you are all mad. Stop being so childish."

Titus stops his reading and sits back down. For the first time since his arrival that morning, there is stillness. No singing. No calling out. No interrupting. No demanding. Stillness except for six more who have left in a huff. He stands for the last of Paul's letter to them.

"Put Jesus' sacrifice foremost in your thoughts and actions. He died for you. He was buried for you. He came back to life for you. He appeared to Peter, who had betrayed him. He appeared to his twelve. He appeared to over five hundred mourners at the same time. He appeared to his half-brother, who had denied him. Last, he appeared to me. If he died and was raised, hold fast to this, so he will bring you back to life when you die. You will die like a seed dies. On the last day, God's trumpet will blast, and the world will be judged. You will rise up to meet Jesus in the air with a glorious body, just like a seed grown into a great tree."

Titus looks up. No more jumping up to be seen or heard. Some lean forward, elbows on knees. Others have their heads bowed. Still, others are looking up. And there are the motionless ones with tears flowing down their cheeks. He reads the last of Paul's letter.

"I am going to stay in Ephesus a little longer. Then I will come to you. Respect Stephanas. He was the first Christian of all of you. Listen to him. The grace of God be upon you all. Amen."

27 ~ TURNS AND TWISTS

"**P**aul is here! Paul is here!" Jupo says, hurrying through the gate her mother has just opened for her.

Titus is sitting in Stephan's courtyard, reading one of the many scrolls he always has with him. He looks up.

"Did you see him?"

"Yes. He has just arrived from Isthmia and has a bunch of people with him."

"How many and who?" Titus asks.

"Well, Timothy is with him. But Timothy is always with him. And another man who looks like Timothy but has blond hair. Well, both of them look kind of like you—you're all tall and thin."

"Anyone else?" Titus asks, trying not to show impatience at having to drag the information out of the teenage girl.

"I don't know. One other man I never saw before."

Did you talk to them?"

"I just waved at them, and Timothy called back to me for Father and you to meet him at Gaius' house."

Titus grabs his toga. Tell your mother where I went, then go tell your father.

"I already told him."

Titus walks south toward the market and hears a familiar voice behind him.

"Titus, is that you?"

Titus turns and sees Stephan. "I'm on my way to see Paul. He just arrived. Why don't you come along?"

They continue south past the theater and odeon on their right, then the synagogue-turned-worship place for Christians, then right and out the west gate of the city. They arrive at Gaius' villa.

They are welcomed in, and introductions are made. They meet Aristarchus from up north in Thessalonica, and another Gaius whom they call Clay Gaius to distinguish him from Silver Gaius from up north and Corinth's Copper Gaius. They laugh at the necessary nicknames to keep all the Gaiuses separated.

The men sit around in Copper Gaius' solarium. Titus watches a goldfish that seems to be attacking a lily pad.

"How are things now with the church?" Paul asks. "Any better?"

"They are still judgmental, hauling each other into court, and doing things that are offensive to our more moderate members."

"Will you stay and speak to us?"

"I will do more than that. I will stay and try to straighten out the mess here. A bunch of people with egos. When we are buried with Christ in baptism, we bury our egos. Our egos are not even supposed to be alive anymore."

"Titus, how did they take my letter to them?" he asks.

"Not well. You bawled them out pretty hard in your letter," Titus answers. "They are the largest congregation anywhere in the world except Jerusalem, and are not used to being told what to do anymore."

"At first they did a little better, but now they're back to their old ways," Sosthenes says.

Paul shakes his head. "Pride."

"But I have been working with them trying to be an example of what you were trying to explain, Titus adds. "The fact that my aunt, Chloe, is a member of their congregation has helped a lot."

"Titus, you and I are outsiders," Paul says. "But you have been here—what? A month? Well, long enough you kind of know the people. We need to make the rounds of everyone in the congregation."

"We must have one hundred fifty homes or more among our six hundred members," Gaius interrupts. "How are you going to go see all of them?"

"Gaius, you were my second convert here in Corinth. You and Stephanus have done a fantastic job of converting many in this fine city."

"Well, it's gotten out of hand," Gaius responds.

"Titus and I will be going to visit all of them in their own homes. You asked how. One at a time for as long as it takes. Isn't that right, Titus? And we shall begin tomorrow morning. Where are you staying?"

"My aunt and I are staying with Stephan. You may not know that we grew up together in Antioch."

"I didn't know that," Paul responds with a broad grin.

"He left home and moved to Rome, where he converted to Judaism. Then Caesar expelled all Jews, so he came here where you converted him."

Paul slaps both of his knees. "Isn't that something? You were my first convert in Antioch, and he was my first convert in Corinth. When we get together, we shall celebrate that."

"But for now, Paul needs his rest," Timothy interrupts.

"Timothy loves to baby me," Paul responds. "But I guess he's right. I'm pretty tired. Copper Gaius, do you know where all the members live?"

Gaius nods.

"Can you have a map ready for us in the morning?

"I can have a map of people who live in my neighborhood tomorrow."

"That's fine. We probably won't be able to visit more than a couple families a day. Good night."

By this time, Paul is walking out of the solarium, hanging on to Timothy's arm.

When they are out of hearing, Aristarchus speaks up. "Our Paul has been beaten and kicked and starved and poked and whipped so many times, it is taking a toll on his health. Timothy tells me he used to be athletic. But now he is bent in order to not strain his back, which is full of so many scars I don't think he can even stand straight anymore."

"I don't believe we realized that, did we, Titus?" Copper Gaius replies.

"He was treated so bad up in Philippi and Thessalonica, he had to escape to Athens. He's been there in hiding and resting," Aristarchus adds. "He keeps talking about a man named Luke, who knows medicine, wishing he had Luke around to doctor him more—not that Timothy doesn't do an excellent job."

"So, whatever you do," Clay Gaius says, "Do not slap him on the back if you embrace him. It is all he can do to keep clothes on it. The scars are ultrasensitive to touch, Timothy tells us."

Titus and Sosthenes stand. "You men traveling with him must be tired," Titus says. "I will come back about mid-morning tomorrow so we can begin our crusade of making an out-of-control congregation civilized and loving."

The next morning, Titus is back. Gaius has the promised map for them, etched on a clay tablet.

For two months six days a week, Titus and Paul visit each family in private in their own home.

"Okay, what questions do you have for me?" Paul always begins.

"Here are some things for you to think about."

"Have you offended anyone? Have you gone to them and said you are sorry?"

"Have you been speaking in foreign languages in worship to show off instead of teaching people whose foreign language you now know?"

"Have you been over to the Temple of Poseidon at Isthmia, or here in Corinth to the temples of Apollo and Aphrodite and Augustus and Hercules to try to save them from hell? Or are you spending all your time telling other Christians what to do?"

"Have you been to the jails to teach them about Jesus, or are you sending those who owe you money to those jails?"

"Have you been down to the docks and taverns to talk to the sailors? Do you think you are better than them?"

"Have you been to the athletic fields you have around

here to talk to the Olympic contenders? Have you been to the theater or the odeon to talk to people rehearsing for their performances?

"How many souls have you taught recently? What do you spend your time doing besides showing off how holy you are to your Christian brothers and sisters, so they will envy you?"

"Who do you pray for besides yourself?"

Each afternoon, they go back to Gaius' house where Stephan joins them, and discuss what they have found out that day. Today, Titus and Stephan have had to take care of something for Aunt Chloe.

The following morning, Titus returns to Gaius' villa.

"What do you mean, Gaius is not here?" he asks the old gatekeeper. "Are you crying?"

Titus enters Gaius' deserted courtyard. "Where is everyone? Where is Paul?"

The gatekeeper sits on a marble bench near the gate, his head bowed. Titus kneels in front of them. "What's going on?"

Every muscle tenses. A feeling grows over him like the feeling he had had when he was eleven years old and lost his mother. A feeling he had had again when he was thirty those fifteen years ago and had lost his little red-headed girl.

"Tell me! Tell me!"

The gatekeeper looks up. "They killed him."

"Killed who?"

"The apostle. They killed Paul. Beat him to death."

Titus stands and backs up. He looks around but sees nothing and breathes nothing. The air is thick and dark and full of death.

"Did they get Gaius and the other two also?"

"No, Aristarchus and Clay Gaius left for Athens this morning. My Gaius is with the church here right now. They are praying for courage to go on without Paul's guidance."

"Do you have a horse I can ride across the city?" I don't need a saddle."

"Yes, in the stable. I guess you can take whichever one you want."

Titus goes through the door leading into the stable, the stable hand throws tack on one of them, hands Titus the reins, and Titus takes off in a gallop until he reaches the western gate into the city. He puts his horse into a trot, the best he can do with the traffic in the streets.

As he rides, he sees the face of his dead mother and the funeral pyre. He sees the angelic face of his baby daughter and the little mound of dirt over her grave. He fights tears and panic and anger. *God, where are you? Can't you protect anyone?*

He arrives at the former synagogue where he sees donkeys, horses, chariots, and carts outside. He throws open the doors, and everyone looks back at him.

"How?" Titus shouts. "How could this have happened? Couldn't we have protected him better? Where is his body?"

Gaius rushes back to Titus.

"He's alive, Titus. We thought they had beaten him to death. We were wrong, though I do not know how he survived it."

"Then, where is he?"

"Sosthenes and Timothy rushed him to Athens to see that doctor he told us about—Luke."

Gaius puts his arm over Titus' shoulder. "Come join us. Help us pray for our Paul."

Sosthenes returns to Corinth three days later and sends for Titus, Gaius, Erastus, and Stephanus.

"It was only by the will of God and all our prayers that we still have Paul with us. Well, and the fast-thinking of Timothy, who helped me get him to the Athens Medical Academy where Luke is. I have never seen anything like it. Paul has no back left. All flesh is gone. It is as though he has been skinned alive. We could even see some of his rib bones. Timothy said he has been beaten so many times, the flesh on his back is always fragile. Luke has kept him sedated with opium. He says eventually, his back will heal, but it will just be one big scar."

The men sit in silence.

"Timothy said he would send us messages sometimes to tell us how Paul is doing."

The following first day of the week, the five men sit at the front of the congregation. The loud singing and showing off of languages and prophecies and missions and ministries seem unimportant now. Now all is quiet and solemn and contemplating what is truly important.

The leaders of the congregation take turns praying on behalf of the members for their Paul. Sometimes someone stands and speaks of a personal experience with their apostle. Sometimes they talk of their conversion, but as often they recall a recent time when he and Titus had visited them in their home and just loved them.

"Keep Paul alive."

"We need him."

"May it not be said Paul was taken from the world while in our city."

Two weeks later, a message is received from Timothy for Titus. "Paul is still very weak, but I think he wants you to stay in Corinth for now. Perhaps in another month, he will be strong enough to think through what he wants you to do for him next."

The following week, Aunt Chloe receives a letter from Antioch. "I believe this is for you, Titus," she tells her nephew when he returns home from debating local philosophers at the forum. "The hand is flourishing like a woman's. It must be from Fjorta."

She hands the letter to Titus and returns to her workroom, where she is copying a will for someone in the city.

My darling husband. Greetings from Antioch. How your son and I miss you. But we know Aunt Chloe needs you. We heard Paul has joined you. That is good.

"Do you remember my Fjorta, Stephan?" he asks his host.

"We both do," Arelia says. "She had long blond, almost white hair that fell down her back, not frizzy red hair like mine. And tall. My, she was tall."

"Did you call her your ice queen?" Stephan says,

grinning.

"Indeed, I did. She is still my queen. Our son is taking after both of us. Sirius is almost nine years old now and as tall as, well, as my mother used to be if I remember right."

"Don't let us keep you from your letter," Arelia says. "Stephan, I need you to lift something for me over there."

Alone now, Titus reads the rest of the letter.

I must warn you not to return.

Titus squints and wrinkles his brow. *What's going on there?*

Remember the speech you made at the Western Forum trying to prove Socrates' ideas of an impersonal creator god wrong? Remember the high priest of Apollo sent legionnaires after you? He has stirred up the entire city. The guards at all the gates are on the watch for you. There is a reward offered to anyone who brings you back to the city to stand trial for atheism and for trying to invent a god the Senate has not approved of.

Why do I do foolish things like that? They could have taken it out on my family.

Your father sends you his greetings, though he still does not approve of Christians. Our son prays for you at every meal and every morning and every night. He loves you and adores you and misses you. Tell us what you want us to do. Your devoted wife.

Titus rolls the scroll back up and walks into Chloe's workroom.

"Aunt Chloe, I need to send for my family, but I am uncertain how I will support them. I brought enough money with me to live for a year. I doubt my father will send me money. Perhaps I need to set up a law practice—not to go to court or anything, but to help people make legal decisions. Do you think I will be able to support them?

28 ~ FALSE APOSTLE

"**I**'ve been meaning to tell you something, Titus, but have been waiting to work a few things out first."

"I only have enough money to rent an insulae for my family and you to live for a little while," Titus says.

"Titus, did you hear what I just said?" Chloe asks.

"Huh? Did you say something?"

"Sit."

"Yes, ma'am." Titus sits.

"The possessions of Banker Khryses have been sold. Praetor Basileus has ordered that the money he stole from my Fulvio be paid to me."

"Huh?"

"I have been in touch with someone who will rebuild my house. A few days ago, I hired someone to clear away the charred timber. The floors Fulvio tiled are still good. They need to be cleaned and will never be like they were originally, but they are still good. So, I still have a good foundation. All my builder needs to do is put up walls and a roof."

Titus smiles. "I am delighted things are turning out better for you now. Maybe I did help you a little after all."

"Of course, I want you and your family to move in with me. Things will be a lot like they were when I was helping to raise you."

"Oh, thank you, Aunt Chloe. But I will still need to

support my family. Do you think I could turn one room off your courtyard into an *officium* to receive clients?”

Chloe stands and steps over to her nephew. She kneels.

“Aunt Chloe, what are you doing?”

“Titus, you have more important work to do than council people about wills and deeds. You have been a Christian for twelve years now. You are forty-five years old. You are respected by the brothers and sisters in the church here in Corinth—well, most of them anyway. I want to support you so you can keep doing what you have been doing. The church needs your quick mind and your leadership.”

“Aunt Chloe, I don’t know what to say.”

“There are still members who are not getting along. You need to become a peacemaker and arbitrate between them, so they will love each other as our Lord wants us all to do.”

Titus looks at his aunt, his head tilted and with an uncertain smile.

“Do not question me, young man,” she responds. “I may not be smarter or even as smart as you, but I am still older than you. You will do what I say. Now, go out there and have a long talk with Stephanus and figure out who in the congregation needs to forget offenses and become friends again. Use your arbitration knowledge and talents for the Lord.”

“Yes, ma’am,” Titus says, standing.

“Oh, and when Timothy writes and tells you Paul is asking for you—and he will in a month or so—you will go see him and say how well things are going here so that one worry will be off his mind.”

Titus walks around behind his aunt’s writing desk. “Thank you, dear aunt. You have always been a lifesaver.” He leans over and kisses her on each cheek.

“Go. Get out of here. You and Stephanus have things to work out. Oh, and tonight, write a letter to your wife. Tell her the first floor of my new house will be completed in a month or so. If it isn’t, you will share your tent on Stephan’s roof with them until it is. Now get out of here. I have important work to do.”

When Titus returns to the courtyard, Stephan is back

on his bench, grinning.

"Did you know about this?"

"About what?"

"You know good and well what I am talking about. Aunt Chloe."

"Well, I guess I did. So, are you returning to Antioch now that Paul is gone and things are settled better than they were here? Or are you going to send for them?"

"It looks like they're going to have to come here. Half of Antioch is after me."

Stephan laughs. "I'm not surprised, but I'm not going to ask you what you did to make them mad this time."

"Stephan, Aunt Cloe says you and I need to make a list of people in your—our—congregation who still do not get along."

"Oh, you mean suing each other?"

"Yes, I need to arbitrate between them."

"So, does that mean you want me to question them while you stand out of hearing so you can tell whether they are lying. You never did tell me all your secrets about that."

Titus sits and crosses his legs. He puts his hands behind the back of his head and stares at his friend. "Some things I do need to be closer to them for. For example, if their lips are lying, but their cheeks are not raised, and their eyes are rather blank, I know their smile is not real. Or, if their smile doesn't last longer than to my count of two, I can tell their smile is not genuine, and they are actually quite unhappy."

"You can tell all that? Well, get out a tile to etch the names on. Better yet, one of your small scrolls. There may be more disputers than will fit on a tile. Let me see now..."

The next day, Titus sets out to arbitrate his first case in the name of the Lord. He goes to the home of the first sister. "You have been arguing a long time. Would you mind telling me what it is about, so perhaps I can help you come to an agreement?"

"We live next door to each other. Every time I go up on my roof to clean my rugs, she spies on me."

"Why would she spy on you?"

"She is jealous. She knows I am going to donate a rug to the church, and she plans to donate a larger rug."

"Why can't you both donate a rug?"

"Because it was my idea, and she will get the credit for it."

"Why don't you donate two rugs then?"

"I can't afford two rugs.

"Under what condition would you make friends with her again?"

"Under the condition she drops her idea of donating a rug to the church."

Titus goes next door. "Oh, I don't want to give a rug to the church," the Christian neighbor says. "I want to give it to her. She is such a giving person and is always doing things for other people, I would like to do something special for her."

Titus goes back to the first Christian neighbor's house. "Your neighbor wants to show you her rug."

"No. Never."

Titus opens the gate and lets the waiting neighbor in. She has a cart small enough she can easily move it. "Here," the second neighbor says. "I want to give this to you. We have been friends a long time. I don't want us to fight. Please, take this rug. I bought it especially for you."

"For me? But I thought..."

The two women embrace, and Titus slips away, smiling.

"Well, my first case was easy enough," he tells Stephan that evening. "But the next one is going to be a lot harder. One of the brothers is suing another for slander."

Several days later, Titus heads into the city to find the wronged brother.

"Felix, I understand you have been slandered."

"Indeed, I have, and it came from a supposed Christian brother. He is no brother of mine if he is going to treat me like I am no better than a rat."

"What did he call you, and how do you know he did, and who is he?"

"He is Cyneas. I am a trainer of javelin throwing. I get young men ready for the Olympic tryouts here every other year. He is telling people I was disqualified when I participated in the javelin-throwing competition at the Pythian Games in Delphi when I was younger. He claims I stepped over the line and had to forfeit my honor. He is a liar.”

“And how do you know he has told this?” Titus asks. “How many people have repeated it?”

“Two weeks ago, when I was training three young men over at the circus, several other trainers came over to me and repeated it in front of my students. They even warned my students to find another coach so they wouldn’t be disqualified themselves.”

“Oh, that is serious,” Titus replies.

“It is my livelihood and my reputation. There is no truth in it at all. No one has even tried to verify it as far as I know.”

“Have you tried to talk to Cyneas?”

“He won’t talk.”

“I will go see him.”

Titus goes to the insulae where Cyneas lives on the second floor with his family. It is late afternoon, and the family is preparing to sit down together and eat.

“Hello, Cyneas,” Titus says when the brother answers his second-floor door. “Do you remember me from the church? Let’s go for a walk.”

Cyneas forms a broad grin. “Oh, you’re a lawyer. Just who I need to talk to. Sure.”

They walk outside and sit on benches behind the building where the tenants have communal ovens and stalls for their animals.

“I understand you are being sued by Felix for slander.”

“Well, it’s the truth. If I can save these young men from having their lives ruined by a criminal like him, I will have done my duty.”

“I see. That is quite a lofty goal—protecting our youth like that,” Titus replies. “So, the youth of our city will, of course, be grateful to you.”

“Yes, very grateful.”

“Have people in this city praised you for other contributions you have made.”

“Not really. No one pays any attention to me. But they will now. I will be their savior.”

"Their savior?"

"Yes, and they might even let me head up the parade at the next Olympic Games."

"That definitely would be praiseworthy."

"It's something my children will pass down to their children for generations to come."

"Having a respected name is important," Titus concedes.

"You are right there. People have never thought I was important. But they will now. I'm the man who saved the Olympic Games."

"What else have you done that is important?."

Cyneas stares at Titus a long moment then looks down at the barren ground under their feet.

"Nothing."

"Nothing at all?"

"It's not that I don't work hard. I work as hard or harder than the next man. But it isn't exactly important."

"What do you do, Cyneas?"

"I am the custodian for the synagogue—er, the building the church uses." He pauses. "And I do a good job too."

"I'm sure you do."

Titus stands. "It was good talking to you, brother. I am proud to call you my friend."

"You are? Are you going to represent me in court?"

"We'll talk about that another day, friend."

Titus works his way back over to the circus and finds Felix. He has a different group of students this time—a little younger, and there are four of them. Titus motions to Felix.

"You men keep practicing," Felix tells the boys. "I'll be watching you from over here."

"Felix," Titus says. "Do you know what type work Cyneas does?"

"Yes. He cleans the building the church meets in. It's a huge job, but he gets it done. Everyone likes his work."

"What type of work do you do for the church?"

"I am a deacon. I am in charge of young orphan boys."

"Uh, Felix, Cyneas does not feel appreciated."

"Not appreciated? We don't know what we would do

without him. There is no one that we know of who would come close to what he accomplishes.”

"Have you ever told him that?”

"Don't need to. He knows we appreciate him.”

"How does he know?”

"Well..." Felix stares at Titus, tilts his head, and lets out a big "Ha!”

Titus smiles back.

"We have never told him. So, he's trying to be important by...”

"Exactly," Titus says.

Two days later is the Lord's Day. There is a ceremony. A bronze plaque is awarded. The lawsuit is dropped.

"So, who is next on your list?" Chloe asks Titus the next morning as they break their fast with Stephan's family.

"One of the brothers says one of the other brothers found buried treasure on his land, and he wants it back. Aunt Chloe, I don't like what is happening. I don't like doing all this arbitration. I want to just worship and be happy that I am saved and try to help others be saved when they die. That's all I want.”

"Titus, Titus, Titus," she says. "The church was set down in the middle of an evil world. It is up to every Christian to protect it. It's warfare.”

He looks down at the yogurt he is dipping his bread in, then lets his hand perch over the shared bowl, but he does not reply.

"Remember all those times you, as a lawyer, defended people?" Chloe recalls. "You are now defending the church.”

"Blessed are the peacemakers," Stephan adds. And that is what you are doing. Paul knew you would be perfect for this job. I did too. So did your aunt and...”

"Thank you, friend. I guess I needed that.”

A week passes. Chloe and Titus both arrive at Stephan's house at the same time.

"Chloe, you are filthy," Titus says. "What have you been doing?”

She stares at him and smiles.

"Your house. Of course," he replies. "So, what is going

on over there?"

"I helped them clear away the rubble."

"Why?"

She puts both hands on her hips. "Because, my dear, I wanted to."

"Besides, you didn't have to pay out so much for labor by doing some of the work yourself," he adds for her.

"That too. Have you written your family to come join you here?"

"I wanted to wait until you were farther along on the house."

"What are you two up to?" Stephan asks as they walk through his gate.

"We should be out of your hair, and you can have your storeroom and roof back in a month or two," Chloe announces.

"Are you done clearing away the rubble?"

"No, but it's starting to look better."

"I am sending all four of my children over to help you tomorrow."

"Father, you didn't tell us that."

"Well, Son, I wanted it to be a happy surprise. Now, look happy for Aunt Chloe."

Stephan walks over to a wooden table, looks at his list, then turns back to Titus. "Here's someone else for your list. Actually, it's three someones."

"And none of them get along?"

"It's not that. They get along with each other. But they don't like me or Gaius, Sosthenes, Erastus or any of the founders of the congregation. They don't like Paul, and they don't even like you."

"I've been hated before," Titus says.

"Be careful what you say around them. They are Geylon, Philon, and Pistias. Be careful."

"I think I'll work on the buried treasure problem next," Titus says. "That one is going to take some doing to solve. Maybe by the time things are worked out, those three men will be tired of playing emperor of the kingdom and go away."

It has now been six weeks since Paul was beaten and

left for dead. Titus has not been able to solve all the disputes in the congregation but has at least been able to set up a temporary truce between many feuding parties.

"I'm getting worried about Gaylon, Philon, and Pistias," Titus tells Chloe one evening. "They're too strong for me. I'm afraid they're not going to let some people stay in the congregation who do not cooperate with them. They started out good, but they're changing. They're up to something."

"Have you talked to Erastus about them? He is high enough in the government, they may listen to him."

There is a knock at the gate. Stephan and his family have gone for a walk out in the country. Titus answers it.

"Letter for Titus Pomponius Brennius." Titus takes the letter and gives the messenger a bronze coin. "It is from Timothy," he says, unrolling it. He sits and reads it aloud to his aunt.

"Greetings from Paul and Timothy in Berea."

"I thought they were in Athens," Titus says, interrupting himself.

"Well, keep reading," Chloe urges, flipping her hand like shooing a fly away.

"Luke has consented to be Paul's full-time physician," Titus read. "He needs it. He is now staying in a house Luke's former master, Theophilus, gave him for his years of service. He has set him free."

"You don't hear of masters setting their slaves free just out of love very often," Chloe says.

Titus resumes reading Timothy's letter. "I am going on to Troas, north of Ephesus, and Smyrna to encourage the church there. Paul would like you to come see him in Berea before he leaves to visit congregations in Greece on his way to Troas. He doesn't want to slow us down. Please come. He wants to know how the church in Corinth is doing after his rather harsh letter to them and not being able to stay long on his last trip. Give my greetings to Stephanus, Sosthenes, Erastus, and Copper Gaius."

"Why don't you go now?" Chloe suggests. "By the time you get back, I may be in my new house. And you can send for your family."

The next day, Titus goes to see Gaius about the invitation. "You should go," Gaius says.

"I have one more minor feud to take care of. Then I'll be able to give Paul a happy report."

The following Solday, Titus and Chloe walk south toward the building now being used by the Christians. Stephan's family is scattered both in front and behind them.

When they arrive, Geylon, Philon, and Pistias are standing by the double doors with wide grins. "Welcome, welcome, everyone," they say. "Welcome. Come in. Come in. What a grand day the Lord has given us."

"What are they up to?" Chloe mutters to her nephew.

"They're too happy," Titus mutters back.

When it is time to begin their worship, Sosthenes steps to the front, as usual, to call everyone to order.

"Uh, Sosthenes, while we appreciate what you have always done for us, we would like to suggest a slight change."

Sosthenes stares at Geylon.

"That's okay. Just sit for a few moments," Geylon continues.

The congregation hears the doors into the building open but not close. They turn around to see who has come late. A large man in a white toga with a royal blue band around the border stands in place, the morning sun glowing behind them.

He holds both arms heavenward and marches up the aisle. As he does, he turns this way and that. "Bless you, my child," he says to people sitting closest to the aisle.

He reaches the front and turns around. He is flanked on one side by Philon and the other side by Pistias.

"Brothers and sisters," Geylon bellows. "May I present to you the Apostle Demas. Let us all walk forward and pay him homage as we ought to anyone who walked with our Lord for three long years."

Sosthenes stands. "What are you doing? Stop this."

"I am sorry, Sosthenes, but you are out of order. If you do not cooperation, your presence in this congregation will be jeopardized."

It takes an hour for most of the six hundred members to walk forward and be blessed by the Apostle Demas.

Titus refuses to go. Stephan refuses to go. They look around to identify those who will not go and be recognized by the fake apostle. About fifteen men and their families refuse to acknowledge the charlatan.

Titus is amazed as he watches family after family walk forward, then return to their seats with broad grins. "Thank you, Jesus, for sending us a real apostle."

The congregation, reseated again, raises its collective voice in a glorious hymn.

That completed, Geylong stands before them again. "I have taken the liberty of renting the finest *palatio* in the city of Corinth for our apostle. Nothing is too good for an ambassador of the Lord. He, of course, will receive a stipend from our treasury. You will be pleased to know that he plans to make Corinth his home. Praise God."

Titus is alarmed as he watches the smiles on the faces of most people present.

"Now only that, but he is going to make this the headquarters for all elders in Greece. He will be the pontificate bishop. Other newly-discovered apostles will be arriving soon. Praise God. He has heard our prayers."

The members look at each other as though in mutual congratulations.

"Now, all will be well with the church in this city. We will become so famous, our congregation will grow much larger even than the one in Jerusalem. Praise God!"

"Praise God," the congregation responds.

29 ~ REAL APOSTLE

*L*ate that afternoon, the worshippers are dismissed by their new apostle.

"Titus, you must go to Paul immediately," Gaius says at an urgent meeting assembled in his house.

"We must know how to face this crisis," Sosthenes says.

"Satan lost the battle of feuding brothers and sisters. Now he has a new tactic," Erastus says.

"We need advice," Stephan says. "For once, I am glad Crispus is not here to see this."

"Who is Crispus?" Titus asks.

"He was ruler of the synagogue at the time Paul arrived and converted so many of his congregation," Sosthenes says. "Crispus was finally convinced to become a Christian, and I took over to rule the Jews after him. I am ashamed to say I imprisoned him and did other cruel things to him before I, too, became a Christian."

"It wasn't your fault the cart fell on him," Erastus growls.

"And that his legs became paralyzed and he eventually died from his injuries," Stephan whispers. "Come, Titus," he says louder. "You need to pack tonight and be on your way at dawn tomorrow. Let us pray there is a ship going that way."

Titus arrives in Berea at the port near Mount Olympus. He stares at the mountain as he walks parallel to it, heading west. *There is a time I would have climbed that mountain so I could interrogate the gods. How silly and ignorant can people be? Just like I was.*

Following Timothy's instructions to Luke's house. within two hours, Titus is at the gate he believes belongs to Luke. He knocks.

A tall blond man who looks a lot like Titus' father used to in his youth answers the gate.

"My name is Titus of Antioch and now Corinth. By any chance is a man here by the name of Paul?"

The tall blond man looks both ways beyond Titus. "Uh, what is your business?" the tall blond man asks.

"Would you mind telling him I received Timothy's letter and I—Titus—have arrived? He sent for me."

"The tall blond closes and latches the gate, mumbles something to someone on the other side, and opens the gate again.

"I am Luke he tells Titus. Paul said to let you in."

"Are people still after him?"

"We cannot take any chances," Luke replies. "No one in Berea knows he is here except the church. Come in."

Luke steps aside and lets Titus in.

Paul holds out his arms to his friend, and keeps Titus at a distance as a reminder they must not embrace.

"Oh, Paul. I am so sorry about the, well, beating. I wish we had pressed harder for you to leave Corinth."

"Luke here has been taking excellent care of me. The church sneaks over here on Soldays, so I can worship with them. They are good people here," Paul says, pulling back his arms and trying not to flinch.

Luke shows Titus a place to put down his traveling bags and be seated. It is a bench facing another one with a cushion on it. Paul re-seats himself there.

"Tell me how things are in Corinth," Paul says, humped over a little and leaning with his hands on his knees.

"They have repented of much that they have been doing," Titus says. "But now we have a new problem."

Paul stares at Titus, Titus does not explain, and Paul shakes his head.

"That bad, huh? Satan never lets up on people with the potential to do much good. So now, what has Satan come up with?"

"Some men have arrived announcing they are apostles and you are a fraud. Our treasury for support of widows and orphans has been dipped into in order to rent the finest *palatio* in Corinth for them to have as a church headquarters and to live in. Oh, and to give them a stipend to live in a manner they know the Lord would want them to as representatives of Jesus on earth."

Paul shakes his head and looks down at the simple tile in the courtyard. Silence awhile. He raises his eyes. "And?"

"And they are already threatening to expel from the congregation anyone who disputes their authority."

"No!"

Titus is surprised at the power behind the wounded man's voice.

"This is the church. It is all wrong. He who wants to be a leader must become a servant."

Paul rises from his seat and walks in circles. "Jesus never intended for the church to become a large organization with heads who must be obeyed and paid homage to. Jesus is the only head. No! It is all wrong. They are destroying that which Jesus died for."

Paul reseats himself and is silent a moment. "This congregation had the most promise of any I ever worked with up to that time," he groans. "Satan is attacking them hard, lest they become a light to the world."

"They are bragging and strutting and threatening. They want people to bow down to them and give them the respect Jesus' apostles deserve."

Paul stands, paces, then re-seats himself.

"Paul, you have lost a lot of weight. Are you sure you are okay?"

"Yes, Titus, I am sure. Well, my health is better than my spirit right now." Paul stares at Titus and says nothing more.

How does he do it? Titus thinks to himself. *He is so strong, even after being beaten mostly to death. How does he do it?*

"Luke, do you have a blank scroll? I need to write them."
Luke steps away.

"Timothy will be so distressed to hear this news. They took to Timothy. Not as much as they did you, Titus, but they still liked Timothy. The letter shall be from both of us. I want them to respect you enough when you get back that they listen to you. You've got to figure out a way to get rid of the fake apostle."

Luke arrives back in the courtyard from a nearby room with a scroll, blackener, and pen. He lays them on a table, and Titus takes a seat there, ready for Paul's dictation. He is shocked at what Paul tells the church in Corinth.

"I, an apostle chosen by Christ Jesus and no human, send you grace and peace....To spare you, I am not returning to Corinth....I was hoping, when we fled from certain death in Ephesus, that Titus would meet me in Troas to tell us about you, but he had business in Corinth and stayed....

"Jesus, the image of the invisible God, is all we apostles preach.... We never elevate ourselves. We are afflicted, crushed, persecuted, and struck down, but we are not destroyed. We do not lose hope, even though our body is all but decaying while we are still alive....

"The love of Christ pushes us forward. He became sin for us.... As servants of God, we apostles endure afflictions, hardships, distresses, beatings, imprisonment, sleeplessness, hunger for you. Oh, Corinthians, make room for us in your heart....

"Some among you say my letters delivered to you by Titus are weighty, but my personal appearance and the way I talk is contemptible....

"The so-called apostles compare themselves to other people instead of to God....I never took a single shekel from you, but those so-called super-apostles have come in to control you. Even Satan disguises himself as an angel of light....

"Are they boasting to you? So, then, I shall. I do it to my embarrassment, just to help wake you up....

"I have been in prison and beaten more times than I can count. Five times I have been tortured with thirty-nine lashes each by the Jews. Three times I have been beaten with rods by the pagans. Once I was stoned and left for dead. I have been shipwrecked three times, and even spent a day and night treading water in the sea....

"I have traveled much and been in danger from raging rivers and robbers. I have gone hungry and thirsty, I have been exposed to extreme cold, and I constantly have sleepless nights worrying about the church. I even have a permanent disability that I have prayed for God to remove, but he has said no because what I am and have is enough....

"Therefore, since those super-apostles among you want to boast, I will boast only in my weakness, and be content with insults, persecutions, and difficulties for the sake of Jesus Christ. When I am weak, I am strong....

"Now, for the third time, I would like to come to you, but I do not know if I can. Get along with each other. Live in peace with each other."

He is quiet a while. Titus rolls up the scroll and seals it.

"Return to them, Titus. Take them this letter, and love them for me."

"Yes, sir, I will."

"And do all you can to get rid of those fake apostles."

"I have an interrogation technique that I only use on the most hardened," Titus says. "I have seldom had to use it. Now is the time. They will destroy themselves."

The following day just before dusk, Titus slips out of Paul's hiding place and heads back south to deliver Paul's letter to the Christians in Corinth.

When his ship slides into the Isthmus to dock, Titus senses something strong. And strange. And dangerous. He turns to one of the dirty sailors on board ship.

"Sir, we are about the same size. I would like to buy your tunic and sandals."

"Are you crazy? What am I supposed to wear, bub?"

"I shall give you my toga. It is made of the finest white linen. And my blue tunic. And my sandals. All three for your tunic and sandals.

"Whew-wee," the sailor says, tugging off his fishy, salty, oily, smelly tunic. "Take it." He hobbles on one foot at a time and throws off his broken sandals.

By now, Titus has taken off all but his loincloth—something the sailor does not have on—and the trade is completed.

"Uh, how about a cap or a hood? Might you have either?"

The sailor reaches over as another crewman walks by and grabs his cap off his head. "Here, take his. He owes me a shekel for the last dice game we played."

The anchor is dropped, the sails hauled in, ropes thrown out to the dock to be wrapped around pilings.

"Oh, my leather pouch," Titus says to his sailor friend, getting the finest Egyptian linen toga this side of Athens fishy, salty, oily, and smelly. "I need to trade you my pouch for a basket large enough to carry my belongings. If you do not have a basket, I'll take a wool seed sack."

"Ha," the sailor replies. "You are one strange man. But I'll take whatever you got. Wait 'til the men see me tonight at the tavern. I'll be the envy..."

"Thank you, sir," Titus replies.

"Oh, and one more thing."

"This is getting to be fun. But I have nothing left to give you."

"I will give you enough money to buy it for me and have enough left over for yourself."

"And what might that be, stranger?"

"A mirror. Copper, brass, whatever it is made of, I don't care. At least the size of my hand, but better the size of my head."

"Now, where do you expect me to find a mirror?"

"Sir," Titus replies, "I saw a lady passenger with a mirror. I do not know where she is, but I think she was from Egypt or Libya or Nubia."

"Oh, her. Yeah, I know who you're talking about."

By the time gangplanks have been put in place, Titus has his mirror tucked in his shoddy basket and is satisfied he looks sufficiently disdainful. He looks onshore and spots them.

He disembarks, makes a point to walk past the spies at

close range, and up the hill toward Corinth. After about half a *mille*, he stops at one of the benches the Romans placed periodically along their roads, sits with his legs on the side instead of the front, pulls out his mirror, and holds it out far enough he can see behind him. The spies are still there.

Upon arriving in Corinth, Titus walks over to the South Basilica with its government headquarters attached. He walks onto the portico with its marble columns and statues of the Caesars, and into the lavish foyer. He pauses and heads for one of the doors.

"Sir, you are not allowed in here," a clerk says, hurrying to Titus and motioning for guards to come to his assistance.

The guards stand on both sides of Titus.

"Escort him out of the building. If he refuses to go, jail him," the clerk demands.

Titus holds out his soft and manicured hands. "Are these the hands of a common sailor?" I am not who I seem. I am Titus Pomponius Brennius, and I need to see Erastus quickly." Without warning, Titus calls out, "Erastus. This is Titus. I need you. Erastus!"

The big man opens the door to his *officium* and steps out into the foyer.

"Ha, ha, my friend. What have you been up to?" he says while motioning for the guards and clerks to leave Titus alone.

"Come in. Come in," he says. "I would shake your hand, but, well, you know. So, tell me what is going on. This should be interesting."

"I saw Paul," Titus says as Erastus leads him into his *officium* and directs him to a bench with no cushion on it. "He wrote a letter to the church here. I have it with me."

"Good. Good. What else?" Erastus replies, leaning on his big writing table.

"He gave me enough ammunition, I think we can dislodge the fake apostles and send them on their way."

Erastus walks around his writing desk and re-seats himself. He folds his arms.

"So, what are your plans?"

"First, there are two spies outside who have followed me all the way from the ship."

"How do you know?"

"I know. Now, I need you to arrest them for vagrancy, being that the city does not allow beggars. Then I plan to interrogate them. But let them sit in the dungeon overnight to get them good and scared."

"What do you want them to tell you?"

"Who sent them. Someone sent those fake apostles. We need to know who, so we can discredit them."

"And you think you can get that information out of them. You're surely not planning to torture them."

"I have techniques I can use. I was a good lawyer—at least sometimes. Now, send your guards out, and you will see two men wearing brown robes. It is too hot for robes, and they are probably carrying hidden daggers under those robes. So, the guards must be on the alert."

"Titus, my friend, you are the most interesting and daring man I know."

"Oh, and I need another favor. In case I did not spot all the spies, I do not want to go to Stephan's house and expose them to danger."

"So, you want to spend tonight at my villa. Of course, my friend. I was planning to invite you when you returned anyway. Someone there is anxious to see you."

"Who?"

"Your wife and son. They arrived yesterday. I'll send someone out to buy you a clean tunic and toga and some decent sandals. There are baths at the other end of the government complex."

"But I needed to send for my family when things were ready for them here. Chloe's house isn't completed yet."

"I guess she had her reasons."

30 ~ FACE-OFF

As Titus approaches Erastus' villa just south of the city, his thoughts shift back and forth between interrogating destroyers of the church and seeing his beautiful white-blond ice queen and smart little boy.

Back and forth between hatred for evil and love for good. *I've got to turn one of them off,* he tells himself as he reaches up to knock on the gate with its insignia of Legion III Gallica. *Things are so bad in Jerusalem, part of that legion has been dispatched from the greater Damascus, Syria, led by a Roman senator, down to the lesser Jerusalem led by an equestrian procurator. At least, that's what I hear.*

As he waits, his mind is jumbled again. Now, he thinks of Erastus being stationed in Jerusalem that Passover and helping to crucify his Lord. It is painful for Erastus to tell the story, but sometimes he does anyway, especially in helping people forgive themselves for sins of ignorance.

"Hello, Father."

Titus looks up and sees his son standing on the edge of the roof.

"Get away from there," he hears his beautiful wife say.

"But it is Father," Sirius says.

Still looking up, Titus sees the white-blond hair of his Fjorta, but only long enough for her to grab their son's arm and pull him away from danger.

He looks back at the gate. It is now open with Carpus, retired legionnaire gatekeeper, wearing part of his old uniform. The old man smiles. "Come in, Titus. Some people here have been watching for you."

Sirius dips his head under the elbow of the gatekeeper and lunges at his father, grabbing him around the waist. "We're here, Father. We're here."

Titus pulls Sirius' arms from around him and steps back. "You've grown."

"Of course, I have, Father. My next birthday, I will be ten."

Titus looks beyond his son and watches his ice queen glide toward him. He lets go of Sirius and embraces his Fjorta. They sway back and forth, back and forth as her tears of joy fall onto his shoulder.

"Shhh, my little ice queen. Do not weep. We are together again."

"Hey, what about me?" Sirius demands.

Titus reaches out for their son, and the three embrace as one.

"Und vhy did you not send vor us?"

"Shhh. We will talk of that later."

"Ve vill talk of it now," Fjorta says, holding the face of her husband in both hands.

"Why don't you three go into the solarium where I cannot hear what your excuse is?" the old gatekeeper, Carpus, tells Titus with a wink.

The three sit on benches facing each other in the center. Grand columns circle the garden.

"Time was getting close to send for you, my sweetheart," Titus begins.

"Get to dhe point."

"Aunt Chloe is building a new house, and we were going to send for you when it was done."

"That vas the problem she vas having when she wrote you?"

"Yes. Plus I delivered Paul's letter to the church here, he arrived a little later, and things got very complicated after that."

Titus decides to change the subject to avoid interrogations about the problems. "So, my turn. Why did you not wait for me to send for you? Oh, I am overjoyed to see you, but I wanted things to be perfect upon your arrival."

"Your vadder told us to come."

"My father? What's wrong? Did you argue?"

"No, dhe high priest of Apollo kept trying to turn dhe people of Antioch against you. He even set vire to your *palatio*. Your vadder could not prove it but knew. He said his enemies vould kidnap Sirius und me next if ve did not leave. He gave us dhe money."

"How bad was the fire?"

"It vas near dhe kitchen area vhere ve have dhe well. It did not hurt much."

Titus moves off his bench and kneels in front of Fjorta. "Oh, my love, I have missed you so."

"Erastus said ve can stay here until your aunt finishes building her house."

"You already knew about the house?" Titus asks.

"Of course!"

The following day, Titus goes with Erastus to the government buildings.

"The dungeon is down there," Erastus explains. "I have told the guards to let you use the interrogation room as long as you need."

They part, and Titus descends steps to a dungeon under one of the government buildings. When he enters the interrogation room, one of the spies.

"Well, have you had time to think?" Titus says, quick to not look surprised the man is already there.

No reply. The spy sits on a bench, his long legs out in front of him, his arms folded against his thin chest.

"What is your name?"

"Dolon," the man mumbles.

"I understand you are not from Corinth. Where are you from?"

Silence.

"Do you have family there?"

Silence.

"You know I have connections in this city. I can convince them to not only set you free but to help you go home to your family."

"You know nothing. You have no power."

"Do you see this toga? It can only be worn by Roman citizens. You know that. I have influence."

"So, what?"

"Who sent those fake apostles here?"

Dolon twists in his seat.

"Don't you want to be with your family again?"

"I have no family. You killed them all."

"Who killed them?"

"The Roman soldiers, when they invaded my country."

"Which country?"

"Well, you Romans didn't turn us into one of your conquered lands. You tried, but you didn't succeed."

"Germannica? Is that where you are from?"

Silence.

"Wouldn't you at least want to go back to your people?"

Silence.

"Okay, so I know the fake apostles sent you to spy on us. But who sent the fake apostles?"

Nothing.

"Don't you want to be with your people again?"

"They will kill me if I tell. They kill anyone who gets in their way."

"I can have you slipped out of Corinth by night and onto a ship as far as the north end of the Aegean Sea. Then on north to your people."

Dolon jumps up and backs to the wall. "No! They will kill me."

Hmmm. There's something about that part of the Aegean that frightens him.

"You can go back to your cell."

Titus indicates to the guard on duty to deliver Dolon and bring the other spy.

The door to the interrogation room opens a while later, and a large man with a broad grin on his face enters.

"Sit."

"Well, thank you, kind sir," the other spy says.

"What is your name?"

"My name, most honored one, is Bardas."

"And where are you from?"

"Cyrene, a city of many fishermen. Do you like fish?"

"Are you a fisherman, Bardas?"

"Yes. An honorable position, though not near as honorable as yours."

Titus draws closer to the big man's face.

"What did you say your occupation was?"

"A fisherman. And proud of it."

Titus notices the man's smile is too broad for the occasion, and the outer corners of his eyes are slightly down instead of raised like the corners of the mouth are. As fast as the telltale signs appear, they disappear.

"Hmmm. Uh, well, would you like to return to the waters of Cyrene teeming with happy fish?" Titus asks.

Bardas' artificial smiles re-appears, but his eyes dart to the door as though searching for an escape. "Of, course," he says. The smile is suddenly gone. He squirms in his seat.

"Who sent the fake apostles to Corinth?"

Bardas hugs himself. His chest heaves in and out in rapid pace.

"I can protect you."

"No, I cannot tell you that. Is your toga made of Egyptian cotton? They make excellent cotton in Egypt." His artificial smile is back.

"I could sneak you down to the docks tonight and have you onboard a ship sailing south by morning."

"No. It does not work like that."

Bardas looks down at the floor, still hugging himself.

"You can never escape them. They are powerful."

"Don't you want to go home?"

"Not as a traitor. Not as a dead man."

That evening when Titus and Erastus return to the villa, Sirius opens the gate for them.

"Father. You'll never guess what happened today."

Titus leans over, picks up his son, turns him upside down by both legs. "Tell me what happened today."

"Oh, Father. I can't tell you on my head," Sirius giggles.

Titus lowers his son gently to the tile, and Sirius moves into a sitting position.

Ha, ha. "Moderr wrestled with Carpus."

"I did no such dhing," Fjorta declares.

"Well, almost she did."

"Ha, ha," Erastus responds. "Carpus, did you let a woman get the best of you?"

"No, sir, Centurion Erastus. She surprised me, sir. I was pouring water into that vat over there and didn't see..."

"the snake," Sirius interrupts.

"...so I wasn't expecting the woman."

"You should be grateful I vas nearby und knew how to get rid ov monsters."

"You killed a snake?" Erastus asks.

"Ha, ha. That's my wife for you."

"Vell, if I'm going to keep dhe honor of my vadder und his brodder, dhe king of Jutland, I must protect my people."

"Carpus is not your people," Titus says, laughing and walking toward his wife.

"Well, he could have been."

"So, what will we be eating to break our fast this evening?"

"I vent into dhe city und vound Aunt Chloe's new house. She said it should be done in anodder month. I helped the men unload marble columns."

"You what? How?" Erastus asks, laughing so hard his middle is bouncing.

"I manned one of dhe ropes. I'm as strong as any man."

"Ha, ha," Erastus says, seating himself near the table of food. "I believe it."

"And I told the oxen to be still and not move the wagon," Sirius adds.

"You are such a good boy, Son. Your father is proud of you."

Titus looks over at his wife, She winks. *I will never treat him the way my father did me,* he tells himself.

The next morning, Titus announces he wants to get to know the new so-called apostles better.

"The apostles can read people. They know how to manipulate people and tell them what they want to hear. It is going to take a different approach to find out who sent them."

For the next two weeks, Titus goes into the city every day to pay a visit to the sacred *palatio* where the fake apostles live.

Each morning, Erastus wishes him success.

Titus learns the first apostle to arrive in the city is apparently the head apostle—Demas. He often has his underling apostles out, making the rounds of the membership to maintain close contact with them and to receive any donations they can be talked out of.

"So, which scripture would you like to study today?" Titus always asks. "I brought Hosea with me today. What do you think of Hosea?"

"Of course, he was a good man, but his prostitute wife was a shame."

Each day they discuss as eloquently as any philosopher at any forum of either Athens or Rome. A little at a time, Titus sneaks in his questions.

"By the way, where were you born, Demas?"

"Oh, well, I was born near Jerusalem. The village is no longer there. The Roman troops that invaded the country when they burned Sepphoris twenty years ago, burned our village. So, there is nothing to tell you about."

The following day, another book from the old scriptures.

"Amos was a shepherd just like King David," Titus says on another day. "Before you came here, which of the other apostles did you consult with?"

"None of them. We each have our own way of doing things." Titus sees Demas spotting his looks of doubt. "Well, I did talk some with James and John before I left. But that is all."

Hmmm. James was killed the year before I was baptized. So he definitely is not from around Jerusalem.

The next book for a philosophical discussion of the old scriptures is Jonah.

"He was very courageous to go to the capital city of Jerusalem's enemy to warn them to turn to the original true

God." Demus pauses. "Titus, you have become a good friend. I have grown to enjoy our daily discussions."

Titus is careful not to sound too friends and thus be as deceitful as Demas has been.

"I suppose the Jews everywhere are angry at how fast the church is growing," Titus replies. "Why do you think they are so angry?"

Titus notices Demas flinch. Both his upper and lower lips raise. His nostrils flare, he lowers his brow. But the flinch lasts only moments, and Demas is back in full control.

He steeples his fingers and leans back. "The Jews just do not understand, Titus. They just do not understand."

Another book on another day: The Psalms of David. This time they are walking around the courtyard near the bottom of the grand stairway leading to the second floor.

"He was an amazing man," Demas says. "He really knew how to control people. I admire that in a man."

Titus puts an arm on the shoulders of the fake apostle and smiles. "You and I know power, don't we? I was a toga-wearing Roman citizen, and you as, well, what did you call yourself? An apostle of the Lord Jesus Christ?"

"Yes, we do, Titus. Yes, we do. No one controls us."

Aha! That is what motivates the man, Titus thinks.

"I'll bet people are trying to control you all the time."

Demas stiffens. "Never. It is not the Lord's will that I be controlled."

"Who sent you here?" Titus asks, ambling away from Demus, and looking at the ornate floor as he asks it. He looks up, and Demus is gone.

Oops. I went to fast that time.

Two more weeks of taking his time. Today's discussion is the Jews escaping their slavery in Egypt under Moses.

"He tried on his own to lead his people out, but God wasn't ready for him to do it yet. He needed to train Moses with some life experiences," Titus says.

"True," Demas agrees. "He had to learn how to survive in the wilderness before he could lead his people to live there forty years."

"Demas," Titus says, putting his arm around the big

man's shoulder. "Do you think you were sent to lead before you were ready to do the most important work of your life?"

"What do you mean, Titus?

"My friend. The people who sent you to take over our congregation and destroy it. Come, Demas. You and I both know you are not really an apostle. Those people who sent you are using you. Once you have the congregation in Corinth destroyed, they will turn right around, accuse you to our city fathers, and have you executed for inciting unrest."

Demas takes Titus' thin arm down from his shoulder. "You knew?"

"Of course, I knew."

"Well, I cannot tell you who sent us. They will do as you say, but they will send an assassin down who will kill the other two apostles as well as me."

It has been four weeks. Titus brings the discussion around to King Solomon and his proverbs.

"He inherited his position as king from his father, King David," Titus says. "He didn't have to fight for it. It was just automatically his."

"A man ought to work for his rewards," Demus agrees.

"You know, I have grown to understand you in all our talks. I think deep inside you are an honest man, but are being manipulated by bad people who have convinced you what you are doing is right and good."

"I cannot tell you who they are, Titus."

"I think you have the potential to be a great leader. But you need to demonstrate your leadership away from those evil people who have sent you. I know good people who are leaderless. They could use you."

"Titus, I can't."

"Demas, if I tell you where this place is—it's another country—that needs your leadership and promise to pay the way for all three of you to leave here and go there, will you tell me?"

They are sitting in a small garden in one corner of Demus' courtyard. Demas hangs his head, then lifts it and looks Titus' in the eyes.

"You tell me, and I will tell you. We're friends. We trust

each other."

"Germannica," Titus says. "Caesar is unable to conquer them, but they have suffered the loss of many courageous leaders. They need someone to pull them together. I will pay your way to Germannica."

Titus looks in a small silk pouch he often carries around the waist of his tunic. He hands Demus twenty silver coins. "There is a ship leaving in the morning."

Demus smiles and takes the coins. "Thessalonica. The leaders of the Jews there sent us to destroy you from within. They're all from Thessalonica."

31 ~ CONFUSION

"Aunt Chloe, I do not know how to thank you for all you have done for us," Titus says one evening sitting on the roof of her new-built villa.

"Ah, it is so marvelous up here," she says, not replying. "We're right in the middle where the Aegean and Idumean Sea breezes waft to us from both east and west." Chloe leans back so her hair can move more freely.

"You took on a large responsibility since my father quit sending any support to me," he continues. "I do not know what has happened. I write him, but he does not write me back."

Chloe sits up and glares at her nephew. "Number one, I heard there has been a drought in western Anatolia. Income from your land cannot be that much. Number two, please be careful how you speak of my brother."

"I am sorry, Aunt Chloe. I just don't understand him. I want to."

"Titus, he was thirty-six years old when he lost his wife. By the time he was your age, he had been without her for twelve years."

"I was without my mother for just as long."

"It's different. When you marry, you become as one, just like the scriptures tell us. You do not become one with your children. They are meant to grow up and move away."

"I don't guess I'll ever understand."

"Let's hope you don't. Now relax and enjoy the evening. It is all perfect and marvelous and beautiful."

"What is?" Titus asks with his rational mind.

"The world, my dear. The world. My villa is all paid for with money the bank refunded me, my scribe school is earning more than I need, the church has settled down and is doing well, and I am blessed with you and your family every day."

"Papa."

Titus looks toward the steps and holds out his arms. "And what has my big boy been doing?"

Sirius climbs up onto his father's lap and wags his head back and forth.

"Your son has been memorizing in between turning summersaults," Fjorta says, joining them.

"And what have you been memorizing, my most favorite son?"

"I'm your only son," Sirius says, giggling. "Papa, you are so silly."

"So, stand over there and recite something for me," Titus responds, setting Sirius down and touching the tip of the boy's nose.

"The fruits of the Holy Spirit are love, joy, peace." He turns in place in a circle. "Uh, patience, then kindness and goodness." He touches his toes and swings his arms over his head. "Uh being faithful, being gentle." He puts on his biggest smile. "Annnnd controlling yourself." With that, he stomps his feet in triumph.

Titus and Cleo applaud. "Well, done!"

"Papa, what does controlling yourself mean?"

Titus lifts the boy back onto his knee. "It means, well, when you want to say or do something that would hurt someone, you don't do it."

"Hurt what?"

"Well, it could be their body or their feelings, either one."

"So, does that mean I can't tell my friend he has funny ears?"

"Sirius. You didn't say dhat, did you?" Fjorta shrieks.

Sirius giggles. "No, *moderr*, but I want to."

"So, my dear, you have been reading my copy of the letter Paul wrote to the congregations in my old province— Galatia? What else caught your attention?"

"Vhy did he talk so much about circumcision?"

"It is a sacred initiation ritual into the Jewish religion. There were Jews becoming Christians who thought we Gentiles needed to become Jews before we could be Christians."

"Dhat's silly."

"You two can sit up here and talk the rest of the night," Chloe says. "I am retiring for the night."

"Oh, I won't be here tomorrow night," Titus says, "so tell your maids not to fix me anything."

"Vhere are you going to be this time?" Fjorta asks.

"The twelve elders of our congregation want to meet with the deacons."

"I dhought dhose twelve officers vere our pastors."

"They are. Elders and pastors have the same job, so they are the same office. Anyway, they want to meet and make sure all the physical needs of the congregation are being met."

"Do you dhink you vill be an elder-pastor someday?"

"I will not qualify until Sirius becomes a Christian."

"I'm almost old enough," Sirius says, playing with a ball and listening in."

"Yes, you are almost old enough. When the time comes that you know the difference in right and wrong on your own, you will be ready."

Two days later, Titus passes Erastus on the street in front of the government buildings.

"Oh, Titus. You have got to see this. Come," the city treasurer says with a big grin on his big mouth.

Titus catches up with his friend, and they walk over to the North Market.

"What's that crowd all about?" Titus asks.

"Ha. That's what I want to show you. You will enjoy this."

They draw closer and hear a man's voice.

"Stop feeding your pleasures," they hear a man say.

They work through the crowd until they see a man

stripped of everything but a loincloth sitting on the bare cobblestone. Behind him is a lean-to with a large sheepskin stretched over it.

"Who is he?" Titus asks his friend.

"That, my boy, is Demetrius the Cynic. He has come home."

"He has moved here?"

"No, he was born and raised here. He moved to Rome and has become a close friend of Seneca, advisor to Nero. Ha. Now, let's stop talking and listen to what he has to say this time."

"Fellow Romans," Demetrius continues while seated on the ground, "what good is a fancy cushion to sit on or a marble bench if you can just as easily sit on the ground when you are tired? Does silk or marble make you less tired? And what good is clothing of linen dyed purple? Does the purple dye make you less cold? What good do rings of gold and ruby do your fingers? Do they enable you to take hold of your work better? No, no, and no. Forsake them, brothers. Forsake everything so you may live in harmony with nature."

"Does he really believe that?" Titus asks Erastus.

"Shhh, listen. It gets better."

"Oh, my fellow Romans. Listen to me. You toil all day, and for what? So you can have a roof over your heads? What is wrong with sticks or skins or the stars? You cannot truly live until you forsake everything. Only then can you spend your time absorbing the essence of the universe and determine virtue for all mankind."

"And what do we accomplish by doing all that?" someone in the crowd asks.

"Eternal life with the gods, of course. As soon as you become perfect, you may live with the gods forever, and you will even turn into one of the gods yourself. Honor yourself, my fellow Romans. Honor yourself."

Erastus and Titus wander away. "Don't be surprised if some half-naked brothers show up at worship next Solday thinking they'll be more like Jesus then, even though Jesus never did such things."

Titus shakes his head. "Demetrius actually declares

that, when we renounce all things, we will be perfect, and the gods will have no choice but to let us dwell with them?"

"And become a god yourself," Erastus declares, still grinning.

"But some people will believe him," Titus says, shaking his head.

"Doing without does not stop someone from being jealous or proud or having any other sinful attitude."

A month passes before the excitement of Demetrius the Cynic dies down, and he returns to Rome. It takes another month to convince his followers among the Christians that they cannot earn their way into heaven, and they can never become a god.

Demetrius' followers denounce him, repent, and the church is back to normal.

"Please come to my home in two days for a feast," Nikanor, the man across the street from Chloe, tells Titus one day. "Relatives from Rome have just arrived, and I want to introduce them to some of my new Christian friends. Bring your family. And aren't you friends with Stephan? Invite him for me."

Titus notices Nikanor has recovered his gates with Ebony from Ethiopia and placed copper knocking plates on each one. The day of his feast, his servants hang garlands all along his wall on the street side. In late afternoon, both of Nikanor's gates are opened wide for the guests.

"He is certainly trying to impress someone," Stephan tells Titus as they and their wives join Chloe to walk across the street.

They are led to a banquet hall on the far side of the tiled and columned courtyard. Brass lamps hang from the ceiling, already lit to keep the hall bright when night falls.

A small group of singers stands in one corner of the courtyard singing psalms of David.

Everyone is clad in their finest. The men have new togas draped over their multicolored tunics with the togas being of lighter color. The women wear their stolas of many colors. Titus and Fjorta have loaned to Stephan and Abelia attire to fit the evening.

When Nikanor determines all his guests have arrived, he stands and raises his hands heavenward. "Let us thank our Lord Jesus Christ for this abundance."

The prayer over, he introduces everyone to his relatives.

"Attention, everyone. I would like to introduce to you the Most Excellent Ovid Alexio Krios and his wife, Hesta. Ovid is Flamen of Jupiter in Rome and is a member of the College of Pontiffs. Annnd," Nikanor's smile broadens, "annnd my cousin. So, everyone welcome my illustrious relatives to our humble city of Corinth."

An applause follows.

"Uh, Most Excellent Ovid," Titus says as the first course is being served. "Has your cousin told you about Jesus the Christ, the Word of God who took flesh and dwelled among us a little while?"

"Indeed, he has, uh, I believe I have forgotten your name."

"My name is Titus Pomponius Brennius, sir."

"Yes, yes. You live across the street with your aunt. Too bad about her villa burning down."

"Your cousin and his wife came to our rescue that night and provided much comfort and solace," Titus responds.

"Back to your question, yes, Nikanor has introduced me to his new god."

"Oh, he is not a new god, sir. He created the universe."

"I do believe I have heard that philosophy. I am sure Socrates believed there was only one creator of mankind. Then he turned the details over to the lesser gods."

"There are no lesser gods according to what Jesus taught us," Titus responds. "Instead, he gives all mankind an opportunity to be an adopted son of God."

Titus feels someone's hand touch his. He turns his head.

"Ummm, go easy on them," Stephan mutters.

"This may be my only chance," Titus mutters back.

"Isn't the food delicious?" Nikanor says.

"By the way," Enyo says, turning the ruby ring around on her finger to show better, "Hesta is named after the glorious goddess, Vesta."

"Oh, I know about Vesta und dhe odher virgins," Fjorta says.

"The Vesta Virgins never marry. They dedicate themselves to praying on behalf of Rome or whatever city they live in, as you know," Enyo continues.

"Does dhat make dhem more holy—to not marry?"

"Indeed, it does," Enyo replies. "They are the holiest of all women."

"You know, Titus, I have been thinking about this," Nicanor says. "I think our congregation has been overlooking our own virgins. Perhaps we should have a special service honoring them."

Titus presses his lips together and looks down at his feet. He looks over at his wife and at Stephan and back at his host. He does not reply.

"Something else we have been thinking about," Nikanor says. "We have elders which sometimes we call pastors. Couldn't we also call them our pontiffs? My cousin here, as the prime Flamen priest of Jupiter, is a pontiff."

"After all, they are the fathers of our congregation," Enyo adds. "It really doesn't matter what we called them as long as they keep doing what they have been doing. Isn't that right, Most Excellent Ovid?"

"Well, it would be an excellent start."

"Did you know my son is going to be entering the Olympics this year?" Stephan says in a rather loud voice.

"Good for him," Titus says, his voice just as loud. "Most Excellent Ovid, have you ever thrown a discus? Stephan's son, Tycho, is excellent at it. He has his father's strength and his mother's finesse. He is sure to win the laurel wreath this year."

In the cool of the evening, Titus and Stephan leave the feast. The women have stayed behind to compliment Enyo on her decorations and ask for a recipe.

"What is wrong with Nikanor?" Titus says. "He knows better."

"Maybe he doesn't," Stephan says.

"People start changing this little thing and that little thing, then a little more, and finally we do not recognize the original.”

“Looks like we’re going to have to have a very long conversation with him.”

“Perhaps our wives should come along and help explain things to Enyo,” Titus says. “They are good people and have good hearts, but, well, the church the apostles set up for Jesus is simple. A few elders, a few deacons, sing a few psalms, read a few scriptures, pray, take the Lord’s Supper. That’s all. Simple, simple, simple.”

“Didn’t Paul warn you?”

“Yes, he did. He said it would be among the elders that things would begin to change. Well, not in Corinth,”

The wives catch up with them, and the couples go their own way.

“Aunt Chloe, you should have been there,” Titus says when he walks in and sees the woman who raised him is still sitting up.

“Oh, so they told you?”

“You knew?”

“Enyo has been referring to our elders as pontiffs for the past month. She has even said she loves her husband but, if she could go back in time, she would not marry so she could be more holy.”

Titus and Fjorta sit across from Chloe. “What are we going to do?” he asks.

“We are going to take it as it comes,” Chloe says. “Humans get used to something, then want to change it. They get used to that and want something else. It is human nature.”

“I thought there would be peace in the church,” Titus says, taking his wife’s hand and looking into her green eyes. “You give me peace, my love,” he adds.

“Peace is in dhe heart,” Fjorta says. “Dhere is never peace on dhe outside very long, my *kareste*.”

“Titus, by the way, my scribe students want to learn the Hebrew alphabet. You know Hebrew, don’t you?”

“A little. When do you need me?”

“Tomorrow, if you have some spare time.”

“I am taking Sirius to Isthmia tomorrow and show him the ships.”

"He turns back to his wife. "You know, I think he needs a pony of his own. I got a pony for my ninth birthday. I was so proud of it. My father bought it for me but said it was my mother's idea. He really loved..."

Titus' voice melts into a memory. He turns to his aunt.

"Yes, your father really loved your mother," Chloe says. "That is a precious memory you have of them. Keep treasuring that memory. Protect it and keep it always with you."

It is Solday again. Titus and Sirius walk in front, and the women walk behind them in the direction of the building that used to be the synagogue. It has been added onto because of the swelling congregation.

They walk in quiet. Meditating on what is before them. Meditating on the blood, the body. On the love of the Creator who would deign to walk the earth to conquer Satan and Death as it exists in this material world.

"Papa," Sirius says, holding his father's hand, "when I grow up, I am going to be just like you."

"And what is just like me?" Titus replies, his heart swelling.

"I am going to be as tall as you. I am going to sit around reading all the time. I am going to learn umpteen languages so I can travel anywhere in the world."

"Wait a minute, Son. I don't know umpteen languages."

Sirius grins and forms a half growl and half snicker in his throat. He looks up at his father with the green eyes he had inherited from his mother. "To me you do, Papa."

They enter the building and spend the next two hours worshipping. As always, they take a break for everyone to eat before they resume worship late the afternoon of the Lord's Day.

"Attention, everyone. Attention!"

It is nearly time to begin the late worship. Titus strains to see who is upfront speaking.

"Is he new? I don't remember him," he says to Fjorta.

"He is new. He is a former priest of Poseidon."

"How do you know?"

"Because, dear one, I used to go over to dheir liddle temple—well, it's a lot liddler dhan Corinth's Apollo temple."

"What did you do over there?" Titus replies.

"I vould vait vor him to come out to dhe altar and tell him about Jesus, the great sacrifice."

"Did I know you did that?"

"Yes, you knew. But you vould alvays be reading somedhing, und I don't dhink you heard me very often."

"So, you taught him, and he has decided to leave those old beliefs and be just a Christian. I am so proud of you, my love."

"Attention, everyone."

The congregation settles down and becomes quiet.

"My name is Abaddon. As you know, I used to be a priest of Poseidon. I am ashamed of that and am now a Christian. The sad thing is that I left behind fellow priests, not only of Poseidon but the other so-called gods that we know are not real."

Titus smiles. He looks over at Stephan and winks. He motions to Fjorta, and Stephan smiles again in acknowledgment.

"I am saddened that we have been unable to convert the others and shut down their temples to turn them into widow homes, orphan homes, handicapped homes, homes with food to give away, and so on."

"This man is really going to be an excellent addition to our congregation, Fjorta," Titus whispers.

"Now, having been there myself, I have an idea that might help win them over and save their souls."

"Uh, oh," Chloe says, sitting on the other side of Titus.

"We have seven temples to seven gods here in Corinth: Apollo, our patron god, of course; then Hera, Hercules, Poseidon, Venus, Hermes, and, of course, Augustus Caesar."

"I'm not going to like this," Titus whispers.

"Now, every week, we invite one of the high priests to come take part in our weekly remembrance of Jesus' sacrifice for us. Then, when they make their next sacrifice, we agree to send representatives to attend theirs. That way, they get exposed to Jesus, and we save their souls."

Before Titus can stand, Gaius has appeared in the front. "We welcome you, our new brother, to the church that Jesus bought with his blood. But we honor only Jesus' sacrifice."

"Now wait a minute," someone in the congregation says, standing. "I think he has a valid point. We cannot expect people to participate in our holy ceremonies if we are not willing to participate in theirs."

Someone else stands. "Perhaps we should just have one ceremony a year instead of one a week."

A hand goes up. "Or one a month."

Sosthenes stands. "As one of the elders, I say no, this is not the way. Jesus, our Lord, never went into the temples of false gods to teach, even though he traveled to Lebanon and Syria. This cannot happen."

"But we're just trying to save their souls," the former priest to Poseidon calls out. "We've got to save their souls. Please, my brothers. A little compromise is sometimes necessary."

Gaius stands. "We will convert them with kindness and knowledge of the truth, not compromise. God did not give us the choice of changing anything. He is not the God of confusion."

Titus stands. "Stay the course, brothers, and sisters. Stay the course."

"You will live to regret this," a strange voice behind Titus' family says.

32 ~ THE IMPOSSIBLE

*T*hree months have passed since the last near-disaster within the congregation in Corinth. Once again, things have settled back <u>down,</u> and the <u>congregation</u> has continued to grow.

"Your God is good and kind," people say. "Not like Poseidon and the others who throw lightning bolts down on us when we make a mistake."

"Your God even wants us to be his children."

"And he doesn't demand all those sacrifices. He made the last sacrifice himself. I want to make your God my God."

Priests in the Roman temples are angry. Some think they are even <u>angrier</u> than the Jewish priests were years earlier when Paul first came and introduced Jesus to them.

"The Olympic Games begin in two weeks," Stephan says. "I have bought a tent large enough for both our families."

Titus, <u>Fjorta,</u> and Sirius are visiting with the <u>potter.</u>

"I have been baking bread and making cheese ahead of time so they will have plenty to eat, and hopefully not run out before the week is over," Arelia says.

"Could we, Papa?" Sirius pleads. "You said I am almost big enough and strong enough to enter the games myself in a few years. I've never seen the games before. Can we, Papa? Can we?"

"It would take us several days to get there," Titus

replies.

"You and I could do some things together while the men are gone," Arelia tells Fjorta.

"Vhy can't ve go?" Fjorta asks. "Oh, yes. All dhe men are naked. Vell, I am not interested in seeing a lot of naked men. So, if our men go, you und I vill make our own entertainment."

"So, is it settled?" Stephan asks his boyhood friend.

Titus shrugs. His one dimple shows. "I guess it is."

As they walk home, Sirius takes his father's hand in both of his and walks sideways.

"I'm go-inggg to the Olym-pics," he chants.

"Tonight," Titus says when the family is nearly ready for bed, "I would like our Sirius to read the scripture for us. I have chosen a special one. It is nearly everyone's favorite."

He hands the scroll to his son. Sirius stands and faces his parents and Great Aunt Chloe.

The Lord God is my shepherd.
So, I'll never need anything.
He takes me where there is food.
He guides me to where there is water.
He makes my soul feel wonderful.
He teaches me to walk the path of right
So, he will be honored.

I have no fears of anyone who is bad.
He always protects me.
He is stronger than all my enemies.
He even feasts with me while they watch.
He will be good and merciful to me all the days of my life.
Then, I will live with my Lord God in heaven forever.

Silence.

"Why are you crying, Papa?"

Titus reaches for his son and embraces him. "I am weeping for your grandmother."

"My grandmother who died when you were just a little older than me?"

"Yes. I was eleven. Not a day goes by that I do not long

for her gentle ways and for her to kiss me good night like your *moderr* does for you."

"Wasn't her name Kharis or something like that, Papa?"

"Yes. And you had a sister by that name."

"But she died too, didn't she, Papa?"

"Yes, she died too."

"It is time vor you to go to bed," Fjorta, says standing and offering Sirius her hand.

Titus jumps up. "We will both take you to bed," he says,having recovered and taking Sirius' other hand.

As they walk up the wide steps, Titus looks over the head of his son and mimes his favorite words to his beautiful ice queen. "I love you."

Morning arrives.

Fjorta is up already? Must be baking for our trip to the Olympics.

He peeks into the kitchen area of the courtyard under the linen canopy. "Aunt Chloe. Have you seen Fjorta?"

"Yes, she and Sirius went to the market."

"Well, when she gets back, would you tell her I am going over to see Gaius a while?"

Gaius' villa not being far from Chloe's, Titus is soon knocking on the older man's copper gate. A gatekeeper opens it.

"Ah, Titus," Gaius says, walking out to the courtyard. "What is on your mind this fine morning?"

"Nothing urgent."

"Come sit in the solarium."

"Our congregation needs more copies of the prophecies about Jesus," Titus says, following his host. "This is what we use to prove Jesus was the promised Messiah."

"It would be a fine thing to provide copies to every family, wouldn't it?"

"Well, my Aunt Chloe—as you know—teaches scribing. I wonder if we could hire her present students and former students...What was that?"

The gatekeeper calls from the courtyard. "Come quickly, Titus!"

Titus runs to the courtyard and sees Nikanor, his

neighbor, standing at the gate.

"Hurry, Titus! Your wife and child have been kidnapped!"

Titus, with his long legs, outruns his neighbor and arrives home first. He pounds on his gate.

Chloe opens it, tears flowing down her cheeks, her eyes red and already swelling. She hands Titus a small scroll.

He fumbles with it, drops it, leans over to retrieve it, and sinks to his knees.

To Titus Pompous Barbarionus. You and your wife have blasphemed the great and glorious Poseidon, God of the Seas. You are pompous and a barbarian. You will now pay.

Titus pauses briefly and remembers the strange voice behind him that Sunday. The Sunday when the elders refused to honor sacrifices to the gods as an expression of friendship.

We have your wife and son at the great and grand temple of Poseidon at Isthmia by the sea. You will come here by tomorrow night and sacrifice an ox to Poseidon, begging his forgiveness. If you do not, tomorrow night, your wife and son will be offered as the sacrifice instead.

Titus drops the scroll, stands, and raises his arms above his head. "Noooo!"

His voice echoes around the finely-tiled walls of his aunt's villa, rises to the clouds above, and swirls among the stars.

"Noooo!"

He pulls at his hair, he turns in place, he rushes out his gate and across a field.

"Noooo!"

"He runs. He falls. On his knees. Now up again. Now prostrate in the dirt."

"Noooo!"

"Come, Titus. Come."

Titus thinks he hears the voice of Stephan. The voice is in a fog far away in a darkness he does not fathom.

Stephan kneels next to him. "Come. We will figure something out. We will free them. Just like you freed me when we were kids. You and I are smart. We will figure something out."

"And God?"

"And God mostly."

The word spreads around the city. Erastus, Gaius, and Sosthenes come. Phylidda, the blind former border of Chloe comes, along with Cyneas, caretaker of the church's building, and Carpus, Erastus' gatekeeper. And, of course, Nikanor and Enyo from across the street.

They take turns praying for Titus' family and discussing ways to free them.

"No, I do not think you should come in," Chloe says.

Stephan looks up to see who is at the gate.

"Who is it?" Titus asks, though his own voice seems far away in another state of being.

"It is Abaddon, the former priest of Poseidon here in Corinth."

"You had better leave," they hear Chloe say again.

"Titus," Abaddon calls in. "I'm am sorry. I tried to stop them. They are jealous and angry. The church is taking away all their worshippers and, therefore, all their sacrificial money and goods. They want revenge."

"Go away," Chloe repeats. "Titus, I made the mistake of telling them who converted me to Jesus the Christ. I am so sorry, Titus."

Chloe gradually pushes the gate closed, Abaddon still in the street.

"I am going to join the rest of the congregation now," he calls over the wall. "I am going to pray for them. God will figure out a way to free them."

"First thing we must do is figure out our strategy," retired Centurion Erastus says. "First, we need to send spies to find out where in the temple they have your wife and son."

"It will have to be someone who has not lived here long and who the priests over there do not know," Gaius says.

"Then, we either openly attack, or we slip in during the night."

"I have a new servant just arrived from Spain," Gaius says. "And I have a fast horse. I will send my servant."

Titus looks up at his friends gathered around him. "But, what if, what if you can't get them out? What if I have to choose between my God and the two people I love more than anything..."

His lips quiver, he stands, and paces. Sosthenes rises to go to him, but Stephan indicates for everyone to let him be.

There is another knock at the gate. "I will answer it," Nikanor says.

"Titus," they hear from the half-opened gate. "It is Praetor Basileus. I have come to offer my services."

Nikanor lets him in, and he walks over to where Gaius has offered him a bench.

"I cannot stay, Titus," he says, watching the bereaved man struggle for his sanity and his faith in the middle of Chloe's courtyard.

"But, when they catch the perpetrator of the kidnapping, I do not care how far up in the priesthood he is, he will die." With that, the praetor leaves.

Two hours later, Gaius' servant returns from spying out the Temple of Poseidon in Isthmia.

"It's a giant of a temple," he says to people who already know it. "The throne Poseidon sits on is larger than a palace."

"Emedio," Gaius warns.

"Yes, sir. They were tied to Poseidon's foot."

"Chains? Ropes? Straps? What?" Erastus prods.

"Straps, I think. I'm not sure. Maybe chains."

"How many guards were around them?"

"Two. But I saw four more outside."

"Okay, who are we going to get to attack and rescue them?" Erastus asks, looking from man to man and over to Chloe.

"What about sailors? Someone asks. "They are always trained in case their ship is attacked by pirates."

"They would know sailors we got from the Aegean side," someone else suggests. "What about the port on the Ionian side?"

"Titus, what do you think?" Stephan asks. "Come on,

Titus, We need you to tell us what to do."

Titus takes a deep breath. He strains the muscles in his face to control them. "That would be fine," he mutters.

"I can go there. I can recruit sailors," Emedio says. "How much will you pay them?"

Sosthenes takes a pouch of coins from his waist. Gaius does the same. Erastus makes a donation.

"This should be enough," Sosthenes says.

"If he goes now, he should be able shortly after it gets dark. Then I will lead the attack," Erastus says, now pacing as though back preparing for a battle with the Germanicans. "We should have Fjorta and Sirius free by dawn."

Chloe lets the servant out. Her stableman has a fresh horse for him.

Erastus stops pacing next to Titus. The big man kneels. Gaius, Sosthenes, and Stephan kneel. Everyone kneels.

"Oh, Lord God of heaven and earth," Erastus' deep voice growls. "We are but men. Give us the knowledge we need and the wisdom to use that knowledge well. And, be with this man's wife and son. No family in all of Corinth is as upright and just as his."

They rise and sit near Titus. Sometimes Stephan brings up something funny that Fjorta or Sirius did back in Antioch. Sometimes one of the others brings up something wonderful Fjorta had done for their family. Or something Sirius had recited to them once.

"What if we cannot get them out?" Titus allows himself to say out loud. "What if I have to choose between God and my wife and son? I cannot do it."

Then prayer again. Then low talking and silence and starting all over again.

Sometimes there is a knock at the gate. Can the sailors have arrived already? It is always someone from the church. "Have you heard anything? We're still praying for them."

Overhead, the moon makes its nightly journey across the sky. Halfway to their morning destination, the assembly of friends hear hoofbeats.

"They're here," Erastus says, standing, his head high, his muscles flexed, his hands drawn into fists.

"Titus," he says. "You will lead the charge with me. Come."

"Yes, Titus. You must be strong for your family. Your wife and son need you right now," Stephan adds.

Titus stands. His face shows no emotion other than the swelling of his eyes and the pressing of his lips together to maintain his control.

"I will ride the steed," Erastus explains. "You will drive the chariot so your family will have a way of escape with you. Here is a spear. Are you ready?"

The gate of Chloe's villa is opened, and the two men join the armed and mounted sailors in the street. Being the middle of the night, they gallop through the empty streets to the East Gate. Erastus calls up to the guards, they open the gates of Corinth, and the rescuers sprint forward.

Hoofbeats pound at the ground, thundering, storming, charging. Rushing to the temple of the god that hates a white-blond haired woman and her green-eyed son named after her father.

The horses stretch their necks and legs. Their muscles flex and strain. Galloping to the enemy city. To the enemy god and its priests. To a woman and son taken for revenge.

As the sun turns the sky gray, they arrive at Isthmia. The gates are being opened by the night guards. Erastus and Titus do not pause. They charge through the gates and toward the temple to the non-god.

Just as they arrive, they hear shouting inside the temple. Titus and Erastus charge in, the sailors behind them.

"Run, Sirius, run!" It is a woman's voice.

Her white-blond hair flies as she swings a chain. Over and over she thrashes and whips and strikes at the statue of the god of thunderbolts and storms and drownings and death. A chip of marble flies loose, then another, and another.

Erastus dashes toward them, sword in hand. Titus is beside him with the spear, ready to defend his family.

The temple. So large. Get to the other end. Get to where the god sits. Get to the woman and child. Run. Hurry. Get to them before the enemy does.

Sirius, confused, stands watching his mother. Two

temple guards rush at her son. Fjorta sees just in time and dashes over to Sirius.

A spear is thrown.

The guard's spear.

It hits its mark.

Through her body and into the boy's.

"Nooo!"

Erastus bellows at the sailors behind them. "Take captives," he orders. "Take captives."

The world for Titus moves now in slow motion.

Ears hearing what they do not want to hear.

Eyes seeing what they do not want to see.

Breathing hard. Gulping in air that is hot and hazy and unreal.

Legs straining, stretching, aching. In a realm of time that creeps in and out of reality. He reaches his son and wife, but too late. He drops to the green marble floor and envelops in his arms. Too late.

The sun touches the horizon, temple guards and priests are bound hand and foot and lined up outside the cursed edifice.

Titus carries his ice queen with the white-blond hair falling down away from her delicate face. The queen of his heart, his soul, his spirit. The queen that had brought him back to life. Now the queen that is no more.

One step at a time, he carries his beloved. Gone too soon. This cannot be. A dream. A vision. A forbidden thought.

Come back.

Another step.

Come back to me, my love.

Step into a dream.

Come back. I need you.

Step into a mist.

I want to love you and adore you and shield you.

Into a haze.

Do not leave me.

Into a fog.

Oh, my ice queen.

An abyss.

Come back to me, my darling.

Erastus rushes to the boy and lifts him with his strong arms. The boy never given a chance to grow up. The boy never given a chance to run in the Olympics or recite Jesus' Sermon on the Mount, or give great orations. Always a boy. Forever a boy. Never a man.

Slow, agonizing giant steps. Two men striding to the chariot waiting outside the hated temple of death.

In a mist somewhere, mother and son are laid side by side.

Titus touches the cheeks of his wife and son, and looks over at Erastus.

"She knew," he groans.

"Yes," Erastus growls, "that they would force you to make a choice."

"She made the choice for me."

Titus tries not to breathe.

"She knew."

33 ~ GROPING

*I*t has been two weeks. Titus continues to sit in Chloe's fine courtyard with the portrait of her lovingly set into the floor by her Fulvio—Fulvio, who is forever gone too.

Chloe has canceled scribe classes temporarily. She kneels in front of her nephew.

"I know you do not want to decide, but eventually, you must. What do you want to do? Do you want to stay here living with me and be able to see Stephan whenever you want? Do you want to go to your mother's homeland of Dalmatia or your father's homeland of Gaul? Down to Jerusalem where the apostles are? Back to Antioch where you father is? What do you want to do?"

"I thought I understood," Titus moans. "All those years, I thought I understood my father's grief. I had no idea."

"And now you are becoming your father if you don't quit hiding and do something with the rest of your life."

"He still had his job as supreme judge of Antioch. But that's all he did. Maybe out of obligation. But the rest of the time, well, I guess he was hiding from his...his pain."

Titus' lips tremble. He fights to maintain control. He hardens his face and stares at the floor, daring it to rise up a strike him dead too.

"Are you saying you want to go see your father?" Chloe asks, still kneeling.

"Yes, I guess that's what I am saying," Titus whispers.

"Then, I will contact Stephan. He will want to help you make arrangements. He will miss you."

"Yes. I will miss him too." Titus' lips form a faint smile. "We were crazy kids together." He sighs. "That was so long ago."

The day arrives for Titus to board the ship bound for Ephesus.

"How long has it been since I was home, Stephan?" Titus asks, fighting on the inside to control battered emotions.

"Three years, I think. You didn't expect to be here that long, did you?"

Titus forces a smile. "That was Paul's doing." He pauses. "You know, I think I'd like to see him again."

"What about your father?" Stephan asks.

"Yes. Him too. I need to go see my father. We have never been close since I was, well I'm nearly forty-nine now, so we haven't been close for thirty-eight years. That's too long. Maybe now... Maybe now that we both have..."

"Yes, maybe now you can understand each other and be close again. You need to do this. Well, do you have everything?"

"Yes, I think so." Titus turns toward the ship, then looks back at his friend. "We won't lose touch this time, will we?"

"No, we will never lose touch again. Well, go on before the ship leaves without you."

Titus turns toward the ship once more, then turns back and walks to Stephan. They stare. Titus reaches out and embraces the dearest friend he has in the world. They pound each other on the back.

Titus pulls away and looks no more at Stephan.

The winds are favorable, and the ship arrives in Ephesus three days later. Now, on his own, Titus forces himself to make decisions—whether to rent a horse or walk to Antioch, whether to buy food for the trip or rely on inns along the highway. Small decisions like small steps back to reality.

He decides to rent a horse, buy a small leather tent, and purchase bread, cheese, and a skin of water.

I need to go home. Really and truly home.

He spends the first night in the area of Meander by the winding river after which the city was named.

Did my grandfather really serve in the legions here when the city was a fort? I wonder what my grandfather was like. I'll have to ask my father when I get home.

His night is fitful. Morning finally comes.

Another day of riding along the broad Roman highway, trees on each side sometimes, just rocks sometimes, though he does not notice. He sees a sign that Tralles is just ahead. He decides to spend the night there.

He sits outside his tent and eats a little only because he had promised his Aunt Chloe he would not neglect food. Most he puts back in his pouch. Sometimes he looks up at the stars. The moon is extra large.

My father is strong. He will show me how to…how to do this. Be alone again.

Morning again. Such a busy highway along the Silk Road. People coming and going, seeing and doing. Everyone with a purpose.

I wonder what their purpose is. Do I have a purpose? What is it? My father will help me out of this fog.

He arrives near Nyssa, where he decides to spend his last night. As he sets up his tent, he fights back tears.

Oh, no. I've been in control the whole way. This cannot be happening now. I cannot lose control this close to home. I have to be strong. I have to be a man. I have to make my father proud of how well I am handling it.

He looks up at the stars. *Let me see, now. That brightest star over there—well, the planet Venus—that is my ice queen. And that star nearby, that's Sirius. I know, Jesus, they are actually in heaven with you. But sometimes I need something to cling to. Is it okay, Jesus?*

Titus wakens and sees that the sky is pre-dawn gray. He has slept better than he has the last few nights. *Maybe it's because I'm closer to home now. My father will know what to say to help me. He is so strong. How has he done it all these years? He is so strong. He will know.*

The West Gate of Antioch is before him. He decides to make a brief side trip. He guides his horse down a path to the cemetery. He climbs off and leads it the rest of the way to his mother's grave. He kneels and fights tears. "Oh, Mama. I miss you," he groans.

Titus looks around and sees some wild violets. In a few moments, they are adorning Kharis' grave. There are three of them. *I wish I could do more for you. And Father, he has never stopped loving you. When you died, you took the light that was in him away. Keep his light safe with you, my dear mother.*

He takes a deep breath. "I'll be back. I won't neglect you anymore," he whispers. "I promise."

He remounts his horse and puts it into a trot toward the West Gate. He slows it briefly, just long enough to wave at one of the guards he recognizes.

"Hey, Titus. Is that you?"

"Yes, it's me," he calls out with a grin, "and I'm glad to be home."

"Where are..."

Titus kicks the sides of his horse and urges it into a lope.

Closer to home.

Closer to good memories when everything was just right.

Closer to the man he longs to please more than any man on earth.

Closer to comfort and being shown how to stand up and be a man.

Closer to his father and putting things back the way they belong.

He guides his horse past the theater along the columned Decumanus Maximus. He turns right at the familiar waterfall and hurries past the Temple of Apollo.

Faster. In a gallop now. Home. This is home.

At the Vici Aegeus, Titus turns his horse to the left. He is on the street where he grew up. He sees the other houses the way they had always been. Everything the same. Everything to welcome him home.

Now at his gate. The gate that had always been open to him and always will be.

"Brutus," Titus shouts. "Come get my horse. She needs

some food and rest. Brutus?"

Titus ties his horse up to a ring in the outside wall put there for guests. He steps over to his gate and shouts. "Cornelius, I'm home. Open up, Cornelius. I'm home."

He hears shuffling inside and smiles. *Good old Cornelius.* The handle on the inside rattles, the hinges scrape, and the gate opens a little at a time.

"Yes?" he hears a small voice say. It is not the voice of Cornelius. Standing there is Lydia. Her eyes seem smaller than they used to be. Her voice too. All of Lydia seems smaller.

Titus forces a smile. "Lydia. Don't you recognize me? It's Titus. I'm home."

Lydia smiles and steps back for Titus to push the gate open the rest of the way. They walk through the guest courtyard where his mother's Muse statues used to be. He beats Lydia to the next gate, swings it open and steps into his old, familiar courtyard.

He stands. He stares. His brow creases. He tips his head to one side. He squints. He looks over at Lydia.

"What happened? And where is everyone?"

The water in the proud reflecting pool is down halfway and teeming with green fungi. Some of the floor tiles have been kicked up and are lost. The gilded chairs are still in place, but the cushions are either gone or shrunken and faded from rain and sun. The marble benches are still scattered around but have dirt and cobwebs under them.

Titus turns to Lydia and repeats his question.

"Didn't you notice the crops as you rode in?" Lydia asks. "We have had a terrible drought. It started right after you left. Everyone is gone now but me. I do what I can."

Titus stares at the old maid who had served his family since his earliest childhood. He looks around the once beautiful courtyard where his family had lived its days, and where the church had assembled.

"And my father? Is he..."

"Yes, he is still here. He does not come out as much. The whole city has slowed down, and there aren't even as many trials. He just goes into his *officium* and reads and broods."

"Then he's alive. Then my father is still here. That's all I need."

Titus looks toward the steps and takes two at a time to the second floor. His father's door is closed. He opens it and rushes in. His father looks up and drops the scroll he had been reading.

Father and son stare at each other. The moment lingers in that mist, that dream-like state that both know so well.

The tears return, Titus steps around his father's writing desk and kneels. "Oh, Father, I never knew. I didn't understand. Please, Father. Forgive me. I did not know."

Justus Brennius Antiochus groans.

Titus lays his head on his father's lap.

His father places his old hand with twisted fingers on the head of his son and groans again.

They do not know how long they remain so.

Titus raises his head and looks up into the weeping eyes of his father.

"Father, my Fjorta is gone. And my son. They are both gone. Oh, Father, I don't know what to do. My whole world has been taken from me. I am so lost. Help me, Father. Help me."

Their broken spirits mingle with their mutual tears.

"Oh, my son," Justus finally says. "I cannot help you."

"Yes, you can," Titus objects, surprised at his own outburst. "I never understood. All those years without Mother, without your wife. I never understood. Help me, Father. Help me live again."

Lydia stands at the door that had not been closed. "Sirs, I have a few apricots I got from a merchant in the market who just came up from the coast. And some bread. I made some bread. And a little goat milk. Would you like to come down to eat them?"

The men do not reply.

"I think it would be best. For you both, it would be best."

Titus wipes his eyes and smiles up at his father. "She has spoken."

"That she has," Justus replies.

Titus stands and holds out a hand to his father.

"How old are you now, Father?"

"Seventy-nine and my knees hurt all the time."

"Lydia," Titus says, turning to the family maid, "would you mind bringing our food up here? My father and I have some catching up to do."

The two men walk out to a balcony overlooking the South Gate. They sit but do not speak.

Lydia brings their food to them and sets the trays on the ledge of the balcony.

The men take the food and set it on their laps. Neither eats.

Silence again.

"I had no idea, Father. I didn't understand. Losing a mother is different than losing a wife. I just did not understand."

Justus groans.

Silence.

The sun works its way across the sky.

Silence.

"Father, I don't know what to do. I can't go on living like this. My wife and son were my whole world. And you too, Father. You too. I don't know how to deal with it. I don't know how to fix it. I am lost, Father."

Justus looks over at his son. Their eyes lock. The old man's eyes mist. He presses his lips hard together and looks out toward the now-fading day.

There is still a sliver of sun left when Titus stands with his back to it.

"Father! Why are you doing this? I have spent most of my life trying to make you proud, and that failed. Now I come asking for your advice, but all you do is sit there and groan. Father! I need you. I came a long way. Help me."

Justus looks up at his tall son, who looks so much like Kharis. His eyes mist. "I cannot," he whispers, then drops his eyes to stare at his gnarling hands.

"Quit blaming me for killing my mother. I didn't mean to. It's been bad enough, but do you have to keep blaming me too?"

Justus does not reply.

It is morning. Titus is back on the highway, this time heading south. He works his way through the tight mountain passes at the far western end of the Taurus Mountains.

Seleucia, Sagalassus, Cremna, Perga. At last, he arrives at the seaport city of Attalia.

I've got to get to Paul. Paul will help me.

He turns in his rented horse, finds a ship headed east and south, and purchases his fare to the other Antioch, Paul's Antioch in Syria.

It has now been two weeks since leaving the Antioch of his childhood and youth. The ship that has stopped at every port along the way, docks at last at the seaport serving Syrian Antioch. Titus rents a horse and rides the twelve *milles* to the city proper. He crosses the Orontes River, enters through the West Gates, continues east toward Mount Silpius on the opposite border of the city, and arrives at the synagogue now turned meeting house for the Christians.

He knocks on the double front door, but no one answers. He walks next door.

"Yes?" the big man says.

"I don't know if you remember me," Titus begins, "but I was with Paul when he went to Jerusalem a few days ago and returned with a letter from one of the apostles about circumcision."

"Of course. Of course," the man replies. "Come in. I am Barnabas. I remember you. Come in."

Titus steps inside and is shown a seat in the courtyard.

"I do not want to bother you for long, but I am looking for Paul. His home congregation is here, isn't it?"

"Yes, it is. But he is not here. Actually, he was arrested."

"What?" Titus says, standing. This cannot be. Not Paul." He looks up in the sky overhead. "When?"

"A couple years ago. We do not know where he is now. He may still be in Caesarea. Or they may have put him in a dungeon somewhere else."

Titus sits back down and puts his head in his hands.

"What's wrong, my friend? Is there something I can do to help you?"

"No." Titus' voice is muffled by his hands. "No. I just

need to talk to him."

"It must be very important to come all this way from Corinth."

"Actually, I have been elsewhere, but, yes. There is something I cannot handle. I need his advice."

"Are you sure I cannot help you?"

Titus stands and sighs. "I am sure."

He walks toward the outer gate. "I guess I have no choice but to return to Corinth."

Titus leaves, realizes he still has daylight left, and takes his rented horse back down to the seaport. The same ship he had come in on is still there.

"We unloaded everything and have loaded some things needed back up north, so are headed that way again," the first mate tells Titus. "Is your business taken care of so fast?"

"I guess it is," Titus says.

"We'll be heading back to Ephesus in the morning, then over to Corinth," he explains.

Titus pulls out the money from his pouch and hands it to the mate without saying more.

The winds do not cooperate. It takes five days to cover what should have taken three days. They dock at Myra.

"What's happening?" Titus asks the first mate.

"The winds are too bad. It is too late in the season. The captain has decided to winter here rather than risk the ship. Here is part of your money back. You may want to spend the winter here yourself."

Titus leaves the ship. Unexpected tears return. *Everything is going wrong. Everything I try to do turns out wrong.* He sits on a bench on the docks and watches busy sailors bring down sails and tie them securely for the winter. He watches as ropes are secured around hulls and equipment put in barrels to be taken below for the winter.

Bells. He hears bells. *Can it be all the ships are not going to winter here?* Daring not to hope too much, Titus turns and ambles up the dock toward the sound of the bells. The sails are up. He goes on the gangplank and speaks to the crewman on guard there.

"Are you going to Corinth or Athens?" Titus asks.

"Yes, by way of Crete, then over to Athens and Corinth. If the weather holds up, we'll winter in Rome."

"Oh, thank God," Titus replies. "Here's your money. Will that be enough?"

The fare is agreed upon, and Titus boards the ship. He sets his traveling pouches at his feet and stands by the rail awhile, holding his head in his hands. Tears return. *Always so close to the surface. Why can't I control them?*

He walks around the deck, finds a place to sit, watches the crew at their work, and grows restless again. He stands and walks around the deck once more.

"Titus, is that you?"

Titus turns at the sounds of the familiar voice.

"Paul?"

34 ~ NEEDED

What are you doing here?" Titus asks, staring at his mentor as though in another black dream. "And what are those chains? And these guards?"

"I am determined to go to Rome, no matter what it takes. I will appear before Nero Caesar within the month. Jesus has promised me that," Paul says. "But what are you doing here?"

"I have been to your Antioch. I saw Barnabas there. He asked about you."

"Okay, keep going," the centurion tells Paul.

"Dear, dear Barnabas. The best friend I ever had," Paul replies. "But what are you doing on this ship bound for Italy?"

One of the Roman guards prods Paul to keep moving.

"I am on my way to Corinth," Titus says, raising his voice as Paul is led farther away. "This was the only ship I could find this time of year even going in my direction. I will change to another ship in Crete."

"Get going, Paul," the guard says again, shoving at his prisoner.

His ankles in chains, Paul scoots over to the hatch going below and calls back to Titus. "You are needed in Crete. When the ship stops there, go ashore and help the church in Crete. Elders, deacons, get them organized. Promise me!"

By the time Paul has said his last two words, his voice

is muffled, and the apostle is out of sight.

Titus stares at the hatch. He stares at the remaining guards following his friend and other prisoners down to what he assumes will be the bilge of the ship.

He prays that Paul will be allowed to return above board. It does not happen. Titus walks around among the crewmen.

"I need to talk to your captain. There is someone I need to see."

"We're about to cast off," the sailor says. "You'll have to talk to the captain when we're out to sea."

"Excuse me, I need to talk to your captain."

"He's busy. Get out of our way."

"Excuse me, sir."

"Go below and stay there."

Titus takes the ladder down to the berth deck. He lets his eyes get used to the darkness, then peers among the shadows, hoping to see the prisoners. Only paying passengers are there. He hears bells and knows the ship has broken loose from its moorings and is headed out to sea.

He finds a place to sit and hangs on to the post nearest him as the ship begins the expected rocking in the late autumn winds.

After a while, the pounding of running feet overhead eases. Titus knows they are in open seas.

He climbs back above board. In the wind, he lunges toward the rail and works his way around to the bridge. He calls up to the captain.

"What?" Captain Milon replies.

"I need to see someone."

"The deck is full of people. Pick one of them to see."

"Sir, I need to see one of your prisoners. His name is Paul of Tarsus, and he is very educated and respected and..."

"Go away, I'm busy."

"But, sir..."

"Paying passengers do not have access to the prisoners. Those are my orders, and that's final. So, go away."

"No, this is all wrong," Titus mutters as he works his way from the bridge over to the railing where he has something to hang on to in the wind.

He finds a place with a fist-sized iron ring coming out from it, sits, and hangs on to the ring.

Paul, I needed you. Why this? Oh, God, why is everything going so wrong?

"Don't let the wind get the best of you," he hears an old sailor tell a younger one. "Make it work for you, not against you."

Titus stares at the scruffy leather-skinned man as he goes about his work, bracing himself and otherwise not paying any attention to the wind.

"No, God. Surely that is not your answer," he mutters to himself, raising his knees up and closing his eyes.

Crete? I hate Crete. Well, I've never been to Crete. But everything I hear about it—mostly all those pirates and slave traders. No. I will not go to Crete, Paul.

Titus leans his head back and tries to remember all the terrible things Plato had said about the island. *They seldom if ever read the writings of anyone except their own people. The only kind of dances they have are imitations of warriors. And their men play the part of women with each other.*

Though the wind is close to gale force, Titus manages to stand by hanging on.

How could the church possibly exist in a hellish place like Crete? Livy distrusted Cretans too.

The wind pounds the ship relentlessly. Sometime later—he cannot tell—Titus goes below, finds a pole to tie himself to, closes his eyes, falls asleep, and dreams he has a family again, and they are going for a picnic at Olympia.

He cannot quite tell how many days they are at sea. All he knows is that the winds have died down a great deal.

"Glad the storm has passed," he hears a sailor say.

He goes back on deck and sees what at first seems to be an island, but is a cape jutting out from a larger land. He asks a sailor and is told they have arrived at the Island of Crete.

Well, I won't be staying here long. I need to go see Stephan.

He watches as they slip south and west past a great palace which he learns later is at Zakros. With the new calm winds, they continue west under the shelter of the great island.

Titus sees snow-capped mountains to the north. Even near shore, the mountains are high and steep, leaving few places for a town. *Why would anyone want to live here?*

Passengers stare at one of the few cities along the rocky coast and grow angry.

"There is Hierapytna. The pirates are back. You think you have gotten rid of them, and here they come again. They give Crete a bad reputation."

At last, they float past a town he overhears passengers calling Labena. Bells ring, and sailors grab rigging. Some man the sails. Some man the anchors. Others are bringing cargo above board. Titus sees a small harbor.

"We're docking here," the first mate calls out to the passengers. "Our captain is Jewish, and his most holy day is now. This harbor is Safe Haven."

One of the passengers stops the first mate and asks about going ashore. "Well, our ship is too large to dock here in this small harbor, but we can weigh anchor out here. Our rowboats will secure us to the dock with long heaving lines, then start taking passengers ashore who want to go ashore."

The Day of Atonement, Titus recalls as he watches the ship slip barely into the harbor and drop anchor.

While crew and passengers both rush around, making ready to go ashore, Titus sits, leans his head back against the hull, and dreams of his ice queen.

He is awakened by shouting at something toward the harbor. He stands and watches as some of the passengers lining up to leave. Once again, he sits. This time he pulls his knees up and lays his chin on them.

No. I am not going. I am not strong enough. There are too many things going on in my life. I can hardly get through a day. I cannot do it. Not me. Paul needs to send someone else. Perhaps Stephan or Gaius.

"Are you Titus?"

Titus looks up at a man about as tall as him and with blond hair like his father had in his youth.

"Yes, I am Titus," he says, standing.

"I am Aristarchus. Paul said for me to come up and look for you and hope you were gone. If you were still here, he told me to tell you God has a job for you. Work is healing."

"What does Paul know?" Titus responds, his eyes misting.

"Remember, he is a prophet. He knows about your wife and son. He told me to tell you he lost a wife and son a long time ago in his youth. He told me to say it is time to climb out of your pit and make your wife and son proud of you."

Titus turns and looks toward shore. "Proud of me? No one is proud of me."

"He said to tell you," Aristarchus continues, "that you must go in the strength you have. And if you do not know what that means, look it up. God told Gideon that. God is now telling you to go in the strength you have."

Titus takes a deep breath and turns around to reply. Aristarchus is gone. He looks up at the white billowy clouds bumping into each other overhead.

"I am so tired," he whispers. "Jesus, help me."

"Most of our rowboats have been deployed," a sailor announces. "Come now if you want to go ashore."

The crewman notices Titus watching him. "You going?"

Titus looks at the sailor, back at shore and back at the sailor, though the sailor is now gone, continuing with his announcement.

He walks over to the hatch where Paul had been forced to descend upon boarding days before in Myra.

"You win Paul," he calls down. "But you're wrong! Nothing is healing. Nothing. Do you hear that, Paul?"

Titus purses his lips, takes another deep breath, and marches to the last rowboat going ashore.

"Don't worry, friend. The ship will be going on to Phoenix. The captain told me himself. Remember, he is only going to be here for his holy day."

Titus turns to see another passenger riding in the rowboat in a short, maroon tunic, a green cape, high-topped sandals, and a band around his head to match the tunic.

"Were you talking to me?" Titus asks.

"My name is Zosimos. If you go north and west, you can

walk around the harbor and be in Phoenix by the time the ship gets there after the captain's holy day."

"Really?" Titus asks. "I am relieved to hear that. Perhaps I can see my friend there. How long will they be at Phoenix?"

"All winter," Zosimos replies. "It is a larger harbor and better suited for large corn ships like this one." The man looks up at the sky. "Sure hope the winds behave long enough for them to get to Phoenix."

"That is very good news, sir," Titus responds. *Maybe I can talk Paul out of this whole thing there, and go on to Corinth.*

They say no more until the rowboat docks.

"I am going to Gortyn, the provincial headquarters, and where you need to go first. But my chariot will not hold two people. Do look me up when you arrive. My job is at the praetorium. Perhaps I can find a place for you to spend a night or more before moving on."

"Thank you," Titus says. "If you would point out the road I must take to go to Gortyn, I would be most appreciative."

Within half an hour, Titus is working his way back east along the coast to Labena. It is dark by then. He finds a small inn and spends the night. Before going to sleep, he looks for prophecies about Crete in the scripture scrolls he carries with him. There are none, but there are mentions of the island. "Well, I'll be," he mutters to himself. "The original people in Crete were the ancestors of the Phoenicians of Tyre and Sidon."

That night, he dreams he is on a ship headed for Tyre and along with him is Fjorta. Her beautiful white-blond hair is blowing in the breeze, and she is happy. He sees Sirius climbing the mizenmast. His son arrives at the top and turns into an eagle.

The next morning, Titus heads straight north and into the mountains that rise fast just beyond the seashore.

Why did Paul have to send me here? I cannot do these people any good. How can I appoint elders and deacons when I cannot think straight? I just want my family back.

The innkeeper had said it would take me half a day to get to Gortyn if it were on level land, which it is not. The walk is hard, always winding up and up. The gusts grow and whip around him the farther he climbs.

Titus stops suddenly and looks around, listening. "Must have been the whining of the wind," he mutters. He continues on a few more steps and stops again. He looks around and listens. *This is what I mean. I cannot think straight. I cannot even hear...*

He spots something beside the road and walks over to it. It is a child huddled on his side with his knees under his chin and whimpering. The child's face is streaked with dirty tears.

Tears well up in Titus' own eyes.

"Little boy," Titus says, kneeling. The child does not respond.

"Little boy," Titus says again. He looks around, then up at the sky. He looks back at the child, and puts his hand on the child's arm.

The child opens his eyes, sees Titus, and his whimpers turn to crying.

Titus shifts his legs around and sits on the ground next to the boy.

"Don't be afraid, little boy. I won't hurt you," he says in Latin. The boy does not respond, so he switches to Greek. "Where are your mother and father?"

The boy sits up, looks at Titus, his face distorts, and he breaks out into a wail. He hangs on to Titus' hand and leans his little head against Titus' arm.

Titus puts his free arm across the boy's shoulders and weeps with him.

The boy grows quiet and looks up again at the stranger.

"Did your *mater* go away too?" he asks in almost a whisper.

Titus sniffs and looks down at the boy with the tear-stained face.

"Yes. I lost my *mater* too."

The boy climbs up onto Titus' lap. "Can you help me find my *mater*?"

"Of course, I can," Titus says. "Just tell me where she is."

"She is in heaven," he replies. "Can you take me there so I can find my *mater*?"

Titus draws the boy closer and rocks him. "We cannot go there. It is the place where people go after they leave their body behind."

"Can we leave our body behind so we can find my *mater*? Please, mister."

Titus takes a deep breath and forces a smile. "My name is Titus. What is your name?"

"Sirius," the boy replies.

Titus jerks his head back. He sets the boy on the ground, stands, and steps back. "You're who?"

"My name is Sirius."

Titus tightens his throat, presses his lips together, and looks up at the dark clouds churning overhead.

He kneels in front of the boy, forcing a smile. "That's a very nice name. I used to know a boy a little older than you by that name. Well, I guess you are lost. What were the people doing when you wandered away from them?"

"Putting something in the ground. I didn't like it."

"Where do you live, Sirius?"

"In Gortyn in a very big house," he replies, holding his arms out to show how big the house is.

"Well, Sirius, why don't we wipe our tears, go to Gortyn together, and find your father?"

"Find my *mater* too?"

"I am afraid she is too far away. She is kind of up in the stars. Would you like a drink before we leave?"

Titus shares his water, puts Sirius on his back, and continues on north. He remembers a song his mother used to sing to him and sings it now. The boy falls asleep on Titus' back.

As the sun begins its descent toward the western horizon, Titus sees a city wall ahead. He arrives at the gate.

"Sir, I found this little boy on the road. His name is Sirius. Do you know who his father might be?"

Sirius wakes up. "My *pater* is Karpos," he tells Titus, tapping him on the shoulder.

"Do you know where you live?" Titus asks the boy,

kneeling so the boy can slide down.

"My house is by a statue of a man on a horse."

"I know where that is," the guard says.

Titus takes Sirius by the hand and follows the guard's directions.

When they arrive at the statue, Sirius points at a house. "That's where I live," he says, breaking away in a run.

"Pater, pater, pater," he calls out, banging his little fist on the gate.

Titus hurries to catch up with the boy, and helps him knock on the gate.

A gatekeeper answers it, spots Sirius, calls back, "He's found," and lets the boy and Titus in.

A gray-haired woman rushes to the boy and embraces him, rocking him back and forth. "You're safe. Thank God, you are safe."

She looks up at Titus. "Where did you find him?"

"I am not sure. I have never been to Crete before. Well, I guess I was a day and a half away from Labena."

"Come in, come in," she responds.

As are most of the buildings Titus has seen so far, theirs is made of fieldstone. The courtyard is floored with fieldstone also. There is a second floor, held up with columns painted orange.

"That is where we held the funeral," the lady continues. "His father is still out looking for him." She turns to another servant. "Will you ride out there and tell Karpos he is home and safe?"

"My name is Adronia," she says, turning back to Titus. "I am the child's grandmother. How can we thank you? The wildcats and bears are bad in these mountains. We thought we'd lost both him and his mother."

"*Yaya*, the nice man shared his water with me and everything."

Adronia sits on a bench and lets Sirius climb up onto her lap. "Well, we're going to have to use some water for other things, such as cleaning you up."

"Can the nice man eat with us tonight, *Yaya*? We are hungry."

"Indeed, he can. Further," she says, turning back to Titus, "you can spend the night here and stay as long as you like."

"I am headed to Phoenix. I am supposed to meet a ship there,"

"Do you know how to get to Phoenix?"

"If I stop and ask directions enough times, I will."

"While we are waiting for the rescue party to return, why don't you go with Chariton to clean up," she tells Titus. "We have our own baths. And I think you are about Karpos' size."

Titus rises and follows the servant. When, at last, he returns to the courtyard wearing one of Karpos' clean, blue tunics, another man is there playing with a cleaned-up Sirius.

"There he is, *Pater*," Sirius shouts.

"Don't be so noisy," the man says.

The host sets Sirius down off his lap and stands. Titus recognizes his expression. One of trying to be brave when he is wailing on the inside.

The men approach each other and extend hands and forearms. They clasp each other hard, looking into each other's eyes, now misting.

"I lost my wife recently," Titus whispers. The men stare at each other as though their shared pain will bring back the ones they loved.

"She is with Jesus now," Titus adds.

Karpos steps back. "You know about Jesus?"

"Yes, I do. Would you like me to tell you about him? He will be a great comfort to you."

"I already know about him. I am a Christian too."

35 ~ BROTHERS

"Come sit, my brother," Karpos says. "Oh, this is my son, Balios," he says, putting his hand on the young man's shoulder who looks to be around fifteen.

"I should have known," Karpos continues. "God sent you to us. I have been praying about so many things: How to stabilize our congregation, how to deal with the Jews, and now for my son's life to be spared. You are, indeed, from God."

"Well, it took God shifting many things around to get me here. Among other things, the sky does not seem to be as fair as it was yesterday. My friend is on a ship that will be leaving for Phoenix soon to moor for the winter."

"And, who is your friend?"

"The apostle Paul."

Karpos' eyes light up. "The apostle himself? I have longed to meet him. May I go with you to Phoenix?"

"Of course."

"Well, we have plenty of time. Our congregation needs to meet with you."

"How did your congregation start? Who started it?"

"It started on the Day of Pentecost. I was among the Jews who went to Jerusalem for the annual feast. I am sorry, but I do not believe you are Jewish. Would you like me to explain some things to you?"

The men stay up and talk until the moon is high in the

sky.

Two days later is the first day of the week. Karpos' family is breaking their fast.

"My daughter is a good cook," Karpos says, "but she married recently and is living somewhere else."

"You have a fine family," Titus says, looking down at his yogurt and trying to be an appreciative guest.

"Will you please speak to our congregation?" Karpos asks. "And have some more yogurt to dip your bread in. It has dates cut up in it. My wife..."

The men grow silent and look at each other a moment.

"I think I can do that," Titus says. "Where do you meet?"

"Right here in my home. We meet in the courtyard. There are eighty of us. They should begin arriving soon."

"Pater, may I sit with Titus when we worship?"

"You may sit with both of us," Karpos says, twisting his son's nose and grinning at him.

The Christian brothers and sisters arrive a little at a time. Adronia greets them all with her smile. Many fight back tears.

"Everyone," Karpos says, standing before the assembled congregation, "you may have wondered who this gentleman is, this stranger among us. Well, something besides his name. He is actually an associate of the apostle Paul. He has consented to speak to us this morning."

Titus stands and looks over the group of Cretans who, just a few days earlier, he had scorned.

"I see pain in your eyes," he begins. "You have lost a sister, and the wife and mother of this house. Thank the Lord Jesus Christ that you have each other. Most of all, thank him that you will be able to see your beloved one again someday in heaven. It is because of his death and resurrection that we can hope for our own resurrection."

Titus speaks a while and sits back down. The congregation spontaneously begins to sing hymns, some of which are from David's psalms, and some he assumes were composed by some of their own. Teenaged Balios starts some of the new songs for them from his seat.

They share the Lord's supper in quiet solemnity. Taking

the bread and wine as it is passed to them, then meditating.

A few more hymns, and the worship is over.

As in Corinth, the members have brought baskets of food to share with each other for a noon meal.

When everyone has had their fill, and the leftovers placed back in the baskets, Karpos stands.

"Brothers and sisters, Titus is here to help us. The apostle Paul sent him to show us how to appoint deacons and elders."

Titus stands. "You need elders, so you have men to teach you further and to teach others in your fair city. You are to have more than one elder, never just one. He must have one wife and be old enough to have children who understand Jesus' teachings enough they have become Christians themselves. The elders are to be equals, not one over the others."

He watches at the members look at each other and whisper.

"The deacons are to have the same qualifications as elders, but do not have to be able to teach, nor have children old enough to understand Jesus' teachings and be Christians."

More glancing and nodding and whispering.

"If our host has enough clay tablets, you should each write down the names of men you wish to be the congregation's elders, and the names of potential deacons."

Names are written, the men on the list stand outside while the congregation talks about their readiness and willingness.

While the congregation does this, Titus meets with the candidates individually to find out their beliefs. He returns to the assembly and tells them which ones are qualified.

They vote on those Titus approved of, then call the men back in.

"Titus announces the men decided on. One by one, members of the congregation walk forward and give their blessing to each new elder and new deacon."

That night, the wind picks up.

"The Jewish Day of Atonement is over. We need to head

out to Phoenix tomorrow morning. And let us pray another storm is not headed this way. We need Paul's ship to arrive safely in their harbor."

"I will be ready," Titus responds.

"And, by the way," Karpos adds, "about the toga you wear. On our rugged island, unless you stay in one place, it isn't practical. Here is a tunic and cape for you to wear. Bright colors, too, the way we Cretans like them. Winters are fair here but may be coming early this year. Oh, and high-topped sandals. When you get off the Roman road, the bushes and falling rocks can play havoc on your toes."

"Thank you, Karpos. You are very thoughtful. Uh, before we go, there is someone I would like to see."

"Oh? I thought you did not know anyone on Crete before you came."

"I did not. But I met someone when I got off the ship. He told me I could find him at the government basilica. Who is your governor right now?"

"Cornelius Lupus. He wasn't the one you met, was he?" Karpos replies with a large grin. What was the gentleman's name?"

"Zosimo. He said I should ask for him."

"Are you sure? Wouldn't you rather leave him a note? We do not want to be out walking if a storm hits."

That evening, Titus writes a note to Zosimos.

Thank you for speaking to me that day. You have no idea how much I needed those few kind words on an island where I knew no one. I sincerely believe Jesus, the Son of God, sent you to me at that moment. I have been staying with a new friend here by the name of Karpos. If you are interested in knowing more about this powerful Jesus, contact Karpos. May the Creator of the universe—the one and only God— be with you, my friend.

Karpos agrees to deliver the message in person.

The following morning Yaya Adronia gives them a basket of food to take along.

"*Pater,* may I go with you?" Balios asks. "I've never been to Phoenix."

"Me too, *Pater*," Sirius adds.

"Well, let's see what Titus says.

Titus stares at Sirius and kneels. "You are such a brave little boy. You remind me of another little boy I used to know by your very same name, only he was a little older than you."

He touches the boy's cheek. "I think I would like to remember you as you are, and go on my way and remember the other little boy as he was. Is that okay?"

Karpos watches Titus as he stands. "Your little boy?" he whispers.

Titus does not reply. He picks up his two leather bags—one with personal necessities and one with his prophecy scrolls—and steps over to the outer gate.

"Balios, I think you should stay home this time. If we do have a storm, *Yaya* Adronia will need you to help get things out of the weather. And, if I'm still gone next Solday, you can take my place, making sure they have supplies for the Lord's Supper and play host."

The next morning at dawn, Titus and Karpos are on their way out of Gortys. The pass the temple to Apollo and a hippodrome dedicated to the god. They pass the sanctuary of Isis.

"By the way," Karpos says, "see that column standing alone in the middle of the agora? That is a replica of the ancient code of law. It is thousands of years old, but those laws are as good today as they ever were. Human nature never changes."

Titus remains silent.

"When the Greeks came here, they claimed that Zeus had a mistress here in Gortyn named Europa. Apparently, they named lands north of Greece Europa after her. Have you ever been to Europa?"

"My mother and wife were born there. I lost them both."

"Titus, I thought the loss of my wife last week was unbearable. But you, you have lost your mother—was she the first to leave you?

"Yes, I was eleven."

"Then you lost your wife. Well, if you also lost a son, I don't see how you can stand it. And here you are helping the churches on an island you've never been to before. You are a strong man, Titus. A strong man.

"Not so strong. I didn't want to come here. I wanted to go somewhere to be alone and mourn them."

They walk along in silence a while, working their way west.

"But Paul. Paul would not allow that. 'Go in the strength you have,' he told me," Titus recalls. "I have no strength. How could he say that?"

"Who did you lose first? Your wife or son?"

"I lost them on the same day. It's been a little over a month now. But your wounds are fresh, Karpos, and here you are escorting me around Crete."

"It is good for me, I think."

"What happened? Was it childbirth?"

Karpos is silent. Titus waits as the other man had waited for him. They continue walking west some time.

"They drowned her," Karpos whispers.

"Oh, no," Titus responds, stopping in the road and looking into the eyes of his new friend. "Because of Jesus?"

"Because of Jesus," Karpos responds, walking again. "We do not know if it was Jewish or pagan women."

"I am truly sorry."

Karpos takes a deep breath. "She received a message a few days ago. Some women wanted her to meet them in the baths where it was more private.

Bring Us Jesus

"That is all the message said. There was no mention of time, so she handed my mother the message and said she would be back home in a few hours. Then she left."

Silence again.

"That is the last time anyone saw her alive," he whispers.

There is a bench beside the road. Titus takes hold of his friend's elbow and leads him over to it.

They sit side by side. They stare straight ahead. They

grit their teeth. Sometimes one looks up at the blue sky with restless gray and white clouds bumping into each other while the other looks off to the north at mountains already glistening with snow.

Karpos stands and steps away from the bench, both hands on his head. Soon, his shoulders tremble. Groans ascend from deep in the Cretan's throat. He lifts heavy arms and raises his face toward the heavens.

"Why?"

It echoes around the foothills of the mountains not very far to the north, and rests in the hearing of Titus. He puts his hands on both knees and rocks forward and back, forward and back.

"Come." It is Karpos. He is kneeling before Titus. He stands and holds out his hand. "We must keep going."

Titus nods and stands. The men continue walking another hour until they come to a large dark structure.

"Looks empty. What did it used to be?" Titus asks, not very loud.

"A castle," Karpos responds, not very loud either. "We are in Phaistos."

"We're not far from a bay down there," Titus says.

"Yes, that's the Bay of Masarra."

"Looks like a good spot for pirates," Titus muses.

"So, you heard about our pirates, friend."

Karpos puts an arm over Titus' shoulder, smiling again. "You had better be good, or we Cretans will throw you to one of our pirates. Ha, ha."

"That's what you think," Titus responds, poking Karpos in a rib.

"Well, this is where we turn north for a while, friend," Karpos says, jumping away from Titus' threatening fingers. "See that mountain peak up there. That's our very own Mount Ida. It is famous. Did you know that? There is a cave in it. Zeus, father of the gods that don't exist, was supposed to be swallowed by his father, who didn't like him. His nurse hid him in a cave up there so he could grow up to be another god that doesn't exist.

In another hour, they arrive at the north edge of the

harbor and head west again.

"How much farther is Phoenix? And the wind is picking up."

"Three more days."

"Do you think we'll beat Paul's ship there?"

"No."

They walk for the next two hours in silence.

"What was that?" Titus calls out over the sudden gust of wind and pulling his cape closer around him.

"We are out of the protection of the mountains," Karpos calls back, hanging on to his own cape in the new north wind. It will be like this until tomorrow when we get some protection from the next range of mountains."

"Which range? And how many ranges does Crete have?" Titus calls back.

"The White Mountains. And we have three ranges."

"On this minuscule island?"

The men tuck their heads down and fight the cold wind as it assaults them, swirling around down from the north and east, then up from the south and west. Pounding and challenging and not letting up.

They walk on another half hour, leaning into the wind, pushing, fighting for each step.

Titus feels a hand on his shoulder. He looks at Karpos, who is pointing to the south at the bay below with its angry waves rising to grab anything in their way. Pounding and snatching and imprisoning in the deep.

Rain hits. Lightening. Thunder. Karpos heads to the side of the road and down into a gully. Titus follows. They hunker down in the scant shelter, wishing they still had the mountains with their myriads of caves.

"Pray, my friend," Titus calls out. "Pray!"

For the next five days, the men trudge down the road, struggle against the wind, and defy the rain. Bullied by rumbling thunder and threatened by lightning forking out of the sky at them.

Push against that which is stronger than they. Struggle and fight back until the energy is gone. Stumble. Take shelter. Rest when they cannot rest. Lose track of day and night. Walk and trudge and stumble.

One step at a time. Struggle to survive. Let the rain sting their faces. Let the gales knock them over. Keep going. Survive.

The pain. The unbearable pain. The pain that penetrates, buries itself, and refuses to let go. Pain and agony and a heart tearing to pieces.

Sleep that cannot come. Dreaming of what can never be again. Hoping against hope. In a world strange and fierce and empty.

"It see it!" Karpos shouts over the gale.

He points. "Phoenix!"

They work their way into the seaside town. Karpos leads Titus down a narrow street. Turns, then down an alley. He pounds on a gate.

"They cannot hear me!"

Both men pound and shout. And hope and pray. "Let us in. Help us. Help."

At last, the gate is opened.

Titus and Karpos lunge inside and collapse. Hands reach down for them. They are carried by their arms, torso, and legs inside a room.

The door is shut against the storm. Quieter now.

"Karpos? Is that you?"

"Paul. Where is Paul? I've got to see him," Titus says between spells of coughing.

"Paul?"

"The apostle. On ship. Should be here," Titus manages to say.

"No ships here in two weeks. That hurricane is bad. No ship could possibly survive it."

36 ~ AFTERMATH

*T*itus sits up in bed. Sun streams in through a high window. He strains his eyes to look out and sees deep blue skies. He coughs.

The door to his room opens.

"Well, look who is awake," Karpos says, walking in with a large bandage around one arm.

Titus stares at his friend, trying to remember why he is his friend and who he is.

"Where am I?"

"You are in Phoenix. We actually walked some thirty *milles* in a hurricane. Well, not all of it, but a lot of it. My friends have been sneaking something pretty smelly down your throat to help your lungs. You look like you're breathing okay now. Are you?"

"What happened to your arm?"

"In one of those falls we took, I guess I cracked something."

Karpos sits on the side of Titus' bed. "Paul's ship has been lost at sea. There is no way he could have survived. We have been waiting for you to revive so we can have a memorial service for him."

"Do these people we're staying with know who Paul is?" Titus asks, having reoriented himself.

"No, they are not Christians. But, they agreed to hold a

memorial service anyway for my sake. And yours. We are old friends."

Titus pushes the sheet down to his feet, Karpos stands to move out of his way. He swings his feet around, sits on the side of his bed, stands, and grows dizzy.

"Easy there."

Titus sits a moment and tries again. He is successful. He walks out of the room, squints in the bright sunlight, and looks around.

"Well, you're back from the stars or wherever your spirit was lingering," a strange man says. "Good."

"Titus, this is my friend, Bion. Bion is not a Christian. Yet." Karpos winks at his friend. "I promised him the heavens would not collapse if he decided to believe in Jesus as the only God."

"I understand you lost a friend at sea," Bion says, looking at Titus, then at Karpos. If you would like to have a memorial service here, that would be all right."

Titus looks at Karpos. "Are you up to walking down to the shoreline? I think I would like to do it there. But, sir, we also want to help you with any storm damage to your house. Or maybe the houses of your neighbors. It is the least we can do for rescuing us and bringing us back to health."

"You are a little late in your offer. The neighborhood united and helped each other," Bion replies. "Everything is back to normal now. But I thank you for the kind offer. Now, go have your memorial service."

The two men make their way to the docks, then walk out as far as they can. They sit on the very end.

"Jesus, is it okay to send a message to Paul?" Karpos asks. "Paul, I never met you. But I heard you were a good man. You are with Jesus now."

"If you see our family there, uh..."

"Yes, if you see our families there, greet them for us," Karpos finishes for Titus.

"Tell them we are carrying on," Titus says. "Their deaths will not have been in vain. Just like your death will not be in vain, Paul. Isn't that right, Jesus? We will tell of you wherever we go."

The men sit in silence a while. Titus prays.

More silence. Karpos prays.

At last, Karpos slaps his knee. "Well, I guess it's on up the coast to Elyros. There is a church there. I will take you to them." He stands.

"No," Titus responds, standing with him. "You have already done too much."

Karpos stares. "I need this, Titus."

They stare at each other and know.

"Yes, I guess we both do. Well, friend, lead on to—where did you say we are going?"

They leave the dock and walk back up the hill.

You need to do something about your clothes if you want people here to accept you. Togas and fine tunics do not go over here. You need clothes like most people here wear—bright-colored tunics and capes."

They go into a small market to buy fresh clothes in the local style, return to Bion's house long enough to change into their new purchases, offer their thanks and goodbyes, back to the market to buy a basket of food, and begin anew on their journey.

"How far?" Titus asks as they get back on the coastal road and continue west.

"About two days."

"Two hours pass."

"You never told me about your son," Karpos says in a loud whisper.

Silence.

"As you guessed, his name was Sirius. He was ten years old and a very good and smart boy. I was so proud of him."

"Oh, my."

"You said they died on the same day."

"My wife was strong."

"Mine too."

"I don't mean like that only. She was physically strong. And she had a strong will. She was born and raised by the Nordic Sea, and their women learn sword fighting, spear throwing, and anything else they take to."

"I think I have heard that."

"She was trying to convince people Poseidon was not a god. She converted one of Poseidon's priests to Christianity. The high priest kidnapped her and my son then sent me a note. 'Sacrifice to Poseidon, or they die.'"

Karpos stops. "I cannot imagine how to handle that one."

"She decided for me. She broke loose of her chains at the foot of Poseidon's statue, and beat on the statue with the chains. Pieces went flying everywhere. One of their guards came in with a spear and..."

"Oh, Titus. I am so sorry."

They do not talk for the next three hours.

"We have to carry on, don't we?" Karpos says.

"I do not like the answer, but yes, we do. Still, can we not mourn?"

"How much mourning must we do to cure the pain, Titus?"

They walk on until high cliffs appear along the shoreline. Steep places where no city could sit.

The sun descends close to the horizon.

"I see you do not have inns along the road like the Romans provide us in Anatolia and Greece," Titus says.

"I should have prepared for this. But I didn't," Karpos says, standing in the middle of the road looking around with one hand on his head.

"I did. If you noticed the extra pack on my back, it isn't clothes. It is a two-man tent. I may need it more than once on this strange and unpredictable island."

The next morning, the men continue west. The bay has now merged with the Libyan Sea. Once again, to their right, they notice snow-capped mountains.

"Are these the White Mountains you were telling me about?" Titus asks.

"Yes, and we are almost to our destination.

"Beautiful. But how can you have snow in such a warm climate? You are just above the great Sahara Desert in Lybia."

"It's just one of the mysteries of our island," Karpos replies.

That afternoon, they arrive at Elyros. Down the hill to

their left is the seaport of Lyssos that services Elyros. Straight ahead are the baths. They go in, dip both themselves and their dusty clothes in the water. Come out, and lay their clothes in the courtyard to dry in the autumn sun.

Refreshed, they walk farther into the city, purchase a few things at the market, and continue on to the residential section.

"I noticed your cities do not have walls around them," Titus says. "Aren't you afraid of enemy attack?"

"We have the strongest navy in the world, and the seas around us are our walls. What more do we need?" Karpos explains. They walk past a temple to Apollo's sons by a nymph—Phylakides and Philandros.

"How can they worship such immoral gods, even if they were real?" Titus muses.

"They have a temple to Asklepios, the healing god, down in Lissos."

"Don't talk to me about that imposter with his deceitful, treacherous, fake healer priests," Titus says in a burst of anger.

"Huh?

"I lost my daughter under their so-called care."

Karpos stops walking. "You lost a daughter too?"

"I don't want to talk about it. Now, where is the church?"

After several wrong turns, Karpos finally remembers where one of the members lives. He knocks on the gate, and it squeaks open.

"Greetings, Diadalos, brother," Karpos says when he sees the confused look on the old man's face. "You may not remember me, but I am a Christian living in Gortyn. May this brother and I come in? We have walked a long way to get here."

Diadalos runs his hand through unkempt gray hair and forms a smile. "Ohhh, yes, I remember you now. Of course. Of course. Come in. Come in.

He steps back, and the travelers walk into his courtyard. It has the usual flagstone flooring with columns holding up the second floor. However, his columns are painted green.

"Diadalos, this is our Christian brother, Titus. He is

here all the way from Corinth."

"Welcome. Welcome to my home. Come in. Sit."

Diadalos hurries to the kitchen end of the courtyard, brings up a pail of fresh water from the well, pours it in mugs, and takes them to his company with shaky hands. He frowns.

"Did you travel through that storm? No one on any ship could have survived it. You weren't out walking in that weather, hopefully."

"Regretfully, we were caught in it. But we have recovered under the care of a friend in Phoenix, except for my cracked arm—or so the doctor said that is what I have." He holds his bandaged forearm to display it.

"And you, Titus," Diadalos says, turning to his other guest. "What brings you all the way down here from the homeland of my ancestors, the Dorians?"

"Actually, it was an accident. I was returning home to Corinth after being away a month or two and ran into a friend of mine."

"That friend is the Apostle Paul, himself," Karpos interjects. His grin fast goes away. "But he is gone now. He was on board a ship when the hurricane hit. What a loss to the church."

"Was he on his way here?"

"He was on his way to Rome. But when he saw me, since the ship we were on was going to dock temporarily at Safe Haven, he told me to go ashore, visit all the congregations here, and set up elders in each one."

Titus detects a flash of smile. Diadalos shifts in his seat. "Well, tomorrow is the first day of the week. There are fifty of us, and they meet here. Would you like to talk to the congregation then?"

The next day after breaking their fast, people begin arriving. Their host asks his two guests to stand at the gate and greet everyone as they come in.

One man with dark hair, a little ample around the waist, with a thick broad nose and lips, and who Titus estimates to be middle-aged, glares at the two guests. Diadalos introduces him as Stavros.

When it is determined everyone has arrived, the group

exchanges prayer requests and announcements of members in need of help in some way, especially since the hurricane. Psalms of David follow. Then the Lord's Supper with each person taking a bite of unleavened bread to represent Jesus' body on the sacrificial cross and a sip of red grape juice to represent Jesus' blood on the sacrificial cross. Finally, Titus is introduced.

"You have suffered loss, some of you unbearable loss."

Karpos sits in the back and bows his head. A few others do too.

"We need each other in times of loss and sorrow. It is not as though our mutual comfort will make the pain go away, but it does remind us that others care and love us, just as Jesus, our Lord, does."

He sees tears come to the eyes of several in the assembly. He fights his own.

"Why does God allow us to go through suffering? For the same reason any good father does. A good father makes his son stand before him and recite the alphabet, and all the city's laws on a certain subject, or all Moses' Ten Commandments, or all the names of the prophets of God. Does the child suffer? In his mind, he does. But his father is only strengthening him for what is ahead in life. God, our heavenly Father does the same thing."

As Titus speaks, his mind wanders back to those days standing beside the reflecting pool with a statue of Augustus in the middle and reciting before his father.

"Why does God allow us to face material loss? The same reason our earthly father does. Our earthly father involves their sons in heavy lifting, jumping, boxing, and hard labor in order to strengthen them. God, our Father, strengthens us in the same ways, forcing us to rebuild and remake things we have lost."

Again, as Titus speaks, he recalls all the rigors of the games his father put him through as a child.

"God is constantly preparing us for greater and sometimes more terrible things. Why? Satan wants to destroy you so you will blame God and come over to his side where he will plunge us into hell for his pleasure. This world belongs to Satan. We are in a battle with Satan alongside God. He wants us to keep overcoming Satan until, at last, we reach our heavenly home and can enter the gates with our head held high."

Titus dares not pause to think of his losses. He is driven to say what he has perhaps known all along. He is driven to pronounce it, announce it, and believe it.

"God does not bother allowing tragedy to hit the man who is crooked and self-absorbed. He is not worthy of God's attention. Misfortune hits the good man for the very same reason that made him good in the first place. He is good because he is an overcomer of bad things around him. We cannot be conquerors unless we have something to conquer. We cannot have victory unless we have something to be victorious over."

Silence.

Though it is a cool day, perspiration has broken out on Titus' brow. He stares at the congregation as though unmovable. He grits his teeth. He rushes to his seat in the back next to Karpos, and there, for a moment, sheds tears of release.

Silence continues.

One slow step at a time, Diadalos walks to the front of the congregation.

"I think we all needed that after the loss of Paul." He takes a deep breath. "We will be dismissing now. But do not leave. Titus has come here on an important mission."

He leads the congregation in a final prayer, then motions for Titus to come forward again.

Instead, Karpos rises and steps to the front. "First, Titus has been sent here to help each congregation appoint elders and deacons. He helped our congregation do it, and it worked out very well. Everyone seemed to be happy."

Karpos instructs everyone and passes out some clay tablets he had purchased at the market. "Everyone write down the names of anyone you would like to hold the office of elder or deacon and indicate which. Remember, they must have one wife, and an elder must have children old enough to understand Jesus' teachings about right and wrong and have become Christians themselves.”

As the congregation goes through their nomination process, Karpos walks back to Titus and motions for him to walk out to the street with him.

“Are you better now? You were speaking to yourself up there, weren’t you? Well, we both needed it.”

Titus looks at his friend, nods his head, wipes away his last tear, and smiles. “Yes, we needed it. I am better now. We both are. Now, let’s get some elders for this congregation.”

As the two men return inside, they hear an angry voice.

“And just who is this Titus that he should interview potential elders and deacons for our congregation? He doesn’t know any of us. It’s none of his business.”

“Now, don’t go getting upset again, Stavros. Control that temper.”

“I will control nothing. I want to know who gives Titus authority over us. None of the other apostles ever said an outsider has authority over a congregation.”

Titus hurries to one of the leather shoulder bags he has carried with him since Corinth and walks to the front.

“I understand your concern, sir,” he says, stepping to the front. “You have a very good point, and I respect that.” He smiles at Stavros. Stavros does not smile back.

Titus holds up a scroll. “Brother, I have here one of the letters the Apostle Paul himself wrote. It has his signature at the end. He sent it to the congregation in Corinth and gave me a copy. Please inspect it, brother.”

Titus holds out the scroll to the objector, and Stavros takes it. Titus waits while Stavros opens and reads the beginning and ending of it.

“Now, sir,” Titus says, pacing in front of the congregation. “Would you say that was written by Paul?”

“Well, yes.”

“And, sir, would you say those are the kinds of instructions Paul would give? Take a moment and read through more of it.”

Titus stands with his elbow propped up by his hand, and his other hand under his chin. He looks up at the sky overhead, over at the wall, over at one of the green columns, then back at Stavros. "Now, sir, would you say those are the kinds of instructions Paul would give."

Stavros pauses. "Well, yes."

"And, sir, if he gave me authority to deliver his instructions in writing, do you not think he would give me authority to help congregations in Crete appoint elders and deacons? Not take over, but help."

Stavros stands, walks up to Titus, stares at him, then breaks out into a broad grin. "I'm convinced," he says. He turns to the congregation and raises his arms. "I'm convinced. So, let us go ahead and appoint elders—with Titus' final approval, of course."

Titus returns to the back of the room and joins Karpos.

"You are full of surprises. You acted just like an attorney up there."

Titus stares at him and smiles.

"Well, well. So that is what you used to be. I should have known."

The process is completed, and elders and deacons are selected for the church of Christ in Elyros.

The next morning, Karpos gathers up his belongings. "I need to get back home now, Titus. I am going down to the docks to find a ship going to the other side of the bay. My family needs... Well, my family needs me in the same way the church here needs you."

Titus smiles. I think I'll spend the winter here. I can go back and forth between these two cities and help them work through any confusions they may have. Your congregation is going to do fine, especially with you as one of the elders."

"And after here?" Karpos asks.

"Diadalos says the next congregation west and north of here is on the other side of Phalasarna in Polirrinia."

"Oh? Are you sure you want to go there? That area is full of pirates."

37 ~ OF PIRATES & PRIESTESSES

"Are you sure you don't want to take a ship up the coast to Polirirnia?" Diadalos asks.

"No. I'm used to walking," Titus responds. "Besides, you have too many storms on Crete."

"It's spring. Nothing is going to go wrong."

"Well, maybe after losing Paul, I've decided to stay away from ships unless absolutely necessary."

"What a sad, sad loss," Diadalos says, shaking his head and looking at his feet.

"I must leave tomorrow," Titus says. I assume that, if I stay on the highway, I will find it."

"Do not worry, my brother. Stavros has agreed to take you up there."

"Ha, ha! Ole Stavros, who was almost my enemy? And now is one of your elders?"

"He'll come in handy, scaring off any pirates you encounter," Diadalos teases.

"All he'll have to do is growl at them," Titus counters.

The next morning, Titus gathers up his belongings and an empty basket, which he plans to fill on their way out of the city with food.

The expected knock comes, and Titus opens the gate.

"All set to go, brother?" Stavros says.

The two leave, stop at the market,, and go out on the

highway heading farther west. At noon, they run out of land and turn north.

Late on the second day, they approach a harbor.

"Walls? I actually see city walls on Crete?" Titus says. "I thought you had such a strong navy, you didn't need walls." He slaps Stavros on the back and laughs.

"That, my friend, is how the pirates do things. Looming before you is Phalasarna."

Titus stops. "I thought you said the Roman fleet got rid of the pirates here."

"If we had time, I'd take you on a tour. The pirates not only built walls around the city, but also around their harbor. Ships could only enter their harbor through two narrow channels."

"Skip the tour. I need to get to the next congregation. If this is the last one, perhaps I can go back home."

"Where is home?"

"Antioch. Or maybe Corinth."

The two pass the ruins of the pirate haven and cross over to the north end of Crete. See that land jutting out there on our left, and the other one way over to our east? Between those two is Coos Bay, the favorite haunt of pirates all of the world. A good hiding place. The bay is hard to see except from the north entrance to it."

"You can have your pirates," Titus responds.

Well, right in the middle between the two pieces of land, jutting out is our destination. We will be there soon.

Just before the sun slips below the horizon, Titus and Stavros enter Polirrinia, the city dedicated to the goddess of Crete.

"She has many names—as do most gods and goddesses on the island," Stavros explains. "And why not? She doesn't exist anyway. Britomartidos sometimes, Diktynna sometimes and Artemis sometimes. Or some people call her by all three names, so they do not offend anyone."

"I've noticed that. But why so many names of the same thing?" Titus asks.

"Well, we have the language of the original people here. Then we have the language brought here from somewhere in the north where the barbarians live now, which some people call Minoans. And we have the language of the Achians who invaded Crete from southern Greece, and the Dorians who invaded from northern Greece. Everyone was proud and refused to give up their heritage."

"This island gets stranger all the time," Titus says with a twinkle in his eye.

"At least we have Greek now to add to their native tongue. I remember when I used to believe in Diktynna. What a fool I was. Well, I never liked her, so was relieved to find out she wasn't real."

"Why did you change your mind?"

"You know the answer to that. I'm sure it happened to you too. Some Jews from here were in Jerusalem on the Day of Pentecost well thirty-two or -three years ago and became Christians. They couldn't wait to get back here and set us free."

Who converted you, Titus?"

"Paul did. I was thirty-three years old at the time, and I'm fifty now, so I guess it was seventeen years ago."

"If I remember right, the church in this city meets down this street."

"What's that temple up at the top of that hill?"

"You have to ask? It's to 'the virgin maiden Diktynna' as they call her."

Stavros continues looking for the house of one of the local Christians.

"Here we go. I remember the gate had the symbol of a fish on it."

Stavros knocks. No answer. He knocks again. Still, no one. Titus joins him, pounding on the gate.

A small peek door opens.

"Who are you? What do you want?"

"Well, I am Stavros from Elyros, and this is Titus. We are Christians and understand you are too."

"Don't say that word," the voice responds.

"What word?"

No answer.

"Oh, that word."

"Well, we are your brothers and have come to see you from the church…"

"Don't say that word," the voice demands.

"We have traveled a long way and would appreciate it if you would let us in so we can rest with you," Titus interjects.

"How do I know you are who you say you are?"

Titus looks at Stavros. "Hmmm, seems like I've heard that one before."

Stavros grins, then responds to the voice. "We have come here on behalf of the Son of God."

"Which god?"

"The only God. The Creator of the world and lover of your soul."

"How do I know you didn't make that up?" the voice demands.

Stavros looks at Titus. "Do you want to give it a try?"

"Sir, I was sent here by the Apostle Paul. Wait one moment, and I will give you proof." Titus reaches into his leather shoulder pouch and brings out a scroll. He unrolls part of it and holds it up to the little window.

"Do you see the beginning of this letter? It says 'Paul, an apostle of Jesus the Christ by the will of God.' See that? Paul gave me this letter to deliver to the church in Corinth."

"Yes," Stavros interrupts. "And he wouldn't have entrusted Titus here with this letter unless he was his friend and representative whom he trusted."

Stavros looks over at Titus as he re-rolls the scroll. "It worked on me," he says, grinning.

The little window in the gate closes, they hear scraping of a bar, and the gate opens just far enough for a man to slip through.

"Hurry! Someone might see you," the voice says.

They step inside, and see a man with apparently his wife and two small children standing behind him.

"We did not mean to frighten you, my brother," Titus says. "What is going on? Are you in danger?"

"You haven't heard?" the man who seems to be in his late thirties says.

"Heard what? What is going on?" Stavros asks.

The young man turns to those behind him and mutters. "It's okay. Go to your rooms. Quickly."

Standing facing the two strangers, Titus notices their reluctant host is shorter than both him and Stavros but is well built. He does not speak or move.

"Nero burned Rome."

"He did what?" Stavros asks.

"He not only burned Rome but now he is blaming the Christians for it."

"How did you learn that?" Titus asks.

"A ship came in with the news just yesterday. These are dangerous times. What if Nero sends his legionnaires all over the empire to round up Christians and kill us all?"

Titus sits on a bench near the gate and sets down his pouches and the tent on his back. He holds open his cape. "I have no weapons. Here are my bags if you would like to search them."

Stavros sits on the bench with Titus and replicates his reassurances.

"My name is Kleitos, I don't need to search you, and I am sorry for the way I treated you."

"I would have done the same thing if I were young and had a family to protect," Stavros says.

"Kleitos, we would like to meet with the church in your city. Would that be possible?"

"The church meets in my father's home. I do not know how many will show up the next time we are scheduled to meet for worship."

"Can you get word to him? It is very important. Titus is here to help you appoint elders and deacons."

"Wait until tonight. I can slip through some back streets and get to his house. Pray for me tonight."

Titus insists on sitting up in the small courtyard all night. He lets Kleitos out, then bars the gate after him. He re-seats himself, closes his eyes just a moment. Then it is morning.

Titus jerks awake with the soft tapping on the gate. He opens it, and Kleitos enters.

"He got the message," he tells Titus.

"And?" Titus inquires, embarrassed he had not been able to stay awake for him.

"He said definitely we are going to meet for worship on Solday, and no one is going to stop us."

"Titus smiles. I think he is right."

Four days pass. The morning of Solday, the family shares his morning fast-breaking food. His oldest son is to go with Titus and show him the way. The daughter is to go with Stavros and show him the way. Last, Kleitos will go with his wife.

It takes most of the day for everyone to arrive for worship. Meeting in a courtyard, Pallas announces they will whisper their psalms. Scriptures are read. An hour is spent praying for Christians in Rome and elsewhere in the world as well as Crete.

Titus explains the procedure for selecting elders and deacons. It is dark by the time the final decisions are made. It takes the congregation half the night to return home, one household every half hour.

The next day, Stavros bids everyone goodbye, walks down to the dock, and takes a small ship back south and to home.

Pallas has been appointed as one of the elders. His son is now a deacon. Pallas asks Titus to move in with him where he has plenty of room. Titus obliges.

"Please stay with us a couple of months," the elder tells Titus soon after his move. "You aren't in any hurry to get anywhere, are you?"

Titus looks up at the sky, and over to the blue pillars holding up the second floor of the elder's home. "A few months ago, I was. But, much has passed. The least I can do is keep the teachings of Paul alive, even though he is no longer with us."

One day two months later, Titus asks the elder about the temple at the top of the hill. "It is to the goddess Diktynna, I understand. What do you know about her? Well, not her, since she does not exist, but the stories about her?"

"Well, she was born in Mount Ditka."

"Where is it? Down there in the White Mountains?"

"No, it's on the other end of the Island. But it's the people here that venerate her the most."

Pallas leads Titus to his solarium where they sit around a lily pool.

"Believe it or not, I was baptized in that pool. Well, most of us were. Anyway, back to that witch everyone calls a goddess. They say Mount Ditka is where Zeus was born."

The elder rolls his eyes.

"Her priestesses say she nursed Zeus, although the patrons of another goddess say their goddess nursed him."

"So, why do people at the west end of the island worship her instead of those at the east end where she was supposedly born?"

"Even our own historians differ on that. But mostly they claim King Minos in the east wanted to ravage her. Instead, she ran from him. But he kept pursuing. So, in desperation, she jumped off one of our myriads of cliffs into the sea and there was rescued by fishermen in their net here in the west."

"People believe that?" Titus asks, shaking his head.

"The priestesses are very powerful. Our local government does nothing major without consulting with the high priestess."

"Isn't that the way it always is?" Titus says. "The patron god or goddess rules the rulers."

"Jesus could set people free of all that."

"Has anyone tried to at least teach the priestesses? Priests of other gods have been converted."

"Not that I know of."

The following day around mid-morning, Titus puts on his sandals.

"I am going for a walk," he tells his host.

He walks through the city, then looks to his northeast toward the tallest hill surrounding it. The hill is steep, and the road to it winds back and forth back and forth to make it manageable for human or even animal travel.

As he draws closer to the temple of Diktynna, he hears the sound of dogs or wolves or whatever they are. *The temple is surrounded by forest, so is a habitat for many such wild animals,* Titus thinks.

Though he sometimes stumbles as he walks, he keeps his eyes on the temple.

Hmmm. A lot like the temple to Artemis in Ephesus, but smaller. And the columns have been painted orange and blue. Quite spectacular, I must say.

He holds out his hands as though in supplication, palms up, to indicate his peaceful intentions to whatever priestesses must be watching him from the other side of the columns.

As he draws closer, he can just make out the statue of the goddess' presence. She is standing with a bow in one hand and reaching behind her for the quiver and an arrow. Just like Artemis. She wears a short tunic tucked under kilts like what the Egyptians wear but two-tiered and almost ruffled. Like Artemis. At her feet is a dog.

He hears a dog bark coming from the surrounding woods and pauses. All is again quiet.

He steps forward. Another bark in the distance. He stops again. Quiet.

The grand steps up into the temple are immediately in front of him. He takes the first step but pauses before putting both feet on it. No sound.

Another step. Arms still extended. Hands still palms up. Gazing at the grand imitation of Artemis.

A third step. Fourth. Fifth

Barking. Barking and growling.

Titus jerks around and looks over to his right. He sees them.

He turns and jumps down to the bottom step and takes off in a run.

Still barking and snarling. Coming closer.

He looks back and sees a dozen dogs like the one next to their goddess' statue. Teeth now bared. Snarling, snapping, straining to get to their prey.

Titus stretches his long legs and wishes he were at least forty again.

Closer they come.

He runs straight down the hill, sometimes on rock and weeds, sometimes on a bit of road.

Running. Escaping. Breath fast and short. Neck veins bursting. Lungs burning.

Teeth bared. Snapping at the heals.

One gets him in the heel.

Titus stumbles and falls. The dogs surround him, biting at his arms, his legs, his back, his neck.

"Stop!"

It is a soft voice. A delicate voice. A firm voice.

The dogs whine and back away, walking in circles now around the priestess.

"That will teach you to not spy on us. You did not have permission to come here and defile our goddess. Shame on you. Now leave, and never come back. If you do, you will die."

Titus stands. He falls.

He looks down and sees all the blood. He must get back to town before he has lost too much of it.

On his knees now, he crawls.

Closer. Closer.

The edge of the city draws near. He cannot go on. He stops. *Keep going. Get to safety.* He begins anew to crawl.

He reaches the bottom of the hill but is still outside the city.

"Help," he cries out. "Help me, someone."

A boy runs up to Titus. "Did the bad priestess get you? I will go get my *pater.*

Titus does not know how long the boy is gone. The next thing he knows, it is dark. No one has come.

Awake again, he crawls closer to the edge of the city.

His arms, his legs mangled by the fangs of the holy dogs. Neck bleeding—ultimate goal of the dogs who sought to destroy him. Torso scratched from trying to move where he should not be.

Oh, Jesus. I was...just trying to...to help them. To free...them. Save...them.

Father. Where...where are you, Father? Ughhh. I need you. Come help...me...ughhh....Father. I'm your, your son. Remember? Your son...ughhh...needs you...Father...

38 ~ MESSAGES

Shadows and monsters and blackness. Lights. Mist. Fog. Swirling. Spinning. Floating.

Songs. A mother's songs. Laughter. Of a beloved wife. Giggles. A little boy. Cooing. A tiny red-headed girl.

Clouds. Rainbows. Flickering stars.

Jesus? Is that you, Jesus?

Shimmering. Softness. Silk.

Angel wings. Hovering. Who are you?

A mighty throne.

Falling. Kneeling. Weeping.

A river so sparkling and clear and cool.

Fire. Hurt. Pain. Burning.

Ashes. Light. Blossoms.

Running. Climbing. Scaling.

Exhaustion. Tears.

"I am amazed he is still alive. How long has it been?"

"Three weeks," Pallas tells his son. "We have treated his wounds with honey. Your mother had some molded bread and used it as a starter on other pieces of bread, then put that on his wounds. It has helped much. But he still has not woke up."

"He just lies there and groans and flails his arms," Dione says, pushing back her black hair and straightening her orange skirt for something to do with her hands.

The three watch the tall and now very thin man with a new beard who had come to strengthen them. Now it is his turn.

"I don't think he wants to wake up," Kleitos says. "Before Stavros left to return home, he took me aside and told me this man has lost his entire family."

They continue to sit and watch and silently pray.

"Look! I think he just opened his eyes," Dione says. She stands and takes Titus' hand.

"We're here, Titus. You're with us. The church has been praying for you. Wake up, Titus."

"Yes, wake up," her husband says. "The church here needs you."

Titus' eyes flicker again. He opens them, squints, and closes them.

"Come on, Titus, sweetheart," Dione says.

Titus' eyes open wide. He looks around.

"Fjorta? Is that you, Fjorta?" His voice is scratchy and uncertain.

"I do not know who that is, sweetheart," Dione replies, putting her hand on his forehead.

Titus looks over at Dione, and tears come to his eyes.

"Was she your wife?" Dione asks with her soft voice, as gentle as the touch of her delicate cool hand.

Titus nods, yes.

"Well, brother," Pallas says. "You are a brave man to face those priestesses like you did. No one in this city would have dared wander up there."

Titus wrinkles his forehead, trying to re-orient himself.

"Yes," Pallas says, "you are one brave but foolish man. Everyone admires you so much, we have had several visitors worship with our congregation. We told them they could take a peek at you as you slept, but no more."

"So, I guess you accomplished some good after all," deacon Kleitos says with a smile.

Titus raises his head, then lowers it again. "Easy there," Pallas says. "You're weak. We tried forcing some juices down you, but it wasn't enough to keep you from getting thin. Would you like to try again?"

Pallas walks around to Titus' side, slides one big hand under his shoulders and grasps Titus' forearm with the other. "A little at a time. That's right."

Titus is now sitting up and feels his face.

"Yes, you have sprouted a beard, friend," Kleitos says. "I'm sure Mother will help you cut it, then shave it off."

Titus looks toward a high window, the door out of his room, and at the three who have nursed him.

"I, I have work to do. I cannot stay here."

"Woah. Take it easy," Pallas says.

"I'll bet you're starving," Dione says. "I have some broth I will bring you. If you don't throw it up, I'll bring you some stew."

She leaves the room.

"I need to leave tomorrow."

"Do you have any idea how long you have been in this bed?" Pallas asks. "Three weeks. Now, you do not have to do anything tomorrow."

"Three weeks? No, I have to leave. Paul gave me a job to do. I have to do it. I have to make him proud. No. That's not right. He's dead. But I have to continue his work. He was depending on me."

"Here is your broth," Dione says, bringing in a large mug. "Drink this. Then we will work up to something more substantial."

Titus drinks the broth with just sips at first, then gulps it. He hands the mug back to his hostess and nurse and smiles.

"Well, that brought some life back into you. I will be right back with the stew."

"Is it day or night?" Titus asks.

"It is day, but will be night soon," Kleitos says. "And that reminds me, I need to get home. I will come back tomorrow."

"You have my son to thank for your survival," Pallas says. "He is the one who found you. But it was morning when he did. You must have been laying out there all night. Your guardian angel must have sat with you through it and sheltered you under his wing."

"Here is your stew," Dione says, returning. It, too, is in

a mug.

Titus slowly swivels around, sits on the side of his bed, and takes the mug. He swallows then chews alternately and impatiently until the mug is empty. He hands it back to Dione.

"I want to stand up and walk around," he tells Pallas.

His host reaches around Titus and puts his big hands under Titus' arms. With combined efforts, Titus stands. He looks straight ahead to stop the dizziness, then turns toward the door. Pallas hangs on to one arm.

Titus takes short steps out to the courtyard and sits on a bench. He looks down at his legs, holds his arms out, and inspects his bare chest. He touches the areas that are half wound, half scar. "I guess those dogs really got me."

"I guess they did. But, by the grace of God, you survived. God has more work..."

"That's what I just told you. I have to visit the other congregations. I have work to do."

"Well, when you are tired, let me know," Pallas says, "and I'll help you return to bed."

"I need to shave," Titus says.

Dione heats some water while Pallas gets out his razor. By the time they are done shaving him, it is dark.

"Go on to bed," Titus tells them. "I will be fine."

The next morning when Pallas and Dione come out to the courtyard, Titus is dressed and has his leather shoulder bags and tent sitting out.

"You said Kydonia had a congregation, and it is only half a day's walk from here. I can find it." He stands.

"No, you don't. Sit back down," Pallas orders. At least stay and break your fast with us. Then we'll discuss our plans."

Just as they are through eating, there is a knock at the gate. Pallas answers it.

"Does a Titus Pomponius Brennius live here?"

Pallas turns and grins at Titus. "All those names are yours?"

"It must be a message from my father. I knew he would find me. He wants me to come home when my work here is done."

Titus stands, becomes a little dizzy, and sits again.

Pallas pays the messenger.

"It's taken some doing to find him," the messenger says. "I started out in Phoenix. The instructions that came with the letter was that I go to every city until I find you. Some money was left for my expenses. It's a good thing I found you now because I've just about run out of the man's money."

Pallas gives the messenger a tip, closes the gate, and hands the scroll to Titus.

"Yes, sir. My father found me. He wants me to come home."

Titus breaks the seal, unrolls part of it, and reads. Immediately he looks up at Pallas, his eyes wide, his mouth gaping.

"Well, does he want you to come home?" Pallas asks.

"It's from Paul. He's alive!"

"What? Are you sure it's from Paul?"

"Yes," Titus responds, muttering as he reads. "He calls himself a bondservant. Has he been in dungeon all this time?" He reads on.

"I need to be quiet to read this. He is reiterating the qualifications of elders and deacons. I want to make sure I have been doing this correctly."

Pallas remains silent, but watches Titus as he mutters and reads.

"Ha, ha," Titus finally says. "Paul quotes Epimenides: 'Cretans are always liars, evil beasts, lazy gluttons.' What do you think of that, Pallas?"

Pallas laughs. "He definitely has some Cretans figured out right, especially our pirates. The Romans came in and killed a lot of them, but we still have their now-grown children to deal with. Have you run in to any of them in your travels yet, Titus?"

"Not yet, but I'll continue to be on the lookout," he mutters, back at his reading.

Pallas waits.

"Hmmm.   He is apparently sending Tychicus and Artemas—they're from Ephesus—to follow up on my work. Oh, and he says Apollos and Zenas will be passing through here, apparently on their way to Alexandria since that is where Apollos is from. Apollos was apparently a great philosopher in Alexandria. Zenas is a lawyer. Wonder why I haven't met him before."

"Would you allow me to read his letter when you are through?" Pallas asks.

"And, when my work here is done, he wants me to meet him in Nicopolis. That's way up in Macedonia. I've never been to Nicopolis. My mother was born north of there in Dalmatia."

Titus stares at Pallas, then around the courtyard, and finally down at his packed bags.

"I need to go to Kydonia now. If you take me, that would be fine. If you do not, I will understand and find it myself." Titus stands.

"Oh, all right," Pallas says. "Sit back down while I get my cape and have Dione put some food in a basket for us. We should be there by noon, and that will be enough time for me to return here before dark tonight."

Soon, the two men are on the road headed east.

"The people in Kydonia claim theirs was the first city ever build on Crete. No one can disprove it. So, maybe it is so."

Titus shakes his head and grins. "He's alive. He's actually alive. Paul, how do you do it?"

"You haven't heard a word I have said, have you?" Pallas replies.

"Huh?"

Most of the rest of the way to Kydonia, the men do not talk other than Titus shaking his head now and then, grinning and muttering, "Paul is alive. Isn't that something? Paul, how do you do it?"

"Well, we're almost there," Pallas says when the sun is high in the sky. "They say the founder was King Cydon, son of Apollos and King Minos' daughter. This is their cemetery we're walking through now. Odd place for it, but the city is old and, well, I don't know why they put it here. But the statues scattered around are fine. Too bad they're mostly of gods and goddesses that don't exist. Just beyond the cemetery is the home of one of the Christians here. I can deposit you there and be on my way home."

"Paul is really alive," Titus responds under his breath. He looks over at Pallas. "How about that? He is really alive!"

"Okay, I think this is his house," Pallas says, knowing Titus is still not listening to him.

"That means I can accomplish a few things before dark," Titus responds.

Pallas laughs, stops, and knocks on a gate. The gate opens.

"Yes?"

"It's me, Pallas. It hasn't been that long since we saw each other. Let us in, Stavros."

The other man stares at Pallas a moment, then smiles. "Well, come in," he says, stepping back to open the gate wider. "So, how are things down in Polirrinia?" He looks at Titus. "What happened to you?"

"Things are normal in Polirrinia, and this is Titus who the priestesses sent their dogs after to tear apart," Pallas replies. "They tried, but Titus is stubborn and survived."

"Well sit, and tell me why you came."

"I wanted to come here," Titus explains. "I was sent here by the apostle Paul. How long has your congregation been here?"

"Since the beginning. Some of our Jews went to Jerusalem for Pentecost, heard the prophecies had been fulfilled of God coming to earth to rule us, were convinced by their miracles, and were baptized. Three thousand baptized that day. We haven't done that well here, but we are doing quite well."

"How many are in your congregation?"

"Near one hundred. More than that sometimes. We are too large for anyone's home and did not want to be separated, so bought a warehouse by the docks and meet there."

"Paul would be proud of you," Titus says. "I am too."

Pallas stands. "Well, I am no longer needed here, so I leave you with the peace of Jesus Christ, and will be on my way."

Titus and Stavros walk Pallas to the gate. Titus embraces Pallas. "Thank you for saving my life," he says in his ear while pounding him on the back. I can never repay you, but Jesus will. Somehow he will."

Pallas leaves, and Titus sits back where he was. He questions Stavros about the members and explains his purpose in coming. He pulls out Paul's most recent letter and reads it aloud.

For the next three days, Titus and Stavros discuss qualifications of elders and deacons, and any problems the congregation may be having.

On the third day, Stavros hosts a reception for Titus. People come and go throughout the day.

"God bless you, Titus, for coming and advising us."

"Titus, will you speak to our congregation on the next Solday?"

"If you run into any congregations in your travels around our island that need help, put them in touch with us."

All day, brothers and sisters come and meet Titus. Stavros hires a gatekeeper because of the steady flow of people arriving or leaving.

"Is this where a man named Titus lives," a stranger asks at the gate."

"Yes, it is."

"The high priest of Apollo is anxious to meet him. Can he come with me now? It is urgent. His advice is needed."

"I overheard you. I am Titus. If it is urgent, of course, I will go with you. Who, again, did you say needs me?"

"The high priest of Apollo himself. He said to hurry."

Titus explains to his host what is happening, then leaves with the man at the gate who he assumes is one of the lower-level priests.

They hurry down the street, turn left, then head for the harbor. Titus sees a citadel on a hill overlooking the water. Also on the hill is a grand temple to Apollo.

Titus turns to start up the hill, but the messenger motions for Titus to follow him closer to the water.

When they arrive at the docks, the messenger takes Titus to a ship.

"They have lowered the gangplank for you."

"Why here? Why not at the temple?"

"Privacy. The high priest wants privacy while he talks to you. Go on now. He is waiting for you on this ship."

Titus turns and walks up the gangplank. He pauses, looks back at the messenger, then steps onto the deck. He is relieved to notice the anchor is still down, and ropes are still around the pilings.

He walks around the deck, waiting for his instructions. A hatch opens, and a hand beckons him. Titus walks to the hatch, turns, and climbs down the ladder. Once on the lower deck, all becomes black. He looks up. The hatch is closed. He climbs up the ladder to reopen it. It does not budge.

"We have him," he hears someone above say. "He'll not escape."

39 ~ PORTALS

*I*n the blackness, Titus wonders. Had he left his bed too soon? Had he rushed off from Polirrinia too soon? What is going to happen to him now? And his work?

He does not know how long he sleeps.

Squeaking and scampering of rodent feet all along the hull. His wounds swell. Despite the coolness below, his wounds feel hot. Perhaps this time they will kill him. If not the wounds, the priests of Apollo. *Am I that dangerous? Satan, stop interfering!*

He leans his head back onto an upright beam and once again falls asleep. This time he dreams. Dreams he is on a ship and it is floating on clouds toward heaven. He has a strange crew of three, but he loves his crew—his wife, his son, his daughter. No! There are two more in his crew—his mother, and a shadowy man he thinks is his father. They climb out of the ship, slide on their own through the clouds, and leave him behind. Titus wakens. He does not know how long he has been gone this time.

His wounds itch and feel as though things are crawling on them.

He looks overhead for cracks in the boards to determine whether it is night or day. He supposes it is now night. Does it matter?

He hears footsteps. The hatch opens. It is not night after all, but shadowy. The priest who had brought him here—the trickster—calls down.

"You hungry?"

Titus does not reply. *Is this another trick?*

"I believe I asked you a question."

Still, Titus says nothing.

"I was given orders to take good care of you and fatten you up. The slave sale is in two weeks. You've got to be in good shape for it."

"Number one," Titus responds, standing now, "Why me? Number two, if you want me to look good at your slave auction, you're going to have to get me out of here. The rats have their eye on my wounds."

"What wounds? I did not hurt you. Everyone knows that."

"Let me out of here, and I will show you."

"Can't do that. You will escape."

"How long have you been a priest of Apollo?"

"One year. Why?"

"Then, why don't we have a debate on which is the best of all the gods? Just let me out, and I promise not to run."

"Everyone lies."

"I don't. Why don't you hand down a chain with a hook on the end? I'll put it around my waist, and if I try to escape, you jerk me back."

Silence.

"Well, it is a little lonely up here in this deserted ship."

"Why is it deserted?"

"I don't know. Maybe someone is going to build it bigger. Well, if you promise to not run away. Wait here."

The hatch is closed back, but Titus can hear chains being lifted and dropped in different parts of the deck.

"Okay, this one should work," the priest says, dropping it down to Titus. When you can assure me you have it securely hooked around your waist, I will let you up."

Titus smiles. *How old is this fellow? Is he that gullible? Maybe he inherited his priesthood from his father.*

"Okay, you can let me up." Titus climbs the ladder.

You'll have to sit right here," the priest says. "The other end is attached to the ship's anchor."

"Maybe you're not as lacking as I thought," Titus says.

"Lacking in what?"

"Is this my dinner?" Titus asks, sitting next to an open basket with bread in it.

"Yes, help yourself."

"So, who am I supposed to be sold to?" he says, digging through the basket.

"I don't know. They don't tell me important things. But, between you and me, I think you are going to be given as a present to the high priestess you insulted down in Polirrinia."

Titus pauses in his eating. He looks at his bread, squints, and looks up at Apollo's priest.

"Scary thought, isn't it?" the priest says. "I'd hate to be in her clutches."

"You know my name. What is yours?"

"Apollon."

"Really? That's really your name?" Titus says, grinning and chewing.

"My father named me."

"So, Apollon, why are you a priest of Apollo? Why did you choose him among all the thousands of gods out there?"

"I didn't choose him. My father did. Our family has a long line of ancestral priests of Apollo. I am proud of my family's genealogy."

Titus remembers back what Paul said in his letter to him. "Avoid foolish genealogies," he had said.

"So, you did not choose to worship Apollos. Your ancestors chose for you."

"Yes, I suppose so."

"What if all your ancestors were wrong?"

"That's ridiculous. If you are through eating, you need to go back down in your hole."

"Now, wait a minute," Titus says. "If you want me to look good for the slave auction or whatever you are setting me up for, you've got to keep my bites from getting infected. Look how red they are. They weren't that red and swollen yesterday."

"I guess you're right, but I don't know where to put you."

"How about leaving me right here?"

Priest Apollon stares at Titus a moment, looks around,

steps over to a long rope, brings it back, ties it around each of Titus' feet separately, and the ends to the mizzenmast.

He gets smarter the longer I am around him, Titus thinks as he leans his head back.

He opens his eyes. *How did it get to be morning?* He squints and looks around. "Hey, wake up there. I need to break my fast."

Priest Apollon groans, opens his eyes, stretches, pushes off his blanket, stands, and stretches again.

This time, the two men eat at the same time. Priest Apollon has yogurt with his bread.

"So Apollon," Titus says, shoving the last piece of bread into his mouth, "how do you know Apollo is the best god other than your father telling you he is?"

"I don't know," the priest says, picking up their food baskets and setting them by the gangplank.

"Have you investigated the other gods?"

"No."

"Then how do you know? Aren't you taking a big chance? The gods are jealous of each other. They could cause you to catch a plague, and you would never know why."

"The oracle at Delphi would send me word."

"And where does the oracle get his information?"

"From the Pythia. Everyone knows that."

"So, she swoons and speaks unknown tongues, and the oracle knows what she is saying in that gibberish."

"Of course. Everyone knows that."

"What if you had her speak her ecstatic sayings to one oracle, that one leave, then she speaks the same thing to another oracle. Do you think they would interpret what she said the same?"

"I don't know."

"I grew up in a city with a temple to Apollo. The priests were always sending to Delphi for the answer to a quandary. I asked a friend going with them once to perform this experiment. So, you know what the result was?"

The priest stands and walks to the other side of the empty ship and sits. He does not return.

Titus leans and looks around. *Hmmm. I wonder how*

many man-lengths this ship is. Twenty? No, more than that. Forty. I'll bet it is forty man-lengths long. So that would make the width..."

The sun is high in the sky.

"Hey, over there. I need some help with these dog bites. How about finding a sponge and a bucket and bringing some saltwater over here to put on them? It will be good entertainment for you—watching me howl in pain."

Priest Apollon stands and walks over to his charge. He stares without saying anything, finds a bucket, dips it in the Great Sea, and bringing it back full. He throws the water on Titus, sets the bucket down, and returns to his spot.

Titus recovers from the overwhelming response to his request and sputters. "Come back here. Don't you want to hear about the God I chose?"

"No," the priest calls out over his shoulder.

"Okay, so let's talk about your god for a while. I understand he is the embodiment of truth. That's why he was chosen to deliver the answers to mankind's greatest questions. Is that true? That he is truth?"

Priest Apollon stands and returns to Titus. "Yes, Apollo is the embodiment of truth and light and goodness," he says, sitting in front of his prisoner.

"Would you say truth and good are both part of the same light? Don't worshipers of Apollo says he is light, like the light of the sun?"

"Yes, he is light, and light is truth and goodness."

"How good is Apollo?"

"He is also a god of healing. He is very good. Just sacrifice to him, and he heals you."

Titus is not smiling. "I don't want to talk about that anymore. Go away."

"Good. I don't like you, anyway." The priest returns to his spot at the stern of the ship.

Titus leans back. "Jesus, help me face this. Just thinking that god's name tears at my heart. He is not a healer. He is a destroyer. He destroyed my little girl."

"What are you over there mumbling about?" the priest calls over his shoulder. "Shut up."

They are quiet the rest of the day.

When the sun reaches the horizon, Priest Apollon returns. "I shouldn't have..."

"No, it was my fault," Titus interrupts. "We both have deep feelings about our faith."

The priest opens a new basket that had been left by the gangplank in place of the empty one.

"What about your God?" the priest asks. "Which one did you choose?"

"First, he was not the son of Zeus or any of the Olympic gods or the gods of the barbarians or Chinese or Parthians or anyone like that. They had multiple sons. My Jesus was the only begotten son of Jehovah God, creator of the universe."

"You know the name of the creator of the universe? No one knows that. Everyone knows something was the original cause for the stars and planets and the earth to have been created, but no one knows his name. People just calls him the First Cause."

"Well, now you know. The creator of all things is Jehovah, and his Son was and is Jesus. He had no other sons like the gods of the nations do."

"But how do you know his name?"

"He wrote his name. Well, his prophets wrote his name. He gave his name to the great prophet, Moses, sixteen centuries ago."

"Really? Homer is the oldest author I know about, and he wrote some eight centuries ago."

"And that is where people get most of their information about the gods—other than what the priests tell the people to believe. And where do the priests get their added information?"

Titus stands, swings his arms around, pivots his head, flexes his leg muscles, and sits back on the deck.

"I already told you: From the Pythia and oracles."

"And, since no two oracles interpret the Pythia's ecstatic tongues the same...Okay, I'll back away from that. Would you like to know what Jehovah means?" Titus asks.

"Of course."

"Remember how Plato and Socrates and everyone else

says there was a First Cause that created the stars and planets and earth? Jehovah means The Self-Existent-One, or I Am That I Am.”

“Your Jehovah was the first cause? He has a name? Wait until I tell the other priests.” Apollon puts his hands on his head and looks up at the sky. “He has a name. Do you hear that, seagulls? Do you hear that, world? He has a name!”

The priest stops celebrating. “Is that when he created the stars and everything?”

“Oh, no,” Titus says. “He created the stars and everything long before that Homer wrote. He created them at least forty centuries ago, and maybe earlier than that.”

“No. No one could know that.”

“I know. In the writings of the true prophets, the prophets of truth, is a Book of Beginnings. It is based on writings left by Abraham, who was a young man when a very old man, Noah, died. And Noah was born shortly after the very first man in the world lived. The very first man, by the way, was named Adam.”

“No, you’re making this up.”

“I have personally read the Book of Beginnings. I have a copy of it and would be happy to show it to you.”

“Oh, no, you don’t. You’re not tricking me. I would have to let you loose. And if I did that, I would lose my thumbs, my eyes, and maybe then be burned at the stake. No, sir. You’re not tricking me.”

“Well, I have some praying to do to my Jehovah, so if you will excuse me,” Titus says, realizing Apollon needs some thinking time.

“Me too. I have some praying to do to my Apollo. See you tomorrow. Maybe.”

Left alone, Titus looks up at the early evening sky. He spots a large star and thinks about his ice queen. He notices another star nearby, almost as bright and thinks of his mother. Tears return to his eyes, as they are still wont to do. “How I miss you both,” he whispers.

Titus sighs and twists around in his rope and chains and can barely see his guard. “Jehovah, he is thinking about you. Help him.”

Morning. It is raining. Titus opens his eyes and sees Apollon standing over him with an empty bucket.

"Oh, did I disturb your sleep? I need to get those bites healed." He sits in front of the still-surprised Titus and grins.

He looks through this day's fresh supply of food. "And I need fatten you up more. So, guess what? He throws some chunks of meat at Titus.

"What's this?" Titus asks, holding up the white chunk.

"Fat. Fried fat. Eat up."

"I don't like fat."

"I can always draw those ropes around each foot farther apart and see how long you last."

"Okay, okay. But, give me a while. I can only eat a little at a time, or it will come back up."

"As long as it's gone by tonight. You'll have another batch tomorrow."

"What are you eating?"

"Oh, grapes, and dates, and cheese and olives. Tasty," Apollon replies with a large grin.

They eat in silence. Titus takes a bite of his fat and, rather than chew it, swallows it whole. Between bites, he looks up at the seagulls and envies them, especially the ones flying with small fish in their clutches.

Before he is through breaking his fast, Apollon disappears down the hatch.

That's a switch. Maybe I should slam the hatch closed like he did me. Well, maybe not.

"You had better not slam the hatch closed like I did you," he hears from below." You'll be left to rot and won't be discovered until you are just a skeleton."

"You do have a point," Titus calls back. "What are you doing down there in the dark?"

"I'm not stupid. I brought an oil lamp with me. I heard they stored gold down here before they brought the ship in to be rebuilt or torn down or whatever they plan to do with it."

"So, if you find gold, will you desert me on this old ship and travel around the world?"

After a while, Apollon returns above board. "The sailors must have gotten what was left behind—if there ever was any left behind. Or maybe they were lying."

"Maybe your Apollo would know. You could send word to Delphi and find out."

"You have a very good idea, there, my friend. But I would need some of that gold to pay the oracle. They do not prophecy free."

"Being prophets and priests have their benefits, don't they? You do know all the high priests of all the gods live in palaces. And you obey them and collect offerings for them and make them rich."

"Well, they deserve it."

"And how about Apollo? Does he deserve all the sacrifices made to him?"

"Of course?"

"Apollon, Apollon, Apollon," Titus replies, shaking his head back and forth. "How can you honor someone who claims to be a healer and so good?"

"Because he is good."

" When the satyr Marsyas competed against Apollos in a music contest," Titus says, " he had her flayed alive for daring him. When he and Poseidon helped a mortal build the walls of Troy and were never paid for their help, Apollo ordered a pestilence on the city."

"Well, he was good in other ways," Apollon says.

"In what ways? He was supposedly the virgin god. But he pursued and ravished many a virgin. He and Hermes alternately raped Chione. He even took a boy to his bed— Hyacinthus. How can you worship an animal like that? He acts worse than most humans I know. All the gods are just overgrown humans with more power than the rest of us mortals, so do whatever they want. They are not good, they are not righteous, they are not pure."

Apollon throws his empty basket at Titus, stands, and stomps away. This time he is on the other side of the ship. He stays out of sight and gone the rest of the day.

Titus does not receive his feeding of fat. When the stars come out, he lays his head over and dreams of his family. And his father. And the priestess. And the dogs.

"Okay, can your God do any better?"

It is morning again. Apollon is already seated in front of Titus with the two baskets.

Titus squints and rubs his eyes. "How long have you been staring at me?" he asks.

"I said, can your God do any better?"

Titus sits up. "Jehovah, the eternal First Cause, put his words in a human body so he could walk the earth with us. When his words became flesh, we called him Jesus. Jesus was the purest man who ever lived. He went about doing good. He healed people of diseases. He made people's cut-off arms and legs grow back. He raised the dead back to life. He never sinned."

"Never? That's impossible."

"It is impossible for humans, but he was part of God in a human body. Did you know some jealous priests crucified him? But, number one, he forgave them in the middle of his suffering. Number two, they couldn't kill him; he came back to life. There are hundreds of eyewitnesses who watched him die, then saw him alive again."

"How can that be? Witnesses, you say?"

"Apollon, why don't you become a Christian?"

40 ~ BREAKING AWAY

Apollon stands and looks back toward the city where he serves as priest to an evil god.

"Apollon, that Apollo you serve, he does not exist. God is not evil. Someone made the whole thing up about Apollo and all those other so-called gods. Claiming to be high priest of a god gives men power. So, they frighten people into following whichever god they conjure."

Titus stands, but cannot reach his guard. "You know God cannot be evil. He creates, not destroys. He gives life, not death."

Apollon runs to the gangplank, rushes across it, and disappears into the city. The last Titus sees him, he is still running.

Titus looks around him. "I can get out of the chains easily enough," he mutters. "Just unhook myself. But those ropes."

He looks around for some way to cut his legs free. He sees what is left of a sword to his left, but it is too far for him to reach. He searches everywhere he can see but fails in his pursuit.

He sits. *I have to figure something out.* His hand falls on Apollon's basket. He feels the knife his guard had used to cut his bread and begins to saw the ropes. The knife is not sharp. All morning he saws. At noon, he breaks free.

Well, I cannot leave now. He goes below deck, though before doing so, he gouges the knife around the hinges enough they are loosened to avoid being trapped down there again.

When it is sufficiently dark, Titus climbs the ladder, slips down the gangplank, and heads for the home of Stavros. Arriving, he raps on the gate. No one answers. He raps harder and longer.

"What do you want and why are you out at night?"

"Hurry. It's me. Titus. I have escaped. Get me inside."

Titus hears the scraping of the bar and rattling of hinges, then slips inside.

The usual oil lamps are lit on each column. Titus looks around. "Apollon, is that you?"

Apollon stands, walks toward Titus, embraces him, and pounds him on the back. He steps back, then, and looks Titus in the eyes. The former priest of Apollo is weeping.

"Thank you. Thank you for releasing me of the hold Apollo had on me and my family. I want to go back to my father and grandfather and tell them what you told me. I am free of all the slavery the gods put us through, and now only belong to the First Cause and his Son, Jesus the Christ."

Stavros walks up and puts one of his hands on each of his guests. "He was even baptized in my reflecting pool," he says with a grin.

"Come sit over here," Aello says, pointing at a grouping of benches around the reflecting pool. "I will bring some nectar out for your refreshment. And, Titus, you look terrible. I will bring you some cheese."

"That will be fine, ma'am," Titus says.

"I'm afraid your skinniness was my fault," Apollon says.

"No, I was skinny before that."

"Tomorrow is the first day of the week," Stavros says. "I have been reading the letter Paul sent to you and have passed the word around that we need to appoint elders and deacons. So, the congregation is ready."

The following morning before daylight, Stavros sneaks Titus over to the warehouse the congregation had bought to worship in. He takes Titus' belonging with them along with a mid-sized pouch for himself.

"You need to leave right after worship and appointing elders and deacons. It is an eight-day walk to where the next congregation is. Yesterday afternoon, I bought tickets for two aboard a small ship that is going to Knossos this afternoon. We will be on it."

The Christians arrive, Stavros introduces their new brother in Christ, and some of the members share with him their shame in believing in their own gods that do not exist.

They worship.

"Rather than eat our mid-day meal," Stavros says afterward, "we need to decide on who we want as our elders and deacons. Then Titus and I need to leave."

Four elders and eight deacons are chosen by consensus of the entire congregation. Someone who is tall puts a cape with hood over Titus so he can hide his identity until on board a ship. They bid him goodbye.

Titus and Stavros are now on the ship sailing east.

"How long have you been here now, Titus?"

"Two years. Paul was right, after all."

"Right about what?"

"Oh, something private and wise."

Just as the sun starts its descent down the sky, the small ship arrives in Heraklion. They disembark and walk through the city toward the mountains.

"How far are we going?"

"It will be dark by the time we arrive. The ship will be returning to my home tomorrow at daylight. So, I need to get you duly delivered to the church in Knosos so I can get back home to my wife tomorrow."

They walk farther.

"What is that over there? It's falling down."

"An ancient palace complex. Some say it is the oldest palace on the island. It was built by the Minoans when the rest of the world was just learning about culture and had no idea what writing was. Well, except for Egypt and Persia. Perhaps you can come for a tour after you settle in here. It is very impressive, especially with all the colorful columns and frescoes. Now they build palaces with white stone and put white columns all around them. Not here. Quite interesting."

"Is the city of any size, what with their palace deserted?"

"Much smaller than it used to be, but large enough."

They pass the palace and work their way into the town to a neighborhood of houses. They zig-zag down several streets.

"Well, here we are. The brother's name is Tarosias. You will like him."

Stavros knocks on the rickety gate. They hear shuffling of feet. "I'm coming. I'm coming."

Introductions are made, the men are fed by Charra, Tarosias' wife.

The next morning, Stavross says his goodbyes, wishes Titus continued success, and urges him to stay out of trouble.

"For the rest of the week," Tarosias tells Titus once they are alone, "I would like to take you to the homes of our members."

"I would like that."

"Are you sure you are up to it? You look a little thin and pale."

"I will fatten the boy up," Charra says, straightening her skirt.

"Dear, he is more than a boy. He looks to be uh, about how old might you be, Titus? Do you know?"

"I am over fifty," he says.

"Well, I am going to feed you beans and cheese all day today," Charra continues, "and potatoes and cheese all day tomorrow."

"Doesn't he get anything good like grapes and dates?"

"Of course, he does. But first, he has to eat his fattening food. By the way, dear, I am going back to the market today to get some fabric to make a new blouse."

She notices Titus staring at her.

"Oh, my clothes? This is the traditional clothing of the Minoans when Knossos was great. If I want a new idea for a skirt or blouse, I just go over to what is left of the palace and tour the rooms with the adventures of the royal family painted on the walls. I like history, don't you?"

"I suppose," Titus says. "By the way, what you are wearing is quite interesting. So, your women don't wear tunics here?"

"Tunics are boring. We like our ruffled skirts and blouses."

The rest of the week is spent fattening Titus up and visiting the members. They visit three household a day.

"Was it my imagination that everyone was analyzing my face?" Titus asks halfway through the week. I didn't think I had any scars on it."

"It's not what is on your face, but what isn't on it."

"Huh?"

"You surely noticed all us men are wearing beards. We have a Samaritan background, you know."

"No, I did not know that. What are the Samaritans?"

"We are Jews the Assyrians left behind when they conquered the northern part of the Jewish kingdom seven hundred years ago. There weren't enough of us to keep the land from growing up and wild animals moving in. So, the Assyrians sent some of their people to live among us. Of course, since there were so few of us, we intermarried with them."

"I did not know that. It seems that would have complicated Judaism," Titus replies.

Charra walks out to the men with something to drink. "This is goat's milk. Very fattening, Titus. Very, very fattening. Drink up. And husband, you only get half a mug. You're fat enough."

"I am not fat," Tarosias objects.

Titus gulps down his milk and hands it back to his hostess. He stands and walks around the courtyard.

"I am getting to like everything being so colorful in Crete. Everything in Antioch where I was born, and Rome and all other empire cities is white—white houses, white clothes."

Charra brings out another mug of milk for Titus, and he re-seats himself.

"Indeed, it did complicate things," Tarasias says, continuing their earlier conversation. "Our ancestors added their Assyrian gods to their belief in Jehovah. But I want you to know that many of us have forsaken those mixed beliefs and have returned only to Judaism."

"I suppose that is good," Titus responds. "But you are no longer Samaritans, now that you are Christians."

"We are having a controversy about that in our congregation right now and, sadly, it is tearing us apart."

"Which are you?" Titus asks his host.

"Which what?"

"Are you both Samaritan and Christian, or just Christian?"

"By birth, I am Samaritan, but not by faith. I am Christian. But I fear I am in the minority. Titus, can you help us?"

Titus smiles. "Would the authority of an apostle help you?"

"Would it ever. Which apostle?"

"Paul. I have in my leather shoulder pouch some prophecies of the Jews, and three smaller scrolls with letters Paul wrote himself."

"What could bring us together?" Tarosias asks.

"The one that addresses your problem is the earliest one I have of his. He wrote it about twenty years ago, soon after I became a Christian."

"Does it cover beards?"

The men finish up the week visiting each family. They warm up to Titus, even those who were suspicious of him at first.

Solday arrives. "We will be worshipping at the home of Noach. His is the largest home among us. He is also the leader of those who want to combine their Samaritan beliefs with their Christian beliefs."

"I hope you can handle controversy and pressure," Charra adds. "Noach can get pretty hot-headed. He's been that way all his life."

They arrive at Noach's house and are greeted with warmth and curiosity.

"Tell me, Titus," Noach says, sitting beside the visitors and putting his arm over his shoulders, "how long will to be here? When are you leaving? Not that we are anxious for you to leave, of course."

"I do not know," Titus responds. "I will be here as long

as I am needed. I am no longer in a hurry to leave as I was when I first arrived. You Cretans have apparently won my heart."

"Well, that's nice," Noach says, standing again.

He walks to the front, raises his arms, and without warning opens with a benediction. "Oh, Jehovah, most mighty..."

His prayer is long, but has a note of longing in it too, Titus thinks.

The psalms of David are sung. Songs that seem to be traditional Cretan tunes are sung.

Another brother stands and reads about Abraham and his son, Isaac.

Titus is grateful he has spent some extra time reading the Book of Beginnings lately.

The Lord's Supper is kept with its unleavened bread reminding everyone of Jesus' torn body on the cross, and its red wine reminding everyone of Jesus' blood flowing a little at a time out of his body.

Noach rises again. "We apparently have a guest with us today," Noach says. "I had not heard about it until two days ago, the day before the Sabbath. He apparently has been invited by one of our brothers to speak to us today."

The man looks over at Titus and smiles, then to Tarosias next to him and glares.

"He doesn't like it when people don't go to him for permission to do things," Tarosias whispers to Titus. "He doesn't like me very much right now."

Titus pats Tarosias on the knee. I think things are going to turn out just fine," he tells his host.

"...And so, we hand the service over to this Titus."

Titus rises. He walks to the front of the group, holds out one hand to hold his elbow, and puts the fingers of his other hand under his chin. He paces and looks at the floor. He hears shuffling of feet and whispering. He paces longer. More shuffling, louder whispers.

"Abraham!" Titus shouts. "Abraham, the great prophet and ancestor of half the world. Abraham, the prince of God. The man whose faith towers over all, and is surpassed by none."

He pauses long enough to allow the congregation to nod in agreement.

"But," he says, forefinger pointed heavenward, "when did God give him the reward for his faith? Was it while he was a young man still living in Ur?"

He waits for the congregation to shake its collective head.

"No! Was it when he moved out of Ur and traveled hundreds of *milles* north to Haran when he was seventy-five?"

More head shaking.

"No! Was it when he moved at last to his promised land and settled in Bethel?"

"Again, head shaking.

Titus ducks his head, looks both ways, and whispers as though telling a special secret.

"How about when he was eighty-five years old and finally had a son?"

Adamant head shaking.

"Do you mean to tell me his son by the slave woman was not God's reward?" he asks, still whispering.

"Well, how about when he was one hundred years old and had a son by his wife?"

The congregation smiles and nods its approval.

Titus stands straight again and smiles back at them. He takes special note of Noach. So far, Noach even agrees. He overhears Noach whisper to the brother next to him, "Aren't you glad I invited him?".

"So, are you saying Abraham received the reward of his faith when he was one hundred years old? And that reward was Isaac, son of promise?"

He puts his elbow back in one hand, holds his fingers up to his chin, and paces. All is quiet.

He turns and faces the congregation.

"But Abraham was called Father of the Faithful and father of the son of promise before he was circumcised."

Whispering among the congregation. "What is he talking about?"

"Is it more important to say we are sons of the Father of

the Faithful because of our faith, or sons of various tribes of Israel because of our circumcision?"

The congregation squints its collective eyes in confusion.

"God," Titus shouts. "God did not say the whole earth would be blessed by all the sons of Abraham. He said the earth would be blessed by one son. That son is Jesus Christ, descendant of Abraham and descendant of God Almighty."

"Now, see here," Noach says, standing.

"Brothers and sisters," Titus continues over the muttering, "Noach here is a man of wisdom. He can tell you that, if we keep the part of the Law of Moses saying we must be circumcised, we must keep the entire Law of Moses. It is all or nothing. If we circumcise because the Law of Moses says so, then we must return to having sacrifices of bulls and goats and lambs for our sins. And we must return to stoning people for adultery, and all of the other six hundred laws in the Law of Moses."

He does not give time for Noach to respond.

"Noach here will tell you that Jesus was the Lamb of God, the final sacrifice. No more Law of Moses unless Jesus repeated it in his teachings."

Titus notices people turn to see what Noach is doing. He is half up and half down, not sure what to do.

Titus lowers his voice. "Brothers and sisters, we must thank God for releasing us of those laws which were impossible to keep anyway. All the laws did was show us how sinful we are. Now let go. Let go, brothers. Let go."

His voice becomes guttural. "Who is blessed then? Those who try to bring back the Law of Moses? Blessed are the pure in heart, for we shall see God. Blessed are we who mourn, for God will comfort us. Blessed are the gentle. Blessed are the merciful. Blessed are the peacemakers."

Silence.

Titus returns to his seat.

Silence still.

Members of the congregation turn to see what their self-appointed leader has to say.

He is gone.

41 ~ FAME

Members turn to each other, questioning and wondering what just happened.

Tarosias' teenage son, Avraham, begins singing from his seat. His sister next to him joins in. Then his parents and Titus. Others look back at Avraham, smile, and they too join in.

Harmony once more. Sweet harmonious voices joined together in love for each other and their Jesus.

Tarosias stands. "We shall now have the Lord's Supper. Remember what Jesus said just before his sacrifice for us: Love one another...

They sing another psalm of the beloved David, "sweet psalmist of Israel," take up a collection for the poor in their city, and then a final prayer.

Titus resumes his place up front. "I am visiting on behalf of the apostle Paul, all the congregations of the churches of Jesus Christ on your island to set up elders and deacons. Other than the obvious excellence in Christian life and knowledge, both elders and deacons must be the husband of one wife, and elders must have children old enough to be Christians themselves. So, do you want to do this together as a group or in secret?

"Let's do it now while we're all together," one of the brothers says.

"Do you have suggestions?

"What about Noach? He already leads us."

"He gets mad too fast."

"He knows the scriptures."

"The ones he wants to know."

"Well, I suppose we could ask Tarasias to be our elder."

"No, Tarosias replies. "Titus said there must be more than one."

"What about Cyneas?"

"He's too quiet."

"He came to my house while I was still a follower of Pluto and explained the true way of Jesus. Don't you remember?"

"He came to my house in private and explained the way and how to become a Christian."

"Me too."

"Well, we have our two elders it looks like," one of the men says, standing. "Any objections? Hold up your hand. None? Who wants Tarosias and Cyneas to be our elders?" All hands go up.

After the selection of elders, the group pulls out baskets of food and eats a mid-day meal together before worshiping again afterward.

That evening Titus walks out of small room where he had spent the previous nights.

"My work here is done, and I am sufficiently rested from my, uh, unexpected adventures in the previous two cities. I must leave tomorrow. Where is the next closest congregation?"

"Dreros," Tarosias says. "It is a good two days to the southeast of here."

"How do you normally go there?" Titus asks.

"Not by water, if that's what you're thinking. We are right in the middle of the flattest and most fertile part of the island—between Mount Ida and Mount Ditke—the Heraklion Plain. We should be able to make it in two days if we leave early."

Indeed, it does take two days. The breeze comes in off both the north and south of the island, meet in the middle, tease each other, and flow through the hair of the travelers.

Titus does not even pull out his tent. No need to find a

soft spot away from rocks and sea spray.

"Well, Dreros is just ahead. This congregation seems to be doing as well as any of the rest of us. But, all the congregations are autonomous, so it's like families—we outsiders do not always know."

"What's that mountain up ahead?" Titus asks.

Mount Ditke. Half of Cretans claim Zeus was born there, and the other half claim he was born behind us on Mount Ida."

"Plato, Socrates, and all the other philosophers claim our ancient fathers were sons of the gods, so we have to take their word for it. They claim there is no other way to know."

"And Dreros is walled," Titus observes. How did that happen since all I have heard since arriving is that the sea protects its island?"

"What do you think happened? The Romans. They don't trust anyone."

Titus stares at Tarosias.

"Ohhh. You're a Roman, aren't you?"

"I'm afraid so."

"Well, you are an exception, I must say."

They approach the city gates, and the guards do not move.

"I guess we are free to enter the city of those Romans who don't trust anyone," Titus says.

Tarosias slaps Titus on the back. "Ha, ha. You got me there. Oh, come look at this."

They approach the forum.

"This column is their city's oath. It lists everyone they are supposed to be enemies with and warnings not to get involved in any controversies that tear away at their great city."

"They don't take any chances here," Titus laughs. "To be my friend, you have to hate my enemies. Ha."

They turn left down the next street, follow it two blocks, and turn right.

"I believe this is the house of Xenos," Tarosias says, knocking on the gate.

It squeaks open. A uniformed gatekeeper greets them.

"Tell your master I am Tarosias, an elder from Knossos, and this is Titus, associate of the apostle Paul."

The gate closes back, they hear muffled voices, and it opens again. This time the gate is opened wide, and they hear a husky voice.

"Oh, am I glad to see you," Xenos says. He is tall and round with black hair and a broad hooked nose.

"I am surprised you remember me, Xenos. It has been a few years. Is your wife sick? Is there anything I can do?"

"Not you," he objects, smiling. "It's you, I am glad to see," he says, turning to Titus.

"Oh, am I glad to see you." This time it is a woman's voice.

"I assume you mean Titus," Tarosias responds. "Well, everyone, may I introduce you to Titus?"

Xenos shakes hands and forearms with Titus while wife Aello holds out one delicate hand to be grasped only by the fingers.

"Come sit," Xenos says. "Oh, and we are very glad to see you too, Tarosias. Thank you for bringing Titus to us."

"Is there something wrong?" Titus asks.

"Ha! He asks if there is something wrong. What's wrong, dear friend, is Noach."

"He's here?"

"He is here in all his boorish glory. He rode in on his horse yesterday and has been making the rounds of all the Christians in Dreros."

"Oh," Titus and Tarosias say in unison.

"He is nothing but trouble."

"What does he want?" Titus asks.

"He wants to take over our congregation. He wants to push out anyone who does not agree with him."

"About what?"

"About anything. But mostly about his deserving to be leader because he is a Levite, direct descendant of Abraham through Noah's ancestor, Levi."

"So?"

"He has half the members frightened to death. He is telling them that, if they do not follow him as the appointed leader because of his birthright, they will go to hell."

Titus shakes his head back and forth and narrows his eyes. "Okay. I'm going to have to give him the treatment."

"What treatment is that?"

"Do you have any pirates nearby?"

"Ha! Why do you want to know?" Tarosias asks.

"Yes, actually, we do. They are in the port of Hierapytna, south of Lato."

Titus pulls out a map of the island he has made, identifying where the congregations are. "I am going to Lato next. I will probably be leaving your fair island from there. But you know for sure pirates are there in Hierapytna."

"Oh, yes. We have a famous one right now—Anicetus. He started out rebelling against Rome in the Black Sea north of Anatolia. Then he slipped through the Dardanelles and pesters ships on the Aegean and Great Seas. We have him until he gets bored again."

"What is he like?" Titus asks.

"He is a dandy dresser. Wears all white a lot—short white tunic with a short toga thrown over his shoulders. Has a leather belt with his loyal knife attached to it. Wears a band of pure gold around his head to keep the wind under control. Yes, a real dandy dresser."

"Is it well known he is down there?"

"Not yet. Has only been there a few days."

"And, where is Noach staying?"

"At the finest inn in the city. He says he bought a house here and is waiting for the owner to vacate."

"He has not. He does not have enough money for two houses," Tarosias objects.

"It is too late to go see him right now. And we are in need of a bath and change of clothes.

"I have a bath here in one of my courtyards that you are both welcome to use."

"Thank you," Tarosias says. If we can avail ourselves of it tonight, I would like to be back on my way home first thing in the morning."

"I tend to think Titus has some mischief swirling around in his head," Xenos says. "Why don't you stay around for it?"

"Oh, I've seen what Titus can do. He definitely will handle your situation for you."

The next morning, Tarosias leaves before Titus is up and ready. When he comes out to the courtyard, Xenos stands and grins.

"And what have we here, Titus?"

"If our friend, Noach, wants to be impressed, I shall impress him."

"So, you are actually a Roman citizen. Only Roman citizens are allowed to wear togas. Our procurator is the only Roman citizen in our city. Anicetus down in Hierapytna isn't supposed to wear one, but he hates all Romans anyway, loves to mock them, and dares them to come aboard his ship to arrest him."

"I was born in Antioch, which Augustus Caesar made free. Everyone in our city is a Roman citizen."

"Well, take a little food to break your fast, and I will deliver you to ole Noach."

"If he is at an inn, I will buy him something to feast on. If the inn is not too hard to find, I believe I will walk there alone."

Having received directions, Titus leaves Xenos' house and walks up the street back toward the forum. He walks slow, his head held high, his steps long and sure.

By the time he arrives at the inn, several pedestrians have run ahead and reported the aristocrat's approach.

He steps up onto the veranda and is met by the proprietor.

"Welcome, sir. We are honored to have you as our guest."

"I am meeting someone here," Titus says. His name is Noach. I do not know if he has any other names, but he is here from Knossos. I plan to break our fast together. Kindly show me to a private feasting room if you have one."

"Indeed, we do. Follow me."

Titus is escorted to a small room with four reclining couches formed in a circle with a low table in the middle. The proprietor orders a servant to take away two of the couches. "I trust this will be satisfactory."

"That is fine," Titus responds. "Now, here is a silver coin. I would like you to bring your finest for our feasting."

"Very well, sir. And would you like me to send in our lyre player? She is quite good."

Titus flinches. Uh, no."

The proprietor leaves, and two maids come in to deliver new wine, grapes, and figs to begin with. Titus stands at a high and wide window.

"Jesus, give me wisdom. Help me save your children here."

Titus reclines on one of the couches, takes a few figs, and lays them on a silver plate, both of which had been brought in during his prayer.

"I am honored to see you again, my friend," Noach says, entering the private room. As soon as he has a full view of Titus, he stops. His grin broadens. "Indeed, I am honored."

"Please," Titus says, pointing at the couch.

Noach stares at the empty couch a moment, pulls on his Samaritan beard, sits on it, and swings his feet around.

"If you are right-handed, you may wish to lean on your other elbow," Titus says.

"Oh, uh, yes. Of course," Noach says, shifting and trying to keep his orange-and-green striped tunic from twisting.

"Help yourself to whatever they bring you," Titus says. "The quality of their food here is exquisite."

"Oh, uh, that would be fine," Noach replies. He reaches for a grape, then draws his hand back. He furrows his brow. "Are you sure..."

"I am paying for this, Noach. I am a very rich man."

"Oh, I can tell you are," he replies, reaching now for everything on the table between them and piling them high on his silver plate."

"I hope you were not offended by anything I said up in Knossos," Titus says.

"Oh, of course not. You mean my leaving early? That was because I had an appointment down here and saw the service was going to be, well, longer than usual. My, uh, servant was waiting for me with my horse."

"Tell me about yourself, Noach?"

The Samaritan grins and nods his head several times. "You may be surprised to know this—or maybe not—but I am one of the leaders of the Kingdom of Israel."

"You mean Palestine?" Titus asks.

"Yes. That is what outsiders call it. Not that you are an outsider, of course."

"Of course."

"Anyway," he says, taking a bite of cheese, chewing it, and swallowing it as fast as he can, "I was born to be a leader of Israel. I am heir to it."

"You are an heir. I am impressed," Titus says.

"I am a Levite."

"I thought you were a Samaritan."

"Well, they aren't really the same. You see, I am actually Jewish. But I had an investment in Knossos, got to know some of the Christians there, and decided to blend in and become one of them."

"They aren't persecuted?"

"Oh, no. I have protected them from persecution by the other Jews in the city. So, anyway, you can stop calling me a Samaritan. I am a proud Jew and heir to the enviable tribe of the Levites."

"I am of a proud tribe in Anatolia—the Okondiani Tribe, and descendant of the great...Well, you do not need to hear all that. Let us return to you."

Noach stares at Titus, his eyes wide, then returns to his normal. "You may not know this, but the Levites are in charge of the grand temple in Jerusalem. It is so magnificent, sitting up there all white on Mount Moriah above Mount Zion, you can see it for *milles* before even arriving in Jerusalem."

"Is that so? I heard the Jews are in the middle of a great rebellion against Rome down there."

Noah dips his bread in fish sauce and takes a bite. "I was born to lead," he says, refusing to acknowledge the rebellion report. "You saw how well I led the congregation in Knossos. Now I am moving here so I can lead the congregation in Dreros."

"I thought you were a Jew."

"I am. But I am also a Christian. You can be both, you

know."

"No, I did not know that," Titus says, sipping some of his new wine.

Noach takes advantage of the pause and pops two large figs into his mouth.

"Yes. You have to become a Jew first. Then you can become a Christian. Christianity is just a sect of Judaism."

"Is that right? Are you sure?"

"Well, anyway, I came here to guide the leaderless congregation of Dreros. They need me, Titus. They need me."

Titus sits up, feet on the floor. Noach notices and follows his example.

"Noach. I know a place not far from here that could use a man like you. The church is not there yet, but with your leadership skills, you need to go there and try."

"But the Christians in Dreros need me."

"My friend," Titus says, now standing. "I am Titus Pomponius Brennius. I know where your skills can best be put to use."

Noach stands too and salutes Titus.

Titus walks toward Noach and puts an arm over his shoulder.

"Noach, your place is in Hierapytna. I know these things."

"You do?"

"In fact, there is an old rebel down there that needs you to tame him. His name is Anicetus. He is a fine dresser and is captain of a fine ship."

"He is?"

"You need to go down there, straighten him out, and calm the fears of the people that he has come to take over."

A servant walks in.

"Ma'am, will you please take our food and put it in a basket. This fine gentleman is going on a little trip."

"I am? Oh, yes, maybe I am."

"You have not had time to purchase a home here, so this is perfect." Titus pulls out a small pouch with coins in it. "When can you leave?"

"I guess I can leave right now," Noach says.

"Down there, you will get the kind of treatment you so richly deserve."

The servant returns, scoops the food in the basket, and hands it to Titus.

"I believe that is for this gentleman."

The maid hands it to Noach and leaves.

"Did you say you came here on horseback?" Titus asks.

"Why, yes. He is a fine steed."

"I'm sure he is. Let me walk you to your room to get your belongings. By that time, your horse should be ready."

Titus follows Noach to his room, helps him pack his belongings in a large basket, and walks beside him to the stable.

As Noach rides away, Titus hears a familiar voice.

"How did you do it?" Xenos asks, walking up from behind Titus.

"Pray for him, Xenos. That man is so mixed up. I got him out of a situation where he can only lose, and his confusion about his self-worth can only grow worse. Pray that he will come to understand the words of Jesus, 'He who wants to be first must be servant of all.' Only then can he become the man he wants to be."

"I suppose you're right," Titus.

They walk back to Xenos' house.

"Could you call the congregation together this afternoon for a special meeting?" Titus asks. "We need to talk about elders and deacons for your congregation, and I really do not want to wait until Solday. I am beginning to feel anxious to go home. Maybe someone there needs me."

42 ~ SURPRISES

"**I** am glad the meeting went well and that you now have elders and deacons," Titus tells Xenos the next day wearing a blue tunic trimmed in green and red and fitting in with Cretans again. "Are there any more congregations on the island?"

"From what you tell me of the cities you have been to, there is one more," Xenos replies. "It is at Leto. Come sit and break your fast with me."

Titus takes a deep breath and sits on a bench across from Xenos. A platter of bread and shared bowl of yogurt is in front of them.

"You look tired, Titus. Are you well?"

"No, I'm fine. I am beginning to want to go home."

"Where is home, might I ask?"

"I guess you could say I have two homes. I was born and spent over half my life in Antioch of Anatolia. I spent quite a few years in Corinth, where I have many good friends. That is where I was headed when I met the apostle Paul on board the ship, and he said the church here in Crete needed me."

"So, where will you go when you leave here? Back home to wife and children? They must miss you after having been gone from them so long. Am I right?"

"How far did you say we are from Leto?" Titus asks.

"Oh, I was prying. Forgive me. Leto is a southeast three-day walk from here. You have to go through the foothills of Mount Ditke. Leto is a seaport."

"Then, that is perfect. So, how is the congregation in Leto doing?"

"Well, our congregations are autonomous, but we do hear things sometimes. Apparently, one of their members is in some kind of trouble and may even be in dungeon."

"Why? What did he do?"

"That is all I know."

"I would like to leave tomorrow morning," Titus says. "I can go alone. You do not have to accompany me."

"Oh, yes, I do. Walking through the foothills of that mountain can be tricky. Plus, it has unexpected storms. I am going with you.

"Thank you, brother," Titus says.

That night, Titus dreams of his white-blond haired lover, his red-haired daughter, and his smart and energetic son. They are at the top of Mount Ditke, and Titus is trying to get to them but keeps slipping in the snow. Someone comes up behind him and gives him a push. It is Titus' father.

The following morning, Titus steps out to the courtyard with his three packs – two leather shoulder bags and the tent on his back.

They walk out through the south city gate and head toward higher ground. Titus is quiet the first day out.

"Did you know I used to be an attorney, what people used to call an arbitrator?" Titus says on the second day.

Xenos grins and pounds Titus on the back.

"I rather guessed."

"How?"

"Stories about you have been circulating around the island for a couple years now. You have handled some rather impossible situations. You are becoming a legend on Crete."

"Well, I hope not too much of a legend. I hope the elders in each congregation keep their members following only the teachings of Jesus and his apostles and not start making up dignitaries for the church our founders never intended."

"Oh, I'm sure they'll control themselves when recalling the days when Titus walked among us."

Titus stops and glares at Xenos. "I am serious. I ran into the problem in Corinth where some new Christians wanted to name the church's officers after the Roman system of government. They even wanted to have Vesta virgins to be married to the church or Jesus or something like that, and call them some other name All Christians are the bride of Christ. What are those people thinking? Xenos, you cannot let that happen.

"I won't, Titus. Neither will any of the other elders. We will get together and coordinate our efforts and make sure it does not happen."

"No! That is exactly what I am talking about. Your congregations must remain autonomous. Don't start organizing anything else."

They resume walking and are quiet a while.

"I have worked too hard on this island. The apostles have worked too hard. Jesus gave too much for us to start changing things. They set up the church the way they wanted it. Any more or less changes the pattern. Keep the pattern pure, Xenos. Keep the pattern pure. Promise me."

"I promise you, Titus. Sometimes my enthusiasm gets the best of me."

"Use your enthusiasm to teach people and save their souls. Then you won't have time to make changes and get away from the pattern. If there get to be too many for you elders to handle, split off, and start a new congregation. Then it will be up to them to appoint their own elders and deacons and become autonomous and completely separate from the mother congregation. Simple."

"Yes, when you put it that way. A while ago, before we changed the subject of our conversation, you said you used to be an attorney."

"Yes. But now I am supported by my aunt Chloe. Her husband was a master tile artist. Even laid tile in the middle of their courtyard that was an exact likeness of my aunt. He was incredible. She is widowed now, and I am anxious to see her again. She is in Corinth."

"I see. Did you know my wife and I went on a vacation to Corinth once? It was when we were young and..."

Mid-day the third day. The sun is high in the sky, and there is a strong breeze.

"I smell seawater. That and those seagulls up there tell me we are almost to Leto," Titus says.

"Did you guess that Leto was named after the mother goddess of Apollo and Athena, her twins?"

"Yes, I guessed as much."

"There is an old city and new city. We'll be passing through the ruins of the old city. The new city is closer to the water. The Romans came in and fortified the new city with walls."

"I guess they didn't trust the sea for protection as much as the Cretans do," Titus say, grinning.

"I guess not. Anyway, it is a busy seaport. The congregation is unique. It has all kinds of people from many walks of life—rowdy sailors, potters, shepherds, bankers—you name it."

"And they get along?" Titus responds.

"Don't know how they do it, but they do get along. Too bad about that Christian in dungeon. We'll find out what the situation is when we get there."

They are quiet the rest of the way into the city. Xenos watches Titus. His lips are pressed together, the veins in his neck are protruding, his eyes darting everywhere and nowhere.

"We need to pray more often, don't we?"

Titus looks over at Xenos as though he had forgotten where he was.

"Indeed, we do."

When they arrive at the city, they pass through the main gate into a courtyard, then another gate at the other end, and into a second courtyard. When they pass through the third gate, they see they are in the city proper, but it is sprawling and has many hills. Ahead of them are stone steps going down into the valley and center of the city.

On their right are terrace houses with the roofs acting as verandas for the houses above them. At the bottom of the steps is a columned portico with benches in it. Titus and Xenos find a bench and rest momentarily.

"Well," Titus says, "I see a temple to Leto on that hill to our right. Shall we go left?"

The men walk past a sanctuary and public cistern with steps down to it. On the other side, they see what seems to be government buildings.

"And, of course, they will have an eternal flame to the goddess Vesta inside so she will protect the city," Xenos says.

They continue walking past the villas. On the other side, the houses become smaller. They arrive at a gate with a fish on it and knock.

The gate opens, and a woman about the age Fjorta would have been had she lived, stands before them. "Yes? Are you the attorney we sent for? Come in?"

"I am sorry," Titus responds, "but I do not believe we are who you think we are. We are Christians from Dreros and Corinth."

"Who is it, Desponia?" a male voice calls out. "You know you should not open the gate without finding out who it is. Oh. Is that you, Xenos?"

"Yes, it's me."

The two men walk to each other, embrace and pound each other on the back.

"And this is our brother, Titus."

"Oh, I heard you were making the rounds of the congregations. You've been here a couple years by now, haven't you?"

"It seems longer," Titus replies with a smile.

"Come in and sit," Desponia says. "I will bring you something refreshing to drink.

Horos takes his guests to the solarium and they sit around a reflecting pool.

"So, how has the congregation here been doing since I saw you, Horos?"

"Not too good. We have been hit from both sides. The Jews persecute us awhile, then the followers of Leto and her twins—you know, Apollos and Athena—come at us. A couple of our members lost their jobs, another one lost his house to a creditor who suddenly decided to collect on a long-term loan, and half the shops at the agora will not sell to us. It's so rocky here, it's hard to grow your own food, though some members with houses on flat ground can. But, I do not wish to burden you with our problems. We will survive."

"What about the member who is in dungeon? Did we hear right?"

Horos bows his head. "Yes, you heard right."

"What were the charges?" Titus asks.

"Theft. But he did not take that money."

"Theft of what?"

"A tariff booth down at the docks." The tax collector swore he left thirty-five silver coins in his booth when he closed up one night, and the next morning it was gone."

"That's a lot of money," Xenos says.

"A year's wages for many people around here," Horos replies.

"His wife and children are desperate," Desponia says, arriving with a tray on which is a pitcher and three goblets. "Of course, they are not going to let him out of dungeon until he pays it—or someone pays it."

"We have been collecting money from the other Christians here every Solday," Horos says. "But with so many other hardships, we have not collected near enough. We just keep praying for a solution."

"He could die in that dungeon," Desponia says. "The conditions are terrible. Most men do not last more than five years in there with the rats and snakes."

"What day is it? I have lost track," Xenos asks.

"Four days before the Lord's Day," Horos replies.

"Then, if I leave first thing tomorrow, I will be home in time. "I am sure you and Titus will find much to talk over."

The next morning after Xenos leaves, Titus asks Horos if he can visit the brother in dungeon and then the owner of the tariff booth.

"I do not know if the guards will let you in the dungeon," Horos says.

"They will."

After breaking their fast, the two men walk back down their hill to the center of the city and to the dungeon under the government building.

"This gentleman would like to see Argos."

"Stand back," the guard orders, aiming his spear in their direction. "You are not allowed here.

"Uh, sir," Titus says, standing as tall as he can and with his chin a little thrust forward.

"I have important business with Argos and demand access."

"Who are you to demand anything? Stand back."

"I am Titus Pomponius Brennius, Roman citizen."

The guard stares at Titus a moment. "Can you prove it?"

"If you will allow me to return to the home of Horos, I will bring something back with me to satisfy you. However, that would be wasting my time. I demand to see the prisoner and now."

The guard looks around. He lowers his spear. "Go on in. This other man stays."

The guard pounds on the iron door, and another guard opens it. "Take him to Argos."

The second guard grabs keys and a torch and leads Titus through a second iron door. As they progress down the narrow corridor, the stench hits Titus. He hopes the guard did not hear him nearly wretch.

What Titus estimates to be halfway to the end, the guard stops. "Step back, Argos. You have company."

In the dim light, Titus can see Argos stand and move to the back of his cell.

The guard unlocks the gate, lets Titus in, and locks it back. "Yell when you want out."

"My name is Titus," he tells Argos as soon as the guard leaves. "I used to be a lawyer, and want to see if I can help you."

"Why?"

"Because more importantly, I am your brother in Christ."

"Well, they say I stole thirty-five pieces of silver from the tariff booth. I never go down to the docks. I didn't do it. But someone is claiming I did."

"Do you know why?"

"Who knows? I may have made someone mad, and they

are punishing me for it.”

“Or just because you are a Christian.”

“Probably that.”

“Well, I am going to see the tax collector now. Is there anything else you want me to know?”

“Will you pray for me? I’m really scared.”

Titus puts his hands on Argos’s shoulders and prays for him, then turns and calls out to the guard.

“You won’t forget me in here, will you?”

“I will return. I promise,” Titus says while the guard is re-locking the barred gate.

Back outside, Titus rejoins Horos, who puts his hand over his nose and mouth. “Sorry friend, but you brought the smells out with you.”

Titus steps back. “He is very frightened, and he should be. I could possibly send for the money to pay off the tax collector, but conditions down there are bad, and it may take a long time to hear back about the money. I do not see how he could live another year. How long has he been down there so far?”

“Two years.”

“Which way to the docks? I’ve got some investigating to do.”

The two men leave out the main gate and down the steep road leading to the Mirambello Bay.

They walk along the docks asking at each tariff booth which one was robbed.

“I was.”

“And your name, sir?”

“Why?”

“I am trying to figure out a way to get your missing money back to you,” Titus says.

“Oh, well, my name is Balios. So, are you going to get my money back for me?”

“When did the theft occur?”

“Two years ago. I remember it exactly. I had thirty-five silver coins at the end of the day when I closed up. The next morning, they were gone.”

“And how do you know it was Argos who took the

money?"

"He is the only one who could have. He was hanging around down here by himself when I closed up. All he had to do is wait a while until it was dark, slip in, take the money, and disappear from the docks."

"So, the money was taken shortly after you closed. Not in the middle of the night or just before you opened."

"I told you. He was the only one left at the docks near my booth when I closed up. Why would he go home, then come back, steal the money, then go back home?"

"And where exactly does—or did he live?"

"I don't know, and I don't care. He stole it, and I want it back."

"Thank you for your time," Titus says. "I may return to ask you a few more question."

"Just get my money back."

Titus turns to Horos. "While I am down here, I need to find out which ship is going to Corinth and purchase fare," he says.

As Titus approaches the ship, he passes two passengers standing on the dock and overhears them.

"Paul assured us Titus is here on Crete, but how are we going to find him?"

Titus stops. He turns around and stares at the men. He steps toward them.

"Uh, pardon me, but did I hear you mention Paul and Titus?"

"Yes, you did. Do you happen to know Titus?"

"I am Titus. Are you, well, are you by any chance Apollos and Zenas?"

43 ~ MIRACLES

"*T*itus? Yes, yes. I am Apollos."

"And I am Zenas."

"You are a lawyer, aren't you, Zenas?"

"Someone must have told you my secret," he replies.

Zenas is short and graying at the temples of his dark hair. His nose is pointed, and his lips naturally turn up on the corners.

"Who do you have here, Titus?"

"Oh, these are the men I was telling you about, Horos. Paul, in his letter, said they were coming."

"Just passing through," Apollos explains in his low voice. He is of average height and has thick Egyptians hair.

"Welcome to our island for as long as you care to sojourn here," Horos replies.

Titus looks over at Horos. "They could at least stay one night while they are way to Alexandria," he hints.

"And that night will be spent in my home. Come, gentlemen. Follow me."

"Uh, did you leave anything on the ship?" Titus asks.

"No, we have everything with us that we need," Apollos says.

"So, what kind of law have you been practicing, Zenas?" Titus asks as they walk up the steep hill to steps into the city.

"I do whatever is needed."

"Have you ever defended a criminal?"

"Like for murder? No."

"How about theft?"

"I have that."

"Uh, Horos, we need to stop by the dungeon on our way to your home."

"What's going on here?" Zenas asks. "We are just going to be here overnight, then it's on to Alexandria as planned."

"Zenas, this man is a brother in Christ."

"Oh."

"Persecution here is bad. Zenas was one of their targets. He was framed for stealing thirty-five pieces of silver and has been in dungeon two years while his congregation tries to come up with that much money. Until now, he has not had an attorney because, of course, he cannot afford one."

"Lead on, then. We must not let think he has been deserted."

"Apollos, why don't you come on with me, and they can catch up later?" Horos says.

They split up. Titus uses his most authoritative voice to get both him and Zenas into the dungeon. Sometime later, they come back out to the street, coughing and trying to get rid of the stench now battering their lungs.

Back at Horos' house, the four discuss the situation.

"I am so close to home," Apollos says, "I can give you the rest of my travel money. The ship we came in on is continuing on to Alexandria tomorrow, and we have both paid our fare all the way there."

"Well, if Apollos will support me until I can get some work in Alexandria, you can have the rest of mine also," Zenas says, pulling out his money pouch.

Titus stands and disappears into the room Horos has given him to sleep in. He returns and hands Horos his money pouch. "I am ashamed I have held out. I thought my needs were more important than Argos'. Here, add this to their contribution."

"I am overwhelmed by your sacrifices, brothers," Horos says. "I really am.

Desponia enters the courtyard where they have been talking. "Who have we honoring our home now?" she asks her husband.

"Sweetheart, these men are Apollos and Zenas, brothers on their way to Alexandria. I am overwhelmed. They and Titus have just donated all they have to help Argos pay back the silver the officials claim he stole."

"Oh, we must take it into the city and pay it to the clerk right now," she responds. "His widow—she catches herself with her slip of tongue—his wife will be so encouraged."

"Grand idea, dear. I shall do that while our guests rest."

"You gentlemen must be hungry," she tells the guests after her husband leaves. "I will bring a tray of cheese and grapes out to you. You do like cheese and grapes, don't you?"

"Did you already have your fare for a ship back to Corinth?" Apollos asks.

Titus is quiet a moment. "Well, I guess not. I will be staying to do some arbitration work until I have enough for fare."

"How long will that take?" Zenas asks.

"I do not know. Well, I have not helped them select elders and deacons here yet. That will be the first thing on my list of things to do."

Horos returns. "The clerk was impressed. He does not understand why so many people would help a proven thief. I explained two things to him. Number one, he is not a proven thief. Number two, Christians always come to the aid of each other, just as our Lord Jesus Christ taught. 'Even if we are mean to you Christians, you keep doing things like this?' he asked. I told him there is no end to the love of Christ and his followers. He has his curiosity up. Now let's see if he is strong enough to become one of the persecuted ones."

"Uh, Horos, it looks like I will not be able to return to Corinth as soon as I had hoped."

"Oh, that's right. That was your ship fare you gave me. Well, you stay here as long as you want."

"That is most kind of you. If you need any legal papers drawn up, let me know. And I would appreciate it if you would spread the word around the city that my services are available."

"Indeed, he will," Desponia says, coming in with a tray of cheese and grapes for everyone. "What are your plans for tomorrow?"

"I would like to go back down to the docks and interview the accuser, the one who claims Argos took his money. Zenas, would you come with me? You may have some insight into something I missed."

"Certainly. We are not in that much of a hurry to get to Alexandria, are we, Apollos?"

"We must stay and help our brother."

The following day, Titus and Zenas leave Apollos and Horos behind to trade stories of their youth and walk down to the docks.

As they pass the ships tied up there, Titus thinks he hears a familiar voice. He turns around and walks closer to the voice. The man turns and the two men lock eyes.

"Tychicus? Is that you?"

"Titus! Friend! Brother!"

The two men walk toward each other, embrace, and pound each other on the back, easily done with both being tall men.

"Paul sent me to replace you," Tychicus says. "He said you are doing a fine job of helping the congregations appoint elders and deacons."

"Ha! How does he know? I haven't written him. Though I suppose I should have."

"That's Paul for you. Oh, he is out of prison now. Nero freed him. The emperor said the whole accusation thing by the fanatical Jews—as he called them—was ridiculous, and he was not going to let those rebels tell him what to do. Things are pretty bad in Jerusalem, if you didn't know. More legionnaires are being sent down there from their headquarters in Syria to control them."

"Well, you are here, and I am very glad to see you," Titus says, putting an arm over Tychicus' shoulder. "And how is the banking business?"

"Fine. I have good employees and can leave home periodically because of them."

"You are going to be surprised at who else arrived yesterday," Titus says. "Apollos and Zenas."

"Really?" Tychicus responds. "Apollos baptized me in Ephesus the first time."

"The first time?"

"Well, he did not know at the time that Jesus had arrived. So, he baptized us into John the Baptist's baptism. When Paul came shortly after, he baptized us into the Father, Son, and Holy Spirit. It will be grand seeing Apollos again. I really respect the man."

"Ahem."

Titus turns.

"I believe I am tagging along with Titus," Zenas says.

"Oh, in all the excitement, I forgot you. Sorry, Zenas. Uh, Tychicus, you may as well go with us if you're going to take my place. You need to know what is going on."

The three men find Balios and interview him.

"He is definitely lying," Zenas says as they head back up into the city.

"What's going on?" Tychicus asks.

They explain the situation to him. "He has been down in that dungeon two years. You know what the conditions are. He cannot survive much longer," Titus explains.

"Take me to him," Tychicus says.

The three walk over to the dungeon.

"No! I draw the line. You are not going to bring someone else in to see that thief. No! Absolutely not!"

Tychicus pulls out his money pouch. "Would a bronze coin make it worthwhile to you?"

The three are admitted, talk to Argos, pray with him, and assure him they will get him freed somehow.

"You are bringing us a household of mighty soldiers of the Lord," Horos tells Titus when they arrive and introductions are made. "Xenos is going to wish he hadn't left so soon."

"Tychicus is going to take my place on the island, so will need your help," Titus says. "Oh, and I took him to see Argos."

"How much money is still lacking?" he asks Horos.

"Well, I believe we have paid the value of about nine

pieces of silver so far."

Tychicus pulls out his money pouch. He pours his silver coins into his hand, then counts them out on a nearby table. "Will that be sufficient to bring him out of that death hole?"

"Brother!" Horos replies.

Titus smiles. "Tychicus is a banker."

"Jesus has sent you here for such a time as this," Horos replies.

"You can pay me back by telling me all about the congregations on the island," he tells Horos.

"Horos and I both will," Titus says. "I was going to be leaving this week, but something came up and I will be here a little longer."

"I thought you would be anxious to return home. You have been here at least two years," Tychicus replies.

"Oh, my. I think I have neglected a very important duty," Tychicus says. He looks in one of his leather pouches. "Here it is. Titus, this is a letter for you. Actually, there are two letters."

"Must be Paul making sure I do my duty here," Titus replies, reaching over and taking the scrolls. "Don't know who else would be writing other than Stephan."

Titus opens one scroll, jerks his head noticeably back, stands, and walks to a corner of the courtyard.

"Is something wrong, Titus?" Apollos says. "We're here for you."

Titus glances up at them, then back at his letter. He turns his back on them. No one talks. He reads for a long time.

"The scroll wasn't that long," Zenas whispers. "What's he doing? Must be bad, bad news."

At last, Titus turns and faces his friends. "It's my father."

"Oh, no."

"Not that. He wants me to come see him. He has been distant from me for the past forty-two years since I was eleven and my mother passed away."

"So, it's good news," Tychicus says. "Isn't it?"

"It has to be good news. Well, I will go there first, then go to Corinth. Necapolis, where Paul wants me to meet him, is not that far from Corinth."

Silence.

"Of course, it means I will have to work a little longer for my ship fare."

"Aren't you going to open the other letter?" Tychicus asks.

"Oh, yes. I forgot."

Titus breaks the seal and unrolls the scroll. He reads and looks up at his friends.

"He has sent me a banknote for my ship fare and traveling expenses."

"Uh, oh," Horos says. "The bankers here will not have anything to do with Christians."

"Horos, take me to see one of your bankers," Tychicus says. "And, Titus, you come too with that banknote."

The three men are gone an hour.

"How did you convince them?" Zenas asks when they return with the banknote cashed.

"I own them," Tychicus says. "So, it looks, Titus, as though you will not be able to train me after all. Horos here will be stuck with the job."

"Horos," Titus says. "Could you call the church together tomorrow? I need to finish the job Paul sent me here to do. I will help them appoint elders and deacons, then my work will be complete.

"I can do better than that," Horos replies. "It is only mid-day. We have a message chain. All anyone has to do to get emergency news out to everyone is tell our five coordinators. They start the chain, and usually within an hour, everyone has been informed. I will go into the city right now and inform our message leaders."

"Oh, I forgot something important," Titus says. I cannot leave yet. I have to defend poor Argos. If I can prove he is not guilty, his accuser will have to pay him double—seventy pieces of silver."

"Uh, Titus," Zenas says. "Apollos can go on to Alexandria without me. I will stay here as long as it takes to prove him not guilty."

"You can?"

Horos slaps his knee. "I have never in all the years I have lived, seen so many amazing things come together exactly at the right point in time and from so many directions. If this isn't miraculous, I don't know what is."

"I will walk you part of the way into the city," Titus says, "then go on down to find a ship going north hopefully tomorrow. I hope it isn't too late in the season."

The evening is a whirlwind for Titus. Elders and deacons are duly chosen, and Apollos and been kind enough to preach one of the most eloquent sermons anyone has ever heard, even if it isn't Solday.

The next morning, Horos, Desponia, Apollos, Zenas, and Tychicus walk with Titus down to the harbor. When they arrive, there is a strange thin man with pale skin and sunken eyes sitting on the ground near the ship's gangplank. Next to him is a small woman and three children.

"Oh, that is Argos and his family," Desponia announces.

Titus kneels in front of the brother, still weak from his ordeal. "God answers prayer," Argos whispers to Titus.

"In ways we never dream possible," Titus says, clutching his father's letter.

As the ship takes Titus home, he thinks back to his mother and father as they were in their youth. He thinks back to his ninth birthday. He tries not to think of what happened when he was eleven, but cannot help it. That is when they had grown apart, each in their own agony. Even when his little girl had died, his father could not express any sympathy other than being there at her grave.

How could I not have understood? It took the loss of my Fjorta to understand. Then it was too late.

And Sirius. My smart little boy. I tried not to be like my father. I tried to give him all the attention he needed. Did I?

For five days, the ship works its way from island to island and then up the coast of Anatolia.

Time. Why does there have to be time? Well, I've waited forty years, I guess I can wait four more days. Well, six, since I'll have to travel the rest of the way to Antioch after I get off the ship.

Titus tries to sleep to make time go by faster. When he

sleeps, he dreams his father has become an eagle and has flown away. Or his mother has turned into a star.

He remembers the storms on Crete. The storms that had taken his Paul away. And the ship that had brought news that Paul had survived. Miracle of miracles.

God, how do you do that? Silly question.

He leans onto the ship's rail and watches the seagulls following the ship and hoping for a morsel for their dinner.

The days. The hours. The minutes. The only conversation he hears among the crew and the passengers is how Nero was assassinated. "Now, the fighting begins between everyone who wants to be the next Caesar."

"Keep him alive until I get home, Jesus. Keep him alive."

"Who? Which one do you want to be the next Caesar," a passenger says who overhears Titus.

"My prayer was for someone far more important than Caesar," he tells the passenger as he walks over to the rail.

At last, the ship arrives at Ephesus. Titus tucks his now-worn letter from his father into his pouch with the other important scrolls, gathers up his other pouch of personal necessities, and his tent.

Onshore, he approaches a stable that rents horses. "How much for your fastest horse?"

"Not anything you can afford if you plan to ride him to death."

"I'm sorry. I guess I sounded too desperate. I will take good care of your horse. But, I still need your fastest one."

The exchange is made, and Titus gallops around the south side of Ephesus and onto the highway. Just after dark, he stops, waters and feeds his steed, sets up his tent, and tries to sleep.

Some time during the night—he is not sure—he rises, takes down his tent, examines the horse to make sure he is rested enough and resumes his journey home.

At sundown on the second day, he sees ahead the gates of home. He gallops through, waves at a familiar guard, and slows his mount to a trot. He passes the familiar theater, turns right at the artificial waterfall, passes the temple of Apollo, and turns twice more.

Home. He is home. He dismounts and looks at the familiar gate. What will he find? Is his father still alive? Had he wanted to see Titus on his death bed? Will his father love him again?

44 ~ HOMECOMINGS

At least the gate has been cleaned up, he thinks as he knocks on it.

"Who's there?" he hears from the other side of the gate.

"Cornelius? Cornelius? You're back? Let me in. It's me. Titus."

The old hinges do not creek and open the gate soon enough.

Cornelius, though as feeble as ever, has a new uniform on. "Welcome home, Titus. Your father will be overjoyed to see you."

Titus pauses and stares. "Overjoyed?"

"Indeed, yes, sir."

Titus passes the old man, hurries through the outer reception area where his mother's statues of the Muses and Apollo used to be. He throws open the inner gate and sees the old courtyard clean, fresh water in the reflecting pool, pots of miniature evergreen trees placed between the columns, and Lydia calling up the familiar stairs.

"Master, your son is home!"

Before Titus has a chance to start up the steps, he hears his father at the top.

"My son, there you are!"

Justus, makes his way down, one step at a time, hampered by his arthritic knees, but with a smile.

Titus stares. How many years has it been since he has seen his father smile?

When Justus reaches Titus, he holds out his arms. Their eyes lock, both of them misty. "Come to your father," Justus says.

Titus holds out his own arms, and father and son embrace. They rock back and forth a few times, and Titus remembers how his mother used to hug him that way in the distant past.

They pull apart and stare at each other, both smiling. Titus pulls away and shakes his head, now only half smiling.

"I thought you were dying, Father. And what has happened to you? You're different. I haven't seen you like this for forty years. What is going on?"

"So much has happened, Son. Come sit here. Let us talk."

They sit in their usual gilded chairs by the pool, facing each other.

"First of all, it finally rained. This past year we have had more prosperity in Antioch than we have had in years. The crops are amazing and bringing wealth back to us."

"And the second thing?"

Justus stares at his son and moment. "How do I break the news to you?"

"You got remarried?"

"No, no. Nothing like that."

"Then, what?"

"I, well, I became a Christian."

"You what?"

"When? How? Who? Well, I know the how, but when and who convinced you?"

"The first thing I was told I had to do is forgive everyone who has done me wrong or who I thought had done me wrong, and the second thing was to ask forgiveness of everyone I had wronged."

They would not let me become a Christian until I at least started the whole forgiving process.

Silence.

Justus grows serious and leans forward in his chair.

"Son, I regret all those years I neglected you. I buried my emotions, my heart, my soul. I buried you when I buried your mother. I even blamed you when there was no one to blame. I am so very sorry, Son. Will you ever be able to forgive your old father?"

Silence.

Titus stands and walks to the gate, then back again.

He forces a confused smile. "When did it happen?"

"About a month ago," Justus replies.

"That's all? You've changed this much in a month?" Titus sweeps his hand around.

"No, the rains came back last year, and that helped. But it was last month I became a Christian."

"Who? Where?" Titus reseats himself across from his father.

"Ephesus."

"Ephesus? What were you doing in Ephesus?"

"Antioch is growing so prosperous, I was chosen to go to Ephesus to see if there were any bankers who would like to move here."

"Bankers? You met Tychicus?"

"Yes, I met Tychicus."

"He is the one who taught you, converted you, and baptized you?"

"The very one."

"When he delivered your letter, he did not say he even knew you."

"I told him not to tell you."

Titus stands and paces again. He pulls his fingers through his thick reddish-brown hair. He looks down at the cleaned-up tiles, up at the sky over the courtyard, over at the stairs on which his father had so often run away from him.

He feels his father's presence.

"Oh, Son. How I have longed for your forgiveness. How I have prayed for God to forgive me for what I did to you. Can we ever be father and son again? Is it too late for us?"

Justus stands and holds out his arms. "Please?"

Titus, now fifty-three years old, steps closer, falls into the arms of his father, and weeps. Their tears mingle with their hearts.

At last, Justus pulls away. He smiles. Titus smiles.

"Well, now, what shall we do first? Go riding together? Oh, I know what. Wait here."

He steps toward a small room Lydia lives in. "Oh, Lydia. Do you have it?"

"I gave it to Cornelius to polish up for you."

"Oh, Cornelius. Do you have it?" Justus asks.

Cornelius walks out to the courtyard with a bundle inside a silk bag and hands it to Justus.

Justus carries it to his son with both hands outstretched as though he were carrying an infant in them."

"I believe this is yours."

Titus takes it and reseats himself.

Justus sits across from him, leaning forward and grinning.

"My lyre? You've had my lyre all these years?"

"Your birthday lyre. Do you remember any of the songs your mother used to sing? Let's sing them now."

The rest of the evening is a dream. Titus wonders when he will wake up.

Morning comes. He sees his lyre next to his bed. He splashes water on his face and takes the stairs down to the courtyard. It is still fresh and inviting.

He sees Lydia. "Is my father up yet?"

"No, he rises later than he used to. But he will come down in a little while. Don't you worry, Titus. He really has changed. It is almost as though your mother was back among us."

"Perhaps she is in some way, Lydia."

Justus comes downstairs an hour later. "Tomorrow is the Lord's Day," he says.

"Did you invite the church to begin meeting here again?"

"Better than that. The new prosperity in Antioch has also helped the church. We went together and bought the old synagogue."

"The Jews are gone?"

"Not completely, but they lost so many members to Christianity, they were having a hard time keeping their building up. And Jerusalem is so full of problems right now, they are unable to send help."

"Then, tomorrow, you and I will worship together," Titus tells his father.

Another week goes by. The kind of week Titus had given up hope would ever happen.

Sometimes happy. Sometimes remembering when. Sometimes sad.

"Father, I never understood the pain you endured when you lost Mother."

"I know, Son. But I never lost a daughter and a son. God spared me that. How old would your children be if they had lived?"

"Well, little Kharis would be around twenty-seven years old now. So, I would probably be a grandfather, and you would be a great grandfather."

"And Sirius?"

"He would be I guess close to seventeen." Titus leans back in the gilded chair. "Our lives would have been so different if..."

"Yes. Perhaps God took them to keep them from some kind of tragedy they may have faced had they stayed here," Justus sighs.

"Or perhaps they are having more fun in heaven than they would have here. By the way, how old are you now, Father?"

"I'm seventy-nine years old, and not too bad for my age. Plus, I'm eating better now that Jesus and Tychicus have helped me break through my dreadful shell."

The second week ends. Justice notices a subtle change in Titus.

"You are growing restless, Titus. What is it?"

"Paul. He is the one who taught and baptized Fjorta and me a long time ago and came by here a few times after that. He is the one who sent me to Corinth to help straighten out some major problems there. Oh, and did I tell you I ran into Stephan there? Oh, my. We enjoyed being together again. Neither one of us had changed at all."

"No, I think you forgot to tell me about Stephan. So, he

turned out all right after all?”

“You may remember he moved to Rome to study under a philosopher about our age. He did well. Anyway, it was Paul who sent me to Crete. That’s where I have been for the past two and a half years.”

“And now he has another assignment for you,” Justus replies, not smiling.

“I am needed, Father. He said he was going to spend the winter in Nicopolis. If I can find a ship this late in the season across the Aegean to Corinth, I will go there and visit with Aunt Chloe and Stephan and the church there. Ephesus is about four days across the Aegean to Corinth. Nicopolis is about two days by ship past that. So it will take me a good week to get to Paul.”

“Do whatever you think best, Son.”

“Father, these past two weeks have been heaven on earth.”

“For me too, Son.”

“But now, I am needed.” Titus looks at his father, whose eyes are watching a dove sitting on the ledge of the pool, and understands.

“Yes, we do need each other. But others need us also, just like all those years the city needed you as its praetor to be its supreme judge and leader. Now I am needed by the church kind of in that way.”

“Go upstairs with me and help me pack, Father.”

“Well, I want to continue to support you,” Justus says, watching his son gather his most important scrolls together. He notices Titus included his letter to him down in Crete. “Son, you are making me proud.”

Titus stops, stands straight, and stares at his father. He steps over and embraces him. His shoulders tremble. Justus puts his old arms around his son, and pats him.

His body calms, and Titus draws back, tears still in his eyes. “You have no idea how many years I have longed to hear you say that.”

“I knew that, Son. But I was so absorbed in myself and wanting to punish the world for taking the love of my life away, I couldn’t. I was being selfish.”

Titus gathers up his two leather shoulder pouches and his tent and takes them down to the front gate. He goes over to the public stable where he had turned in his rent horse upon arrival and rents a different horse to return to the coast.

The following morning when he starts down the stairs to the courtyard, the steps are white. He looks down. The entire courtyard is white.

"Snow?" he says to himself. "It never snows here."

"Well, looks like it did this time," Justus says, standing behind him. "Perhaps Antioch needs you more this winter than Paul does. Corinth and Nicopolis will still be there next spring.

"So, we wasted our goodbyes last night?" Titus says.

"Looks like it," Justus replies. "Come back inside. I have something to show you. I forgot to show it to you before. Well, it wasn't finished until yesterday."

They walk up the corridor to Justus' *officium* and pass it. Justus opens a door that used to belong to Kharis. "Do you like it, Son? It is yours. The writing table is of cedar and ivory. Over there are cubicles for you to put your scrolls in. Over there are shelves to put your baskets of supplies on."

"How did you know it was going to snow today?" Titus asks.

The winter passes. Titus is called on often to preach for their congregation, just like at the first. Justus sometimes does but says his eyes aren't good enough anymore, and Titus is a better speaker than him.

Spring arrives.

"It has been good, Father. You have made me very happy."

"Yes, it has been good. Very good. We have made each other happy. God indeed blessed us, especially with that snowfall we had."

"Well, I'm glad it snowed."

"By the way, I want to keep supporting you. Here is enough traveling money to get you to Corinth, and enough to get you on to Nicopolis. If Paul sends you somewhere, let me know."

The men smile, embrace one another, and Titus steps

over to the gate.

"You know, you always looked so much like your mother—those big eyes, your broad straight nose with the tip turned down, and your one dimple."

"Don't forget my pointed chin," Titus says.

"Yes, and your pointed chin."

Titus leaves. He stops at his mother's grave, then heads for Ephesus.

A week later, he is at the isthmus and walking toward Corinth. He passes the Temple of Poseidon, stops, stares at it, and whispers, "I will always love you both."

Once back in Corinth, he walks west a few streets and arrives at a familiar gate.

"Hey, Stephanus. Do you have any pots for a traveling man?"

The gate opens, the two friends grin and hold their arms out to each other. They embrace and pound each other on the back. "My family is at our booth at the market. As the family slave, I stayed home to make more pottery. Come in. Sit."

They sit on wooden benches Stephan has sanded down and put enough coats of oil on that they shine.

"I didn't know you were back," Stephan says, wiping his nose on his shop rag. "I must say you look better than I thought you would. You were in pretty bad shape when you left here."

"Yes, I was. My heart was crushing the life out of me. My father was no comfort, so I went in search of Paul. We met by accident on the same ship, and he told me to go into Crete and help them set up elders and deacons in each congregation. I was in no shape to do that. I just wanted to run away from the world."

"But you did stay, didn't you?" Stephan says, coughing into his hand.

"Do you know what he told me? 'Go in the strength you have.' Turns out that is what God told Gideon when he asked for a miracle. Not long after I resigned myself to staying, I met a man—probably not by accident—whose wife had been drowned for being a Christian just a few days before my arrival. It was exactly what I needed. And I think I helped him too.”

“So, you are okay,” Stephan says, sniffing.

“Better. You will never guess what happened to my father and me. He became a Christian, asked my forgiveness for shutting me out all those years, and we have spent the winter together doing father-and-son things. Well, it was about forty years too late in some ways, but a late miracle is better than no miracle.”

“So, why didn’t you stay in Antioch?”

Titus does not reply.

“Oh. Paul again,” he says with a brief cough.

“He wrote to me while I was on Crete and told me to meet him in Nicopolis. Corinth is on the way. Maybe he wants me to tell him how the work on Crete went. Hopefully, he will recommend that I return here.”

“So, how long will you be here in Corinth?”

“Two or three days. I want to go see my Aunt Chloe. She will be happy to hear about her brother. Is she well?”

“Yes. Except she is more stubborn than ever. And hardheaded,” he replies with a sniff.

“Over what? Are you okay?”

“I’m fine. For one thing, your aunt has plenty of money now since that settlement with the bank, but she keeps insisting on running that scribe school.”

“Ha! I cannot wait to see her. I think I will do that right now. But I will stop by on my way out of the city, friend.”

Titus leaves his boyhood friend’s house, walks past the synagogue that now serves the church in Corinth, and turns left at the temple of Hera. He walks past the odeon, and arrives at his aunt’s house. A maid opens the gate.

“I am Titus, Chloe’s nephew. Is she here? May I come in?”

“Whose voice do I hear?”

Chloe joins the maid at her gate and opens it wide. “Well, come in. I want to hear all about your adventures the past three years. You look well.”

They embrace, and Chloe rocks him back and forth like his mother used to do when he was a little boy.

“Sit here and tell me what you have been up to. You

were so sad when you left, but now you look very happy. What happened since then?"

Aunt Chloe, you will be most happy when I tell you: Father has become a Christian."

"Praise God," she says, standing and swinging in a circle in place. She reseats herself. "Tell me all about it."

"We have made up," Titus says, not answering her question. "He has asked my forgiveness, and I have asked his for not understanding all those years what it is like to lose a wife. Then we spent the winter doing, well, being father and son."

"So, what are you doing here? Why aren't you back in Antioch?"

"Well, Paul seems to have this hold over me," he says with a grin. "He always tells me how needed I am and how proud he is of me. I did not intend to stay in Corinth, but I did. I did not intend to like Crete, but I did."

"So, he has another assignment for you."

"I don't know. But it is likely. He is in Nicopolis and sent word to me to meet him there. That's why I left Antioch and am coming through here. I will go on tomorrow if it is okay for me to spend tonight with you."

"Of course, it is. I have left your room unchanged."

The rest of the evening is spent telling Chloe all his adventures and misadventures on Crete. The following morning, Titus packs up his things and heads to Stephan's house to say goodbye to him.

"I'm coming with you," Stephan announces.

45 ~ THE ATTACK

"**W**ell," Titus says as they head toward the West Gate of the city, "I guess I have enough money to buy us both fare on a ship down the Ionian Isthmus and over to the Adriatic Sea itself, then up to Nicopolis."

"I feel ambitious," Stephan says. "Let's head north to Athens. That way, we don't have to go by ship at all. Then all we have to do is bypass Athens, head west, bypass Delphi, go on to the coast and then walk north to Nicopolis. I love the mountains."

"How did you know I don't like ships? And Stephan, why do you always have to be right?"

As they work their way north, Stephan's cough grows worse.

"Are you okay?"

"Oh, it's nothing. Just came on me two days ago. It'll be gone by tomorrow."

Two days later, they are just west of Athens and have run through all the boyhood misadventures they can remember.

The morning of the third day, while Titus takes the stakes from the tent and folds it up, Stephan sits on the ground. With a knife he carries with him, he cuts away sprouts from the two branches he has found on the ground. "They will make perfect walking staffs."

On the wide Roman road again.

"I love the mountains. Don't you, Titus? Ah, yes."

"You had better love them. Mount Parnasos is the highest mountain in Greece. Of course, we won't be climbing the mountain. That's where Apollo's priests sell their lies about his oracles to people by the thousands every year.

On the fourth morning, Stephan stands outside their tent, wiping his nose on oak leaves.

"Is that blood?" Titus asks, having just crawled out of the tent himself.

Stephan grins. "Nothing to worry about, pal. I am getting overweight, and losing a little blood will be good to slim me down a little. You don't want me to get pudgy again like I was when we were kids."

"Bleeding to lose weight? And where did you hear that one?" Titus growls.

The road grows steeper as they progress. The sun is now high in the sky.

"Whew," Stephan says. "I'm a little out of shape. You've been scaling the mountains of Crete for two or more years while my legs have grown flabby under my potter's wheel."

"Let's rest," Titus suggests, "then slow down. Paul will still be there when we arrive—I think."

"Good thing we have these walking staffs I made us," Stephan says, his breathing short and forced.

An hour before the sun touches the horizon, Titus looks over at Stephan and notices his face is red and he is wet with perspiration.

"We've gone far enough for today," Titus says. "Just sit while I set up the tent.

Stephen stumbles over to the side of the road, drops to his knees, and collapses.

Titus hurries to him, rolls him over onto his back. He pulls out his waterskin, lifts Stephan by his shoulders. "Here, drink this. You're hot all over."

Stephan does not open his eyes.

Titus pours water on his kerchief and pats it on Stephan's face, arms and legs. He raises Stephan's tunic to cool him off there and sees the lower right side of his front is swollen.

He notices Stephan is clutching something in his hand. It is his kerchief full of blood.

Titus brings his tent over, secures it with pegs on one side, lifts his center stake over his friend, and draws the tent to the other side, pinning that down also. With his tent set up around Stephan, he finishes securing it to the ground.

And Titus prays.

During the night, Stephan struggles in his sleep.

What are his visions? Children hurt and cannot get to them? Wife dying in childbirth. His pottery business being burned down? Oh, Jesus. Help him. Enter his awful dreams and give him peace.

Morning comes. Stephan is calm. Too calm. Titus puts his ear to Stephan's chest. His heart is still beating. He dabs him all over with cool water again. When he raises Stephan's tunic, he sees red spots all over.

"Hey, what are you men doing in that tent?" someone calls out from the road. "I saw you here yesterday."

Titus crawls out. "My friend is sick with a high fever. I'm not sure, but he may have Typhus. He is strong. He will recover in a few days.

"Is it catching?" the man says, sitting up on his cart. "We don't want anyone with anything that is catching. He could start a plague."

"I do not think so. At least, I have not caught it. We'll be okay."

"You should take him to Delphi," the man on the cart says. "They have a temple of Asclepius there, the god of healing. People lay their sick in his temple all the time, and they always get well. If not, the great temple of Apollo is right there. He's the father of Asclepius, you know. If one doesn't help your friend, the other will."

"I'm sorry," Titus says, fighting back his anger at how the fake gods had promised to heal his little red-headed girl. "I am a Christian. Those gods do not exist except in stone. They are not real. Leave us. The creator of the universe will heal my friend in his own time. Good-bye."

Titus does not wait for the man to leave. He returns to

the tent and dabs cool water on his friend again.

"There's a spring not far from here," the man calls after Titus. "If he sleeps by the spring, you can give him a drink more often."

Titus hears the cart's wheels heading on up the road toward Delphi.

For the next two days and nights, Stephan lingers in his fever. *Maybe I should take him to that spring.*

Titus looks around and finds the spring the man on the cart had told him about. He goes back to the tent, crawls in, then back out of the tent pulling on the mat Stephan has been sleeping on. Once out, he picks Stephan and his mat up like a baby and carries him to the spring.

This isn't a bad idea. It's cooler here. I can dab the cold water on him more often.

The rest of the day, Stephan mutters and picks at his tunic and the air as though trying to get bugs off of him.

That night, Stephan sleeps better. He is quieter. *The fever must be breaking.*

When the morning sky turns light gray, Titus leans over to dab more water on his friend.

Stephen is gone.

Titus stands and rushes to his tent. It is still there. He looks inside to see if Stephan had gotten well and crawled in on his own. The tent is empty.

"Stephan! Stephan, where are you? Stephan, where did you go?"

No answer. Titus stumbles around among the rocks that rise on one side of the road where the mountain grows steeper. He returns to the road and calls down the deep gully on the other side of the road.

"Stephan? Did you fall? Where are you?"

He climbs down into the gully as far as he can without falling down its steep sides. He returns to the road and backtracks everywhere he has been. "Stephan!"

Someone rides by on his horse.

"Did you see a man who may have been stumbling down the road?" Titus asks the horseman. "He is sick and feverish and would have been barefoot."

"Sorry. Haven't seen anyone."

"Where are you going, may I ask?" Titus inquires.

"To Delphi. I left a sick father there a few days ago and am going to see if he has been healed. Do you think your friend may have revived and gone there to thank the gods?"

Titus is quiet. "Uh, sir, would it be possible for me to ride with you?"

"Climb on."

"Can you wait a moment while I pick up my tent? It will fit on my back. My baggage is not heavy. I will pay you."

"You do not need to pay me. Come, we shall look after our sick together."

Just as the sun is setting, they arrive in the vale just below the mountain sanctuary of Apollo, Son of Zeus, and at the exact center of the earth.

"If he is not here, maybe one of the Pythias will seek Apollo's oracle. He will be able to tell you where he is."

"Thank you," Titus says, sliding off the stranger's mount. He takes out his money pouch.

"No, I do not need your money. Go with the gods."

The stranger leaves and Titus looks around. He sees an inn and enters.

"I am looking for my friend. He is average height, has thick brown hair, and kind of round face, brown eyes..."

"Whoa. That describes half the world. Sorry, I can't help you."

"He is sick and feverish and sometimes thinks he sees things that aren't there," Titus adds.

"Sounds like he needs to go up on the mountain and get healed. Check there."

"He cannot go by himself," Titus retorts. "Excuse my outburst."

"Maybe a priest saw him and took him up there to be healed."

Titus leaves the inn and looks around. He sees the market and walks over to it. "Have you seen a man who is red with fever walking around here?"

"If he's red with fever, he would be dead. Go away."

"Have you seen a man who is red with fever walking

around here."

"Sounds like he need Apollo. Check up at his temple."

"Have you seen a man who is red with fever walking around here?"

"No, but I see one of Apollo's priests riding by on his cart right now. All their carts look alike."

Titus hurries to the man on the cart.

"Have you seen a man who is red with fever?"

"I believe one of the other priests brought a man in like that last night. Said he was left deserted by the side of the road."

"That's my friend, he was not deserted, and I had him by the spring where the priest told me... Where is the road up to Apollo's sanctuary?"

"Follow me. I'm headed back up there now. I would offer to let you ride with me, but these are sacred carts, you understand."

Titus follows the priest, easily keeping up with his horse with his legs made strong on the mountains of Crete. An hour later, they arrive.

The grand Temple of Apollo dominates everything. Titus estimates it must be forty man-lengths long.

"When you get to the temple, turn left and at the end is the temple where the sick are laid out. If he is gone, Apollo must have healed him."

Titus eyes Apollo's temple as he walks toward it, shaking his head and gritting his teeth. "Why?" he calls out. "Why do people believe in a piece of stone and a girl who spouts gibberish and priests who pretend to know what she says?"

He notices people staring at him, switches his thoughts to Stephen, and turns left. He passes a government building, then comes to the healing temple. He goes in and looks among the sick lined up along both outer walls and down the middle. In the third row, he spots Stephen, who is still oblivious to the world.

He raises Stephen's shoulders, puts his other hand under his knees, and stands with his friend in his arms.

"What are you doing?" a priestess says, rushing over to

them.

"I am taking my friend out of here."

"You cannot do that."

"But I am doing it."

"Help!" the priestess calls out. "Help!"

Titus rushes out the front of the healing temple, sees a gate out of the sanctuary ahead of him, and despite Stephen's weight, runs with him.

"Stop him! Stop that man!"

Titus can hear priestly guards running after him.

"Halt. You there! Halt."

Out the gate. Ahead of him is a continuation of the hill on the right and a steep gulley on the left. "Jesus, help us." He steps over to the edge of the gully and jumps, Stephan still in his arms. Titus rolls and lets go of his friend. When he stops rolling, he looks up at the road then the place he thinks Stephan will be.

He sees priestly guards rushing down the road and looking on both sides of it. Titus realizes his two leather traveling pouches have survived the jump and puts them back on his shoulders. He spots his friend and crawls to him. A bush is right there, and Titus shields his friend with his body. Stephan groans.

"Shhh," Titus whispers. "You can talk later."

When the guards give up, Titus decides it is time to leave. He cannot climb back up to the road, so decides to walk along at the bottom of the gulley, hoping for a break where he can climb back up.

"Wha?"

"Shhh, before I drop you and let you walk," Titus says.

"Wha? Let me down."

Titus stops and sets his friend on the ground. "I have to say that you have the hardest head of anyone I know. When we jumped off that cliff..."

"We jumped off a cliff?" Stephan mumbles.

"Well, it wasn't exactly a cliff."

"Where?"

"We are in Delhi, and you have had a fever. Looks like that cold spring did help you. I doubt they did anything for you in that Asklepion temple."

"I was in a temple? Let me down. How long have I been..."

"Two weeks if you count the days you were sick and wouldn't admit it at home. We may as well lean our heads back and try to sleep here. In the morning, we'll look for a way to climb back up the hill."

The night is hard. No tent for shelter. Rocks and sticks and stones for a bed. Titus puts a shoulder pouch under each of their heads for a pillow.

When the distant sun turns the morning sky light gray, Titus comes to a full awakening. "Climb on my back," he tells Stephan.

"No."

"You will do as I say. You are too weak to walk, and we have to get away from this place."

With Stephan on his back, Titus works his way along the bottom of the gully until he sees a break in it and a way back up to the road. He scales the hill and is back on a flat surface. He sees a bench on the side of the road, lets Stephan down onto it, and sits beside him.

He hears wheels and puts his arm around Stephan, guiding him to bushes behind the bench.

The wheels come closer. Then he sees it. It is a cart, but unpainted and drawn by a small donkey.

"Stay here," he tells Stephan. "And try not to fall over."

Titus goes out to the road and stops the cart.

"Sir, I have a...well, I have need of transportation. May I buy yours?"

"Of course not."

"How much?"

"I told you no."

"Would twenty bronze coins be sufficient?"

"No."

"Thirty?"

"No."

"I can give you my last silver coin. It is worth far more than your cart and donkey. Would you take a silver coin?"

"You must be desperate, sir," the stranger says, smiling.

"If you are willing to part with a month's wages, I'm willing to let you."

The man climbs down off the cart, Titus hands him the silver coin, and the man turns around to walk back the way he came.

Titus goes to the side of the road behind the bush and gets Stephen, who is trying to stand.

"Here, big guy. Lean on me. We're going for a ride."

Titus situates Stephan in the back of the cart and snaps the reins. He hopes they can make it to the Ionian Sea before nightfall.

Two days later, Titus sees ahead of him a large bay coming in from the sea. "I think we might be here," he tells Stephan.

"It's about time," Stephan says, waking from a nap in the back of the cart. "Stop here."

"Why? What's wrong?"

"We do not want Paul to think you have a sickly friend," Stephan announces. He climbs over the bench and sits next to Titus.

"What are you doing? Get back there. You're still sick."

"I refuse to be sick any longer. Just go. You know, Paul is the one who baptized me."

"I forgot that," Titus says. "No wonder you wanted to go with me to see him."

They arrive at a city gate and realize they are in Actium. "Nicopolis is north of here right across that little strait. You can get a ride of a ferry to cross it. Then the city will be right on that peninsula where the ferry lets you off."

"I see it ahead," Titus says soon after leading his cart off the ferry. Half an hour later, they enter through a city gate and stop at an inn. Titus goes in but does not stay long. "He has no idea who Paul is."

"What about Christians or Jews?"

Titus goes back in. "He told me where the Jewish synagogue is," he says, stepping up to the cart. "Let's start there."

Titus guides the cart down several streets and stops in front of the building described by the innkeeper.

"And you had better stay out," they hear a man up on the portico say.

Another man is backing away from the first and shaking his fist. "I tried. By the Lord Jesus Christ, I tried. Your blood be on your own hands."

Paul turns to see who might have heard him. He looks up on the cart where two men are waving at him.

"Titus? Stephen? It's about time you get here, he shouts. "I'm leaving tomorrow. Winter is over. Headed for Colossae, Ephesus, and Troas next. Follow me."

"We're not riding while you walk."

"I live next door!" he calls back to the two younger men.

Titus and Paul talk most of the night about Titus' successes on Crete, along with his challenges.

"I see you're not wearing those silly Roman togas anymore," Paul observes.

Titus smiles. "They were expected in Antioch, sometimes in Corinth, but impractical on Crete."

"Yes, yes. It was expected in Tarsus where I grew up, but I got away from that when I went to Jerusalem to school as a youth. Now tell me some more about Crete."

While the men talk, Stephan sleeps.

"Take Stephan with you," Titus tells Paul. "He's been sick, but he'll be all right now."

"Corinth is on the way. Sure. It will be nice having a traveling companion. I'm supposed to meet Timothy in Ephesus. I will be most happy to take Stephanas with me."

Silence a while.

"Oh. And you? I want you to go on up to Dalmatia."

46 ~ CHANGE OF PLANS

*T*he following morning at dawn, Paul has possession of Titus' cart and of Stephan. They are at the docks.

"I'm sorry we did not have more time together," Paul tells Titus. "I thought you'd be here before winter. Well, reuniting with your father is important. Good for you. A blessed thing. I never had that kind of relationship with my father. But, no matter. I expect to hear great things from you."

"Yes, my brother. I will make you proud of me."

"Oh, not me. Make our Lord proud of you. I am unimportant."

"Well, pray for me as I shall you."

"I already do, my son. I already do."

Titus turns to Stephan, fresh from a good night's sleep, and able to stand on his own for a while.

"Well, my dear friend," Titus says. "Since we grew up, it seems we are always saying goodbye."

"It does seem that way. But we kind of made up for it those years in Corinth."

"Yes, we did, my friend. They were good years. Perhaps you can bring your family up there to Dalmatia and visit me if I stay too long."

"That's enough, you two," Paul says. "There are a lot of sailors scrambling on your ship, and a lot of bells ringing. You'd better get on board while you can. And Stephanus, get into our illustrious cart."

"Good-bye, my friends," Titus says. "Good-bye."

Titus turns and walks over to the ship and up the gangplank. He turns at the railing to see if his friends are still there. They are. Titus waves. Paul and Stephan wave back. As the ship slides away from shore, he watches his two dear friends grow smaller and smaller onshore as they lead the cart away.

Titus walks around the ship a while. "Pardon me, sir," he says to one of the sailors. "How long will it take to get to Dalmatia?"

"Probably three days if the wind is right."

"Thank you, sir."

He looks around for a place that will be out of the way of the busy crew and sits. *Jesus, help me not be lonely. I'm always saying good-bye to people. No mother. No more wife. No more children. Well, thank you for my father. I have my father back. But then you called. Keep my father safe. And Aunt Chloe and Paul and Stephan and Xenos in Crete and...*

Titus realizes the sun is high in the sky. The nap has been his first deep sleep in a long time. *Thank you, Jesus, for that.*

He stands, walks around a while, and returns to his seat on the deck. Despite having lost his tent in the fall below Delphi, he had managed to keep his two leather shoulder pouches with him. He pulls out the letter his father had sent him down in Crete, closes his eyes a moment, then opens them back and reads it.

The next day is a repeat of the first. He begins to look off the bow of the ship, wondering what Dalmatia will be like. He tries to remember the stories of his mother that her father had told her about life there.

Let me see now. She was of the Dardanian Tribe. Who were their gods? Seems like Perun was their supreme god, their god over all the other gods. Hmmm. I must learn more about him, so I can explain the superiority of the true God to their Perun. Seems as though he liked to throw thunder and lightning around. Oh, and he had a cosmic battle with the dragon, sometimes a serpent, and named Veles. And don't they have some kind of three-headed god?

A shocking memory comes to Titus' mind. He does not know who told him but must check it out. "Uh, excuse me, sir," he says, stopping another sailor. "Is it true that the people who live in Dalmatia never bathe, and they live in caves?"

"I suppose so. I never get off the ship when we're up there. Too many people."

"What about music?"

"Sometimes, I hear flutes at night when the dockworkers are sitting around."

My mother was a refined lady. Those cave stories have to be made up.

On the third day, he realizes spring has not quite arrived in Dalmatia. *I'll have to buy a cloak or cape when we get there. Hmmm. I heard they wear capes made out of fur. Wouldn't that be something? Stephan would laugh at me."*

"We're docking here," Titus hears the first mate announce. "We're docking at Endirudini. The bay is perfect."

"Uh, sir, how important is this city?"

"I don't know if it even is a city. It's just the name of one of their tribes. A larger tribe is farther north another two days. Haven't you ever been here before?"

"I'm sorry, but I haven't."

The first mate shakes his head. As he walks away, Titus can hear him muttering, "I feel sorry for that guy."

When they dock, the sun has almost disappeared. The enthusiasm Titus had felt around Paul has melted into confusion.

I knew there were congregations in Corinth before I went there. I knew there were congregations on Crete before I went there. I know nothing about Dalmatia except what my mother told me. She never lived here. Maybe she was wrong. Help me, Jesus. I do not know what I am doing.

The ship docks and the gangplank is lowered. Titus looks around for the other passengers going ashore. There are none. He is the only one. It is a dark night. He looks around for a market place where he can buy a cloak or cape and perhaps another tent. He does not see one.

What if they were right and everyone lives in caves?

He sees a small light ahead of him back off the seashore and walks toward it. When he draws close, he sees it comes from a shack. Titus goes to the door and knocks.

A bulky man taller than Titus wearing a dirty plaid tunic opens the door and growls. "What?"

"Dear," Titus hears in the background. "Quit scaring people." She speaks in a backward form of Greek.

A petite woman walks to the door, and the one who Titus assumes to be the husband steps back and clomps over to a bench by a fire in the floor.

"You look like you just got off the ship. Am I right? We have a lot of confused people stop by here when they first arrive. Why don't you just come right on in? We'll feed you and send you on your way to wherever you want to go in the morning."

Titus smiles. *Thank you, Jesus, for leading me.* "Yes, I would appreciate it. If the ship had gotten here in the daylight, I might have been able to find where I am going then."

The petite woman steps back so Titus may enter. He looks around. *At least it isn't a cave.*

"Just set your bags over there," the woman says.

"No, thank you. I just have the two bags, and they seem to be attached to my shoulders. I will be fine."

"Well, sit over here on this nice bench. Just lean back against the wall and relax. I'll bet you are hungry. I have some cheese on the shelf. I will bring you some. And while you're waiting, here is a mug of tea to relax you."

The woman takes an iron pot hanging over the fire in the floor and pours its contents into a mug. She goes over to a shelf, takes down a small jar, and pours some of its powdery contents into the mug. She stirs it and hands it to Titus.

"The Lord Jesus led me to you tonight. You may not know him, but he knows you. He lives in heaven and knows everyone."

"That's nice, dear. Now drink up your tea."

....Titus opens his eyes. It is morning. He realizes he cannot stand. He looks around and realizes his legs have been tied to the bench, and his arms are behind his back. Something is attached around his neck, apparently to the wall behind him.

"No! You can't do this!" he shouts.

The petite woman walks in. "Did you have a nice sleep? You were unable to eat last night, so I'll feed you this morning. We want to fatten you up."

The bulky man follows her, goes to the pit in the floor, adds kindling, and gets the fire started again.

"Why are you doing this?" Titus asks. "I did nothing to you."

"Oh, it's not what you did to us. It is what you are going to do for us. You are now our slave. We are going to take you to one of those cities you outsiders do not think we have, and sell you. My, we will get a good price for you. You're not too young, but you're tall and strong and seem healthy enough."

This time I cannot use my name and my aristocracy to impress them. What could impress them? I have no idea.

"Jesus loves all kinds of people, whether you live in a villa or in a wooden house, or even a cave."

The bulky man, wearing the same plaid tunic as the day before, grunts.

"Shut up," the woman says, her smile of the previous evening now gone.

"I have money," Titus says in his desperation. "You can have it all."

"We already have it all," the bulky man growls. He holds up Titus' money pouch and grins.

The man and woman sit at the table and slurp their thin porridge.

Think of something to say. Keep talking. Uses the wits you were born with. "Do you ever think about God? Did you know he loves you? You don't even have to offer sacrifices of whatever you sacrifice to your gods. He just wants you."

"Why? So the river god can drown us, or the mountain god crush us, or the sun god swallow us? Your god is no different than all the others," the petite woman replies.

At least I've got her talking, Titus tells himself. "But the God I want to tell you about created the rivers and mountains and sun. There are no individual gods in all those things. They have no power over your soul. They have no mind; so, how could they? There is only one God, the creator, and he just wants to love…"

The man turns from his porridge with the rag he had been wiping his nose and mouth on and stuffs it in Titus' mouth. He laughs at Titus' expression and clomps out the door.

Jesus, why did you let Paul send me here? These barbarians are unreachable. Help me escape. Help me find a way. I'll go back to Crete. I'll go to Parthia. I'll go to China. Just help me leave this place alive.

The door opens again, and Titus can see a wagon hitched to one of the largest horses he has ever seen. An abundance of hair is around its huge hooves.

The bulky man steps over to Titus, grins wide, unties his arms, legs, and neck, and throws him over his shoulder. He clomps back out of the shack and throws him in the wagon bed on his back. He climbs up in the wagon, puts a knee on Titus' chest, and hooks chains around his wrists that are attached to the wagon bed. He does the same thing at his ankles.

"At least take that awful rag out of his mouth," the petite lady orders the bulky man while handing him something. When the rag is out, a chunk of bread is stuffed in his mouth. "Don't choke on it, dear," she says.

The two climb onto the front bench and head away from the Ionian Sea.

On the rocky soil, the ride is rough. Titus tries to hold up his head so it is not bumped so often. His neck grows tired. He gives in to it. After a while, the sun is in his eyes.

He has managed the lump of bread in his mouth and gradually eaten it. The petite woman watches him, and as soon as he consumes all the bread, she climbs back to him and stuffs his mouth with more bread.

"We have to keep you fattened up."

Night comes. Titus is cold. The couple stops at a shack by the road that looks similar to the one they were in by the seaside. They go in, close the door, and after a while, he sees smoke coming out of the center of the roof.

Lord, what is going to happen to me? Help me escape.

Please. I cannot be a slave. I cannot. Slave to you, yes. Not to anyone else.

Morning the second day. The cold has kept Titus from any deep sleep. The routine begins again. Titus senses they are in hills now and that they are headed farther into them.

The hills become sharper and higher. The wagon seems to be zig-zagging.

"I hope the River Tara isn't frozen yet," the petite woman tells the bulky man.

Higher up into the hills. Zig-zagging more. Bumps and jolts. Titus tries to will the pain in his head away. It does not work.

Night. Another shack like the others.

Once again, the couple goes inside, Titus watches smoke rise up from the middle of the roof, and longs for a chance to escape back to civilization.

He closes his eyes to dream. Dream of his ice queen. She has turned into an ice sculpture. He tries to get to her so she does not have to be so cold, but a mountain appears between them. He climbs the mountain. It is full of fresh snow. He keeps sliding back down. He hears her. "I'm so cold. I'm so cold."

It is morning. Titus wakes himself. "I'm so cold. I'm so cold."

Another lump of bread stuffed in his mouth, and they continue on. Farther into the mountains. Steeper now.

"The River Tara should be just ahead," the petite woman says. "Just follow it down to the valley, and we will be there. Probably tomorrow."

The wagon crosses the river. The water seeps up into the wagon bed. It feels like ice on Titus' back.

The sound of mountain waters rushing downward grows louder. He hears the sound beside the wagon until the sun is low in the sky.

Another shack. He tries to flex his muscles so his arms and legs are not so numb. Instead, he can no longer feel his arms and legs.

Morning again. *Lord, God, why aren't you helping me escape?*

Bumping again. Groaning, squinting at the sun overhead. Wishing he were truly warm again. Trying to dream, but afraid to.

Some time along the way, Titus senses the wagon is not tilted as much. Mid-afternoon, he realizes the wagon is not bumping as much.

The sun grows warmer. He smells barley grass. He hears sheep. A horse gallops nearby, and someone calls out a hello as it passes.

Just as the sun rests itself on the horizon, the wagon comes to a halt. Titus cannot see a shack. Maybe it is farther from the road this time.

The man and woman climb out of the wagon.

"Well, here he is," the petite woman says. "The first man to get off the ship in two weeks. Wait till you see him. A fine specimen."

A refined-looking man arrives and looks into the wagon bed. He has white hair. His face is square, and he is clean-shaven.

"What have you done to him? Has he had no more clothes on than this, even up in the mountains?"

"We didn't have an extra coat, and we needed our blanket for ourselves," the petite woman says. "Besides, slaves don't need to be warm."

"Unchain him!"

The bulky man leaps up into the wagon bed and unchains Titus. Titus tries to raise himself to a sitting position, but cannot.

"Help him sit up. And he had better not be injured, or I will not pay you full price."

"Oh, you won't see any injuries. We even fed him."

The bulky man puts a rough hand under Titus' back and lifts him to a sitting position.

Titus rubs his wrists but finds his arms weak and unable to even extend themselves.

The man with white hair calls out. "Someone come help this man out of the wagon." He looks at the bulky man and adds, "Not you."

Soon two younger men arrive from a nearby manor

house. One climbs up on the back wheel of the wagon. "Do you think you can walk?"

"I doubt it," Titus replies.

The man climbs the rest of the way into the wagon bed and lifts Titus from behind, holding him under his arms. A second man lifts one side of the wagon off. The first man swings Titus around so he is seated on the edge. He takes Titus' limp legs and pulls them around so they dangle over the side of the wagon.

"Okay, now you're going to have to trust us," he says, pushing Titus forward.

Titus is caught by the second man on the ground and lets Titus lean heavily on him while he holds him up under his arms.

The man in the wagon jumps down, and each man lifts one of Titus' arms over his shoulder.

"Try to walk with us. We'll hold you up some, but we cannot hold your entire weight. This will be good to get strength back in your legs," the second man says.

As they start walking, Titus can hear the white-haired man discuss money and the wagon leaving.

At first, Titus drags his legs.

"No, don't do that. You have to help us out. Put your feet flat on the ground and walk with us."

"Our master is good to us but can have a temper when he grows impatient. You do not want to make him angry."

47 ~ DISCOVERIES

*T*itus follows their instructions, and the feeling in his legs begins to return.

They continue across a large barley-grass area, and he realizes they are nearing a manor house in the Roman style, though made of native stone rather than cut rock. It has columns across the front, which Titus assumes had been imported.

The three enter a side door that opens to a large room with pallets on the floor. They lead Titus to one of the pallets and lower him.

"I'd like to try sitting up," he tells them.

"Well, this is home for the rest of your life. And, by the way, I am Ragwald, and this is my friend, Gervas. We are spoils of war from Germannica."

"And what am I spoils of?"

"Rome hasn't had any good wars lately—well, except for the one down in Palestine with the rebel Jews. They don't like Rome ruling them any more than we did. So, we have no idea why they grabbed you."

"Were those people who brought me here..."

"Yeah, they were slavers."

"Who is your master, and what does he want another slave for?"

"Our master is Anostas. He served with the Eleventh

Roman Legion, as did his father. He inherited this plantation from his father. The land was granted for loyal service upon retirement."

"And?"

"We have no idea why he wants another slave. If he wanted many of them, he would have gotten them from Palestine. But, apparently, he wants just one. We can never guess what he has on his mind."

"What do you two do?" Titus asks.

"As you probably figured out, the slaves involved with his household sleep and eat here. Those who work the fields have their own buildings," Ragwald says. "I keep records of the income from the crops and how much is spent feeding and clothing all the slaves."

"And I am his personal physician," Gervas says. "But now, you need to rest."

"No. I have been resting too many days," Titus objects.

"Then I shall stay with you and massage your legs and arms to build up your muscles again. No, first I shall feed you. You must be starved. And probably thirsty. Master has an excellent cook. He inherited her from his father. I will go to the kitchen area and see if Ris has any dried fruit. It's too early in the season for fresh. And I'll look for some wine to help you digest it."

When Gervas leaves, and there is no one left in the big room, Titus scoots over to the wall. He leans his shoulders on it as he raises himself up a little at a time. Now standing, he looks out the window.

Crops and trees and mountains. No people that I can see except those in this isolated manor house. Lord, how am I supposed to tell Dalmatia about you while a slave in a place no one ever heard of?

Three days after Titus' arrival, he receives a message that Master Anostas would like to see him. Gervas gives him directions. A servant opens the door into the *officium* for him.

Titus stands before his new master holding his head up and trying to feel like the aristocrat he was long ago back home.

Anostas is seated behind a large cedar writing table and

looks up. He sets down the scroll he had been reading.

"Well, I am not sure what to do with you. I was expecting to receive a new crew of workers for my fields who I was told would be former sailors. Instead, I get one person, and your hands tell me you have not done any or much work with them. Further, that little bit of gray at your temples tells me you would not do me much good out there anyway. Do you have any suggestions what you can do for me? What has been your occupation?"

"I was an attorney, sir."

Anostas' head jerks back, and he furrows his brow. "You were what?"

"An attorney. However, I stopped doing that about ten years ago, and now I travel—or used to travel—around telling people about the one and only true God and his Son, Jesus Christ, which are actually one and the same."

"What is the name of your God?" Anostas asks.

"He is not my God. He is the God of everyone in this world and of the entire universe which he created. His name is I AM."

"Well, that's fine. What else can you do? Do you speak any other languages?"

"I can speak Greek and Latin fluently, though Latin is my mother tongue," Titus responds. "I also speak a little Hebrew and a slight amount of Dalmatian."

"Dalmatian. That is interesting. How did that come about?"

"My mother was Dalmatian—or rather, her father was. She was born in Rome."

What tribe of Dalmatians?

"I believe she was the Dardanian Tribe."

"I am on land of the Siculotae Tribe, but have heard of them. Well, go on."

"She taught me a few words when I was a child."

"Then she died?"

"Then she died."

"Hmmm. If you travel around trying to convince people to believe in your God, you must be an orator. Am I right?"

"I did excel in oratory at the university in Pergamum."

"And you write well, I assume."

"Yes, sir. I write best in Latin, but also very well in Greek. I never learned to write in Hebrew or Dalmatian."

"What is your name?"

"Titus Pomponius Brennius."

"Hmmm. Brennius. That sounds familiar."

"He invaded Rome a long time ago, then he and his people settled from Rome all the way over to Anatonia where I lived. He is my ancestor."

"That long string of names, including your ancestor, certainly is not doing you any good now."

"No, sir. I suppose not."

Anostas steps out from behind his writing desk, walks around it, and looks Titus in the eye. He turns and returns to his desk. "That will be all for now. You may leave."

It has now been three days since Titus spoke with the master and explained to his two friends what the master and he spoke of.

"If he cannot think of anything useful I can do for him, what will he do to me?" Titus asks Ragwald.

"He certainly is not going to feed and clothe you for nothing. He'll either sell you to someone else, put you out in the fields, or execute you. If he executes you, he'll let the farmhands do it for him."

The master's messenger walks into the room. "Calling Titus. Calling Titus. Your presence is required by the master."

Titus stands, takes a deep breath, and walks forward. *Is this it, Lord? Did you send me here to kill me? Let me die well, Lord.*

"I have decided to make you my personal secretary. I believe you will come in handy." Anostas rises from behind his writing-table, walks around it, and paces.

"We will start slow, of course, but build from there. You can check my deeds for me and all other legal papers I have to make sure they are in my best interests."

He stares at Titus. "I have been thinking of writing about my experiences with the Eleventh Roman Legion. Perhaps I will let you interview my slaves from different nationalities and write things about their culture. Of course, your writings will be authored and signed by me."

Months have passed. It is summer. Titus has settled in and is relieved that, at least, his skills are being well used. He tries to tell people about Jesus, but thus far, they have not seemed very interested.

During the hours he is not writing for his master, Titus walks outside and across the barley grass surrounding the manor house. He sometimes watches the sheep keeping the grass low and fattening themselves up to be sacrificed for food and clothing.

Most of all, he sits leaning against a tree and watches the River Tara flow by or the mountains loom in the distance. Sometimes he thinks of his Fjorta, his little red-headed girl and his smart boy—all taken from him far too soon.

All alone now. Limited in who he can talk to and, therefore, limited in fulfilling his mission of telling people about Jesus and saving of their souls from hell.

"Is this it, Lord?" he whispers. "Never to escape beyond those mountains or down that river to where it flows into the sea? Did my life as Titus Pomponius Brinnius end when I stepped off that ship last winter? Am I no longer me? Am I lost to the world? Will no one I loved ever know what happened to me?" He fights the unmanly tears. "I am all alone."

The summer passes. Titus is busy with his master's projects. He lives one day at a time. He survives one day at a time. He exists, and that is all.

Today Anostas is dictating to him.

"Let me see now. We were up against the Germanicans. No, it was the Frisians. Well, just say it was the Germanicans."

The master begins to cough. "Oh, my throat is getting scratchy. Would you go to the kitchen area and ask Ris for a mug of water for me?"

Titus sets down his writing material, goes out into the corridor, and to the door leading to the kitchen where he has so many times enjoyed smelling the fresh bread as it is baked.

"Hurry," his master urges.

He goes through the door and looks around, not having been allowed in the kitchen area before. "Uh, where can I get a mug of water for our master?" he calls out.

He hears a crash and turns in that direction. "I'm sorry, did I startle you?"

The woman before him stares, not trying to pick up the tray and its contents. She sucks in breath. Her head jerks back. She raises her hands to her cheeks. Her eyes are wide, and tears come to them. Her mouth drops open. She closes it again. Her lips tremble.

She has big eyes, a broad straight nose with the tip turned down, a pointed chin, and one dimple in the middle of it.

She holds out her arms and forms a trembling smile.

"Titus? My son, Titus?"

Titus stares at the woman staring at him. He squints, stares, and steps back. He presses his lips hard together.

She steps toward him.

"Titus? Is that you?"

Titus stares still.

She takes another step toward him, her arms still outstretched. "Oh, my son. My son. I'm your mother—Kharis."

Titus takes another step back. "What? You can't be. My mother died…"

"No, I did not die in that earthquake."

"You know about the earthquake?"

"Before it happened, I was accosted by two rough men. They put a bag over me, and one of them threw me over his shoulder. I heard the falling rocks, and they were able to get out of the way of the earthquake in time. They were slave traders."

Silence.

"Oh, Titus, I know it is you. When you walked in, you looked just like my father. Titus, please, Son, come to your mother."

Mother and son trying to conceive the inconceivable, trying to grasp the impossible, trying hard to believe.

Titus' lips tremble. He looks up at the ceiling, tears fast forming. He looks to one side. He looks back at the woman before him. She steps toward him again.

He stands still. She steps closer to him. In slow motion, he raises his arms as though in a dream. She draws closer.

They look into each other's eyes.

Titus knows. He steps forward and wraps his arms around his mother, lost so long ago when he was but eleven years old.

He lays his cheek on her now gray hair, and she leans into his chest, embracing and both weeping and trembling. They sway back and forth, back and forth, as they had done when Titus was a boy back in Antioch.

Others in the kitchen area have stopped their work and stand around the two, smiling and crying. The door to the kitchen area opens.

"What's going on in here?" Anostas demands. "Where is my water? I'll have him flogged."

"Sir," one of the cooks says. "this is Ris's son. Titus is her son. They have not seen each other since he was eleven."

Anostas stares. "She's not dead?" He watches the two in their sacred moment and forms a grin. "Well, the gods are full of surprises, I should say. Let them have their time together. One of you give me some water."

Titus does not hear the other cooks talking. He does not hear his master talking. He does not hear anything except his heart crying out to his mother.

At last, they draw apart. Both with a trembling smile, each forming their one dimple.

"The master said to let you have your time together," one of the other cooks says. "So, get out of here."

Titus looks down at Kharis and takes her hand. "Come."

He leads her out onto the barley grass. He puts his arm around her and looks down at her as they walk. "I never thought I would be tall enough to look down on my mother," he says, his lips still unsteady.

"Oh, you grew up to be so handsome," she says.

They face each other and embrace once more, swaying back and forth, back and forth.

They pull apart again, and he takes her to his tree.

"I have a thousand questions for you, Son."

"And I have a thousand answers," Titus replies. "First, I know you have wondered about Father."

"Is he still alive?"

"Yes, he is."

"Let me see. I am seventy-one now, so he must be eighty-one. Is he still handsome?"

"Indeed he is, Mother, and…"

"How I have longed to hear you say that word to me."

"Mother," he whispers. "Mother."

"So, you were telling me about Justus. How did he take my death?"

"Not well at all. He cut off the whole world. He continued to do his job as praetor of Antioch and did it well. But, when he was not doing that, he was up in his *officium* with the door closed and not talking to anyone."

"Surely, he talked to you."

Titus is silent.

"Oh, no. I was afraid of that. Did he blame you for my death?"

"Kind of. And so did I. I have fought my feelings of guilt my whole life. If I had only left Father's hearing early and delivered the lyre myself…"

"Then you would have either been caught in the earthquake and killed for sure, or kidnapped by the slavers. At least, this way you got to grow up and be normal."

Titus looks down at his mother, embraces her, and they are silent a while.

"Who helped raise you? Lydia?"

"Father sent for his sister."

"Chloe was a good woman. I liked her. If I had got a chance to choose who replaced me, it would have been Chloe. So she was good to you?"

"Very good, Mother."

Silence.

"Did you have a funeral for me?"

"Yes. We identified you by the lyre at your side—or whoever it was we buried. I wonder whatever happened to the family she really belonged to."

Silence.

"I got married." He says.

"You did? Is she nice?"

"She was nice."

"Oh, no. She died in childbirth?"

"No, I will tell you about it, but not now. I just want to absorb finding you after all these years."

"Children? Do you have grandchildren for me?"

"Mother, I will tell you about them later too. I promise."

"Oh, my son. What have you been through?"

Titus forms a grin before he loses control of his emotions. "Do you remember any of the songs you used to sing to me when I was a boy? Would you sing one to me now?"

The afternoon is enveloped in a misty dream of shimmering bliss and remembering and absorbing a renewed love.

"Do you think there is any way to notify your father? Anostas will never let us go free. But Justus could possibly come here to us, even if it is under pretense of being someone else."

48 ~ TO THE ENDS OF THE EARTH

*F*ive months have passed. Jerusalem, the temple, and all the rebel Jews have been destroyed.

"There is some kind of excitement going on outside," Gervas tells Titus, taking a break on his pallet from his work. "Hurry, Titus. You'll miss it. Some man in a silver chariot. Hurry."

Titus sits up and walks outside. He sees four legionnaire equestrians in front and four behind a silver chariot with one horse harnessed to the front and one tied to the back.

The man in the chariot steps out. As Titus draws closer, he sees the man is wearing a white toga with purple edging.

Gervas and Ragwald, running across the barley grass ahead of Titus, have almost reach him. Titus hears the voice of his master and stops to allow him to go ahead.

"Welcome. Welcome," he hears Anostas pronounce to the stranger.

Titus hears his father's deep voice. They speak to each other in Latin.

By instinct, Titus steps aside and does not approach the chariot or his father.

As his master and his father turn toward the manor house, Justus glances at his son but does not acknowledge him further.

"I come to you with greetings," Justus tells Anostas, "from your illustrious Governor Marcus Pompeius Silvanus Staberius Flavinus."

"Well, greetings to him too," Anostas replies, putting an arm across Justus' shoulder. *Please, Lord, give my father patience and wisdom. He promised me he had changed.*

The master and the aristocrat disappear in the front entrance. Titus rushes back to where the pallets are, to the opposite door, out to the back corridor, and into the kitchen area.

"Mother. Mother. Come quickly."

At the sound of her son's voice, Kharis hurries over to him. "You sound so much like my father," she says, her one dimple showing.

Titus stands before her, both hands on her shoulders. "Mother. He is here."

Kharis stares at her son. He says nothing more.

She sucks in a breath. Her eyes sparkle, then mist. "Justus? My Justus is here?"

She turns to the others in the kitchen. My husband is here. My Justus."

The newest maid steps over to Kharis. "You cannot meet him wearing that. Come with me. I still have the tunic they kidnapped me in. It is not the fanciest in the world. It is blue linen with some fringe on it. Come."

"Wait for me," another maid calls out, carrying a pitcher of water and a bowl with soap in it.

Titus goes back out to the main corridor. He listens for voices to determine where the men are. Not having large courtyards as they do in the south, Titus walks past each room he thinks they may be in.

At last, he hears them. He paces between the door and the intersection of corridors, where he can see his mother when she arrives.

"Hey, you." Titus turns. It is Gervas and Ragwald. "Here is a wet cloth. Wipe your face and put on this..."

"Thank you, I believe I need the wet cloth," Titus says, "but what I am wearing is sufficient. It is who I have become— a slave, if not of man, then of God."

Titus' two friends stand along the wall of the corridor, grinning as they watch Titus resume pacing.

After a short while, they hear giggling from the intersecting corridor.

"Oh, I'm so nervous," Titus hears his mother say. "Do I look okay?"

"You look fine," both of the cooks say in unison.

Titus meets her and holds her at arm's length. "Mother, you look beautiful. Father will fall in love with you all over again."

"You mean he stopped loving me?" she grins, her eyes sparkling. "Oh, I'm so nervous."

Titus steps around beside her and puts his strong arm across her shoulder. "You are going to be fine. In a few moments, your jitters will be gone, and only your heart will be flittering."

Kharis slaps him on the chest. "Oh, go on. You're making me feel like a new bride, and you are giving me away."

"I guess you are, and I am," he replies.

She stops. "Oh, I hear his voice." She looks up at her son, the tears of happiness starting.

"Now, Mother, if you cry, you will make your eyes all swollen and ugly. Think mean thoughts, like when you used to spank me for wading in the reflecting pool."

They stand before the double doors where the men are visiting.

"So, you see, sir," Justus says, "the governor has given orders that these two slaves be immediately freed."

"He can't do that. They're mine. I bought them legally."

"Of course, you will be reimbursed. I do not know how much you paid for them, but the one hundred pieces of silver in this pouch should more than make up for your loss."

Titus can wait no longer. He knocks on the door and flings it open. He steps behind his mother, puts his hands on her shoulders, and announces to the other end of the large receiving room, "Father! Your wife."

Justus turns and stares at the doorway.

"Your wife? That is your wife?" Anastos questions.

Justus groans, and his eyes mist.

"My darling, how have you been all these years?" Kharis whispers.

The old man walks with slow, even steps toward the love of his life who he had lost so long ago when they were young and happy.

Kharis cannot wait longer. She runs toward her beloved, and they embrace, rocking back and forth, back and forth.

At last, they pull apart, look into each other's eyes, and embrace again. Titus steps over to them and envelops them both in his long, strong arms.

"Well, I'll be," Anastos says, scratching his head.

"Just look at that," one of the cooks says.

"True love reigns forever," the other cook says.

"Family," Ragwald mutters.

"At least someone is truly happy again," Gervas says.

"Go on. Get out of here," Anastos proclaims, still confused but happy with his enlarged purse.

Justus and Kharis walk toward the door. Titus stays behind. "Sir. Now that I am free, I would like you to bring all your slaves and paid servants together. I have something to tell everyone."

Anastos does not answer.

Justus turns toward the retired equestrian. "If I were you, I would do as he says," he calls over his shoulder.

"Okay, but after their work is done. At sundown, you may address them on the barley grass if you don't disturb the grazing sheep."

Out in the corridor, Justus embraces his wife and son once again.

"Come with me," Gervas says. "I have a private examination room and storeroom for my medicinal herbs. You can have your privacy in there."

"Wait, Justus says, embracing his wife again and calling over her head. "Son, would you go to my chariot and bring back the two baskets of clothes. Oh, and tell the legionnaires they can camp here tonight."

When Titus returns with the baskets, they go on into Gervas' examination room. The three sit and talk. Mostly Titus lets his parents talk.

After a while, Titus interrupts them. "I believe I need to go somewhere else and let you two talk in private."

"No. Please. Stay here with us," Kharis says. She looks at Justus and receives his approval.

Titus stays with them a while longer, then stands. "I believe my congregation is assembling. I must leave now."

"What is he talking about, Justus? He has a congregation?"

"Father will explain it to you. Then you can join us."

As the sun sets, Titus stands before the three hundred and fourteen slaves of Anostas.

When his parents join them, Justus is wearing a plain tunic of green with embroidery along the hem and neckline.

"I cannot begin until the master comes," Titus announces.

Ragwald stands. "I'll get him."

Soon Anostas is seen running out of the manor house.

"What did you tell him?" Titus asks when Ragwald returns and sits in front of him.

"I told him Justus Brennius Antiochus demands it," he says with a grin.

"How did you know my father's full name."

"I overheard him introduce himself to the master."

Titus looks toward the assembly and raises his hands.

"I come to you on this glorious evening to give you freedom."

His voice echos around the mountains.

"Now, wait a moment," Anostas says, standing.

"Sit down, sir. Listen to what he has to say," Justus barks. Kharis giggles.

"Your whole life, you have been controlled by gods that are really Satan, the enemy of your soul. Jesus is the lover of your soul. He was the Word of God that took the form of flesh to come to earth and collect your wages for your sins—death. Soul death, and eventually body death. He collected those wages to set you free."

Titus pauses. He looks over the crowd and down at his parents. They smile, he raises his arms, and continues.

"He not only collected the wages, but he came back to

life. Right in the cemetery. He had been dead for three days, but he came back to life."

Gasping in the crowd. Muttering. Wondering.

"How?"

"He was the Word of God in human form. Satan brings death. God brings life."

"How do we know you aren't making all this up?" one of the farmhands shouts.

"I am personal friends of a man who voted for him to be put to death, then saw him after he came back to life. I have met others who saw and talked with him both before and after."

"How do we know he was really dead?"

"Roman soldiers crucified him. Most of those soldiers are still alive. And can tell you,"

"How can we come back alive after we die?"

"You have to tell God you are sorry for all the bad things you ever thought or did."

"Even our thoughts?"

Titus smiles and continues. "You have to be sorry for them and promise God you will try not to do them again. Then, you have to believe Jesus really did die in your place and come back to life."

"I believe," someone in the back of the crowd calls out.

"I believe," someone over on the left side calls out.

"I believe," someone says, running toward Titus.

"Everyone who believes and wants to become a follower of Jesus the Christ, come forward."

Titus steps back as people come toward him and kneel.

"I hope you all are kneeling in prayer to the only true God and not to me. I am only a messenger," he tells those immediately in front of him.

"Now, tell me if you believe Jesus really was the Son of God in flesh. If you do not believe it, go on back."

Everyone who is on his knees says an enthusiastic yes, many with tears.

Titus estimates there are close to one hundred who have believed. He calls to his father.

Justus stands and walks over to his son. "I see you need

some help here. I will take the small ones. You take the larger ones."

"How did you know?" Titus asks.

"I'm your father, remember."

Titus turns back to the crowd. "Everyone, if you are truly sorry for your sins and want to live a better life, and if you truly believe Jesus was the Son of God and have confessed it, you can do one more thing. Follow me to the river.

As the crowd walks, Titus mingles among them, smiling and patting them on the back. "You no longer need to fear those false gods. They do not exist. Only Satan exists in them. But Jesus has overcome Satan. You are free, my friends. You are free."

The crowd spontaneously shouts, "We're free. We're free."

Once at the water, Titus announces that, since they have died to their sinful nature, just like Jesus died for their sins, they can now be buried in a watery tomb, just like Jesus was buried.

"Annnnd," he announces with a combination of gusto and glory, "you will rise up out of the waters of your tomb, your soul reborn, just like Jesus rose up out of his tomb."

He looks at his father, who steps over to his son's side, embracing his wife.

"Form two lines," Titus announces. "Those of you who are thin and short, form a line in front of my father. Those of you who are fat and tall, form a line in front of me.

The lines formed, Justus turns to his son. "There is someone I must baptize first."

"Who?" Titus asks. Then he sees the smiles.

"Your mother."

Titus turns with his back to the two lines and watches as his parents wade out into the waters of the River Tara. He hears his father repeat the words Jesus himself had commanded at baptisms. "I baptize you, Kharis Sejanus Brennius, in the name of God the Father, Word, and Holy Spirit."

Titus meets them in the water and the three embrace. "Well, now my parents are now my brother and sister," he whispers.

"Hey, give us a chance," they hear onshore.

As the moon rises high in the sky, Titus sits on his pallet, knowing it will be his last night there.

"Gervas and Ragwald, I expect you to be the leaders. My father will send you a copy of things the apostles have written about Jesus' life and their own inspired teaching. Guide them carefully. Coming from my father, ole Anostas will obey his instructions and give them to you.

"Titus, you have changed our lives," Ragwald says.

"Little did we know when we rescued you from that wagon and helped you walk again," Gervas adds, "that someday you would rescue our souls and help us truly walk."

"Uh, we have written letters to our families. They are rich and, when they find out where we are, will surely be able to buy our freedom as your father did yours."

"I will find a reliable ship going south and give the captain instructions on how to find your families."

"They will pay the captain well once they receive our letters."

It is morning. Titus had not slept except for a brief dream of walking beside his Fjorta with Siera holding his father's hand and little red-headed Kharis holding her mother's hand.

When the sky turns silvery, Titus rises and walks to Gervas' examining room. His knock is soft. "Are you up?" he whispers.

The door opens.

"We are up and ready."

Titus, with his father and mother, walk out of the manor house for the last time and onto the barley grass still wet with dew.

"Are we going back to Antioch?" Kharis asks.

Silence.

"Oh, I see. My men have plans."

They walk toward the river and the silver chariot and extra horse tied behind, four legionnaires in front and four in back.

"Son, your horse is saddled and ready for you. You are

the leader. You tell us where."

"Paul told me the preach everywhere in Dalmatia, and that is what I intend to do," he says, mounting his horse.

"That is fine, Son. When we arrive at Salona, I shall return our armed guards and thank the governor for the use of the legionnaires and his name. It is a large and grand Roman city."

"So the rumors that all Dalmatians live in caves is not true after all," Titus laughs. "Well, I think Dalmatians are going to be very receptive to only one God."

"By the way, how did you find us?" Kharis asks her husband.

"Didn't he tell you? Titus apparently convinced his master to buy urns from Stephan in Corinth, and slipped a secret message in it for me."

"Stephan? He's in Corinth? Is he still a potter?"

"The best," Titus calls back to his parents from his mount ahead of them.

"No!"

"What do you mean, no, Mother?"

"This is all wrong. Get out of the chariot."

"Dear, what are you up to?" Justus says, following her out with a grin.

"You two," she says, calling up to two of the legionnaires. "Off your horses."

"Kharis?"

"Right now. Off your horses."

The two legionnaires look at Justus, and he nods. They dismount.

"Now, you two ride in the chariot," Kharis says, still in command.

"Now, Justus, help me up on that horse."

"Ohhh." The old man smiles and obeys.

Titus' parents ride up to Titus, one on each side.

They resume their journey north.

"After a while, Son, if you are good, I will sing you a song," his mother says.

The procession continues down the road toward the sea.

"By the way," Justus says. "After we have covered

Dalmatia, what then?"

"Jutland. I would like to go on farther north to Jutland. My wife, Fjorta, would have liked that."

"I think she would too," Justus adds. "I'm so proud of you."

"You still have not told me very much about life with your wife and children," Kharis says as the three ride side by side.

"Well, the first time I met Fjorta, she hit me in the eye, and I immediately fell in love with her. She was my ice queen with white-blond hair and..."

THANK YOU

Thanks for reading my book! I'm so honored that you chose to spend your precious time with my characters. You are appreciated. I'm an independent author who relies on my readers to help spread the word about stories you enjoy.

Would you take a few minutes to let your friends know on Facebook, Pinterest...wherever you hang out online? Also, each honest review at online retailers means a lot to me and helps other readers know if this is a book they might enjoy.

I welcome contact from readers. At my website (below), you can do so. You can also sign up for my monthly newsletter (below) for half-price paper and 99c ebooks for the whole family - novels, non-fiction, storybooks and first peek at my newest release.

GET ALL 8 BOOKS IN THE HISTORICAL SERIES

INTREPID MEN OF GOD

Novel 1 ~ Lazarus: The Samaritan
Novel 2 ~ Paul: The Unstoppable
Novel 3 ~ Luke: Slave & Physician
Novel 4 ~ Mefiboset: Crippled Prince
Novel 5 ~ Joseph: The Other Father
Novel 6 ~ Michel: The Fourth Wise Man
Novel 7 ~ Stephen: Unlikely Martyr
Novel 8 ~ Titus: The Aristocrat

HISTORICAL BACKGROUND

GAULS, after whom the Roman province of Galatia was named, invaded Anatolia (Turkey) in 390 BC after conquering Rome. In 188 BC, it came under Roman control. In 25 BC, Augustus Caesar created the province of Galatia. The province was divided into three counties—Pisidia, Lycaonia, and Galatia.

BRENNIUS was the chiefton of the Gauls who invaded northern Italy and Anatolia. His followers split off, part settling in Italy and part crossing over to Anatolia. In my book, I made Brennius a direct ancestor of Titus and his father, and therefore, their family name.

OKONDIANI TRIBE among the invading Gauls located itself where Antioch and nearby cities were. They would have been the ancestors of many of the citizens of Antioch.

ANTIOCH was first settled by citizens from the city of Magnesia just below Ephesus. It was declared a free city by the Romans in 188 BC, meaning anyone born there was automatically a Roman citizen with all its privileges. Unlike other cities around the Empire, citizens of Antioch were considered aristocracy and spoke Latin. Several of its citizens became Roman senators.

THE DARDANI TRIBE OF DALMATIA lived north of Greece, and this is the heritage I gave Titus' mother. Although considered barbarians, they had a love of music.

TITUS POMPONIUS ATTICUS, after whom I gave our Titus his second name, was a friend of Cicero.

LAWYERS. I made Titus a lawyer because he was sent by Paul to three areas where they were having church problems. He was an arbitrator, which is what Roman lawyers were often called at the time. At first, arbitrators/lawyers were just volunteers, but by Titus' time, they were being paid.

ARISTOTLE, SOCRATES, PLATO, CICERO, SENECA: I read Plato's *Laws* (304 pages), Cicero's *The Republic & the Laws* (288 pages) and *Moral Goodness* (100 pages), Senaca'd writings on *Clemency, Providence*, and *Anger* (c. 200 pages), Aristotle's Metaphysics Book 12, *On the Existence of God,* and *Timaeus* on how the universe and human body parts were formed by the gods by Socrates as reported by Plato, and *Phaedo* on the last discourses of Socrates regarding the afterlife as reported by Plato. Since I made Titus a lawyer, I needed to know the laws and what government offices existed.

PRAETOR. I made Titus' father Praetor of Antioch, meaning he was the Supreme Judge. Citizens got to choose their own judges, and these judges were just volunteers and did not know the laws very well. It was up to the praetor to educate them in preparation for whatever case they were to judge.

TOGAS were the official "uniform" of Romans, though only the aristocracy was allowed to wear them. They were long pieces of white cloth wrapped around one shoulder, and brought around under the opposite shoulder. If they achieved high status, they were allowed to wear a purple border around their toga.

AUGUSTUS CAESAR was sanctified and declared a god by the Roman senate (the only body allowed to announce a new god). On the side of Augustus' temple in Antioch was engraved every major undertaking and battle won by Augustus during his lifetime. This played an important part in this book.

PAGAN GODS were overgrown humans with more powers than humans. Homer in BC 800 named many of them. The gods were created by national leaders in order to control the people. Priest-hoods were political positions. A flamen was head of a local temple and god. A flamenica was a female head.

PERGAMUM was famous for its library, second largest in the world behind the one in Alexandria. Pergamum was also famous for inventing the animal-skin parchment which replaced the reed papyrus.

AMMONIUS in Pergamum later became the teacher of Plutarch in Athens. He was about Titus' age.

JUTLAND was the homeland of Titus' wife. Jutland was in the northern part of today's Holland. I chose that background because I wanted Titus to use some of his arbitration skills to convince Antiochians to accept an outsider.

STEPHANUS, Titus' boyhood friend, eventually went to Rome and studied under Gaius Musonius Rufus. Gaius taught philosophy during the reign of Nero, and about the same age as Stephanus. Paul said he baptized Stephanus in Corinth (I Corinthians 1:14f)

COLLEGE OF PONTIFFS WERE officials even before the Roman Republic which began in 509 BC. Originally advisors to the king, they then became advisors to the Roman Senate. They controlled lists of deities, their ceremonies of appeasement, and records of all magistrates. They also controlled the calendar, determining all political and religious special days. Membership was typically offered to the wealthy and politically powerful and was for life. The leader was the Pontifex Maximus. Julius Caesar was the first emperor to call himself the Pontifex Maximus. When Christianity became the official religion of Rome, Pope Leo I around 440 AD adopted the title Pontifex Maximus to emphasize his authority.

VESTAL VIRGINS were priestesses of the goddess Vesta who took a vow of chastity, so they could reflect the purity of the state. Their attire was partly that of a bride. The order was the last holdout of paganism in 394 AD in Rome.

PIRATES everywhere found haven in Crete. Among them was the infamous Anicetus who died in AD 69.

CRETE was a challenge to study because of the earthquake of AD 365 that buried part of eastern Crete under water and tipped the island so that the western side rose over twenty feet above the water. Cities Titus may have visited to help congregations establish elders existed then, but do not now.

DALMATIA TODAY IS CROATIA, SLOVENIA and the former Yugoslavia. At times, it was controlled by Hungary and the Ottoman Empire. In II Timothy 4:10 just before his death, Paul wrote of Titus going there.

TRAVELS.   The Apostle Paul mentioned Titus being in Jerusalem (Galatians 2:1-3), in Corinth (2 Corinthians 2:13; 7:6-14; 8:6-23; 12:18), in Crete (Titus 1:4), and in Dalmatia (2 Timothy 4:10).

ELDER & DEACON qualifications and church organization are taken from *Titus* written by the Apostle Paul. Being visited by Tychicus, Zenas the lawyer, and Apollos is taken from Titus 3:12-13).

DALMATIA covered the northern part of present-day Albania, much of Croatia, Bosnia and Herzegovina, Montenegro, Kosovo and Serbia, The Romans called it called it Illyricum. It became a Roman province in 27 BC. Although the cities were Romanized, the urban areas kept their social and political traditions as well as their gods. They were extremely superstitious and fearful.

BUY YOUR NEXT BOOK NOW

HISTORICAL NOVELS FOR ADULTS

THEY MET JESUS Series of 8
http://bit.ly/TheyMetJesus

INTREPID MEN OF GOD Series of 8
http://bit.ly/IntrepidMen

HISTORICAL STORYBOOKS FOR CHILDREN

A CHILD'S LIFE OF CHRIST Series of 8
(Parallels Adult *They Met Jesus*)
http://bit.ly/ChildsLifeOfChristSet

A CHILD'S BIBLE HEROES Series of 10
http://bit.ly/Bible-Heroes

A CHILD'S BIBLE KIDS Series of 8
http://bit.ly/bible-kids

A CHILD'S BIBLE LADIES Series of 10
http://bit.ly/BibleLadies

DISCUSSION QUESTIONS

CHAPTER. 1: Think back to your childhood. What was the happiest day of your life that you will never forget?

CHAPTER. 2: What failures in life (or tragedies) do some people unjustly blame themselves for? Why do you think they do that? Have you ever done it?

CHAPTER. 3: There is a book out called "Hurt People Hurt People." (http://amzn.to/2u6hFOr) After sympathizing with someone, did they retort, "You DON'T know how I feel"? Do you think part of it could be bragging "My hurt is so great and magnificent your hurt will never measure up"?

CHAPTER. 4: Titus was highly intelligent and dared enter the adult world when he was just fourteen years old. Did you ever do something "grownup" when you were still child?

CHAPTER. 5: Even though Titus entered the adult world early and handled himself well, he was still a kid socially. Do you recall any books or movies about an intelligent young person who did not know how to handle himself socially with others his age? Or did it happen to you or a friend?

CHAPTER. 6: Do you remember telling or hearing ghost stories around a campfire or at a party or even at a cemetery when you were young? What can you say to a child who was truly frightened and cannot sleep?

CHAPTER. 7: Today we have urban legends that appear on the internet, although sometimes repeated in conversations, articles, or speeches as true. How can a person track it down to see if it really happened?

CHAPTER. 8: Sometimes people's reputations can be "murdered" in gossip, articles, on Facebook, etc. Did anyone ever do this to you? How can you counter it, or should you try?

CHAPTER. 9: Did you have a best friend in school? What kinds of things did you do together? If you have been separated since then and tried to resume your friendship, what was it like?

CHAPTER. 10: Tell about your first love. Was it based on something silly or serious? Was it based on the physical, emotional, or spiritual. How do these things make a difference?

CHAPTER. 11: Have you ever tried to fit in with people who were not like you? What was it like for you? How did they try to make you feel welcome? Or did they? What helped the most?

CHAPTER. 12: In the story, Titus' daughter was dedicated to a Nordic goddess, a Greek/Roman goddess, and Jehovah with the hopes of not leaving anyone out. If you dedicated your child to someone, who and why?

CHAPTER. 13: Do you know anyone who has lost a child? What can help get the parents cope with it? What do they normally tell themselves to bring the pain to some kind of resolve they can live with from then on?

CHAPTER. 14: Pagans were taught (Hindus, Buddhists and Shamanists still are) that there are thousands of gods. Jesus gave his apostles the power to perform miracles to prove Jehovah was the only God. We cannot do that today. Look up "archaeology and the Bible" and "Jesus prophecies fulfilled" to see what is used today to prove the God of the Bible is true.

CHAPTER. 15: Can we do whatever we want in Christian

worship? That is the trend today. Are we worshipping ourselves by doing so? Find a concordance and look up in the New Testament "sing," "pray," "scriptures," "give," "teach," "break bread" (the communion) and see what you find out.

CHAPTER. 16: How can being handicapped bring glory to God?

CHAPTER. 17: In the early church, some wanted to claim the old Law of Moses was still in effect, and insisted Christians be circumcised. Today, some people want to dip back into the Law of Moses for tithing, a separate priesthood, candles, incense, etc. Look up Galatians 5:3 and James 2:10. What do you think?

CHAPTER. 18: Have you ever accidentally do anything that threatened the lives of others? Have you ever known someone to kill a person in an auto accident? How can a person deal with the feelings of guilt?

CHAPTER. 19: Did you ever lose your faith or at least question it? Most people have, but just do not admit it. How can admitting it help you? Have you ever helped someone with lost faith?

CHAPTER. 20: Do people usually recognize when they have been given a second chance at something? What are some second chances you have experienced?

CHAPTER. 21: Are victims sometimes accused of "making" someone do wrong to them? This is usually the excuse of bullies. Look again at the book, Hurt People Hurt People and talk about it.

CHAPTER. 22: Have you or someone you know prayed for years—sometimes decades—for someone to become a Christian. Do you think appeals to that person now and then through the years helps?

CHAPTER. 23: Have you ever belonged to an organization, but had to leave (much to your regret) then ended up with something better?

CHAPTER. 24: Remember your best friends in childhood? Have you met them in adulthood after years of separation? What was it like?

CHAPTER. 25: Tell about a time you ran up against the "big guys" in some organization. Were you successful? Have you heard stories of those who were? Even movies?

CHAPTER. 26: Did you ever have to be the bearer of bad news? How did people treat you? Do you think it depended on how much they were able to accept the bad news?

CHAPTER. 27: What is it like to lose someone who is very important to your congregation, the Christian world, a social organization, your family?

CHAPTER. 28: How can a wolf in sheep's clothing ease into a congregation or some other organization? What is it like for people who refuse to accept this new leader?

CHAPTER. 29: How can outside assistance help create doubts in the minds of star-struck followers of a wolf in sheep's clothing?

CHAPTER. 30: Interrogators of enemy leaders have an almost impossible task of breaking someone who is unbreakable. Titus used a method used by today's interrogators. How could you use that with your wolf in sheep's clothing?

CHAPTER. 31: People who insist on being leaders often give themselves grandiose titles in order to make themselves seem more important. What are some titles you have run into in clubs, congregations, etc.?

CHAPTER. 32: Do you know anyone who has sacrificed

"everything" for someone they loved? If you don't, perhaps think of a historical event. Also, think of Christians in hiding in hostile countries.

CHAPTER. 33: Sometimes it is good to look for understanding by someone who has gone through what you have. Sometimes it backfires. Think of your worst life experience. Do you think you could help someone else going through that?

CHAPTER. 34: People in deep depression feel they can never laugh again. They feel life has come to an end. What are some things that could bring someone out of a deep depression?

CHAPTER. 35: Tell about a time when you shared a pain with someone else who had experienced the same thing. What things did you do to help each other cope?

CHAPTER. 36: Tell about a time you won someone over who didn't believe you. How ingenious did you have to be?

CHAPTER. 37: Do you have any friends who started out as enemies? What is your relationship like?

CHAPTER. 38: Have you experienced an illness or injury when you refused to let it keep you down? What was it like trying to force yourself to resume your work?

CHAPTER. 39: Our mothers and grandmothers used to tell us, "You can catch more flies with honey than vinegar." How did Titus lead his kidnapper one step at a time to the truth and his voluntarily setting him free?

CHAPTER. 40: Have you ever felt cornered and just slipped away out of embarrassment? As you look back, you may think it is funny now. Would you like to share it?

CHAPTER. 41: Think about a time when a group finally got rid of a troublemaker. Were you able to forgive that person?

Remember, forgiveness is not condoning, but hoping for a better life for that person.

CHAPTER. 42: Sometimes we think we are making a great contribution to a congregation by being on a committee or holding office. Jesus went out to "seek and save the lost." Do you think, if you were busy doing that, holding office or being on a committee would really matter?

CHAPTER. 43: What is it like running into old friends or even people in general you admired in the past? Share it.

CHAPTER. 44: Do you think a person can change almost overnight? Have you seen it happen? Has it happened to you? What is it like?

CHAPTER. 45: Has anyone ever given you an assignment that seemed too difficult or even impossible? Were you proven right, that nothing will work out as planned?

CHAPTER. 46: Think about the important things you do. Who do you try to make proud of you by doing them? Is there anything you are doing that God would not be proud of you for? If so, how could you change it?

CHAPTER. 47: Have you ever experienced feeling completely defeated, then something good and unexpected happened that made the difficulty worthwhile after all? What do you think of the Providence of God?

CHAPTER. 48: Think back on your childhood. What did you want to do when you grew up? Is there some way to make that come true late in life, perhaps in a different way than you had planned?

ABOUT THE AUTHOR

Katheryn Maddox Haddad spends an average of 300 hours researching before writing a historical novel—ancient historians such as Josephus, archaeological digs so she can know the layout of cities, their language, culture, and politics.

She grew up in the northern United States and now lives in Arizona where she doesn't have to shovel sunshine. She basks in 100-degree weather, palm trees, cacti, and a computer with most of the letters worn off.

She is author of 77 books, both non-fiction and fiction. Her newspaper column appeared for several years in newspapers in Texas and North Carolina ~ *Little Known Facts About the Bible* ~ and she has written for numerous Christian publications. For over twenty years, she has been sending out every morning a daily scripture and short inspirational thought to some 30,000 people around the world.

She spends half her day writing, and the other half teaching English over the internet worldwide using the Bible as textbook. She has taught some 7000 Muslims through World English Institute. Students she has converted to Christianity are in hiding in Afghanistan, Iran, Iraq, Yemen, Uzbekistan, Somalia, Jordan, Tajikistan, Sierra Leone, Pakistan, Indonesia, and Palestine. "They are my heroes," she declares.

With a bachelor's degree in English, Bible and social science from Harding University and part of a master's degree in Bible, including Greek, from the Harding Graduate School of Theology, she also has a master's degree in management and human relations from Abilene University. She is a member of American Christian Fiction Writers, Historical Novel Society, International Screen Writers Association, and is also an energetic public speaker who can touch the hearts of audiences.

CONNECT WITH

KATHERYN MADDOX HADDAD

Website: **https://inspirationsbykatheryn.com**

Facebook: **bit.ly/FacebooksKatherynMaddoxHaddad**

Linkedin: **http://bit.ly/KatherynLinkedin**

Twitter: **https://twitter.com/KatherynHaddad**

Pinterest: **https://www.pinterest.com/haddad1940/**

Goodreads: **https://www.goodreads.com/katherynmaddoxhaddad**

GET A FREE BOOK

Sign up for Katheryn's monthly newsletter with half-price books for the whole family and insider tips on what's coming next.
http://bit.ly/katheryn

JOIN MY DREAM TEAM

Members get the first peek at my newest book and have fun offering me advice sometimes. I have a point system of rewards for helping me get the word out. Check it out here: **http://bit.ly/KatherynsDreamTeam**

www.ingramcontent.com/pod-product-compliance
Lightning Source LLC
Chambersburg PA
CBHW031731180726
48283CB00005B/1466